FAITH
A Life Interrupted

Sharon Follows

◆ FriesenPress

One Printers Way
Altona, MB R0G 0B0
Canada

www.friesenpress.com

ISBN
978-1-03-917258-6 (Hardcover)
978-1-03-917257-9 (Paperback)
978-1-03-917259-3 (eBook)

1. Fiction, Romance, Contemporary

Distributed to the trade by The Ingram Book Company

TABLE OF CONTENTS

CHAPTER ONE
The Meeting

Faith stood on the rocky cliff with the sun shining on her sunburned face, the wind took her hair, and it whipped like fire lapping at the sky as she stared across at the tip of the pillar rock that jutted out from the water. Tall grass blades bent under the command of the winds in the fields around her, rustling. It filled her ears like thunder rolling across the sky, as it swayed and moved, like the water below her feet.

Closing her eyes, Faith drew in a heavy breath as her mind flashed with memories of the day she'd first met Archer on the beach. Not this one, though. This was where he'd fallen in love with her, proposed, and where they had shared many tender moments, she was now struggling to forget.

That day her blue sun hat had been taken by the wind as she bent to pick up a piece of sea glass. *Oh, lavender!* Faith thought. Then, *WHOOSH*! A gust of wind pulled it from her head and her hair with it. "Oh!" Faith squealed as her hat blew to the edge of the shore.

Chasing after it, Faith bent to pick it up and *WHOOSH*! the wind came again, lifting her hat high into the air. When it finally landed on the water just out of reach, it began to flip like a tossed coin, all the way across the surface. Faith watched in slow motion, until it settled out on the waves, much too far for her to go for sure. "Damn," she breathed out and flopped her arms.

Archer had been out for his morning swim and hearing her disdain about the hat, whipped his head looking around to see the fuss. After all, he did think it was just he and Trevor there.

Seeing Faith on the shore, watching her hat flipping on the waves, he waited for it to finally land, then dove in swimming towards it, fast as he could. He really could swim like a fish. His mother had always told him so.

Underwater he looked for the shadow on the surface above him, then pushed hard and reached. Finally with the hat in hand, his head burst through the surface. Flinging his hair sideways, water sprayed through the air in a fine mist and the droplets flashed, like diamonds in the rising sun.

Faith couldn't believe her eyes. *Such a daring rescue,* she thought, as he started in towards the shore.

Tickled on the inside the whole time Archer splashed towards her, Faith was reminded of the stories her mother would tell about dashing heroes and pirates. Her fantastic tales of sea captains and mermaids captured her as the two of them hunted the shores for glass. The truth of the glass, though, was just as fascinating to Faith as the stories her mother made up, speculating all the while about where the glass pieces may have come from.

Now that Archer was closer, Faith could see him much better, and it made her heart flutter as he said, "This must be yours," a little out of breath.

The nearer he got to her, caused her heart pound harder and Faith felt her face blush.

Smiling he said, "It's definitely not mine." Then breathing out hard, he let out a, "Wooooo lordy!" passing the hat back to her and with a funny face continued, "It's not really my colour."

The coolness of the water drifted off his skin and down over hers. She, nearly as breathless as him now, mustered up the ability to speak.

"Oh, thank you so much. I doubt I'd have gone after it. The water is cold today and I'm not as strong a swimmer as you. That was quite something."

"Yes, the water is chilly. Gets the heart pumping, though." Not one to brag about his skills, Archer just usually deflected credit. For nearly everything. It was just "stuff" he did.

"That was nice of you."

"You're very welcome and it was nothing really." he answered, then waving his hand to gesture it wasn't a big deal, he added, "I was already there."

Faith laughed again as the wind came under the hat attempting to snatch it from her once more, but she swooped her hands together to catch it.

Hat in one hand, jar in the other, half of the glass flew from it, looking like the water Archer had shaken from his hair. Reacting quickly, he stretched his hands to help, but it was no help at all.

"Aaarrghhh," he grumbled as he caught but one, then bent down to pick up what he could see. "It's not your morning, is it?"

"It appears not, but there's lots of the day left to turn it around."

"Good point," he agreed happily to her positive outlook.

As Faith bent down with him to re-collect the glass, Archer picked up a few pieces and jostled them before passing them to her.

"What's this?" he asked picking up what looked like a stone. "You collect rocks?"

"Well, *that's* a rock," she giggled taking a white chunk from her jar and passing it to him. "*This* is sea glass." she added holding what looked like a black rock as he got closer to look but didn't see anything special.

"And this?"

"This is also glass."

Holding it to the sun knowing he'd have to get very close to see it or have to pass it to him to look for himself, Faith wanted him closer but was nervous. He was *very* handsome.

"They both look like rocks to me."

Then, Faith passed it to him motioning to take it to the sun as she had just done. Archer follwed her instructions as she explained to him how the glass was tumbled by the ocean taking the sharp edges off, eventually being considered a gem by glass hunters.

Holding it between his thumb and forefinger Archer moved it to the sun as she'd done. Like magic, the deep emerald green showed itself to him. The outside was dark and frosty, but the light made its true colour shine through. *Like people*, he thought.

"This is amazing," he exclaimed in surprise investigating her jar while she rattled what was left in it.

"While I can see the colour in those ones, this one looks like a rock."

"Some do. It takes a trained eye to see these kinds. Sometimes even I'm fooled. I find myself throwing away a lot of rocks. I can't pass them by now, though. I'm addicted to hunting."

"It's funny I haven't heard of this before. I live on the beach, really."

"I can't *not* see it," Faith laughed.

Archer helped her pick up what he could find, he then watched as she picked up what he'd missed. He hadn't even noticed them right before Faith's finger plucked them from the sand. It was like she'd cast a spell and brought them from invisibility.

"Wow," he kept saying, inspecting several of them.

Faith mentioned to him that her mother told fantastic tales, weaving a story about where the glass came from, as he helped to pick up what he could find.

The glass clinked as Faith put them back into the jar and he noticed her nails were chipped and jagged. Seeing Archer notice, she felt insecure and so took her hand and wiped the sand from her fingers on her capris.

"It ruins my nails digging through the pebble beds. I really should have a digger. I just get excited."

Archer loved people and always tried to help when he could, so ignoring her verbal insecurities, asked what she did with her collections.

"Well, I have it all through the house. I put them in glass jars on the windowsills. Some I make into jewellery or suncatchers with wire. Some are *very* rare," she answered, holding another to the light. "Those ones I keep in a special cabinet. These will just stay together till I get back home. I'm just here on vacation. So, the special ones will have to wait to join their new family in the cabinet."

"*That's so neat*!" he exclaimed as another guy ran up close to them.

"Hey, bro," he said simply, and ran up towards the dune.

"Hey, Trev. Be right there."

Waving, he just kept going as Archer turned back to Faith and nervously said, "I'd better go. Was nice to meet you and cool to hear about the glass and your mom. Like . . . *really* cool! Hope you enjoy your stay on our island."

She gave him butterflies and he pushed them down as if they'd fly from his mouth when he spoke.

"Nice to meet you too, and thanks again for bringing my hat back. I doubt it would have fared as well in the ocean as the glass does," Faith laughed.

Archer bowed that she was welcome as his friend beeped the horn from the other side of the dune. "I hope the rest of your day is excellent and the hunting goes well."

Archer smiled once more before taking to the dune himself. He'd run right up and over it like it was nothing. Faith had a time of it about halfway up. *Stallion*! she thought and sat down on the sand with a sigh. What a dreamboat he was to her. The day had already turned around having met him. She hadn't even asked his name and grumbled about it. "Not that he would be interested in me," she whispered.

Putting on her sunglasses, Faith went to the water and rinsed the glass in the jar to get some of the sand out. People had started coming over the dunes then and she listened to them as they talked, and children shouted.

Sitting back on the sand, Faith laid onto her elbows and watched some dogs running around playing with each other, while people strolled the beach. It wasn't long before she smelled a barbecue had been started and once the food was on the grill the scent made her hungry. *Time for lunch*, she thought and rose to leave. She'd only had a coffee for breakfast.

Hat and jar in hand, Faith headed towards the dune. A couple walked by holding hands and smiled to her saying "Morning."

"Morning," she replied back with a nice smile.

It was sweet to see but made her feel lonely, and jealous. They weren't young. In fact, they were seniors who adoring looked at each other.

She still hoped to find the love of her life, even if not the man of her dreams. To still be in love at their age, the way they were, was a beautiful and rare thing.

Faith turned, walking backwards a few steps watching them a minute as they strolled up the sand. He put his skinny arm around her as she put her head on his chest.

The moment touched Faith's heart but also made her feel a little more alone. If that was possible.

She and Jonsie had split up a little over a year ago now and she'd turned down a lot of men in the time after. None of them had really interested her, and even if they did, Faith felt scorned and wanted nothing to do with romance or men.

Living in a small town, word spread quickly about the breakup, and she found herself being asked out regularly. Even when just grabbing a few things at the market or getting cough syrup at the pharmacy. Dating made her so nervous she didn't even know how to go about it. She and Jonsie just happened. They'd not dated per se. He'd taken her out a few times, but it was normally just hang out and watch movies or she'd cook. Eventually it just made sense to live together. What was she even thinking?!

After catching him in bed with her best friend, that horrible morning, Faith wanted space more than anything, but was beginning to look forward to trying again soon. Maybe.

Happy she'd found out he'd cheated before they'd gotten married, was a godsend. And Lacey? Backstabbing witch. She'd pat Faith on the back now and then. *No doubt looking for the soft spot to stick the knife*, she thought now.

Her hands wiped clean of them both, Faith had no one now, and that was alright with her. *Better to be alone than a sheep in a pack of wolves*, she thought going up the dune to her car. It always started out easy but halfway up she struggled a bit. Even a month later now it was *still* hard. *How'd that guy run up it so easily?* she thought, as her speed slowed some.

Wiping sand from her feet at the car, Faith started it up and was thankful she'd parked in some shade. It would have been an oven. At 6 a.m. it was already twenty-five degrees. Now it was close to 9 a.m. Maybe just some toast for brunch and a smoothie.

There were stands set out by farmers all along the way, where she could get fresh strawberries, or that oh-so-good blueberry preserve she'd gotten a few times before. It didn't last long. Her favourite berry in the world, made into a "not quite jam, not quite jelly" treat.

The house next door had homemade breads and biscuits. Muffins and fresh eggs. That woman sure knew how to bake. Warmed biscuits, melted butter, and that preserve was about all she could bare.

Two pieces never enough, Faith went through them both in a day, not daring to buy more than one of each at a time, afraid she'd be as big as a house before the summer ended.

Rounding the turn just before the cottage, she decided to grab what she needed from the stand and have just one biscuit, while writing her novel awhile. Then maybe treat herself to lunch at the diner. It was so cute with its old-fashioned look and the red stools.

Approaching the preserve stand on the roadside, Faith took money from her pocket and dropped it into the cash box they left out. The honour system in the country made her feel a sense of safety. Prince Edward Island seemed laid-back, and their ways were sweet.

Called "the friendly island", being there showed her just how friendly it was. Everyone said "hello," or,"hey," on the streets as you passed them. They'd hold the door open for you, even if you were nearly a half a block away, it seemed. Some would even ask "How ya doing?"

Small sea-shanty towns scattered across from tip to tip, with several farmers markets in Charlottetown, Faith found many things she loved about the island. Handmade leather belts and wallets, homemade soap and lotions, paintings, pottery, jellies and preserves, fresh baked breads, veggies, local meat producers, and foreign foods already prepared to eat on the picnic benches outside, while musicians played jigs, reels, and folk music.

Then there was Kate the Spice Lady. One of her favourites. She had everything Faith would ever need and told her the funniest things. She might be silly, but she sure knew her stuff. Whatever you wanted to know and some you didn't. Like how you could kill someone with certain parts of a plant, then mentioning that people called them witches. Full of knowledge, she could really talk for days.

Thinking on it now, Faith figured maybe one day this week a trip to town was due to restock the cottage with spice and maybe go to the diner for lunch. She'd been there for a month already and had only done a few things.

Calling her trip "a vacation", Faith would confess she was there as more of an escape, but if anyone asked her seriously . . . it was to start a new life.

Living in the city with Jonsie and working as a self-employed cleaner, Faith hadn't really lived until now. The houses she cleaned were huge and she'd worked hard to make a living at it, but now, wanted one for herself. Aiming to make a career change wasn't the safe thing she'd always done. Something had to give, though.

One day, during the winter, high winds had taken the power out, so Faith messaged the day's clients that she'd reschedule, after waiting over an hour for the power to come back on.

The whole day was screwed now, she'd not be done in time. Everyone out of power had gone home from work also, so she didn't feel bad about calling it a day. It would end up being quite a while before anyone had gotten power restored. The country being hit the worst.

Pulling into her driveway, Faith saw Lacey's care covered in snow. What was she doing there?

Hoping she'd popped in to visit; Faith checked her messages. Lacey hadn't mentioned she'd be by. Faith wanted to deny it, but in her heart, she had a sinking feeling something else was going on. She'd been there for awhile for sure; the snow was thick on her car.

Faith just sat and watched the snowflakes land on the windshield until it had cooled off so much, they'd stopped melting and clouded the view. Lacey must have been there since she'd left that morning.

Having been in the driveway now for almost an hour, nothing moved. Faith sat until she couldn't see out the window anymore and sighed.

Feeling sick to her stomach now, as she got out of the car, one set of tracks going to the house had almost filled in, but for the pucker on the surface.

The snow crunched under her feet, and her heart speed up the closer she got to the house. Now pounding in her ears, Faith wasn't prepared for what, she hoped, was definitely *not* going on. "It's not happening. It's not happening," she kept telling herself, as if it would just go away.

Opening the door, though, she saw Lacey's boots. Then her shirt, a sock in the hall, and a bra. She knew . . . *oh, yes* . . . she knew. There was no denying it now.

Shaking, Faith picked up the landline and called Jonsie's cell, then listened as it rang in their bedroom. Not even caring that her boots were making a puddle on the floor she stood there waiting. Nothing mattered just then and when it went to voicemail she hung up. Feet shuffled a moment and then it was dead silent.

Well, then. This may turn out to be a long day, Faith thought and took a bottle of wine from the fridge and grabbed a glass.

Sitting at the island, still in her boots, she poured a full glass, prepared to wait as long as it took. The bathroom in the hall under the stairs, there was no way Lacey would get out without passing by it, or the kitchen, and Faith wasn't leaving. No way!

Hours went by. Two, three . . . four! It was dark now and she was quite drunk. Refusing to budge from her seat, it was all she'd done besides a few trips to the bathroom in the hall.

She was *not* going upstairs. That was a sight she didn't want in stuck in her head. The imaginary scene was enough. Not real.

Pouring another glass, Faith set the empty wine bottle beside the other four empty ones. She'd chugged nearly every glass, liquid courage, and had no longer thought the term when she heard the stairs squeak.

Lacey came down the hall, round the corner, then skulked into the kitchen to face her judge. Awaiting her sentence in one of Jonsie's shirts, Lacy looked at the floor.

Faith opened her mouth and breathed in, and Lacey could have sworn she was about to scream at her or at least *say* something . . . but didn't. Faith just took another sip of wine and flung her hand, pointing a bony finger for Lacey to get out.

Slinking to get her clothes from the floor and put on her boots, she looked at Faith and sighed, "For what it's worth . . . I'm sorry I . . ." but Faith cut her off with a swoop of her hand again, limp-wristed, like she was weary of this conversation.

"Faith . . ." she tried again, but Faith put a finger to her lips and softly whispered "Shh" glaring at Lacey in a way that would have made Satan himself cringe.

With her tail between her legs, Lacey walked out and closed the door quietly like that would make things better. She knew what Faith was like when she was set off and, only seeing it once, it was more than enough for her to back down.

Faith sat at the island and waited for Jonsie to show himself. How could she not have seen this coming? How long had it been going on? Who started it? What was she going to do about it?

Questions spun her drunken mind. With every right to haul off and crack that fucker right in the mouth, she fought the urge, wanting to hear his explanation.

When he came into the kitchen some time later, Faith was fuming. Using his narcissistic ways, he did his worst and looked as though he didn't care at all that he'd just crushed her heart and destroyed her whole world, then just picked up his keys and left. Why did he always make her feel like everything was her fault? Unworthy.

Again, she fought with the idea that Jonsie could have made her croon over him instead of belittling her. Making her feel an option instead of a priority.

Faith started to wonder what she'd done to cause this, then shook her head. *I'm not at fault here*, she reasoned with herself.

Standing up, angrier than before, she thought, *give your head a shake, girl*! before calling a cab to get a motel for the night. Or two. It wasn't far and she could walk over the next day when it was dark to get the car. *If* he hadn't smashed it. Faith knew his temper, but right now it didn't matter. Nothing did.

Settled into the hotel room, she ordered food and more wine from the local go-fer business. Sometime in the wee hours she fell asleep on the blankets, still as angry as the fires of hell, and not caring for what tomorrow would bring.

Not long after the front desk rang to remind her about check out. Not ready yet she booked another night, then went back to sleep for awhile.

Mid-afternoon, waking with a bad hangover, Faith poured more wine, and ate a cold egg roll. Thinking back, the power had come on some time yesterday and she hadn't even noticed what time. Did the microwave beep while she'd gotten drunk in the kitchen?

With nothing that needed to be done today, she texted Jonsie: *You'll be moved out by the weekend*, was all she disclosed in her message. Not caring what he had to say back, nor where the hell he'd go, as long as he left, he could walk out in front of a train for all Faith cared anymore.

Deciding to keep the room until Sunday, she rang the desk to let them know. Best to just avoid the whole fiasco that was sure to happen if they met face to face.

She knew he had lots of money to get a place. He never paid for anything, and probably had a nice stash. The house was hers anyway. Her mother had left it to her and was already fully paid for. Jonsie had no stakes in it. *Thank God*! He'd have had her tied up with lawyers for an eternity over it. Just to get even. She knew his ways. Even if he was in the wrong, he always acted like he was entitled to have some final move or say.

When her hangover subsided some, Faith took a shower, despising the cheap conditioner they gave. It was never enough, as hair was past her waist, making it felt squeaky instead of smooth.

After having it wrung out enough, Faith called a cab and went to the mall for toiletries and clothes. She wasn't going to set *foot* in that house until he was out. After dark, she walked back and picked up her car to work on Monday.

Only doing what was needed that week; work, eat, and shower, that Friday the decision was made to put the house up for sale. There were too many memories that she just wanted to forget and move forward. It was all that bounced around in Faith's head for the next five days.

She'd get a good price for it too. The market had boomed a few years before and people were getting a small fortune for what she'd have called a hovel. The renovations were desirable too. Modern and clean looking.

Jonsie didn't do much to help her around there. Ever! Cooking, cleaning, *or* renovations.

In the beginning he'd helped, but that soon died like the attention he'd given her to win her over. She had decided it was time for a change. A *whole* life change.

Faith mentioned it to her clients, as she went along, that when the house was sold, she'd be done with cleaning. They wished her well and hoped she wasn't ill or acting too rashly.

Telling them she was fine, Faith really wanted to say, "I have dreams and I think they need a push."

To them, all she implied was that she needed a change, with as much confidence as she could muster.

Truthfully, Faith had no idea what she was doing, but it was better than staying there and stagnant. Always doing the safe thing, look where it had gotten her. Mediocre job, in a mediocre house, with a cheater fiancé, and a backstabbing, so-called, friend. She was so over it.

With no real plan, she decided to coast off the house money and thought of what would make her happy. Like, *truly* happy.

Remembering her teacher would say, if he could give Faith 110 percent, he would have, and after passing out an assignment, he'd waited eagerly for Faith's papers. Faith had a way with words and the teacher would be engrossed in her stories, so thought, maybe she should try her hand at writing. But what?

Recalling a dream she'd had, that jarred her for months, even now three years later it still made her teary-eyed, so thought maybe she'd make it a novel. If the plan failed, she'd just start cleaning again. That wasn't an issue.

Settled on it, Faith thought maybe a vacation was due. She'd never really done that.

Her mother, Linda, was young when she'd had the car accident and died soon after.

Watching her mother become frailer by the day until it seemed she'd just vanished, Faith thought that she hadn't noticed how life can be taken in a heartbeat. She should have been living her best life and taking chances.

Remembering her mother's last day, Faith was certain Linda wasn't in her body anymore anyway.

Just seventeen, the lawyers tried to get her out of the house, claiming Faith wasn't capable. Even before her mother passed, they'd plead with her that she was too young to keep it. That it was too much responsibility. Really, all they wanted was to get her out and make whatever they could from Linda's estate, but Faith dug her heels in as they pushed her around.

Refusing to budge, they made multiple attempts to get her into a group home. Still, she refused.

With a part-time job she'd gotten the year before, Faith had savings, only needing to pay for food and utilities, until she graduated. Linda had made sure she'd gotten enough insurance to pay off the house and funeral costs with a little left over for Faith, to get her through her grieving time. Why didn't she have that grit with Jonsie, that she'd had with the lawyers?

After the lawyers had taken their share from what her mother had left for her, Faith struggled just to pay the land taxes and utilities. That's when she met Jonsie.

He was generous in the beginning and stood up for her. Offering to pay some things until the cheque had come from her mother's insurance company and she accepted his help. Now, he owned her. Really, though, she loved him. It was him who saw their relationship as a transaction.

One day Jonsie said he'd heard there was good money in cleaning and pushed her to give it a go. Scared to leave the steady paycheque, Faith fought him for a year, saying it was too risky and she needed the benefits that came from her job at the company.

Soon after, she'd caught wind that the company was bought out and they'd be downsizing. One of the last hired, Faith knew she was out for sure and a lull in money wasn't something she could handle. So, now being less risky to her, she decided to try the self-employed cleaning, which turned out for the better. Eventually filing as a business she had full-time work for double what the company paid. Clients were also very grateful for her. That hadn't happened at any other job, plus, she was always overworked and underpaid.

Jonsie had moved in with her by then and when he saw Faith was making good money and had savings, he stopped paying for his share of anything, saying he forgot. She'd just cover the bills herself and wait for him to pay her back. Sometimes he did. Sometimes he didn't. A lot of times he didn't though, nearly stopping altogether.

A few times she mentioned it and Jonise lost his temper reminding her who had taken care of things after her mother had died, then commented that Faith was a bitch and that all she wanted was money. The truth was, she was barely making ends meet now.

Soon after, she had to stop shopping. There wasn't enough anymore for her to splurge or even buy dearly needed clothes. All the pants she had for work had been eaten away at the knees, eventually needing replacing by things she felt comfortable in, until it began to require her nice clothes.

It wasn't long before she was dressing like a slob around the house and stopped going out other than to work. During cottage season, Faith used the money to update the house. Thankful now she'd done that, it was in better shape, and she'd be able to get a decent price for it. Without his help. She'd show him now that she didn't need him like he'd accused her of.

At the end of the work week, Faith began packing her things. Drunk most nights, she'd just sleep on the sofa. It was comfy and she didn't want to sleep in the house, much less in the bed.

Her only fear was that Jonsie would come back and start fighting with her. Not knowing what he might really do, she didn't want to find out.

Although she was a boxer, it was just for sport and recreation. Once, he'd pushed her and soon found out what she was capable of, and Faith felt awful about it. She didn't want to have to hit someone. Especially in anger, having worked that all out after she'd met Usha, before graduating.

He'd sucked it out of her that one time, though. Pushing and pushing. Egging her on and then backing her into a corner physically. She socked him an uppercut he'd not soon forget.

Thinking about Usha now, warm memories flooded her mind of how nice she was and mature for being just sixteen. It was only one summer that she came as an exchange student, but they'd gotten close.

Now and then Faith thought of her and wondered where she'd ever gone and what she might be doing, as memories floated through her head.

Usha's hair was so black and shiny, her brown eyes and the sharp white that came from her mouth when she smiled. As beautiful on the inside as she was on the outside, Faith laid on the sofa remembering her.

Pondering life and putting all the furniture for sale on marketplace was all she could do for now. Only keeping what was needed, the rest was packed away, then shipped to storage soon after. It took some stress away and the tension left her. Nothing for him to break.

One day a client mentioned they knew of a house in the country for rent. Being friends, she had told them of Faith's situation with selling the house and presumed to save it for Faith until she called.

Making haste, she took it without even seeing it. She wanted out of that house! The owner hinted; it was tiny but cozy.

To Faith? It didn't matter how small. It was all she'd need until her house sold. Then, the vacation!

Before the spring Faith was signing papers. The buyers didn't even want to negotiate the price. Over half a million dollars, which she thought was outrageous.

Figuring she'd overprice it so they could beat her down, they didn't. Free of it, Faith went back to her tiny place and cooked a lovely celebratory meal.

While eating, she flipped through a magazine she'd had a subscription for which mentioned a place called Prince Edward Island. A great travel destination surrounded by beaches. The north shore with its white sand and cool waters. The south had red sand and warm water with sand bars. It also had art up to Ying yang. Just what she needed. The article said it was known for its friendly people. Typing it into her laptop,

Faith wanted to see and read more about it. *Charming*, she thought.

Reading enough, the next thing was to find a place to stay and book the travel plans. It happened quickly. Money wasn't an object right now. Finished with her clients and no family or friends to be concerned with, nothing was holding her to this place, now that she'd sold the house. Having never been on a train, she thought it would be interesting. Another train would bring her car the next morning.

Booking a hotel in Halifax, Faith could take in some sights while waiting on the car, then take the ferry to The Island.

With everything booked, she sat back going through site after site, gathering what was needed to fill the summer with. Joining social media pages where people had posted pictures of sea glass, Faith chatted with them about where the best places were. Off her rocker or on a goose chase of sorts, she didn't care, she'd have the time of her life.

CHAPTER TWO
Archer

Archer woke up and got ready for his day as usual. Yoga, meditation, reading the paper with coffee, his swim while Trevor had his run, then a nice breakfast. They alternated days driving.

After spending so much time at the gallery, while Johanna was away, Archer had the loft installed with a kitchen and full bath above his office, overlooking the gardens. His bedroom above that, with full skylight. It was less lonely there.

Trevor had always lived down the road, they'd gone to baseball camp together and he helped Archer build a diamond for the community after hitting it big with investing. He was still in high school, but it came to him like a second skin. Intuitively he would buy and sell, just at the right time, taking money here and there from his account to help kids who wanted to play sports. Those whose parents couldn't afford gear.

Teachers would mention children with gifts for the arts while attending community events. Archer was always there to help them realize their potential. He also sponsored a team and put a lot of time in with them, as he spent a lot of time alone. When money began accumulating, he'd used it to build the gallery.

Archer's high school sweetheart, Johanna, a model, would always be off on photo shoots travelling the world. Sometimes he'd go with her to see some of the cities.

He'd ask her often when she'd be ready to settle down and have children of their own, but she'd always talk about the next photo shoot, saying she wasn't ready yet. He wanted a family badly but didn't want to push.

As time went on, Archer asked less and less. Eventually using up his patience, he'd find his limit. When it seemed like Johanna was stalling, he'd call her on it. "Come. Sit," he'd say to her when he needed to have a heart-to-heart. That day it went like this.

"Johanna, dear. We've been together for ten years now, I'm pushing thirty and have made more than enough money. Neither of us ever has to work again, really," he suggested calmly. "I know you love me, and I love you but . . . I really want to get married and start a family. I see you with Greta and Jonah. You're so great with them and it makes me feel good. I see how happy and content Derek and Brett are and it makes me sad that I don't have the same. Those kids have changed my brothers so much. I know you see that too."

Sighing, he continued as she rolled her eyes. She's lucky he didn't see her do it either, he'd have lost his ever-lovin' mind. He was trying hard. His dad, Roger, had warned him about Johanna. Archer ignored him in the hopes she'd come to see it his way at some point, so continued.

"I want that for us and hoped maybe you'd give me an idea when we might start our own family?"

Johanna rubbed her temples knowing where it was going, and Archer could see her answer already. It was nothing new.

A little upset now he said more sternly and as caringly as he could spare. "Are you ever going to stop modelling? You party all the time. We're adults now and I've waited for nearly eight years now." Being totally honest he tried suggestions.

"I just feel like you're never going to settle down with me. You keep dodging the issue and I need to know. Maybe you could take a course and get other work here that you'd enjoy, something that gives you more time at home. I mean we'll vacation. If you still want to travel, you can. I'd stay home and take care of things if you needed time away, or you don't have to work if you don't want to. I just feel like I'm in limbo and hanging onto prayers at this point. I'm growing weary of it."

"Oh, my god. Archer. Why are we having this talk again?!" she complained. "I love our life the way it is. Though I could do with a lot less talk about babies . . . to be honest I'd hoped you'd just drop the subject at some point. I don't feel like anything is missing. Am I not enough for you?"

Whining, Roger called it. Johanna was selfish and he was on to her. Archer wouldn't hear him, and it made Roger cringe every time she did it. Archer was just now beginning to feel the same.

"Yes, darling. You're enough. You always were," Archer declared lovingly, still trying to be calm and considerate. "It's just when I see Brett with Greta, how he goes to her dance classes and does her hair, the way she looks at him and cuddles in," Archer said then, talking with his hands. "Derek and Jonah do everything together. Derek loves going to his games and even practices his lines with him for drama club, leads his Scout camp, no one could have seen that coming. Children change a person, and lives, for the better and . . . I want that, Johanna. With you."

Searching her eyes for the truth, hand over his heart as he felt it breaking, Archer almost knew the answer, seeing her attempt to avoid him again as usual.

"I just need to know if you'll ever make that decision. And if so, then when? Two years? Three? *Ever*?" he asked, a little more frustrated now. "I'll wait but I need a solid answer. You can't keep ducking out on me with this."

Johanna knew his tone. She'd better tread lightly but was running out of reasons. Best to tell the truth, or something close to it. Maybe buy a little more time.

"Well . . ." she responded, breathing out a sigh of relief. "I was waiting to tell you, but I guess now is as good a time as any. I've been offered a job in the States for a role in a big soap opera. We'd have to move there."

Archer was shocked.

"*The States!? Are you kidding!?*"

Johanna got excited when his eyes opened wide.

"*I know, right?* I'll be famous! You could walk the red carpet with me, meet some stars and famous musicians! Maybe that favourite singer of yours . . . um, I can't think of their name . . . Anyway, it doesn't matter! You'd be famous too. You're with me," she cooed with a huge smile and hands clasped together.

"I can't believe you just said that . . ."

It made Archer's heart slowed a few beats though. He'd been afraid to ask again. Sometimes she'd flip right out and not talk to him for days. Slamming all the drawers and mumbling.

"What? Wouldn't you be proud?"

"I'm already proud, Johanna," he affirmed touching her hand. "I can't think of a thing better than to have a little one following at your feet, though. I dream of the three of us playing and laughing. Fixing scraped knees and drying their tears. Having meals together. Holding them when they're sick. I can't even say all the wonderful things that roll through my mind. It makes my heart pound to think of it."

Archer's eyes now with a dreamy look, he waited. When she offered nothing, he kept going.

"I imagined being there for you through it all and how much I would admire you. Taking care of you and waiting on you hand and foot while you create life. It's such a miracle. It would bring us even closer together."

Johanna had heard this all before.

"I'm starting to think though that I'm being a fool about this and it's making me upset."

That she'd never heard, though.

"My body is all I have, Archer. I've seen what it can do. I would be worth nothing then," Johanna maintained, touching her heart. "I'm not going to ruin it with stretch marks and sagging skin. My tits would be ruined! I know how you love them too."

She was sly and trying to bargain with him now.

"Our child would *not* devalue you, Johanna! I've waited so long now it's breaking my heart. I'd love your body just as much as I do now." Archer argued seeing her obvious manipulation. He was cross, and on to her. "Nothing is more valuable than love, but I don't think you get that. I want that in my life, and I want you. It could be so amazing. I'd do anything for you. You know that."

"Anything except drop the subject of children," she groaned. "We already have an amazing life. I don't want it to change. Babies are a lot of work. For at *least* eighteen years . . . and . . . what if they come out retarded or something?"

Archer stood up fast and put his hand on his forehead to keep his brain from exploding. What a nasty thing to say. Especially about his possible child.

"*What*? You know what's hard work, Johanna? Dealing with your work all the time. Being alone so much. You're always gone. You dismiss my dreams," he said with an elevated tone and pacing the floor. "I never know if you'll change your mind and, frankly, I'm sick of waiting. You always leave me hanging. *That's work!*"

"Jesus, Archer. Calm down!" Johanna shouted throwing herself into the sofa. "I've just had the offer of a lifetime and I need to commit to my dream. I've wanted this forever!"

"Your dream? What happened to us?" Archer asked with his hands up.

"You know what I mean," she said quietly, as if to not poke the bear more. She wanted her way, and she knew how to get it from him and always played him like a fiddle.

Archer looked out the patio doors. "This means you're taking the job? You'll live in the States, and I'll live here?" he asked, almost resigned to his fate.

"Nooo," she begged, getting up from the sofa and putting her arms around him from the back. "You come with me. It will be amaaaaazing . . ." she soothed and snuggled her face into his shoulders. That usually did it.

"I have a life here Johanna. With you. The business, family . . . the diamond and the kids. The team. You expect me to just drop everything and live in Hollywood?"

Johanna didn't know what to say. She'd never heard him like this with her before. She always got what she wanted, never considering he made sacrifices for her happiness. This was beginning to be work now. "You know what?" he spoke tenderly. "Okay . . ."

Johanna squeezed him, feeling her victorious win with her acting. Her career depended on it. "*Oh, yay*! I'm sooo happy you see it my way!"

Archer took her arms from around him and threw them to his side hastily. "Oh. Well . . . you know . . . it's not hard to figure out. Nor a hard decision to make. You want what you want, and you don't care who you step on to get there. I think you should take the job. While you're at it, you can forget about me. I want someone who wants to have a family and be around. It's obvious you're not the one. What a waste of time," he muttered walking away.

Johanna was horrified. "Archer, noooo. Don't be like that!"

"Johanna. Yes. I'm done having this conversation with you. This discussion is over. You're used to getting your way, but not this time."

With that, Archer put on his coat and headed for the door. "I'm going to stay with Trevor. You figure out what you're going to do and let me know."

"*You selfish bastard*!" Johanna screamed as he walked out the door.

He just turned back and speaking softly said, "Yes, Johanna. This time I am and it's long overdue. It's always been about you."

With that he quietly closed the door. He was finished. The click of the latch like the cocking of a gun.

Johanna also had had enough and left that night, never coming back but sent a few texts over the next short while before leaving for New York. Always saying she was thinking of him and crying. That she needed him and wanted him to come to her. That'd she'd forgive him.

That she'd forgive me? Whatever the fuck that meant, he'd think and deleted the message. There'd been too many late-night discussions about this, and Archer had finally put his foot down and wasn't backing out either. The messages stopped soon after. He knew she'd gone to New York.

Wishing her good luck in his heart and hoping she found her dreams to be, as she'd hoped, Archer put all his focus into the gallery and the local teams. He spent more time with friends and family and quite liked it that way, figuring when he met the one, he'd recognize her. Johanna wasn't it. Nothing short of that was acceptable now and he was done taking women on their word. That was a tough and costly lesson in his opinion. Whoever it was would need to show it before he'd give his heart fully next time.

The one for him would take an interest in his dreams as he would in hers. That they'd teach each other, grow together, and bring wonderful things to the table for "them."

Compromise. Compassion. Someone with a gentle, motherly nature. Ready to commit to something bigger than just the two of them. And so, Archer spent several years single after that. Fine with it . . . mostly . . . The gallery, successful now, and being the owner, Archer came and went as he pleased. His staff was competent and knew what he wanted. They worked together like a well-oiled machine. Carla did most of what was needed but checked with him for final say.

Tonight, he'd booked a wonderful musician to play in the cafe while people ate and had woken up excited to go down for a listen later on.

When pulling into Trevor's, he was already set to go, per usual. Trevor loved his time on the beach, just running off the pudge he'd gotten from Dora's cooking. Staying fit until after they were married, then working hard to keep his shape, her dinners were more than his body could take. Dora called him fluffy and didn't mind it. He did, though.

"Saw ya pull out," Trevor said getting into the car.

On Archer's swim he was pleasantly surprised by this woman and her runaway hat. She had a calm but excited energy about her. So open and gentle. That fiery hair. Those green eyes. Having not introduced himself, Archer now hoped he would bump into her again.

After they'd left the beach, he dropped Trevor off at the house. "Later, buddy. I'll text when I'm ready to go in the morning," he told Archer, tapping the hood of his Camaro.

"Ya, dude. Enjoy your day!"

A few days a week Archer enjoyed getting to the gallery before the staff to go over inventory and make plans for bare spaces on the wall. Sometimes he'd just sit in the gardens and take in the peace of it all. He'd built it close to town in case the cafe ever needed supplies. Best not to keep guests waiting or disappoint.

Now and then he'd sit in the gardens and just watch people. Lovers holding hands, others smelling flowers and commenting on the fountain. He didn't bother fencing it in. Always open, he built it for people to enjoy. He loved their smiling faces.

Remembering that the woman on the beach had said she made sea glass art, Archer made a note in his phone to check that out, always on the lookout for new things. If he were lucky, somehow or some way, he found her, he could feature her in the gallery. Even better, get to know her some. Thinking she seemed sweet and delicate; he regretted not introducing himself. What could he do now? Nothing.

Sighing, Archer checked the logs and pushed it from his mind. "*So* much to do, so much to do," he muttered. Then thought, *better to just get to it*, then after taking some stock he went back to collect envelopes from the office that Carla had put on his desk as outgoing. Checking his schedule once more for time, Archer left the office whistling, and it echoed through the gallery hall.

The post office was all he needed in town, the rest was emails and phone calls. The day was getting hotter, and he was glad he didn't need to roam the streets for long. Saying hello to a few people in the gardens, Archer strolled through lazily before hopping in his car.

Town was small but took forever to get around. People stopped on the streets to talk in their cars. Tourists were crossing on every corner it seemed, along with seniors going out for their daily walk.

It was so small in fact most of the people he went to school with had moved away for better jobs, with not much else to do but fishing and farming. There were few office jobs or grocery clerk positions and only one pharmacy, which had the same pharmacist forever. Since he was a kid, really.

People didn't usually stray too far from work they'd gotten. Even gas attendants. Not the best job in the world but when you got one you kept it. Everyone was so predictable to him now. Like staple.

Anyone wanting a career had to move to the main part of The Island, as that's where the university and college were.

Because he'd done some travelling when Johanna had photo shoots, Archer seen a lot of the world. It was not only beautiful but educational and he learned a lot about spices, dishes, traditions and cultural norms.

Wine being part of most of the meals, he'd became a connoisseur and studied all the different lagers, wines, and spirits. Potters Peek wouldn't support his taste and so he relied on tourism to carry the weight of the gallery and cafe.

Farmers and fisherman were happy with their bacon and eggs, mashed potatoes, burger and fries, or pizza. It gave him a good idea of who was local. They usually never ordered the pulled pork on brioche with the topping of dry coleslaw or the samosas with sweet chili sauce.

Tourism is what made the gallery truly lucrative. Tourists all wanted to immerse themselves in the sea-shanty life, and there were lots of places where they could get that. Archer wanted to stand out, though. Many had a taste of the good life, and he knew they couldn't eat lobster and mussels the entire visit. He'd be there for them and anyone who wanted to venture into the flavours of the world.

Thirty million dollars went through the island every summer, though he may have been using a modest number. He hadn't checked in a couple of years and made a note to refer to that later.

Having drifted off into his thoughts, he suddenly realized he'd made it to the post office. With his sanity intact, he parked the car. Quick in and out, he shouldn't break too much of a sweat. The heat was soaring quickly.

Archer sent off the mail and returned into the busy streets. The smell of coffee in the air, as he left the post office, drew him right in, so thought, he could do with one. Ada made the best.

There was always a good feeling when he walked in. Like when he was a kid, and his parents would take him and his brothers for lunch on Sunday after church. Before leaving home, he continued to go with them out of respect. It was hard to break the news to them that he wouldn't be attending church anymore. Roger and Debbie were disappointed and prayed he'd change his mind. Like it was a phase.

Archer just felt like there was more to life, and in his travels, he'd learned about the Buddhist traditions. Their approach to spirit was interesting. Much sounder and more logical to him.

Finding peace and feeling grounded, he adopted the theology but not the customs. It took the fear of God from his heart and replaced it with an unconditional love, that, with time, allowed him to feel a healthy relationship with his creator, understanding that no one knows for certain. He was going on a feeling, just like everyone else. His main goal was to be intellectually honest, and it was hard to talk to his parents about it. They'd been immersed in Christianity from birth. Both model followers. No doubt, no questions. Unless it related to the bible and knowing God more deeply. Archer couldn't swallow it.

Now and then they'd ask him to come to church and he would. To make them happy. When they asked if he'd come back for good, Archer always told them that he felt he was making the right decision for himself.

They fought with his reasoning and stated that there wasn't a choice. You either followed Jesus or you went to hell. Other options were of Satan.

He'd reinforce that, if God wanted him back in church he'd surely tug at his heart, and he'd let them know. Always open to receiving, what *they* called a "revelation", Archer assured them that he loved them, and that God would be heard, Usually satisfying them.

When at dinner, he observed their beliefs and prayed at the dinner table. In his own way, of course. Not that he was better than them. He just thought differently. Many paths, one truth, he believed.

A very gentle man, Archer enjoyed listening to people talk about their ideas and concepts. Live and let live was his philosophy. Religious history had been fraught with violence. Groups trying to make others believe as *they* did. He'd not be that person, nor would they have his support. In his opinion no one needed "saving."

After watching some theological debates between atheists and theists, he'd concluded that followers mostly just carried a herd mentality and wanted nothing to do with it.

It wasn't anger he felt for it, though it did upset him. It just wasn't for him, and Archer followed his own heart, leaving others to do the same. The path of peace and as little chaffing as possible.

Knowing he'd experience what he allowed, he became deliberate. Beliefs being something you tell yourself over and over. Mantras. It was all anecdotal anyway! Wisdom came over him then and Archer suffered living in Potters Peek.

The people were simple and had their ways. Few changed. "Life is complicated," he'd say to himself to sooth his loneliness. But today . . . he just felt like bacon and eggs.

CHAPTER THREE
To Town

With her blueberry preserves and biscuits, Faith pulled into the cottage, and straight away put on the coffee she'd bought from the farmer's market. While it was in the grinder, she remembered the line of customers and how it went all the way down the corridor and out the door into the parking lot. The poor man, run off his feet, and struggling to hear orders over the hundreds of people talking.

Enjoying the scenery, she watched as people cut through the line, some stopping to talk or peruse the booths around her. Elbow to elbow, the people met old friends, and sometimes the line would be cut. Every time, Faith worried she'd lose her place. It took nearly an hour to even get close. She'd considered forgetting about the coffee, but it smelled so good!

The kitchen, now overpowered by it brewing, mixed with a hint of the ocean, as she opened the windows. It was humid out, but the sound of the ocean called to her. She was sure going to miss this place.

When the coffee maker finished and made its gurgling sound, Faith spread butter on the biscuits and popped them in the microwave, then opened the jelly jar and the honey that was for sale beside the preserves. Flavourful in her coffee with milk.

The microwave beeped and she poured the preserves on the steaming biscuits. It was thick but still runny. Nice on a warm English muffin too when she ran out of biscuits.

Preferring homemade wares, Faith only used the grocery store for things she couldn't get at the market. With her snack, sea glass and a towel, she went to the living room. Setting the food on the table to spread the towel on the floor, she sighed contently. The normal ritual when she returned with glass.

Dumping the jar of glass onto the towel Faith got her black flashlight. Now and then she'd find uranium pieces. She'd seen it in a magazine once and went through her entire collection which took days with what she had collected. They were sneaky little things. Some you could tell right away, some were what she called "sleepers," as they looked like any other regular piece, until the black light hit them.

Now and then she'd go through the jars, missing them occasionally because she had so much and got completely lost about which had been sorted through.

Now seated, Faith took a bite of the biscuit and wiggled a little happy dance, then sipped coffee. Delighted, her fingers sifted through the pile to find the lavender piece, as her mind drifted away to the handsome stranger. The piece she was after when the wind took her hat. Humming a tune, she went through the pieces and found no sleepers.

"Darn it," Faith grumbled and relaxed back on the front of the sofa.

Finishing the biscuits, she thought they tasted like more, then went to her laptop to get it started. The internet was slow being so far from town, so she just left it to make the other biscuit. Returning, she checked to see if there was anything from her publisher but all she found were twelve emails from Jonsie.

"God, will you go away?" Faith asked out loud, and clicked them right into the bin, having stopped reading them months ago.

All he ever said anyways, was that he wanted to make it up to her, or how sorry he was. Until he got angry. Then he'd say she was an idiot and that she'd never be anything without him and to just keep fooling herself. Then always stated that she's eventually end up begging him to take her back. Realizing Faith wasn't going to respond, he started putting things into the subject line knowing she'd see that.

Blocked on her phone, she now considered making a new email address to get them to stop all together. He had no idea where she'd gone, and she didn't care where he was, finally getting some peace and happiness, that was all that mattered now.

Not sure if she even wanted to leave the island, Faith toyed with what it would take to stay. Even if for a while longer. It was so nice here and she loved the beaches. Which took her back to that devilishly handsome man.

Faith was about done letting Jonsie phase her. She had a book to do, an island and art to enjoy. Now this gorgeous man to think about. Maybe she'd run into him again and ask his name next time. If he was single, ask him out, or make friends just to be in his company.

Questions buzzed in her mind. "What if I met him again? What would I do? Would I ask him out? I shouldn't have let him get away like that." Then muttered, "Faith, get a grip on yourself!"

Another of Jonsie's numbers showed up, and doubting herself, Faith figured it was best to just forget about it. What *would* he want with *her*? She'd have a lot to fix about herself before taking on any relationships.

"Even just a fling?" rang in her head which made her laugh. She never was one to sleep around or she could have done half her town after Jonsie left. Emotional connection was the most important to her when it came to relationships.

Sighing, Faith put it out of her head and cursed Jonsie for messing her up more than she was when he'd met her.

That's what predators do, though. They find a weakness and extort what they have to, to get their control. She felt like a wreck about it, but also knew she could have been a lot worse for wear if she'd stayed.

"Asshole," she grumbled out loud.

Thinking about him gave Faith a headache, so she took a few pain relievers and a hot bath, which usually helped. Today, though, the feeling lingered and her insecurities surmounted. Needing to take responsibility for staying so long, as to take her power back, he'd really done a job on her, and that was the whole point of coming to PEI.

Time for a reset and finding out how hard it was to get rid of his brainwashing, maybe a trip to the gallery would make her feel better. They had music in the café, from what she'd read in the pamphlet on the entrance table, after arriving at the cottage. It sounded amazing!

It was late in the afternoon now and the gallery sounded great. Music and dinner with art, plus a stroll through the gardens. How could she not go?

Pulling out the list, Faith double-checked the local entertainment guide. It was time to start hitting the town. Making a schedule to see musicians and plays, she then bought what she needed. No going back now that it's paid for. If she had to force herself to go out, she would.

Going back to the pamphlet, Faith read more details of the gallery. Paintings, pottery, glass work, soap, carvings, and more, the brochure said. *How much more could they possibly have?*

Having been here for weeks already, the end of August seemed to be nipping on her heels. Two months left. The book was nearly done, and Faith felt as though she'd made excellent headway. A little ahead of schedule, actually, and she needed some R&R.

She'd been to the diner a few times. It was sweet with its old-fashioned bar stools and rounded counter. She wasn't sure if it was a new building or if they had just kept it very well.

The farmer's market was a weekly thing. The tiny towns were adorable, but Charlottetown, with the downtown streets filled with tables and canopies, wonderful food carts, and musicians everywhere, was the bomb.

Once there was a young girl playing guitar. Maybe fifteen. Her voice was amazing, the guitar playing was beginner level for sure. The strings buzzed because she wasn't pressing hard enough, and her fingers looked clumsy. Faith loved every second when she strolled by checking tables and wares.

Feeling a sense of pride for the young girl, Fith dropped a hundred-dollar bill in her jar. The girl noticed and her eyes opened wide as she stopped singing to say, "*Thank you so much!*" then continued her course.

Faith gave her the peace sign and mouthed "You're doing great," then kept moving through the street. Though she had a long way to go with the instrument, her bravery was something Faith admired and wanted to encourage her, wishing she'd have gotten even a *little* encouragement along her own path.

Getting ready, the sound of lapping waves was like a stadium full of people at a concert in the open. The thought of success, with the book, made her decide to spend, just *one* hour, on it every day and rarely needing prompting to get it done, she'd gone head-first into the deep end and had to make time to do other things. Like eat and sleep.

Ready to go to town, she just needed the book out of the way. Pulling with all her might to get into the book deep, she focused, but then . . . "I wonder if he's at the beach often."

Sighing she commented out loud, "*So intrusive!*"

No progress was being made, but inward, Faith felt like a schoolgirl again. It was nice and it reminded her of Tony. She had such a crush on him for years and then a few weeks before school ended, he'd finally noticed her and they talked at a party, had a brief encounter and then he was gone.

Wondering what had ever happened to him, Faith sat back in her chair. He'd left so suddenly to be with his grandparents in Florida and never even told her. It made her feel rejected and disposable. Her self-esteem was always so poor. He'd brought her to life that day and she missed him. They'd had so much fun. How he'd ravaged her and opened her eyes to a whole new world. He told her to call him enthusiastically, but then was never home when she did. Or at least that's what his parents said. Then she heard he'd left the state.

Distracted now, Faith got up and closed the laptop. She *had* to finish this book. Today wasn't the day, though.

It could mean a whole new life. Fame. Fortune. Trips around the world maybe. This cottage was a like a dream house to her. Like the ones she'd cleaned. All of what happened, seemed to her, like a sign.

Hindsight being 20/20, Faith could see how life had pushed her here. Remembering the dream that inspired the book, she thought of the AI character she was in it.

It had a definite feel to it. She knew her body wasn't real, but her feelings were. All the AI had real emotions and it hit her like a rock. She was woken from the emotional intensity and the sound of her tears hitting the pillow in quick succession. Tick, tick, tick, they went. Automatically, Faith just picked up her phone and recorded what had happened. Her voice wispy as she struggled to speak as she was completely devastated that her lover didn't recognize her and attacked. Many times over, they fought.

She'd felt every ounce of pain in the dream as though it were real. with a first-person view. Faith listened to the recording a hundred times, still feeling the desperation, pain, and grief. That night, though, she cried for hours as quietly as she could. Try as she might to stop, Faith found she was inconsolable.

Jonsie never even noticed her get out of bed. A wreck, she went and sat on the sofa, weeping and sobbing until the sun came up. Dreading having to go to work she was so exhausted as it shook her to the core.

Even now it made her feel sad, though not as intensely. Imagining loving someone so much, and how she'd felt about Jonsie, Faith now wondered if maybe it was a premonition of how he would eventually betray her, or that she didn't love him the way she was capable of loving. Sure, she'd be sad, but it wouldn't end her world. Not like this emotion.

Remembering the handsome stranger and how he'd listened so intently to her ramblings about the glass and her mother. How he was so very sweet not to interrupt and seemed genuinely interested, Faith somehow felt, she should expect that from her man.

Jonsie was always so jealous when she was happy or excited, always saying something to ruin her mood, cutting her off in the middle of a story, even if they had company. Always asserting his dominance over her, his self importance took precedence over her feelings. Recalling it all now, it's mostly what made her feel broken and insecure. Even after Usha boosting her confidence, Jonsie undid it all. Somehow, she'd agreed with him, not knowing it at the time.

Hot chocolate always brought her comfort and so made a large mug of it. Her mother would do that when she saw that Faith was feeling down. After Linda died, Faith started using alcohol, but fixing the house was costly and hot chocolate was much cheaper than whisky.

Taking the steaming mug in her hands, Faith went to the patio while trying to let the feeling fade from her mind before hitting the road.

After finishing it, she only felt a bit better. Going to the mirror, she put a splash of colour on her eyelids, mascara, and a soft pink lip balm. Not much for heavy makeup, Faith's features became sharp with the tiniest bit, but still soft.

With full and thick hair, she wore it extra long, and the reds flashed in the light. Even when it was messy, she got compliments on it. They were the only compliments she'd ever gotten. Jonsie never, "*Stop*!" Faith told herself and grabbed a soft summer dress from the closet, then looked for the new sandals she'd bought last year but never did wear.

Smoothing the dress she slid on the sandals, grabbed the keys and hopped into her white Mini Cooper with the red racing stripe.

It was the only thing she'd ever splurged on and loved it so much. It was fast and when she stepped on the gas her belly would fill with butterflies but would only do it for a minute. Not much for breaking rules, it gave her a rush to do it, now and then, making her feel free. Jonsie always wrangled her and, "*Stop!*" she shouted out loud this time.

Faith's memory went back to her being in school as she drove to town. How she always felt left out until Usha came to town. Being an exchange student and always alone, one day she'd asked to sit with Faith in class after hearing the kids put her down behind her back. Faith had just turned into her locker to try and drown out their voices.

Usha saw how hurt she was so had gone to Faith saying hi, but she didn't hear Usha over the noisy halls. Keeping her head in the locker, pretending to dig things out, Faith dried her eyes and when all the kids had left the hall, silence came. As Faith closed the locker door, she saw Usha standing there.

"You mind if I sit with you in class?"

Faith thought maybe she was feeling lonely too and agreed. They ate lunch together that day and over the school year they became the best of friends. They'd hang out in the park sometimes and Usha, feeling like she could talk to Faith about the other kids now, said, "Faith. I see how the other kids treat you."

"It doesn't bother me." Faith said a bit snarky.

Usha expressed what was in her heart then. "Yes, it does, Faith. I see the look on your face when they call you a loser. I want you to know something, though," she smiled. "They're wrong."

"What if they're not, Usha? What if I am the loser they say?"

Taking Faith's hand to soothe, Usha shared her thoughts. "People come from so many kinds of homes. I should know. I've been in a lot of them."

Faith looked at her confused but wanted more. She didn't see Usha's point but wasn't sure how to see herself the way Usha did.

"It's very diverse and . . . well . . . people who have never lived anything outside of their own homes, with their own friends, in their own town, are doomed to continue the monotony that as their basis to judge others for not being like them," she informed Faith and looked over her glasses with those eyes. "It's very small-minded and shallow. You'd do well to understand they deserve pity and understanding. You should never look to them as a role model. What they're doing is from a small and prejudiced viewpoint and when they put you down, it's not you, it's them. It's not bravery or strength that makes them do that. It's insecurity. You don't fit into anyone else's box but your own. You're beautifully yourself and their opinions don't matter. Nor do they know you like I do. And I think you're amazing."

Faith was crying now. "How . . . did you get so wise, Usha? You're just a teen like me and I don't have thoughts like that. It's something my mother would have said," she told Usha wiping tears from her face. "I miss her so much . . ." she cried.

Usha took over wiping the tears for her and hugged her there on the swings as the cool kids walked the street on the edge of the park, yelling, laughing, and calling them dykes and lesbos.

Faith hung her head, but Usha took her face and picked it up to look into her eyes. "Don't let them dull your shine," she whispered and kissed her on the mouth. "You'll do better than they ever will."

She stared deep into Faith's green eyes, now red with tears, and kept wiping them from her face. When Faith finally stopped, Usha kissed each of her cheeks and stated, "Tenderness and kind acts don't mean anything more than someone cares. Those kids will talk about what just happened and I did it to make you stronger. For you to remember. When someone says mean things to try and hurt you, there will also be someone who won't see you for anything other than the beautiful creature you are. Keep them in your focus. That shame doesn't belong to you so don't take it. It belongs to them."

Sitting back on the swing she continued. "I don't care what they think or say. I care how you feel. They don't bother me. I just wanted to prove that to you. They are living their own tragedies in their own lives and are probably powerless. Trained into their beliefs and feeling like they're above others. Deep inside they know they're not. So, they try to insert their power into the lives of others out of their own weakness. Misery loves company,".

Faith's mother had said the exact same thing to her, but now . . . it began to make sense, and she felt better.

That summer, Usha left, and Faith never saw her again. She also never let the other kids make her feel bad again. She had Usha's kiss, which was so much more important. It let her escape them every single time. Until Jonsie. He took her power often. Many times, he succeeded, but sometimes not. It took time, but he eventually wore her down until she just felt shame all the time.

He'd called her sea glassing stupid, and now this made Faith angry again, though it also helped her feel stronger. Mind now back to her car, she let the thoughts disappear into the background and found the feelings she always got hunting for sea glass, playing her guitar, or when making soap.

Faith loved those things and Jonsie made attempts to ruin that saying it was immature, she was wasting her time, that she was an amateur and complained that he smelled like a woman all the time.

The essential oils filled the house and permeated the walls over time. She'd always gotten compliments on the smell and knew he probably did too but didn't like the feeling he was out of control and wanted her to stop to gain control.

She didn't let him take that from her, though. They were the only things Faith really held her ground on.

She never told anyone about Usha or that tender moment, and how the whole world stood still. Just them on the swings as she sang to Faith's soul.

Faith listened to Jonsie about money because he was smart about it. His being stingy was a different topic. Money smart, business smart, he was tactical and ruthless and had no conscience. That should have been a red flag for her.

Imagine if I'd married him, Faith thought. Realizing the favour Lacey had done by stabbing her in the back, she thanked Lacey now. She was free of Jonsie now and it was all that mattered.

Breathing deep, the smell of fresh-cut grass, which reminded her of watermelons, drifted into the car.

With the possible success on her mind, Faith sank into the seat reminding herself how well she'd done, despite those who wanted to see her fail.

She was strong. More than they gave her credit for. More than she'd even given to herself, until just now. With no awareness of how strong she'd come to be, though, Usha had told her. "You can be, do, or have anything you want. You just need to believe you can and conjure up the emotion of it already being done."

That's why Faith had started the book, guitar, and singing. She'd once heard a university professor say, "You can learn to love something you're good at or you can learn to be good at something you love. Failure is when you let adversity convince you that you won't succeed. All will go according to the depth of your desires. You may be on your deathbed when it happens, and that's okay. Don't give up on your dreams. They will build you up. There's a chance that your confidence will either make others attack you because they're jealous, but to some, you will give hope. Life is what you make it."

He was very passionate about what he said and had her convinced. Taking on all life threw at her though wasn't as easy as it sounded. All anyone saw of her was her tough exterior.

Faith stepped on the gas as if to run away from her thoughts. They were persistent. The car hugged the long turn tightly and just before she reached the sign saying, "welcome to Potters Peek", she slowed back down.

Driving through town Faith took in the scenery of their quiet ways. No hustling but bustling with tourists. No one sitting on the streets begging for money. She was slowly falling in love for sure.

Pulling into the parking lot of the gallery, she took in the building. It was gorgeous with its old barn board exterior and concrete statues on the lawn. Ornamental glass flashed and reflected the sun in the windows as Faith passed them by, looked for a parking spot. It was full but she noticed a sign that said, "parking on the side" and found one near the back.

Now out of the car, she noticed another sign that read "gardens" with a gold arrow carved into the old barn wood. *Ooh, gardens*, she thought closing her door, suddenly feeling much better.

Rounding the back of the building there was a wooden walkway which led to a pond. The boardwalk went up and over it with a railed bridge.

Grape vines draped over the trellis cover. Crossing it, Faith noticed signs all over the place.

The one on the bridge read "Pinot Noir" and continued below. "This is one of the most widely used grapes for red wine making. It is a variety of the Vitis Vinifera species. A top pick for wine enthusiasts for ages. Originating in France, this wine pairs well with food rich in hot sauce and a wide variety of cheeses. This wine is produced in-house and can be served with cheese made from PP Cheese Company located in Potters Peek. "It's a gouda life", it read after, which made her chuckle. Ask your server for complementary samples." It sounded great, and Faith noted it. Maybe give that a try with her meal.

The smell of flowers wafted on the breeze that blew through her hair and tickled her skin. It was very hot, and the occasional breeze was refreshing. The trees rustled a bit and Faith found it relaxing. . . and someone *smelled . . . fucking amazing*! It came on the breeze then disappeared. It was musky and dark. Faith couldn't help smelling everyone who went by, after saying hello. Nearly obsessed, she felt *enchanted* by it.

People roamed the gardens. Their chatter and laughter touched her ears gently behind the fountain that tinkled into the pond. She took in the feeling of it deeply, walked down from the bridge, then followed the path, trying not to get lost. Reading some of the signs and touching them, she thought being on the island made her stop and appreciate more. Even textures.

Not able to hold herself back, Faith bent and touched some of the flowers gently. They had wonderful, bright colours and the petals were delicate. Taking her time, she slowly strolled saying, hi, to everyone she crossed. Then smelled them. The scent burned into her mind now.

As she approached the back of the gardens there were people gathered round and clapping. She watched a minute and saw them shuffle around with cameras and caught a glimpse of a couple who had gotten married. The photographer was arranging their hands and tilting their heads for the perfect shots. They never took their eyes off each other but for a moment.

The bride was smiling and crying, and the groom kept wiping her tears as she giggled nervously. Every time he wiped her face, she'd get worse and then laugh—then everyone laughed with them and saying, "Awww."

Faith smiled and thought *That is so sweet*, and put her hand to her chest, feeling emotional. *Don't cry, don't cry*, she kept telling herself. But she did. A little embarrassed, she put her head down and put the back of her fingers over her mouth, creeping away slowly to give them privacy *and* to stop herself from tearing up too much. Thankfully only a few fell. Happy ones.

Looking around Faith saw the entrance to the cafe. Arrows were painted on the walkway made from huge slabs of sandstone. Likely from the shores of the island. She could smell the food now and was delighted by the blends of spices, only making some of them out.

She hadn't tried many things in her life, being a creature of habit. Usually burgers, fries, or pasta. She *was* making an effort to change that too. This was just what she needed.

Walking in, the sounds of people, dishes, and laughter floated through the air. A young musician playing classical guitar captured her attention.

Typical in his appearance, he wore a crisp and wrinkled cotton top with laces on the front covering his caramel skin and leather straps on his wrists. His long blond and shaggy hair bounced as he played. Every now and then his face would crinkle, and he'd bob his head and rock. Totally lost in his music. They all seemed to do that.

When he stopped people clapped, then Faith heard someone speak to her.

"Hi. Can I help you?" a woman behind the podium asked. "Have you a reservation?"

"Oh. Reservation. I wasn't aware of that. I don't have one."

"We'll have a table available in an hour or so if you'd like to make one."

"Yes, please!" Faith said excitedly.

"For how many?"

"Just myself."

"Okay, and the name?" the server asked holding her pen ready and looking at the beautiful black book with gold trim, waiting.

"Leone," Faith answered and spelled it out.

The server reached under her stand and passed her a pager.

"Very good. I'm Sara. You can take this and when your table is ready, we'll page you. I'll be here when you get back. If you like you can see the gardens and roam through the gallery. I'm sure there will be enough to entertain you as we prepare for your return," she said with a genuine smile.

"I have no doubt."

Thanking her again, Faith was excited to go and take a look around.

"See you shortly. Enjoy your time here." Sara wished before Faith had fully turned away.

Going back out into the gardens Faith thought, *So classy*, as she stepped back onto the boardwalk and looked to see which way to go. A sign pointed the way to the gallery, so she followed it, then walked down a short hall.

It opened right up and spiralled stairs ran from the second floor right the way down into the basement level. *Probably best to start at the bottom*, she thought, as to not get lost. The place was huge and was packed with art, but skillfully placed.

A man in a suit walked around with glasses of wine on a tray. He asked people if they would like to try the "on the house" wine and told them about what they had as they tasted it.

Eyebrows raised as they swallowed then nodded, he nodded back and continued. Smiling the whole time he spoke, Faith thought how happy he looked. All the staff were actually she'd noticed and when he'd made his way to Faith, he offered her one.

"Sure. Thank you," she expressed as he held out the tray.

Choosing a white wine, he said, "Excellent choice," then told her about it.

The sweet fruit filled her senses as she tipped the glass. It was *divine*!

"There are cabinets around to put your glass when you're done," he mentioned as he gestured to the red shelving. "If you have any questions, please feel free to ask any of the staff. They'll be happy to help."

Thanking him, he continued on his way and Faith began wandering the gallery. Picking out some petrified wood coasters, a hand-carved tray of teak wood, and a few pottery bowls she then entered the main area and smelled . . . *soap*!

Following her nose until she saw a display with a wide assortment. Reading the labels, she thought, *Nice recipe*! and then smelled them all. Three stood out above all the others and she struggled to choose . . . anise, spearmint, or chai tea? Unable to decide, she took them all.

The paintings were magnificent. Many ocean and boat scenes. The ones she loved the best were brightly coloured and abstract, but obvious fields and sky. Some of the shores. Looking each one over, taking in the colours, *glorious* was what came to mind. The sharp straight horizontal lines in an ombre effect, were stunning. Susan Christensen, written on the bottom. They filled her with warm emotions.

Turning to find a register, Faith took her purchases to the counter. "It's lovely here. I can't wait to try the food!"

"Oh, in that case we'll hold your purchase and bring it to the cafe. No need to be dragging it around with you. I'll let Sara know."

"Your services are bar none."

"Yes, Mr. Agenta has his ideas about how guests are to be treated and we follow them through faithfully. He likes things to be a special occasion for everyone. It's just his way."

"You must have great reviews!" Faith commented, passing over her items.

"Yes. It grows busier every year. Enjoy the gallery and the gardens and have a lovely day."

Faith walked away feeling special, but also a little apprehensive. Like she didn't deserve it. It was just respect that they had shown her. Why was it making her uncomfortable?

Going back to the gardens through another door, she was greeted by a marble statue of a Buddhist monk bowing and hands together. *Lovely*, she thought and had to touch it. It was smooth and cold. Admiring the details briefly before walking up the stairs, each one had words painted. "You are loved", "You are amazing", "Life is a gift", the last one took her breath away. "Love is learning another's heart song."

Faith remembered the couple in the back of the gardens who looked at each other so adoringly. Closing her eyes, in her head Faith prayed, "I wish you joy, peace, and happiness. May your lives bloom and flourish as the gardens you stand in and your love never die." Just then a breeze came through from the back and chimes rang in the trees. It sent a shiver up her spine.

"You may have just been granted a wish," a voice said passing by and touching her arm.

Wow! Faith thought, watching him go by. Feeling as though she had walked into a dream and wishing the whole of her life had been that way. Then, correcting herself, intimated, "No," out loud and closed her eyes.

I hope that the rest of my life feels this way no matter where I go. Serene, peaceful, happy, and full of serendipitous moments, she thought as another breeze came ringing the chimes.

"No crying. Life is amazing. You are loved. Life is a gift," she reminded herself. How she wanted it all to change. Or stay like this. Just then the pager went off, interrupting her daydream.

The cafe was right around the corner, going swiftly to Sara, she passed her the pager.

"Right this way, Miss Leone," Sara gestured and led the way.

CHAPTER FOUR
Wonderful Surprises

Archer walked down the post office steps and across the street to the diner, Ada was cleaning plates from a table. "Ada, darling!" he greeted.

Blushing she responded, "Oh, Archer, you charmer. Stop."

That feeling come over him, of not having a care in the world. Ada had been there as long as he knew and didn't move as fast as she used to. Her last child gave her a "bummed hip" she called it. Eight boys and five girls.

Her husband had died at sea just after their last child and Ada raised them herself. As the kids got older, they each had gotten a job to help with the house.

She sure did raise them right. All of them kind and compassionate. They'd all chosen professions where they could serve. Doctors, family lawyers, nurses, pharmacists, and child services. All very close to each other and very active in their communities as well.

When Archer's parents took them to the diner as kids, Ada would always have some candy for them that she'd pull from her apron while their parents ordered. She did it for all the kids and made it look like she was hiding it, passing it to them and not taking her eyes from their parents ordering. They'd take it and cup the candy in their fist then put it between their legs like no one saw. Before Ada left the table, they'd have it unwrapped and ready to pop in in their mouths before their parents could tell them no. He could hear the crinkling in his ear even now.

Smiling, he walked to the counter and sat on a red stool.

"It's been a while," Ada mentioned grabbing a mug knowing he wanted coffee. He always took one to-go too.

"Yes. It's been busy at the gallery. It's still quite early and I had errands to do at the post office. I couldn't resist when I smelled your coffee across the street," Archer remarked with a smile while she poured.

Putting down the pot Ada said, "Some things never change."

"Amen to that, Ada. Amen to that!"

Then sipping the coffee, Archer made a face like he'd just fallen in love as she smiled and passed a menu.

"Birt's special?" she asked as though she had to, always seeming to know what he wanted.

"Yes, ma'am. Hit me with it!"

Turning, she passed the paper order to Birt in the back and rang the bell. He scooped it up right away and Ada left Archer to his coffee to tend to other customers.

Archer listened to the bustle around him. A group of teen boys came in excitedly, and when seeing Ada, they calmed right down.

"Okay, boys," she growled to them. "Take a seat."

They shuffled into a booth near the front, and she passed them menus, took their drink order then tended to more customers.

Archer listened to them giggle about his car. A 1986 Camaro. He and Roger bought it when he was young, and they restored it back to original after an accident. She was a beauty. Roger wanted to teach him how to appreciate something broken and make it like new.

Drinking his coffee, Archer watched Ada as she hobbled around filling glasses then took them to the boys as they giggled and whispered behind him.

Birt rang the bell and slid his breakfast on the metal countertop. Ada came right back and took the plate to him. "Here you go, dear. You finish that all up, you look a bit peckish," she inferred with a stern voice and rubbing her belly.

Archer checked his washboard abs. "Oh. You're right, Ada. I will. I think the chef's beginning to nail this," he laughed, picking up his fork.

Loudly, Ada chortled, "I hope so! It's been twenty-five years; he may be catching on!"

"*I heard that*!" Birt yelled out from the back.

Archer cut his eggs and put some on the toast then sliced into it with his fork, laughing about what Birt had said. Classic!

Ada chatted with him about the kids and grandkids when he asked how they were, then listened as he ate. She was so proud of them. Pulling a book from the side of the register she showed him some pictures when not serving people.

Now on his last bite, Ada questioned him, "Will that be all, dear?"

"Well . . . I'll take a coffee to-go."

"I'll get that for you," she said, sliding his tab.

Pulling a hundred-dollar bill from his wallet. When Ada had turned from him, Archer put it under the tab, on top, he put the price of the meal, then got up for a hasty escape. She couldn't growl at him that way for being generous.

He loved her, really. To him Ada was an extended part of the family. He knew she'd get the grandkids something with it. Sure, she was doing fine, now that the kids were grown, having Birt around. Still, it made him happy.

The kids had paid bills for her before she and Birt got together. Ada was over forty then and had one more baby with him. Mary.

Birt and Mary were treated as if they weren't step-anything. Thirteen stepbrothers and sisters. Archer couldn't imagine.

Ada said it wasn't awkward, at all. They just blended from the start. The diner did well. The tip was more for him than for her, he'd told her the first time she growled at him. So now he'd just hide it. He'd learned that it saved him from having to insist. She'd always take it in the end.

Ada turned back with his coffee and a paper bag. "I put in some fresh biscuits and a slice of your favourite pie. It's more for me than for you, really." she winked, totally teasing him, having seen him slide the money under the tab. Nothing escaped her watchful eyes.

"Yer a doll." Archer told her before taking the paper bag and was reminded not to argue with *her*.

"You don't share those, now. We can't have you wasting away on the ladies. There would be a lot of sad ones."

Shaking her head, Ada couldn't understand why he'd been single for so long; she thought it was such a waste. He could have almost anyone he chose, and she was concerned for him.

"Have you met anyone yet, by the way?"

"Well, there was one lady on the beach this morning. So, you never know."

Her face lit up. "Oh, dear. I'll pray for you, love."

"Aww. Thank you, Ada," Archer said as he kissed her cheek.

Giggling like a little girl, it always made him happy to see her face light up as her age disappeared, losing all the things she'd suffered during her time.

"You're an angel. They must be missing you up there," he said then, pointing to the sky.

"Stop now. You get going and come back soon. Bring that girl with you next time so I can see if she'll do," Ada returned, flicking her hand towel at him.

"Will do, Ada love."

There was something about her. Almost psychic. It was like she already had people's orders written down before they said what they wanted.

"Byyyeee," he sang as he left the diner towards the car.

"Bye, dear," he heard her say as her voice was eaten up by the noise of the streets.

Now in the car, magnificently full, Archer groaned when he leaned forward to put the keys in, then started the car.

It rumbled a bit and the boys all put their faces to the window. Revving it a few times, the boys made a ruckus but soon settled, having seen Ada come over and growl at them to sit down.

Laughing, Archer held his belly. "Ooohhhhhh. Too full for that," he groaned and put it in gear.

Off to the gallery now he felt a bit guilty for eating all that grease, as tasty as it was, and decided a walk in the gardens would help. It was a lovely day and he looked forward to it.

Gardeners were tending the flowers when he arrived and went over the bridge. He'd grown the plants in a greenhouse himself and then taken them to the gardens. They just maintained his design.

Strolling through, looking at his empire, he patted himself on the back in his head. Job well done, he supposed.

An old couple stood by the rose bushes. She was smelling them as he rubbed her back. *So cute*, Archer thought.

She stood slowly, holding her back, and he held her arm, then pulled her in and whispered something. She laughed and slapped him on the arm.

I hope to have that someday, he thought and chuckled, then left them to their business, going up the back patio stairs entrance to his office. *Yes, the gallery needs my attention*' he thought and whistled some. He could come to the gardens for a walk later.

Unlocking the side door, and entering, Archer turned the alarms off, then roamed through the gallery area, jotting notes to give to Carla for the staff to move things. He didn't *need* to send orders but enjoyed tending to his fruits.

Scrolling through the upcoming agenda for the week ahead, he noted that Dana was coming to sign off on the consignment they'd discussed. "Tomorrow at 3 p.m. After the market. Dana," Archer reminded himself out loud to plant it in his head.

Seeing her work when he'd gone to the market, he asked all about them. Her intricately carved original animal sculptures fascinated him. She explained how it came to be while also tending to other potential sales.

Archer liked her attitude *and* her work so asked if she was interested in taking him some pieces for the gallery. She excitedly agreed, knowing who he was.

"A great kick to her career," she'd put it and Archer looked forward to seeing more.

Taking in some of the paintings on the walls as he went further through the gallery, he stopped at a painting of a Japanese cherry tree. It was only shades of pink, and thought it was amazing how someone could take two colours and make an exquisite piece with such defined lines.

Noting to make plans to go to Japan and see the festival in the spring, Archer kept moving along. Japan wasn't a country he'd visited yet. The videos and pictures always looked so stunning.

Staff had started to arrive by the time he'd gotten to the front. Greeting them all one by one, he wished them to enjoy the day. It wasn't very often he was around that early and there was so much to be grateful for.

Meditation had taught him to be mindful when doing anything. To be in the moment. Forever fixed on it now since he'd let Johanna go, he realized how much time he'd wasted on being hopeful. Life is too short to entertain mindless self-absorbed people and ones who just complained, never willing to do anything to change it.

Ben the gardener came in first. A deep introvert who loved his job and did it well. Archer gave him the position under him, as tender, letting Ben hire the rest of his staff alone. He had one of the greenest thumbs Archer had ever seen. Even though he was young. He enjoyed being able to put in his headphones and go to work without being bothered much.

"Morning, Ben."

Archer had a sly look about him having just decided to give everyone a raise and his face showed it. They deserved it.

"Morning, sir," Ben answered back, and put his eyes to the floor.

"Have a great daaay," Archer sang back.

"You too . . ." he said in a questioning way.

Archer was acting . . . weird.

Turning towards the upper part of the spiral stairs, Archer took a sip of coffee, raising his eyebrows at his own little secret, then watched Ben as he ran down the stairs to the basement level.

Ben not taking his eyes from Archer, really, with a puzzled look on his face. His fast footsteps rang through the halls and mingled with Archer's slow ones.

As Archer went upstairs, he listened to his shoes clack on the steps and out into the tall ceiling of the wide room. Then, the way his footsteps shooshed on the rug and how the door made that noise when he went into his office.

Delighted, Archer turned all of his attention to the sound of the coffee cup as he set it on his desk. It was very quiet but wouldn't be for long at nearly ten in the morning. The doors would soon open.

Taking a water jug from the closet he filled it, then went out to the patio to his plants, which he kept himself.

After putting the jug back, he took his coffee to the patio and sat on the outdoor sofa taking in the sounds of the fountain splashing beneath him in the pond. There was nothing to be done about time passing everyone by. Archer, was one to seize every moment he could capture.

The water cycled up to the patio, into a small pool to overflow it, then splashed back down. Like rain. He closed his eyes just listening. That woman kept popping into his mind, though. She sure had taken him, and he didn't want to stop the thoughts, so held on to them. She was just lovely, he thought, as he seized her in his mind and fondled the idea of her. Of them. Until his phone rang.

"Hi, Mom."

"Hi, dear. We're thinking of having a dinner sometime in the next few weeks and wondered what your schedule is like. The boys can come anytime. We know you're busy this time of year, so we'll plan around you," she told him lovingly, then asked, "How are things?"

"Oh, good, Mom. You know. Busy, busy. Can I get back to you on the date? I haven't got the schedule up just yet. Fridays can be a little weird. How are you?" he asked and pushed everything aside that had been on his mind.

"Good, dear. Your father is well also. Jonah and Greta have been asking about you and we told them we'd see you soon. I'll call and invite Trevor and Dora. If they can come, we'd love to see them."

He knew that meant he was to coax them to come, maybe just drop a word. They sometimes felt like they were imposing. "I'll mention it to them the day before to see if they can make it."

"Oh good, honey. How was the water this morning?"

"Refreshing. It's better this time of year. Not quite warm yet but not a polar bear swim."

"Oh, I don't know how those people can do that! It would be such a shock," she commented and made a shivering noise.

"I may be tough but I'm not *that* brave."

"They must be suckers for punishment," she said with a tsk tsk.

"Well, they're something," he laughed. "I sure don't get it. Though I'm sure it's exhilarating, it's not on my thrill list."

"Yes. They must be . . . One sec," she murmured and put the phone to her chest. "Well, Dad just came in. I have to get lunch started. Do let me know when I should schedule the dinner, love," she said then, cutting the conversation short.

Archer heard Roger mumble in the background.

"Dad says hi," she repeated.

"Hey, Dad," Archer yelled, knowing Debbie had the phone up so Roger could hear. Water running in the background, he knew roger was probably covered in grease, as he loved working on old cars.

Buying Archer Camaro when he turned fourteen, Roger figured they could get it done for when Archer got his licence at sixteen. It was a piece of junk, really. They'd spent four years restoring it all, and then some. Archer was nearly eighteen when it was finished. He used a few bummer cars before they'd gotten it done, not wanting to shell out a bunch of money into something he would sell tomorrow . . . or next week, which turned into four years. Then took a couple of years more than that to completely finish it. Now, it was a fine work of art. It's why the boys had gone nuts in the diner.

"See you soon, Dad," he yelled. Then heard more mumbling.

"Dad says I love you," Debbie repeated for him.

"Love you too!" Archer yelled back and laughed to himself.

She and Roger were so cute.

"Okay, dear. Call me back. I love you," and kissed into the phone.

"Love you too," he replied and kissed back.

"Bye, dear," she said, then growled something hanging up as Archer was saying goodbye also.

Shaking his head and smiling, Archer could see the scene in the kitchen. Debbie complaining while Roger rolled his eyes and apologized. Most time she didn't make sense to Roger, but he did what she asked anyway. She'd start singing again and peace would be restored.

Carrying on with his day, Archer took a shower to refresh, after that the day flew quickly.

Checking in with Jim about the music for Archer asked when he'd be in.

"Just packing up my gear. Didn't get out of work till three thirty. Always those ones asking more questions at a meeting and holding everyone up," he groaned, "I'm about on my way. Should be there by four."

"Awesome. You know where the equipment is. It'll be nice to come and have a listen. It's been so busy I rarely make it down to see you."

Where had the day gone? It seemed like he'd just gotten into the office.

That taken care of, Archer was just getting up for some of Devon's coffee when the office phone rang. Answering, he had a chat with Dana about their appointment the next afternoon.

Wondering if she needed to bring anything else. Archer replied to just bring herself and she sighed with relief. She'd left her art at the market and couldn't get anyone to let her back in and he assured her it was fine.

When they'd hung up, Archer realized he hadn't eaten since the diner, so called down to Devon to see what he suggested for dinner. After being told, he cheerfully said, "Sounds great!"

Devon said he'd ring when it was ready, so Archer went to the patio and watched people walking around the gardens, paying particular attention to the kids, pondering again all he would do if he was ever blessed with the chance.

Pushing thirty-three now, and having had a few short romances in that time, Archer never felt like they were a good fit for him. Then there were the ones who threw themselves at him. He took a few of those. *A man has needs*, he'd reason then always felt bad afterwards, not wanting to see them after that. They'd blab on about stuff he wasn't interested in, overly dramatic and fouled-mouthed sometimes. He wanted more. *So* much more.

Someone who had interesting things to say, intelligent, and funny. Someone demure and feminine but didn't mind taking charge when needed. Loving, kind, generous. Confident, but not egotistical. Strong but also needing him. Spoiling his woman was something he loved. He just . . . couldn't get his head into the ones he'd tried dating and just stopped seeing anyone. It wasn't fair to them nor to himself.

Devon rang and Archer took the elevator down. Trying to keep clear of the people, he'd peek around quickly to see if they were enjoying themselves and stayed out of the staffs' way not wanting to feel he was looming. He wouldn't appreciate it himself unless it had to be done, so he gave them the benefit of working freely, just poking in briefly to make sure they were doing alright.

Looking into the dining area, Archer glanced around and saw a full house with people in line. *Nicccee*, he thought. Everyone seemed to be enjoying themselves.

Wanting to see how Sara's day was, he watched her point around the dining area and then noticed the hair. Could that be her? It had to be. *No one* had hair like that.

His heart skipped a beat as Sara moved to write in the book and he saw that, *Yes! It was her!*

Quickly, he felt panicked and moved forwards to go to her. His anxiety made him stop . . . *What? Me?* he thought. *I'm the most together person I know.*

Seeing her there, though, had caught him off guard, again, and his true feelings showed. She was sweet and beautiful . . . but . . . this feeling that rushed through him was a little out there. Come to think of it, he'd only felt it a few times before.

I don't even know her. She could be a psycho, he thought . . . but he sure would love to get to know her and find out.

Pacing around just outside the cafe, a voice in his head screamed, *Go, talk to her!* Quietly he whispered "No!", which made people look at him.

Archer then just waved and said "Hi!" with his best smile to those who had noticed. *She's gonna leave! You have to act!* It interrupted again.

"Shut up!" he whispered again trying to hide his desperation and think clearly.

People around him who had heard, did their best to ignore this apparent outward argument with himself, then hoped the mental battle was over, smiling to everyone who may have overheard him talking to himself and decided it wouldn't hurt to approach her. Rubbing his face in frustration, he then brushed his shirt flat.

Don't be a fool, his heart said, and this perked him up. He hadn't heard from that part of himself in forever. So, standing upright, he fixed his hair, and rubbed his teeth. *Be casual*, his heart insisted.

"Casual. Yes . . . casual . . ." he whispered and turned, nearly running into the wall, then cleared his throat and tried again.

I'm good. I'm cool . . . I'm the man, Archer thought to himself reassuringly. Slumping, he admitted he was twitter patted. A wreck actually.

Go, get her, show her how you feel, his heart whispered.

Breaking into a sweat, he walked over saying "Hi" to people he knew along the way.

Archer, bud. Get it together, his reminded himself.

Closer to the podium now, his heart screamed. His mind arguing with itself.

Go fast! The voice yelled.

Go slow, his heart whispered.

Get her now! . . . Be aloof and standoffish! The voice argued.

Don't. Be real, his heart argued back.

Losing his mind, the closer he got to Sara, she moved and there was a little old woman with her daughter. Both his head and heart screamed now in unison.

ShIttTT. YoU mIssEd hEr.

Was he dreaming it? Did he miss her? Should he run to the parking lot? Lost, he just waited for Sara to seat them. He'd just ask her.

Look at the book! his brain said.

That's creepy. Stop! Archer strongly insisted, frustrated with this voice, as Sara came back.

"Sir?" Sara called on him.

"Hey! How's the day going?" he inquired awkwardly.

"It's good! Full house. Has been all day," Sara answered, checking names from the list. "Can I get you something?"

"Oh. No. Devon has food ready. Which is why I'm here," he lied.

"Oh. Shall I get it for you?"

"Umm. No. I'll get it myself. I was wondering, though . . . the woman . . . with the long red hair . . . did she have a table?" he asked almost impatiently as he fought not to look at the book.

Just a peek, the voice said, and Archer stood straight and looked around with an awkward smile.

"No," Sara replied, and his heart sank wanting to run and find her.

Damn it! Go get her . . . Now!, the voice ordered.

"She didn't have a reservation, but she made one."

Yes! He heard in his mind. At the same time, his heart calmed down.

"Is everything okay?"

"Oh, it's fine!" he laughed and leaned on her podium. "She'll be back then?"

"Yes . . . Sir. You're acting weird."

"Oh. Ha! Sorry. I'm just hungry," he laughed. "I mean, I know her a bit and thought maybe I'd put her things on the house."

"Oh, that's sweet of you, sir. She has some things she was buying," Sara informed him.

"Throw those on there too," he insisted happily, then strongly suggested. "Just make it a pleasant evening for her. It would mean a lot to me." he smiled.

Sara had never seen him so antsy. He was almost sweating. No. He *was* sweating.

"Is it warm in here?"

Archer had seen her look at his forehead and knew she knew.

"Well, the a/c is on, sir. I'll check the temp."

Sara moved to go, but he halted her abruptly.

"Oh, no, it's alright. If the guests are fine, it's fine."

"Okay. Well. I should get back to work."

Letting her go to greet the next people in line, Archer happily took to the kitchen quickly. His behaviour was unbecoming of him, unusual, and didn't want anyone to notice.

Opening the kitchen door there was much noise. Dishes clanking, Devon yelling directions, table attendants calling out orders and asking about substitutes, food and sauces sizzling! Devon noticed him come in, though, and rushed for his dinner. "Here you are sir. I think you'll enjoy this."

Smiling he then told Archer all about it, but he didn't hear a thing, so took the plate and lifted it as to say cheers. "Sounds delish! I'll leave you to work. Thanks. You're doing a great job."

"No problem, sir. Enjoy. Any issues let me know." he informed Archer then went right back to yelling orders.

Archer left and peeked through the dining room again. No sign of her, he took the elevator back up and sat on the deck with his dinner. His ears were perked to hear her voice. He remembered it still.

Peek over the side. I bet she's there! The voice insisted.

Ignoring it now, Archer decided to stay seated, eating sparsely, trying to convince his mind to calm down while it kept telling him to check the cameras.

Creeeepyyyyy, his heart reminded Archer.

Archer agreed and when he finished his meal, a thought popped into his head. *What if she was with someone? What if it made a scene that everything was on the house? What if it got her in trouble with a boyfriend? Or husband . . .* What have I done? *Damn. Damn. Please, no.*

Only caring how that might affect her, not that he'd look bad, Archer called down to security using his calmest voice.

"Greg. Please check with Sara about the table on the house. If she's alone, walk her to the car. If she's not alone, just keep an eye out. Any trouble, intervene politely and ring me?"

"Yes, sir. Is everything okay?"

"I hope so. It's probably nothing. I just wanted to have you pay attention, is all," he said to assure Greg, but felt he should explain. Certain he sounded . . . off.

"I'm sure there won't be anything. I'll be in my office. If there is though, I'll be right down."

"Okay, sir."

"And . . ." Archer continued.

"Yes?"

"Don't be suspicious."

"Okay . . ." Greg confirmed but bewildered now.

"Sorry, this must seem bizarre."

"A little, Mr. Agenta."

"Sorry. Just . . . make sure her night is smooth is all, really," he said, trying to back out of the panic he'd just caused Greg.

"You got it, sir."

That was it. Nothing else was to be done. If there was damage, he'd have to deal with it. Embarrassing as it may be.

It was in Greg's hands now he thought as he sat down and smacked his head more. *Could I make this more complicated?* he thought.

CHAPTER FIVE
The Gallery

Faith followed Sara to the table where a waiter was already holding out her chair. It was full and comfortable looking. "This whole place is just amazing. The owner must know what he's doing."

"Oh, yes. Mr. Agenta is very particular about making things pleasant. He's truly amazing. There's actually a booklet about how all of this came together. You may find it interesting if you haven't seen it. Shall I fetch it for you? It's a good read while your meal is being prepared," Sara informed her.

"That would be lovely!"

Pulling out Faith's seat the waiter scooted it in as she sat. Sarah had already left to get the booklet and the waiter introduced himself. "I'm Daniel and I'll be serving you this evening. Would you care for a drink?"

Faith glanced at the menu, then mentioned she'd have the wine and cheese she'd read about in the gardens, and for her meal, she'd have the owner's favourite, whatever it was, then passed him the menu.

Wanting a better peek into the owners' mind, fascinated by the whole place, what a mind he must have,

Daniel nodded and said he'd be back with the wine and cheese as Sara took his place at the table, holding the booklet and asked if there would be anything else. Faith assured her it was all she needed so Sara left to tend to her station.

Faith set the booklet down to look around the cafe. It was beautiful. Plants everywhere. White linen tablecloth. No flowers or flip charts with desserts. Just a napkin, cutlery, and the booklet. Tidy and clean.

Daniel came with wine and cheese and setting it down, he told her about what she'd ordered, how long the meal would take to prepare, and asked if that was all. Assuring him she was pleased, he nodded and told her if there was anything else, to catch his attention. Faith thanked him and opened the booklet.

Taking a bite of cheese, she washed it down with the wine. It was as amazing as the sign suggested. She hadn't expected it to be *that* good. Really having not lived much outside of the ordinary, Faith reminded herself of why she was there to begin with. To start enjoying life, instead of working just to pay bills and be treated like shit under Jonsie's shoe. And Lacey's, she added.

Needing a fresh start, she'd kicked it off with a bang. Coming to PEI was a big step. The slow pace of the island had helped her to settle, but ready for some fun now, the gallery and cafe were just the thing she needed to step things up. Thinking of what she'd do after this, Faith dreamt about travelling, seeing the pyramids, dinosaur bones, and museums, having done nothing in her life but age in that small town.

The booklet open, she read while finishing her cheese and sipping wine. In the gardens section of the booklet, it told of how Archer had taken the seeds from all over the world, planted them himself, and designed the gardens. It told of his passion for other lands and cultures and that he'd taken down an old barn to built the gallery with.

It mentioned his younger days and that he'd started investing as a teen and spent a lot of his time becoming knowledgeable about trading and stocks, with a natural ability to forecast them.

A millionaire before he was nineteen, he'd used the money to get the gallery project started but did what he could with his own two hands. It took three years to complete. He was also a humanitarian and funded many non-profit organizations and groups needing a helping hand. In a quote it read, "If helping hands are needed, I have the hands to help" and "it was his pleasure."

Archer invested in people who were trying to get their own businesses off the ground to become self-employed. He'd put several gifted kids through college who otherwise couldn't have afforded it.

What he loved most was people. Especially children. The greatest achievement in his mind was the first thing he'd ever done. Buying the field in the country and constructing the baseball diamond. He and Trevor worked into the wee hours of the morning and barely slept. His father (Roger) and his mother (Debbie) were so proud of him building a baseball diamond for the entire community. He also sponsored and coached a team: the PEI Hellcats.

Born and raised on "The Island", he loved his home. The rest of the world was beautiful, but nothing compared to PEI for him. His two brothers, Derek and Brett, were married with a child each. Trevor his best friend. They'd always been neighbours. For almost all of their lives, the town rarely saw them separated all through school.

No mention of a wife, girlfriend, or children of his own. No mention of a "partner" either. *Bizarre,* she thought.

How could someone so amazing not be married or have a significant other? Surely there was someone, or, maybe, they didn't like being in the limelight.

Try as she might, flipping through the last few pages, there was nothing. He didn't even have his own picture. Just ones of his works. Faith felt disappointed, then felt bad for him.

Maybe he was more of a private person with his relationship life. But . . . the book had mentioned his family and his friend.

Faith was quickly interrupted with her meal, which was fine with her when the Daniel placed it on the table. It looked amazing. Honey-garlic glazed salmon, rice pilaf, asparagus, and bruschetta. Faith remarked that it smelled amazing.

"It's certainly a great choice," Daniel nodded approvingly, then asked if she'd like pepper and she declined.

Dreaming about what it would be like to do all the things she'd read about him and the things he'd seen, it was strange for her be in this classy cafe, let alone travel all over the world. It was a far cry from what she had known and couldn't imagine his life but dreamed it anyway.

Daniel told her to enjoy the meal before leaving her to it and when she touched the fork to the fish it nearly just fell apart. Soft like butter but firm, it stayed on her fork. Taking a bite, the smell came under her nose first, and once on her tongue, the sweet honey and garlic dazzled and confused. The salmon followed behind, like a slow-burn mystery movie, mingling with the honey and garlic. *So good!*

Finishing the salmon first, Faith then washed her palate with wine. Always being one to eat one thing at a time, she'd usually start with the item that would be the worst when it got cold. Or warm.

The rice pilaf was flavourful but not overpowering as some were. It was fluffy and light. The asparagus was crisp and buttery with some spice she didn't know, the texture a little flaky. It looked like salt but wasn't. Foreign but delicious just the same.

The bruschetta was served with crispy, but not toasted, assortment of tiny breads. The slices, all different colours. No idea what she was eating, she'd never even looked at the menu. Just a quick scan. Words with no pictures.

The goat cheese was soft enough that it spread and didn't crumble. She'd have died if it had and fell on the table, or worse . . . on her dress! How embarrassing!

The musician was amazing and played the whole time she was there. All his songs stirred emotions inside and as Faith sipped the wine, she tossed ideas around in her head about how the music made her feel. How she'd dance to it.

Picturing a waltz, she thought, no. It seemed more romantic than that. Happy to just take it all in, Daniel again interrupted.

"How is everything, Miss Leone?"

"It was brilliant," she told him with a large smile. "I'd never have dreamed something as amazing as this place. It's been a real pleasure."

"*Oh good*!" he clapped. "Would you care for dessert?"

"*Yes*! What would you suggest?"

Glaring at him to tempt her even though she was very full, she figured could manage to roll her to her car if needed, then giggled inside at the thought of them actually doing that. Like a cartoon. That happened to her a lot.

"Well . . ." he whispered. "If I were you, I'd get the cheesecake. It's deadly."

Smiling evilly, Faith quietly said, in a dark tone, "Make this happen!"

Daniel laughed under his sleeve. *This chick is cool!* he thought as he straightened up.

"Very good. I'll be right back."

And he *did* come right back.

"Let me know if there's anything else," he mentioned, still smiling about her joke then sang, "Enjoy your cheesecake."

Of course, it fell apart in her mouth. The creamy flavour delighted her senses. Greatly. Trying not to moan and not sure she hadn't, Faith kept her eyes on the plate and avoided any eye contact. Her belly was beginning to hurt but she was damn well finishing that cake!

Groaning in her head, she took the last bite and barely putting the fork down, Daniel came to take the dishes.

"I trust it was good?" he winked at her.

"It was sinful," she confessed.

"Awesome. Will that be all?"

"Yes, but I do have items from the gallery. I was told they would be here for me?"

"Yes. Sara will bring that with your bill," he confirmed. "Enjoy the rest of your evening."

With that he gave a slight bow and left, and Sarah wasn't long bringing her bag of items and the black leather book with her tab. Setting it down, she informed Faith everything was taken care of, and that Greg would walk her to her car.

"*What*? How? Who? Why?" she stuttered.

"Oh. Mr. Agenta saw you make a reservation and said your visit here was on the house. We don't question his motives. Was everything satisfactory?"

"More than that. I'm just confused, though," immediately noticing as Greg walked up to them.

He was a brute of a man. Very young, though. Not particularly attractive to her but his size was magnificent. She bet those muscles were exquisite in some shorts and no shirt.

"Miss Leone. If you're ready I'll take you to your car," he gestured putting his arm out for her to take.

Don't mind if I do! she thought and stood from her chair as Sara held the back.

Faith put her tiny arm into Greg's large one. It was hard as a rock!

His face had a few scars and he looked no older than seventeen. She knew he was tough, but his face was very gentle and kind looking.

As Greg walked her to the car, he asked how she enjoyed the gallery, then listened as she tried to be brief. He'd only be with her a minute. No point starting a whole back-and-forth conversation, sure he had other things he needed to do.

Simply, Faith told him how she was visiting the island, about the cottage, the beaches, and now the gallery. How she loved everything she'd seen so far. The towns and roads were quaint, the people friendly, and the views were stunning. The red dirt roads were one of her favourite things.

"Oh! It's good you're having a good time here. I forget what an oasis I live in. Working at the gallery and talking with visitors reminds me how fortunate I am to be born here. You'll have to come back and visit with us again." Greg smiled.

Faith pushed the unlock button of the car and he took the handle to open it for her. "I'll close your door. You lock it," he said passing her the bag of goodies. "I'll wait till you're on the road before I head back in."

This took her back, but she'd do as he insisted. "That's quite a service."

"Yes. Mr. Agenta likes things a certain way and we do as we're asked. It's the least we can do. It's a fantastic place to work and he's very good to us. We love him really. He's like . . . my role model."

"Wow. You're very lucky indeed. All of what I've seen is like a dream I wish I wouldn't wake up from . . ." she replied, shaking her head.

"Maybe you should consider moving."

Smiling Greg motioned her into the car holding his hand out for her to take it.

"That's not a bad idea. It's actually crossed my mind."

Smiling as Faith got in the car, with his huge hand holding her dainty long fingers, Greg closed the door gently, then motioned for her to lock it, then mouthed "Come back soon" with a tiny wave as she locked the door.

Car in gear, Faith put her hand over her heart, smiling. As if to say, thank you again, and Greg smiled back. Waving once more, she pulled out and onto the road and saw him head back inside, patting an old man on the back then laughed with his head tilted back.

What a sweet boy, she thought. The whole trip had been sweet. How was she going to go back to Vermont now? Stuffy little town and unfriendly people.

Faith pulled into the cottage road in a food drunk state. Taking her bag, the air moved around inside the car pulling the smell of the soap around with it. It was heavenly.

Once inside, she put the bag on the counter and uttered, "*Wow! Wow! Wow!*", out loud in disbelief of the day. "What did I do to deserve this?"

After opening the windows to let the air in, Faith went to the bedroom to change. It was cooler now and she loved the smell of the salt air. Plus, the waves sometimes came in hard and crashed onto the shore as it lapped at the rocks.

One of them made a blooping noise and on the edge of the cliff, sometimes, she could hear the pebbles roll around over one another when the wave was on its way out.

Slipping into comfy clothes Faith leapt to the bed, throwing herself on it, then twisted a strand of hair around her finger. *Who is this Mr. Agenta?* she thought. "*Idea!*" she said out loud, which she did often. Silent thought with a verbal answer.

Bouncing over to the other side and grabbing her laptop, she flopped it down and opened it. Quickly, she typed in his name and the gallery. Taking forever to load and impatient now, Faith waited a minute then decided to get a drink. Hoping when she got back to the laptop, it would be loaded.

Setting the glass on the nightstand, she sat to have a look. Pages and pages came as she scrolled and drank wine. It seemed like she'd scrolled forever. Here and there she got caught up in some of the art and descriptions, forgetting why she was even there to begin with. Until his picture came up.

Faith's jaw dropped as she set her wine on the nightstand. It was . . . him! "*OMG OMG OMG!*" she screamed, leaping from the bed and jumping around room. She'd found him! Or? Had he found her?

Rather heated now, she did a little shuffle like she'd won something, which she called, a "smol viktory dance." Until it all began to sink in.

"What do I do with this?" thinking out loud and pacing. "I'm lost now. Should I call? *No!* Too immature. I have to do *something*, though."

It must have been near three hundred dollars worth of stuff he'd given her for nothing.

Laying back on the bed looking at his picture, Faith pulled a pillow to her and hugged it thinking, *what to do, what to do . . . What if?*

"What if . . . what?" she asked out loud, then told herself to stop.

He was probably just being friendly and kind. He's way too successful, sweet, and good-looking to be single. Some people just are genuinely interested in others and love to be nice.

That's probably all it was, she figured.

Relaxed now that she'd talked herself out of anything romantic with him, Faith decided to call tomorrow, make a trip over and thank him face to face. "*'Cause that would be awful to see him again!"* she squealed out loud.

Having worked herself up, Faith rolled over and turned out the lights. Then . . . just laid there. It was ten o'clock now. Still some good time to get decent shuteye but laid there staring at the ceiling instead.

Twelve o'clock now. Tossing and turning, she growled that she needed to sleep. Her publisher was calling in the afternoon sometime and there were things needing to be done in the morning. Plus, work on the book.

Soon it was 2 a.m. . . . then 4 a.m. . . . then 5 a.m.! "Go to sleep!" she whispered, a little insane now . . . Then . . . she watched the sun rise.

"Dear Lort!" she groaned and flopped her arms and legs across the bed, finally getting up to make coffee. "Now I'm beat . . . and friggin' bored!"

Did she just say that? *Friggin' . . . friggin' . . . What does that even mean?* Words sounded stupid to her now and she laughed.

Arranging the coffee, Faith thought of how it would feel if your brain didn't work right, and words lost meaning. Or if sight was a bit different for everyone. How confusing the world would be, and the chaos. Maybe something to write about, she thought, and put on the news, then laid on the sofa to wait for the brewer to make its sound. It didn't. She'd finally fallen asleep.

CHAPTER SIX
A Strange Voice of Reason

Archer paced around in his office, sick to his stomach. He couldn't believe she was in his cafe. Should he go say hi? No. No. That would be too forward. *I'll just sit here and do some work*, he thought looking around the office, "What work? I can't even focus," he grumbled loudly while rubbing his forehead. People in the gardens below heard him and looked around at each other.

What is wrong with me? Am I insane? Sunstroke? Food poisoning? he tried to reason. But there was no reasoning. Archer was crazy about her and there was nothing else to it. He didn't even know her, but desperately wanted to. *What if she has a man?* he thought then, making his heart sink.

The voice in his head started again, saying, *Just look in the monitor*, so Archer rushed to do something else . . . anything else! He was *not* going to do that. Better to drive himself completely bonkers before that, so went to the treadmill to try to burn it off and attempting to convince himself he was fine, he wasn't. At *all*. What he felt was "compelled".

To be with her, listen to her talk more about her life, get lost in her voice, hear her laugh, and touch her skin. To take her face in his hands, then into his arms. Archer imagined looking into those green eyes and tucking in that one loose strand of hair she had on the beach, behind her tiny ear.

To sweep the back of his hand across her cheek and watch goosebumps travel across her skin under his touch. To see her lips wanting him to *Kiss her!* the voice screamed.

"Nope!" Archer shouted and jumped off the treadmill. *This isn't helping at all,* he thought and called Trevor.

Nervously sitting on the sofa, with his leg hopping as he bit on his finger, it rang and rang. *Pleassee pick up*, he prayed.

"Hey, brother. S'uuuup?"

"Before I say, this is between us," Archer whispered.

"Okay," Trevor whispered back.

"So. The woman from the beach this morning is in my café."

"Yesss?" he questioned, waiting for the rest of the story.

"Yeah, and . . . I'm losing my mind . . ." Archer continued.

"So, what's up? Do you know her from someplace? You seem off."

"I'm beyond off! More like off my rocker . . . I just helped her this morning and I haven't been able to get her from my head all day . . . and . . . now she's heeeeerrrrrre," Archer said, panic-stricken, which was almost cute to Trevor.

Trevor had never heard tell of Archer not "having his shit together," as he would put it. "Is she following you?"

"No. I don't think so. I mean, I didn't notice anyone following me. I ran errands earlier this morning and had a bite at the diner, then came here. It wouldn't be so bad if she *was* following me. I could do something about it," he sighed.

"Well. Why don't you just talk to her if that's the case?"

"I can't. I don't know if she's here alone and don't want to make trouble for her. You know? I may have already started some by giving on-the-house treatment. I saw her making reservations and lost my head. I even walked into a wall. Like, bro! I'm out of my right mind. I tried to burn it off on the treadmill but got myself all worked up again. So, I had to call."

Trevor pictured Archer nervous and walking into a wall. Nothing had ever tickled him so much about his best friend. "Yeah, well, if I'm the voice of reason for you? You're in some deep kaka," he joked, trying to lighten Archer's mood.

"Ugh. Man! C'mon. I need your help!"

"Okay, okay. Sorry," Trevor laughed. "Personally, I'd just talk to her. You're pretty smooth and always know the right things to say. Maybe make like you bumped into her."

"Trev, man. I gave her dinner on the house. I don't know if she knows it's from the guy at the beach or just some creepy dude now. In any case. She knows that I know, she's here. I haven't felt like this . . . everrrr!!!"

"You've paid for Johanna for way too long now and those other ones never got you like this. What did y'all talk about this morning?"

Archer sighed and paused. "Just sea glass, to be honest," he answered, then regretted not asking for her name again.

"Wow, ummm, okay. Who is she? Is she from here? Like, what do you know?"

Trevor's goal was simply to get Archer's head in a place where he'd think straight. To find a solution. Truth be told, he had no idea how to help the rock of his life.

"I know she's sweet. Funny. Beautiful. Her name is in the books, but I don't want to be a creep, though. You know?"

Working himself back up, after being okay just a moment ago Archer felt in distress.

"Well, that's problematic. Maybe you could try bumping into her again on the beach? Hang around town some? I mean, dude, if you like her, you should find out something."

"Yeah, maybe if I hit the same beach, same time, she might show?"

"May not be a safe bet, but it's something. You want to go early just in case? Or stay later? I can always go home and pick you up later. Not a problem, big guy. Whatever you need," Trevor said caringly. "If that helps," he pressed on. "Or . . . you could go alone . . . or . . ."

"Or?" Archer came back, hopeful.

"Just look in the book."

Archer threw up his hand and said, "I can't, man. I'd be all . . . weird . . ."

"Well. If you feel the way you say, and you called me, it has to be something serious. What if she's the one? What if, like, your souls were born to be together, and they've finally closed the gap?"

Trevor didn't believe in all that jazz, but knew Archer did. Dora was a fanatic. They didn't see eye to eye on those things, but he loved her just the same. Archer too.

"What if that's why you're so out of control? You always had a great intuition. Is that where this is coming from?"

"Yeah. I thought the same. I just hadn't expected to find anyone. You know? Wasn't even on my radar. It's been so disappointing and frustrating; I'd kind of let go of the hope," Archer sighed. "It's been six years."

"It's long overdue, Archer. We all worry about you. I've heard that people find their soulmates just when they've given up hope for expecting to meet them. When they are doing their own thing. You been doing that a long time. Maybe she's caught up to you. You're such a good person and you deserve to have a mate. Someone who reflects the best in you, and you in her. You have so much love to give, and I hate you for making me all sappy right now," he joked.

Trevor was always the kidder; emotional things threw him off but right now, Archer needed his help. Trevor did things in a way Archer didn't understand and he'd have to let him take the wheel if he wanted Trevor's help, so, with confidence he said, "You should do something. I'll pick you up early. You sleep on it and let me know in the a.m."

"*Sleep*!? Sadly, I don't think I can."

"Well, I suggest you make an attempt. You'll get seven hours if ya go now."

"*Damn*! How did it get to be ten so fast. You're right, man. I'll see you in the morning. Thanks for the advice."

"Good stuff, and no worries. You've always been there for me and everyone else. You need to think about you for a change. You only ever need extra hands from me, which is fine, but it's good to be able to be here for you on an emotional level. That's all I'm sayin.'"

Archer could hear Trevor getting awkward now, so said he'd see him in the morning and let him off the hook. Dropping the phone into his pocket, Archer locked up the office and left through the back entrance as not to be tempted to be a "that guy." Even though she was probably already gone.

Then at home, got his clothes ready for the morning and set the alarm. Crawling into bed, he had to work on calming down and so closed his eyes to meditate then wasn't long drifting off.

In the morning he jumped out of bed a half hour before the alarm went off and texted Trevor. *Up man.*

Trevor text back. *Figured as much. I'm ready when you are.*

I'm gonna have a shower. May not swim today. I don't want to miss her. Not taking any chances, he texted back.

Trevor responded, *Sweet! See you at 6, then.*

Archer took a shower and shaved, had a small bite to eat then sat on the porch waiting. He could see Trevor's house from there, having bought the property from him when he lost his job and almost Dora.

Trevor, a heavy drinker once, was quickly running out of money and wouldn't accept any from Archer. Not even a loan. A proud man, though not proud of his behaviour or the drinking. Maybe it was part of his alcoholism.

The guilt of doing what he was doing. Like Ouroboros. The snake eating its own tail. Archer knew better then, than to bring up the subject, though. Trevor always found his way eventually, so offered to buy some of his land at a nice price, hoping he took it.

Trevor accepted the offer and Archer paid way more than it was worth. It was the only thing he could do. Then built a house on it, making himself handy and available for Trevor. Johanna wasn't happy about it. She wanted privacy.

Trevor cleaned himself up soon after that. Dora was overjoyed.

Watching Trevor leave the house, Dora gave him a kiss, then waved. Archer waved back and started the walk down the lane. Trevor waited for him, knowing the drill.

They talked about things on the drive, and Archer felt calmer as Trevor went off to run.

Archer put in one earbud. He wanted to keep the other ear out as he walked on the beach. Maybe just wade in the water a bit, and not really knowing exactly how, keep an eye out for sea glass, but didn't find any. She was on his mind the whole time, making it pass really, really, realllly slowly. Painful even.

Picking up some rocks he checked them for colours against the sun like Faith had shown him, then skipped them through the waves saying, "Nope. Nope. Nope."

Maybe the way she had said she'd done so may times and pictured her doing it.

Birds dipped and played on the shore. Piping plovers. They always made Archer laugh the way their tiny legs ran so fast. They'd tuck in their heads and some of their legs would disappear into a blur. Just short bursts. No doubt trying to save energy.

The tern's dove in the ocean and came up with fish. Remembering seeing one on the beach that was injured, he'd called wildlife rescue and left a message. Not wanting to leave it there alone knowing a coyote would get it, he thought to try to pick it up.

It was fast, though! Faster than he and it nipped his hand then watched every single move Archer made. Like a cat, really. Making the decision it was better not to anyway, he just sat and watched awhile. The eyes were captivating, sparkling with gold around the edges.

The bird's wing was nearly broken right off. Thinking he was probably not soothing the beast; Archer went back up the cliff. After getting to the car, wildlife rescue had called back and said it was probably a juvenile and that they don't have experience with the sand dunes just under the water, usually, crashing into them. They'd get calls four or five times a day about it. Sometimes just getting knocked out and needed a rest, if they were hurt badly, they didn't rehabilitate well, refusing to eat.

Informing him the bird would wait for the tide and go to sea to die, that broke Archer's heart. He wanted to help but now knew he couldn't. Thanking them for calling back he drove away begrudgingly. Nature is cruel along with the gifts it brings. Finishing the thought, he heard Trevor come up behind him.

"How ya doing?"

"*Anxiety*!" he yelled, and Trevor smiled big holding his gut. "Is this how you felt with Dora? Sick to your stomach?"

"Yep," he answered in that Island way of breathing in as he said it. "Pretty much every time I thought of her. Still do after eight years."

"Ugh. That's both awesome and terrifying to hear," Archer laughed as Trevor patted him on the back.

"So . . . you wanna go or stay some?"

"I think I'll hang around a bit."

"I know your determination. I also know that heart matters can make a man stupid and irrational. Dora sent some snacks for ya."

"Really?"

"Ya! Can't have you wasting away. Might have a date," Trevor laughed awkwardly. "Low blood sugars and blabbering. I can see it now," he joked then and covered his eyes.

Archer laughed in agreement.

"Cool. I'll come up with ya . . . and . . . thanks for that. You're a true friend."

"*Relax*!" Trevor said, running up the dune. "It's just juice boxes and Rice Krispie snacks that may or may not be stale."

That cracked Archer right up. He was always joking. No matter what. Probably a stress mechanism . . . or maybe a little mad. If you wanted to find him at a party, all you had to do was follow the laughter.

Trevor went to his side of the truck and Archer followed. After pulling out a cooler and a blanket, he hopped into the truck after Archer had taken it from him, and yelled, "*Call me*!" driving away.

Archer watched the dust from the road drift up and over the trees. When the truck had disappeared, he took his things to the dune and spread out the blanket. Sitting near the edge of it, he dug his toes into the sand saying, "God help me."

Opening the cooler, Archer saw Dora's homemade punch in a mason jar, a massive hero sandwich, and two muffins. Plus a few bottles of water "for good measure," she'd always say. He could hear her voice saying it in his head as he thunk it. Like in unison. Dora had written on the bag with the muffins "two, just in case." Opening the sandwich, Archer took a bite. God damn, that girl was good!

Taking his phone, he sent a text to her. *Thank you, sister! Love you!*

She texted back, *LOVE YOU TOO!!* with a smiley face.

Sitting as people came and went, eleven o'clock rolled around and decided he was probably wasting his time and should get some work done.

Texting Trevor that he should come back, Archer packed everything up and headed for the paved road that crossed the beach drive.

It was a good long walk and he still hoped he'd see her. Trevor was just getting there right when he hit the corner. That was it. Time to go now. Archer put the cooler and blanket in the back.

"Did she show?"

"No. Just locals are all I saw."

"Damn." Trevor said disappointingly.

"It's okay. The sandwich was awesome, though. Great breakfast."

"Ya, I know," Trevor laughed, rubbing his belly. "That's how I achieved my dad bod. Pretty hot, I know. I don't blame you if yer jealous," he smirked looking over his shades.

Archer laughed and punched him in the arm.

"For real, though. I feel lucky to have her. She could have left me, and I would've deserved that. I put her through hell."

"Maybe so. But if you didn't deserve her, she'd have been gone. We see you better than you do, brother. People make mistakes and bad decisions. You're human. You did the right thing in the end. It could have been so much worse."

"I suppose. I had a great support system, and couldn't have done it without you, though, Arch. You did more than you realize," Trevor said a little teary-eyed. "I just hope I can make her dreams come true. She deserves that much from me. We see a specialist on Monday to find out what the issue is."

"Hey, man. You'd have figured it out. You need to give yourself more credit. If I can do anything for you I would do it gladly. I know what you're looking at is expensive. What's mine is yours if you need it."

Trevor punched Archer's arm back after parking and left his fist for the bop they did. Archer obliged and got out of the truck with Trevor saying, "AMARRAW!"

"AMARRAW!" Archer yelled back . . . meaning he'd see him tomorrow.

Chuckling as Trevor left, he went to get ready for work. Having already showered, he dropped his bag inside the front door, grabbed the car keys, and went to the gallery.

CHAPTER SEVEN
Oh, What A Night

Saying his morning hellos on the way to the office, Archer was back in business-mode. He drew up documents for Dana to sign for their agreement about the animal sculptures for the gallery. Getting excited, and feeling they really needed to be seen to be appreciated, he couldn't wait to appreciate the hell out of them.

After finishing the documents, ARcher went to the agenda board to check the schedule. There wasn't anything particularly needing his attention. Dana at 3:00 p.m. and someone named Faith Leone would be in for scheduled appointments later in the afternoon.

"Who is this at five o'clock? Faith Leone."

"Oh, it was a woman who called after lunch saying she wanted to speak to you personally about her meal here. Could be someone who has a complaint. You know how some of them like to tell you themselves."

"Ugh. I hope not," he groaned going back to the list.

Wishing there was something to keep his mind off of her until the appointments were over, Archer usually took pleasure in his work. Today had him a bit disappointed and it got under his skin, noticing how much she'd really affected him. There must be something he could do.

Flipping through the agenda he'd made the day before, Archer crossed off things he'd done and notice the memo to call, "*Mom*!" he hollered and bolted upright. He'd forgotten with the bustle and distractions.

Picking up the phone he called, saying he was free for dinner Friday evening. Debbie would let everyone know and was excited.

After getting off the phone, Archer went down to the cafe to get some of Devon's coffee. The staff called it "No Smack Jack" and teased it was "high test."

Very tired now, the day had just slipped right by him . . . at a snail's pace he felt in the same breath. Coffee would pick him up some, he thought, grabbing his favourite mug.

Up near the loft, he'd added a pottery room and rented it out to people wanting to give it a try.

It became a sociable space for those who needed to get out and meet others who were of like mind. Potter's wheels turned in the background and chatter as Archer passed it going back to the office.

It seemed to him that artists tended to close themselves off sometimes and not notice till it was too late. The ache of loneliness looming about, they would gather in the gallery for coffee, talking more than actually doing art. He'd seen it a hundred times. Easily.

The equipment was expensive, and they made good use of it before taking it on as a hobby. Then kept coming back. Other classes followed behind. Painting, live models, and charcoal. Slowly it took on a life of its own.

Archer would listen to the wheels hum in the room below the office and people's cries of agony when their project failed and flopped on them. "Learning curve," he'd say every time. As the quote goes: "The difference between a master and student is that the master has failed a million times." Most appropriate.

His niece Greta had wanted to "play with the dough," she called it, and so took her in, and they made a mug together with the instructor. It was warped and twisted.

Kind of like Trevor, Archer always joked, but he wouldn't have either of them any other way. The handle was way too small for his fingers, so he'd just put his hand around it like a cup. Every time he saw it, it lit up his heart and he needed that right now.

Asking Devon for some of his magnificent bruschetta, he whipped it up rather quickly and put it on the tray for Archer to take on his way back to the office and thanking him before leaving with the snack, Devon replied, "No prob, Bob."

Dana would soon be there, so he thought, but walking off the elevator into the reception area, Archer was happy to see she was already there and appreciated her eagerness.

Telling Dana he'd be right with her, he put the snack on the table in the corner and asked Carla to bring her in. Food could wait a minute.

Greeting her formally, when Carla showed her in, Archer briefly mentioned the terms of the consignment, then offered her a seat on the patio and something cold to drink, as she read it over. He'd use the time for a quick bite.

Assuring him she was settled, Archer went back in for that bruschetta, after asking Carla to get her iced tea.

When she'd finished reading the contract, Dana sat and looked over the gardens drinking her iced tea, then feeling a bit like she was taking advantage of the hospitality, she got back to the business at hand and grabbed the papers to go back into Archer's office saying, "It's as we agreed and I'm ready to sign."

"Good, good. I'll call Carla as a witness. This protects us both," he told her happily, after wiping his mouth of crumbs, and called Carla in.

Having all signed, Carla gave her a copy and offered to show her out. Dana put her hand out to shake. She was a go-getter and he liked it.

Welcoming Dana to the gallery officially, Archer expressed that he was excited for her and how people's art careers tended to take off once they'd been accepted into his gallery and a few pieces were sold.

This got Dana excited too and she didn't hide it. Pumping a fist, she followed Carla into the reception area, and it made Archer laugh a little as he jotted the note in his phone's agenda to arrange to have her pieces picked up, then wished her to enjoy the rest of her day.

"Very good. You enjoy yours also."

Now alone, he took a glass of wine to the patio, since it was the end of the workday. Carla would be around awhile longer since she'd left early the day before. Attempting to get her to leave at five, she always insisted there was more to do. He loved that she was always so thorough.

It drove Carla nuts, if she felt something wasn't completed and always needed to have things wrapped up before leaving for the weekend. If she needed a Saturday, Archer didn't want to see her before noon and was to be gone by five. Sundays were off the table altogether. That was the deal. If she needed closure, she had to be done no later than seven on a weeknight. He wasn't going to see her overworking herself. Even though it was seasonal.

Looking forward to getting the next meeting over with and claiming his Sunday off too, Archer eased into the idea that it could be a long one, just as the laptop made a ding. With some regret, he opened a new message from Carla, reminding him of Miss Leone. Sighing, he prepared himself to deal with a possible complainer.

■ ■ ■

The sun came beaming in the large two-story patio windows and onto Faith sleeping peacefully on the sofa and cracked her eyes as a bead of sweat rolled down her cheek and into the pillow she was laying on.

"Oh . . . oh," she groaned stretching. It was so hot in there. *What time was it even?* she thought looking at the clock on her phone.

"Eleven twenty! Oh My God!"

Faith scurried to get things together. Opening the web page with the number for the gallery, she copied and pasted it in to call, then went to the patio doors to open them for some breeze.

Taking a deep breath as her thumb hovered over the call button, afraid to touch it, Faith saw her hands were shaking, so sat on the outdoor sofa, staring at the screen.

All of a sudden, her hand twitched and the phone rang on the other end. She didn't even know what to say, but it was too late as the voice on the other end said, "Good afternoon. Island Fantasy Gallery and Cafe. Carla speaking. How may I help you?" in a very pleasant tone.

Faith was speechless.

"Hello?"

"Yes. Sorry. I'm calling to make an appointment with Mr. Agenta, please."

Faith had struggled to gain her composure.

"I see. When were you thinking to come in and what is the nature of the appointment?"

"Well, I'd like to come in today, if it's okay, I'd like to discuss my dining experience."

"Mr. Agenta has an appointment at three o'clock today. What time were you thinking you may be here?"

"I thought maybe around five if it's possible?"

"That would be fine. I'll take your name for the books, and we'll see you then."

"It's Faith Leone."

"Okay," Carla affirmed, repeating her name.

Faith heard her fingers rapidly type and was a tad jealous of the speed.

"I have you in and Mr. Agenta will look forward to your visit. Just note it's after hours. If you could make it brief that would be well. Have a good afternoon."

"Thank you. You as well."

There, she'd done it and was very proud of herself. It was so unlike her, suspicious now that she had more than her share of anxiety, seemingly about everything, only now noticing it was difficult for her to do things like that. Ordering food, going into stores. She'd work on doing better at that.

Mentally Faith told herself to breathe, relax, breathe, relax, making her feel a little better then. Though knew she'd better eat something, it probably wasn't helping.

She'd felt as though someone had taken the wheel when she'd hit the call button and had to press forward. Almost automatic.

Like she was in the sandbox playing and someone sighed saying, "Let me get that for you then." Maybe her guardian angel.

Connecting the phone to the Bluetooth speakers, Faith hit play in her music app, and "I Got the Power" came through the speakers. One of her favourite songs. Fast and cheery.

Yes, I do! she thought, even if someone else had just played the role for her. Sliding across the kitchen floor to the fridge, Faith danced with the biscuits and jelly she'd gathered up and after arranging them, poured some coffee.

It was cold now and needed to be heated in the microwave. While it buzzed and whirred, she got the milk and honey. When it was done, in went the biscuits. While waiting she breathed in the coffee and felt the heat in her hands. Biscuits ready, she buttered them then spread some blueberry preserves on top.

Pouring the milk in the coffee, it swirled around like smoke. Leaning on her elbow, Faith watched it twist around as a peaceful scene came into her head about the coffee house, she'd been to in Summerside when first getting to The Island.

It used to be the town's post office and had been converted. Once into a printer shop and now the coffee house. There were large leather chairs and old wire-wheels turned into rustic tables. The walls were brick and painted white.

Finally in the comfy chair, she took in the scenery, imagining what the building had seen. It had to be a few hundred years old. At least. All the pictures on the walls were black and white. Faith had watched the milk swirl that day too. It was the first time she'd ever noticed, really.

Here, she wasn't herself anymore. Changed somehow. Become more . . . mindful, slowed down. There were so many moments on the island that had made time seem different . . . or . . . maybe it was just her.

Watching the coffee mixing with the milk and drifting off, words flooded her mind, so wrote a poem on the spot, then tucked it in her purse.

She'd forgotten about it until now so made a voice note in her phone to look for it later. It could be a song. That was usually how they were written for her. Occasionally, though, she'd just be playing around with new chords to memorize them, and songs would be made.

Picking up guitar a few years before, Faith found she had a talent for it. It wasn't all, she discovered. It seemed there was no end to her learning and creativity and vowed to try anything and everything that set her heart on fire.

Coming back to the coffee in front of her, it was blending, and the swirls had almost disappeared and begrudgingly stirred it, added the honey, then ate breakfast at the island in the kitchen.

Thinking she should be proofreading the book, Faith found herself just staring at it. Reading some, she didn't absorb a word. Probably best to put it away for now rather than mess it up. Hoping it would help her get that career change, she closed the laptop and prepared to meet Mr. Agenta.

Getting ready, Faith thought of what to do when the trip was over. She wanted more freedom and feel a sense of fulfillment and accomplishment. That dream was amazing to her and imagined that the book she'd built around it would go over well.

The inner critic said horrible things to her now that she had wiped her mind of wonders and daydreams, trying not to doubt herself, Faith remembered hearing the phrase, "things that are akin draw together," and prayed it was true.

Rubbing her forehead, Faith took a bite of the blueberry biscuit and felt satisfaction right there and then. She wanted to be positive and hoped to make an impression on this beautiful stranger from the beach. Then reminded herself to be careful. He could be a wolf in sheep's clothing. Torn, Faith's mind was arguing with itself again. *Good grief*, she thought. *Do you two ever stop?*

Wanting to be positive *and* realistic about this Mr. Archer Agenta, though, she couldn't shake the feeling that something was guiding her. That something incredible was there. If not him, then maybe something else important. Feeling it in her soul she'd see it to the end.

Lack and scarcity having taken much of her life so far, Faith struggled to get into a wealth and prosperity mindset. Here she was though, in this cottage, the pretty bank account, a possible bright future at her fingertips. Literally. She could taste it, but it was like vanilla ice cream. Tasty but not chocolate mudpie tasty.

Her experience versus belief was so conflicting but wanted to believe so badly in manifesting what her desires. Lacking the full understanding Faith hoped she was at least doing *some* things right. If it were anywhere near true, she wanted it. It occurred to her that you don't have to be special or do anything incredibly hard to find success, your dream home, dream job and maybe your soulmate. You just needed to be a better version of yourself and follow your heart. So many wise teachers had said it. All differently, but the meaning held fast.

After nearly ruining her breakfast with a mental fist fight, Faith hopped into the shower then towel-dried her hair, which felt nice as she dragged it down. It seemed to pull them all individually.

The sound of the towel running against her ear was very loud and when it was dry enough to get dressed, she sported one of her new sundresses, making her feel . . . sexy.

Usually not seeing herself that way, it was hard to not pick little things out about herself out that she wasn't happy with. *I mean. Who doesn't?* she thought.

Working to push them from her mind now, many times, Faith tried to settle into feeling the confidence she needed. To see what you would prefer, you must believe before it can manifest. Believe it to see it. How was she going to do that?

Sighing she went for more coffee then opened the laptop with the gallery page still on the screen. Swooning over his picture more, and glancing now and then at the time, her publisher would call shortly, and Faith intended to sit there looking at him until then. Taking in his features and fantasizing about how she could maybe persuade him to pick her up like a feather and drag her, any damn place he wanted to, and have his way, anyway he wanted. His plaything. For just the summer . . . oooh. Wouldn't that be fun?

The joker bartering with the fool in her head, they convinced her that having a romance, with no intentions beyond that, could be acceptable, she could learn to like it with him. Single or not. Just then the phone rang interrupting her devilish plans. A sign?

Faith talked with her publisher awhile, always keeping an eye on the time. Not wanting to cut him off but not wanting to be late, she was trying to start something good for her future, maybe become famous. Financially free would be enough, though, really. She damn well wasn't missing that appointment, though! He didn't have a snowballs chance in hell keeping her later than 3:25.

He'd wrapped up the call before three, which left her plenty of time to collect herself. One more glance to check. The dress hugged in all the right places and flowed off her round hips like a waterfall. The cut was deep and slightly revealing but still classy . . . not trashy. The colour made her eyes pop. A deep emerald green like the sea glass Archer had held to the sun when she showed him.

It was so adorable the way his huge fingers held it so delicately. Like it floated between them. How his shoulder flexed when he drew it to the sunlight like an offering to the gods. Surely one himself.

Eyes squinted, long black lashes shielding him from the glare, he stared hard to get a look at the colour. Faith loved how his face changed when he began to see what she saw. Lighting him up, as it seemed he was inspecting every atom.

She, inspecting him, while he obtained its beauty . . . and *that damn smile* he had as he gave it back to her.

It was one of those moments that Faith had gotten lost in. Like at the coffee house, it seemed in slow motion, she, grateful to have taken in every single detail of it. Passing the glass back to her, his skin touched hers briefly, which ran straight though her body and Faith did her very best to ignore it and giggled nervously as he smiled again, with no idea what she was feeling just then.

She hadn't been touched in so long and just stood there a minute, trying to stay still. Thinking on it now, Faith felt it all over again. Her body responding the same way it did with him in that moment he'd touched her. Did he feel it too?

As it played out in her mind, she looked in the mirror, twirling the dress to see how it flowed, greater things lay around the corner, she hoped.

Mentally sending herself on a mission, prepared for whatever, she was going to pry and find out about him. Ask him on a date if he didn't ask her. No stranger to rejection, she'd not feel bad about it. It'd be what it'd be.

Twirling one more time and smoothing out the dress with her hands, Faith sighed. A content one. "Yes, this will certainly do," Faith smiled and winked to herself in the mirror, then did her eyes and hair.

Thinking she'd have to do this more often "for herself," Faith wondered what had stopped her before. It felt so good. If she hadn't agreed with negative-neds or put so much *faith* in their opinions, she might have been doing this the whole time.

Instantly taking the blame for every bad emotion she'd ever allowed herself to feel, like taking her power back, knowing full well, though, that the work wasn't done. Whatever she gave power *to* would have power *over* her. Now it was time to learn what that truly meant.

Brushing on eye shadow Faith talked to herself in the mirror. "If it doesn't feel good, don't give it any merit. Don't take it on. Don't react. The second you start to feel bad you need to remind yourself: opinions are just opinions. You get to choose how you feel, girl . . . Do you *want* to feel bad? No. We don't. Then just stop it."

That would be easier said than done. There was so much power to take back. Jonsie, Lacey, the kids at school. Those popular girls at the first party she'd ever been to.

That rich girl never knew what hit her either. Faith dropped her fast. Should have kept her hands to herself anyways. She'd learned a lot about herself that day and then was deprived of enjoying any of it. Until now. It was time for a change.

In any case, Faith would articulate herself accordingly with the next man she had, completely done settling for lame-ass one pump chumps, there was no more time to waste, and she had no interest in playing coy or hard to get. How to do that was another story indeed. Right now, though, she had a hunk to admire and praise.

Feeling the super soft bathmat in front of the mirror as her weight shifted, Faith enjoyed it a moment before going back to the task of making herself as irresistible as she could without walking into his office in a garter and heels.

Sliding the gloss over her lips, she leaned in for a good look. They were super full and seemed like there was thick glass or a pool on each of them. Doing her hair up in the Viking style she loved would set the whole look. It was just a few elastics, really. Nothing difficult, but glorious when she pulled small sections out.

Makeup and hair done now, all she needed was to lock up and try to have a nice drive to the gallery and meet . . . Archer.

Feeling she had the upper hand after realizing, she knew his name, he, no clue as to hers. Fair trade. He'd given her gifts and left her wondering. Now it was his turn.

As Faith drove, she fidgeted in her seat. Memories of Jonsie invaded her nice thoughts and ruined her mood. First task of choosing how to feel, this wouldn't be an easy road, but it *would* be worth it. She hoped.

Faith was forever trying to cope with his neglect by doing things for herself. She loved him and that meant she'd take him for better or for worse as they say. Having to imagine what she wanted from him, no other man would do it for her. She was a faithful Faith.

Sometimes wearing tight outfits to entice him, he'd snarl about her looking slutty. *I'll wear whatever I damn want,* she'd think. Never having the courage to say it out loud. Jonsie's anger had showed slowly, and he'd take fits on a dime. She suspected he'd smack her good if she did say something.

Always staying faithful and true to him, she didn't think of leaving. She was in too deep then. Invested. Plus, there was no telling what he might actually do, and, like the teasing she'd gotten at school, Faith learned to just put up with it.

That was the end of it now with this new venture. That treatment, now, unacceptable from anyone. Not a solitary . . . single . . . one. Not from today on for the rest of her life.

Lacey didn't help, either. She always tried to keep Faith in jeans and sweats, humming and hawing about dresses when asked how it looked. Realizing she was jealous that Faith was thinner than her, had longer hair, and always smelled sweet, Faith stopped asking her and went shopping alone.

Until Jonsie stopped helping with the bills.

Lacey's hair was thinning, and she had to go the extra mile. Faith just had to be Faith. Often, Lacey would tell her, "If it were me, I'd leave him. You deserve better."

Faith's cheeks got red, and it soon consumed her whole face the more she thought. Clenching her teeth she snarled, "That little troll. She was trying to get him for herself." How did she not see?

Suddenly making up her mind, Vermont may be her home, but she was ready to leave now. It made her sick to think of even going back for her things, and if she ever came across Lacey, If they ever made eye contact, Faith would lose her mind.

They weren't worth letting go of the peace she'd built being on the island. They were definitely *not* worth an assault charge or losing her reputation with the publishers.

Having something too substantial to lose for the first time in her life, it wasn't worth the risk. It was very fragile at this stage, and Faith hadn't even gotten accustomed to it yet. So much on the line, and in transition, she'd have to do whatever was necessary to keep it going. What she had in Vermont was not living.

Mulling it over made her feel more relaxed. She'd decided, though, that she was never going to look back, then told herself, "You are worth more than the feeling of satisfaction and sweet revenge. As good as it might feel. It's beneath you." Primal emotions had stirred, and they weren't to be ignored.

They'd be excellent fuel for her determination, appreciating their power and usually destructive nature. Not today, though. Never again if she could help it.

Noticing the viewpoint, Faith recognised her growing desire for more happiness, a better life, for . . . peace . . . mindful to not be consumed by hate or anger ever again, new life was born in her now, and she'd do what was needed to keep it alive.

Placing it all away in the back of her mind, Faith was mildly terrified at the thought of being free, but also noticed, it felt a lot like being excited.

Yes! Excitement! Intending for this to be the last day, she'd ever let anything like a new adventure make her fearful. More food for fuel . . . but then . . . hadn't she always been free? It just didn't seem to be that way, having given it away to others so often, she just hadn't recognized what she was doing. No one was ever getting it again, not without a fight!

Acknowledging that she'd put herself on the path to healing in a very powerful way, yet also knowing there'd be old things to battle, now and again, to get where she wanted to go. Faith had asked for this and she'd not betray the promise she'd just made to her future self. It really should have been done years ago.

Her mind back to her car and the sound of the tires on the road, Katy Perry-Firework, came on the radio. Listening to the lyrics, it sang of letting yourself go and showing the world who you really are. All of it. To explode into a burst of light.

Interesting, Faith thought. A new chapter of her life had just begun, and she was ecstatic about it. She'd go into Archer's office like a lion! Stalk her dreams like prey. A powerful hunter, she'd pounce on them with great speed, dig in her claws, and they'd have no choice but to surrender to her will and desire. The rest of the drive Faith spent feeling liberated and in charge.

Once in town, she pulled into a gas station and got out to fill the car. Reaching for the pump, a hand came from behind and touched her. Before he could say anything, Faith had jumped back startled and nearly fell into her car. He'd caught her, though. Right before instinctively punching him in the face.

"I'm so sorry. I shouldn't have surprised you."

It was Greg from the cafe.

Covering her mouth, Faith touched his face as he rubbed it himself. "*I'm so sorry!*" she told him, sucking in through her teeth.

"No. No. It's my fault. I thought you saw me. I shouldn't have surprised you," he said, rubbing his jaw where she'd whacked him. "You pack a wallop!"

Greg had no idea she'd been in boxing tournaments. He'd taken it fairly well. Clueless to what had just happened, he picked up the gas pump. It was like she hadn't hit him hard at all. Putting the pump in her car he said, "I only wanted to keep your hands off this filthy pump."

"Aww! That's too sweet. Thank you. Are you okay?" she asked as if he'd never gotten a punch before from someone, no doubt stronger and more savage, than she'd just been.

"Oh, yes. I'm sure you've noticed my scars," he confirmed pulling his finger across them, watching the price on the pump. "I have brothers," he laughed.

Faith laughed out loud then too.

"You look stunning!" Greg remarked as he quickly looked Faith up and down, then back to the pump.

"Yes. This dress is something," Faith smiled and twirled a bit from side to side. It felt nice running over her legs.

"How much?"

"Oh, it wasn't that expensive."

"I mean in the car. How much gas?"

Faith blushed and laughed hard as she tried to tell Greg she wanted to fill it.

"Full it is then," he chuckled. Then with a serious tone he said, "You seem a little on edge. Everything okay?"

"Me? I'm totally fine. I was just on my way to the gallery to thank Mr. Agenta for a lovely evening. It was really special, and it meant a lot to me. I wanted to tell him in person. You were very charming too, by the way."

"Oh! Mr. Agenta is a super classy guy. What you saw from me is what I learned from him."

Faith's stomach filled with butterflies at the thought of Archer himself treating her that way and then reminded herself that *she* was the tiger this time . . . but who was she kidding? He was going to melt her like a Popsicle in a furnace!

Greg put the pump back and said, "There you go, Miss Leone. It is 'miss,' isn't it?"

"Yes. It's 'miss,'" she answered, taking up her purse. "There was a time when that was going to change. It didn't work out. It's fine, though. I'm actually lucky it didn't. Either way, when one door closes another opens. I'm loving my life, and you played a part in that Greg. It felt nice to be treated like a lady. I didn't realize I deserve that until just last night. Thank you for that."

"*What*?" Greg exclaimed in shock. "A fine woman like yourself deserves the red-carpet treatment. You should have a gentleman! One who supports your dreams and helps you to reach them! A rock. A shelter. A friend," he expressed with great passion, his fingers touching like an Italian telling you what needs to happen and why. He was quite serious. His eyebrows were tight and together. "Eyebrows knit," her mother would have said.

Greg's head bounced as he spoke and searched for words, as though it had upset him that she hadn't realize this, like a big brother might do.

"The world can be harsh. We all need that someone. Don't ever settle for less," he said shaking a sausage finger at her. "I hope, Miss Leone, that you find that. I think . . . I feel . . ." he corrected himself. "I *know* and *believe*, that you would be the wind beneath his wings."

When he smiled the seriousness went, then, looking all around her, he nodded, took her hand and kissed it. "Fair lady, your chariot awaits. You have a date. Have a wonderful evening."

Greg left her and got in his car.

What did he mean "date"?

Something about the way he looked at her made her think he was psychic or something. *Maybe he reads auras*, she thought, turning to go pay for the gas a little dazzled at what he'd just said. He was so young but inside . . . an old soul.

Turning back, Faith asked, "Greg?"

"Yes?"

"Please call me Faith."

"As you wish, dear Faith," he nodded, starting his car.

"Thank you for filling the tank, and again, I'm so sorry about hitting you."

"None of it is a problem. Enjoy your visit at the gallery," he winked.

Turning again, she heard him pulling with music cranked.

Opera? and *What did he mean enjoy the gallery?* She was just popping in and out.

Getting back in her car, she headed for the gallery, her heart could have pounded out of her chest.

CHAPTER EIGHT
A Fine Evening

Now at the gallery Faith exited the car and went straight inside. Looking around briefly she decided to just ask a staff member to guide her to the office. Taking her themselves she was led just past the cafe, and it smelled amazing.

People turned their heads, and she noticed them watching, making her feel awkward then. Was it the dress? Her hair? *Don't trip, don't trip*, she prayed as she led to a hall with elevator and was told she wanted to be on the second floor.

Faith thanked them as she caught a glimpse of herself in the mirror at the end of the hall, barely recognizing herself. She looked . . . amazing. Somehow changed.

Maybe that was what they saw in her. Newfound confidence. It felt nice and Faith basked in it while waiting for the elevator. When it dinged, the door slid open silently to let her in.

Going inside she pushed the button for the second floor, and when the door closed, she suddenly felt trapped and wanted to run, so reminded herself what she was doing. That she could have, do or be anything, her heart said back.

Who was this causing her to doubt herself? Why had she never asked before? It's that fucking critic.

Where'd they even come from? Natural instincts for survival? The nasty teasing and Jonsie? It would have to be put to rest if she were going to be happy.

She was creating something new. Maybe it takes a while to sink in. The way school teaches. Repetition.

Pushing the image she'd caught in the mirror to the front of her mind, Faith held on for dear life hoping she could get her courage back on the short trip to the second floor. *DING!* and the doors opened, right into the reception area where a woman sat typing. No opportunity to change her mind, Faith stepped off the elevator with as much courage as she was able to gather.

Another moment for her to walk deeper into that new life and seize the day was right on top of her as frightening as it was.

Her emotions were all over the place but reeled them in as best she could, doing what she could with her puny army to accomplish her goal. All she could think though was, *See the cute guy and find out what you can.*

The thought of Archer felt warm an helped her find the strength to blurt out, "Hi. I'm Miss Leone. I have an appointment with Mr. Agenta," as confidently as she could muster. It actually sounded good to her. Impressed, Faith stood a little taller and swooshed her skirt. Just a little.

It was significant enough that her fears subsided some. Grown beyond sick of feeling insecurity and helplessness anyway. *Make your dreams happen!* she told herself. *People don't become successful by waiting for it to come and get them.*

How might Archer feel? His success was all around her. Probably more than she could see, and she wondered if this was how he felt all the time. Reminding himself he was a creator. Worrying if he'd make that next target or goal, he'd set for himself. If he even struggled at all. Maybe it came to him naturally. Either way, she was going to find out. Even if this was the last time, she'd ever see him.

Carla looked up from what she was doing to greet her, and Faith hoped she hadn't seen through her, oh so thin, veil. "Oh, yes. I'm Carla. We spoke on the phone. Please. This way. Mr. Agenta is aware you were coming," she informed Faith getting up from her desk, then put a hand on her elbow to lead the way.

Tapping the door gently Carla went in and introduced Faith. "Miss Leone is here to see you," she announced.

Archer turned in his chair as Faith put out her hand to greet him. Archer almost bit his tongue when he stood to shake her hand and officially introduce himself. Body in motion already, his eyes caught hers and it seemed his brain slowly got the message. Then it tried to scream, *It's her!!*

All of his sanity fell out with his words. "So very nice to meet you, Miss Leone," he choked and took her hand, putting the other overtop of it.

That was his way of saying he had control. To her it felt like being wrapped in a warm blanket during a blinding snowstorm when she'd been freezing. He'd just taken the power Faith had worked so hard to get back, right away from her. Both of them now blubbering idiots.

It's just a handshake, Faith told herself and conjured up a feeling that vaguely resembled the confidence he'd just stolen from her. She needed it now feeling as though she'd just lost her phony upper hand.

Carla asked if they needed anything and Faith said water would be nice. She'd suddenly become parched. Archer asked for the same. Him thinking it might help him swallow his heart back into his chest that had just made an attempt to escape and throw itself into her hands to do whatever she wished with it.

When Carla left to get their water, Faith noticed her looking strangely at them so looked at Archer, still clutching her hand. He looked down then to see he was still clutching her hand, then gently let go.

"Yes. Ahem. So," Archer grumbled softly, not knowing what to do with his hands now. "What can I do with you? I mean . . . *for* you today?" he corrected mentally kicking his own ass. This was happening way to often. And it was all because of her. What was he to do?

Faith had him figured out now that he'd just given himself away and looked to the floor to hide a smile. Though when she looked back to him, Archer had regained his composure. He was really, really good.

She took his cue and did the same. On the outside. It was alright, she'd seen his true feelings. Confidence restored fully, Faith laughed and quickly said why she was there, in an attempt to take his obvious pain away, so motioned for her to sit on the office sofa.

Faith thought if she just talked it might help him get focus, that Freudian slip telling her more than he wanted her to know, she wanting all of him. His hands, his lips. His body on hers, or she on his, it didn't matter which. Faith was so frustrated at this point she'd bend her rule about sleeping with someone without having heartfelt emotions. She'd also settle for him giving her some pointers on how to approach her goals. Maybe show her some of his mistakes.

A business relationship wouldn't be so bad. She could be in his presence. Get him on the phone and listen to his wonderfully deep voice and dream of him wanting her but playing hard to get.

Faith was good at fantasizing. A trait she'd built with Jonsie, and she'd make it serve her while waiting for the love of her life to show up. Her strength was mighty when it came to waiting for a man and taking care of herself. A pro with many years under her belt. Jonsie had taught her another valuable lesson. She wasn't going to forgive him, but he was useful for something, at least. It softened her hate for him.

In the end, it would help her step into her new personal freedom in a grander way. Maybe not this red-hot minute, but eventually. It made her relax with a solid plan to get this man and have her way. His way. Any way he wanted.

Faith told him of her treatment the night before in the gallery and cafe. How much it meant to her and how it had made her feel special. Her evening ended with her floating on a cloud all the way home, to be totally honest.

She always told what was on her mind, sometimes getting her in trouble. Maybe tact was something to work on. O maybe he was a kind of trouble she wanted.

Complimenting how charming the staff had been Faith told him how much she loved his island, then to the point added, "However, at the end of the evening, I was shocked to find out that I didn't have to pay for my visit."

"Oh, was that okay? I didn't mean to offend."

"Yes, it was okay. It just took me off guard. I spent the whole drive home confused how it might have happened. It was so generous of you." she answered with a seductive smile, watching Archer squirm in the chair across from her.

He'd put the coffee table between them, as not to be threatening . . . or obvious. Maybe it was serving in the other direction. Faith was sending him signals he hadn't seen in so long. He shouldn't have been so hasty to assume but she certainly could make a move on him. He'd continue to remain a gentleman about it, though and wanted to make sure she knew. He'd watch her, though. Gold diggers and trollops came in all shapes and sizes.

Continuing the conversation Archer said, "Well, it was my pleasure. You'd had quite a time with your hat and sea glass, and I happened to catch you making a reservation as I went down to the kitchen for some coffee. I thought it would make your evening nice. Did the rest of your day go better?"

"Yes, it was quiet and peaceful," Faith told him as Carla came in with their water looking at him questioningly, as if to say, "Is everything okay?"

"Thank you, Carla. Everything is good. Close the door on your way out, please, and you may leave when you wish. I'll make sure it's all locked up," he said, then winked at her.

"Very good, sir."

Knowing Archer had it handled, and it wasn't what she'd been afraid of, Carla turned and left, closing the door with the softest click. It almost made Faith feel as though she'd just been locked in. Part of her worried the other part of her now sat on the edge of her seat. Sure there was going to be a show.

They chatted about things. What she'd filled her time with on her vacation, how long she was staying on the island. Him prying to get all the info he could. A very confident and collected man, she searched his eyes and watched his body language. If he liked her, he had the best poker face she'd ever seen. Faith . . . had nothing!

Archer, on the other hand, wasn't sure about the look on his face at all. Her eyes had captured him again. The way she made him feel was unfamiliar causing him to sink into his seat hard, as if it would protect him. Or maybe help hide his feelings.

Now having gone into some of her personal life, she asked about his family, then listened as he told her of his parents and Trevor.

No mention of a wife or girlfriend, she came right out with it then. "No significant other?" she asked and tried to be casual about it.

"At one time there was. High school sweethearts. We grew apart not wanting the same things from life."

Not sorry at all, Faith said she was sorry to hear that. Maybe there *was* a chance to get closer to him.

Archer expressed it was fine and that life has those lessons and thought maybe it was a blessing now that Faith was sitting across from him. He may have ended up marrying Johanna and this fine creature would be doomed to be the fabled unicorn to him. He'd find out, given the chance.

"I wanted a family, and she was a model. Not the best things to mix together sometimes, I suppose. She was very self-absorbed and felt it would ruin her body to have children," he admitted, but then added, "I don't mean to try and make her look bad to you. It's just the truth and I suppose I ignored that because I loved her."

Faith knew the feeling. She'd done the same. Maybe everyone does. He sounded very down to earth and now they had something in common.

"I've been down that road too. I understand how it feels. It can be hard. My last relationship was like that. Controlling and volatile. I stayed longer than I should have. We tend to do that when we love someone. Not ignoring their faults, but seeing them and loving them anyway, with hopes they'd change their mind and give respect. Then they'll do little things that make you think they see what they're doing to you, so you'll find faith that it'll get better. Being loyal can make you suffer a lot. I'm sorry you went through that."

This woman. *So* caring, mature, wise, obviously loyal. Having gone through similar things they bonded. Understanding each other they both relaxed now. And what she just said, 'find faith'. Had he found 'his Faith'?

Faith and Archer talked about their lives and dreams. He was impressed with her, and she wasn't afraid anymore, he'd made her feel comfortable. For the first time in her life really. Like he was actually interested in her.

Faith, to him, was a delight. She was smart and funny. Her head was on straight, and she'd given him the impression that she found him attractive. All he needed to take another step.

Wanting to talk more he asked, "Have you eaten yet? It's gotten quite late."

Faith looked at the time and gasped. "Oh. I was having so much fun. The time has gotten away from us, I suppose."

"I can order something up and we can eat on the patio," he chimed in rather quickly. "If you like, have the time, and care to stay awhile longer. I'd love if you'd join me. I'm enjoying our talk."

He really wanted to tie her up and never let her leave and didn't care if he seemed overzealous anymore. If needed Archer would throw himself down like the proverbial coat over the puddle. Him being the coat.

The time to act was now. He suspected if he'd idled any longer, she may leave, and his chances might be lost. She was already pausing. Thinking she was looking for a way out, Faith was actually thinking she should go, or she may just jump him. Another time might be better.

Getting awkward and worried he'd get weird, like he'd told Trevor, Archer added, "Unless you have someone you need to get back to. I don't want to hold you up or get you in any trouble."

Faith hadn't mentioned anyone yet but did say her *last* relationship. Was she not in one now? Or maybe it was the time before one she was in? He'd make her come out with it, until Faith said, "Oh. It's just me. I needed to come here alone. I'm looking for something fulfilling and wanted time to figure out what I want and what to do with my life. It's been a bit of a train wreck, to be honest."

Not quite what he was getting at, though his heart skipped a beat. Alone didn't mean single. He'd bought time to try later, though.

"I don't want to impose though," Faith expressed then, feeling like she'd taken too much already.

"You, my dear, are nothing close to an imposition!" Archer assured her leaning forward with so much confidence, it made cower inside.

There! He'd said it! *Now leave me alone, brain*, he thought as it tried to run away with him.

Faith eased into her seat and didn't know what to do with her hands and wrung them. Compliments made her feel embarrassed. She'd usually tell them they needed glasses, but not this time.

"You're too kind," Faith flattered him, still feeling shy.

It was the cutest thing he'd ever seen. And genuine. Other women had said the same thing. They seemed fake, though, and used it. Like he'd just stroked their ego, then trying not to show the actual size of it.

"To be honest, Faith. I actually was hoping I may have the chance to get to know you. I've been thinking about you."

"Well, Mr. Agenta. That would be splendid. You know I'm only here for a short time, though."

"Please. Archer," he said putting his hand to his chest rubbing it. "I'd prefer to drop the formalities."

Putting her hand to her chest as he had done, like the imitating monkeys, wanting acceptance, she said, "Faith."

"Beautiful name for a beautiful woman," he complimented, tipping his head slightly.

As flattered as she was, Faith kept her position. So dashing and as he said it, she couldn't help but think of that hand on her back as he leaned in to kiss her.

It was very powerful, and she thought she may lose consciousness. Swooning like in the black and white movies. Her head felt light, and scrambling to catch herself, it wasn't in time. He'd seen it!

Seeing her embarrassment, Archer got up to let her roam in the cage he'd just trapped her in to catch her breath. When he turned to go to his desk, Faith wiggled in her chair doing her "Smol Viktory Dance" then sat more comfortably, watching every move he made as he grabbed a tablet from his desk.

He smelled so good. She'd have eaten him for dessert after dinner. Wait. That was what she smelled when she had walked into the gardens. She must have been so close to him and never even knew it.

Waking the tablet, Archer pulled up the menu for the gallery, then walked back to sit. Beside her! All sides of Faith's personality ran around screaming in her mind like teen girls at a sleepover after some hunk in a movie had said the right thing, at the right time to the leading lady in the blockbuster chick flick. But fixed herself as best she could when Archer sat and asked what she'd like to eat.

Then, clicking out the side of his mouth, he said jokingly, "Money is no object."

Faith laughed nervously as he passed her the tablet, calmly saying, "It's okay if you're leaving PEI, but if I could spend some time with you, maybe show you around some, I would be deeply honoured. I know a lot of secret places. My buddy Trevor calls them hidey havens," he laughed. She did too. Right from her toes.

There it was. That laugh. Archer hid his contentment but not sure why. He'd have borne his soul and told her everything if she wanted him to. In a heartbeat. Tonight, he'd settle for listening for as long as he could hold her there.

Letting her peruse the menu he asked if she wanted some wine. When Faith accepted the drink, they discussed which to open and settled on a baby champagne.

Passing her the glass of cold wine that was beginning to sweat with the heat, bubbles ran up the inside of the glass like a ghost in the mist through the now tiny beads on the outside.

Taking a sip, it was just as he'd described, and figured he must have written the signs outside himself. Saying it was sweet like juice, Faith had to agree it was. "Oh! A person would have to be careful with this," she laughed. "I'd call this woobly juice."

Archer thought that was absolutely the most adorable thing he'd ever heard come out of someone so stunningly gorgeous . . . and he'd seen a lot of them travelling with Johanna. Beautiful on the outside but some ugly on the inside. *So* full of themselves, he wondered how they had room to love anyone else.

On occasion, he thought maybe they weren't full at all. Just hollow and empty, everything they tried to shove in was to clog the bottomless pit, but seeped out the ends as fast as it went in. He wasn't sure how some of them had even managed to get dressed, let alone, feed themselves.

Faith chose her meal, and Archer chose his then called it down to the kitchen. Devon said it would be thirty minutes, he was just getting another order done but he'd ring and send Greg up with it. Which bought him thirty minutes before the food came and the talking stopped awhile.

Archer thanked Devon, hung up and turned to Faith. "Come see the patio," as he motioned for her to come, then put his hand out for her to take.

She did, and also, did her best not to lunge across the room to do it.

Hand in hand now, Archer stood as she went before him almost introducing her. Pouting to herself when he let her hand go, he then put it softly on the small of her back, turning her into a puddle again.

Jesussss, she thought as it played with her mind and had a hard time keeping herself together now. The bubbly wasn't helping at all. "This reminds me of a quote I read once. 'Won't you come to my garden? I would like my roses to see you.'"

Guiding her to the railing he returned her quote with, "Richard Brinsley Sheridan."

Faith admitted she didn't know and said she had only read it once but it stuck with her.

"No matter where. The medium isn't as important as the message." Archer smiled as the gardens came into full view.

Seeing it all now, Faith could only shake her head. It was nice down walking in it, but what a view he had from here. "Gorgeous," she whispered, then commented about the fountain.

That's where she'd smelled that scent. He must have been on the patio when she came in. Fate was a cruel master but loved it anyways and thought she needed to follow her intuition more. Stop overthinking. That's what brought her here. Maybe, just maybe, it all began before she'd caught Jonsie and Lacey. Maybe she *needed* to catch him to be here.

Heart brimming with gratitude, Faith would do anything he wanted tonight and do her best to accept how it went.

"Oh. You must see this!" he insisted putting his hand out for her to take again.

As before, Archer let her go ahead of him and touched her back. Showing how it came up from the pond, he explained how he'd designed it so the water would come up the tubes that were encased in the blocks of barn board. Holes were drilled where it came out on the underpart of the top beam.

It couldn't be seen that it was a rectangle from below, seemingly it looked like it fell from almost nowhere.

"Genius!" she commented.

It pleased him to see her happy. Just then the phone rang twice. "Food will be up in a minute," Archer told her without even answering it.

This guy was smoooooth . . . and pampered. He deserved it, though. How hard he must have worked for all of this. All Faith saw was the lavish accomplishments. Not his struggles. Asking how he built this. If it was hard or if he struggled with his confidence at all . . . the elevator rang, and Greg got off with their food.

Archer moved his hand for her to sit at the patio table. When she did, he held up a finger saying he'd be right back. Every bit of her taken with this man, her mind screamed. She crossed her legs and sat into the cozy chair trying to find a comfortable position. Nothing about this was comfortable. Desired . . . but not easy.

Faith watched as he took more wine from the fridge and Greg wheeled their dinner in near the patio door on a lovely rustic cart, repeated the meal, as best he could, to Archer.

"Thank you," he nodded and told Greg he'd done a good job to remember it all.

Greg looked up, still confused from the words he'd struggled to remember, and felt proud he'd done well enough to receive a compliment.

Asking if there was anything else, Greg noticed Faith's green dress. She was still there, which got him excited for Archer.

He'd suspected the nature of their relationship when he'd seen Faith at the gas station. Good at reading people, it's why Archer had given him his position.

Greg's mother was sensitive to energies and passed it down to him. No one knew anything of it though.

Why Archer always seemed to be alone was beyond Greg and felt bad for him in a way. He had class and style, was generous and thoughtful, immense knowledge and a great sense of humour. Everything Greg looked up to. His role model. Then Greg realized. He was waiting for *her*. It was the only thing that made sense. Staying available until she was ready for him, Greg saw it all around her earlier that day.

Archer said that would be all and shifted his pants as Greg commented, "You have some great company."

"Yes. She's a delight. She's here on vacation. We met at the beach yesterday. I wasn't sure how to tell why I asked you to treat her as I did. Sorry if it seemed like I was acting oddly . . . I just wasn't sure if she was with anyone, and it hadn't crossed my mind that my gifting her dinner might upset her or get her into some trouble."

"All good, sir. It's turned out for the best. Enjoy dinner." Greg winked knowing now that fate had drawn them together.

Greg left and Archer wheeled the cart out onto the patio. After serving them each, he sat with her, pouring them both a fresh glass of wine.

"Thank you." Faith smiled, then shifted the plate slightly to admire it. "It looks lovely."

"I would say the same to you, Faith. It's been a very, very long time since I've had the company of someone as lovely as yourself. If ever," Archer returned as he took the napkin from the utensils and put it on his lap.

Faith followed his lead. This was all so hoity-toity . . . but who was she to complain. She wanted to share the term with him but wasn't sure what his sense of humour was like yet. Maybe someday she'd tell him. Until then, the lovely dinner in the amazing gardens and sweet wine, was all Faith concerned herself with. If someone woke her from a dream right now, she'd be very angry!

"I find that hard to believe. Look at you. A gorgeous man. So polite and kind. Generous. Successful. This place and what you've built. It's the sweetest dream. The women must throw themselves at your feet."

Archer blushed and stuttered a bit as he cut into the food. He had to look down. those eyes had cut deep into him, and he avoided her question about the women only having eyes for her. They didn't matter anymore. Not a single one of them.

"Yes, it was a labour of love. I grew up quickly and knew what I wanted then went after it aggressively. It was hard to exercise patience. It taught me a lot. Anything worth having takes time. Looking back now at the stages, it's quite overwhelming. It seemed like it took forever. Every piece of this place has a story and I basically 'grew up' here. When I look at each thing has a specific memory. It floods my mind now and then. Some good, some not. It's all me, though."

Talking more as they ate, Faith was getting a better picture of him. The food was as divine as the night before and when they'd finished, he suggested they sit on the sofa where it was more comfortable.

Once seated, Archer reached for her foot with raised eyebrows. Surrounded by his dark skin and silky black hair, he asked with only his eyes as he kept talking with her. Not sure why she asked. "What?"

Moving his fingers for Faith to give her, Archer took her ankle gently and pulled off her shoe, put her foot on the coffee table, then motioned for the other and did the same.

"Relax . . . we're friends now," he smiled, then took his own off and joined her. "Now. What were you saying before I so rudely interrupted you?"

Faith smiled remarking, "I wasn't sure what you were doing, but this is really nice to feel relaxed."

"Good then. I've been successful."

Archer told her of some places she should see while on The Island. They talked for hours, and the sun had gone down long ago. Still, they just kept talking. The wine made Faith feel light-headed and refused another glass when he offered. "I have to drive, and I've already had one too many."

"Nonsense. I can have Greg drive you home. You can go alone. No need for me to see where you live. I have a room in the loft. There's a full bath and I have clothes. I'll be fine to stay here, I mean, I'd never do anything like stalk you or come over uninvited. It's not me."

Which was true. He wouldn't even peek at the books or look in the monitor and had a fight with himself about it, actually.

"Well. I really haven't been like this for a long time and it's very nice. I don't drink much. Some here and there really is all," Faith admitted, leaving it at that. "I'll have one more then if you check with Greg first, though, please."

It made him happy to hear her say that and knew for sure she was considerate. "*Great!*" he commented with a happiness she loved.

Then bouncing up to get his earpiece Archer called down to Greg. Pacing in the office, Faith watched him talk, then listen. Putting the earpiece on the desk he took another bottle of wine from the fridge and she assumed Greg would be driving her.

"Greg is good for anything we have a plan for," Archer confirmed and poured them each another glass. "Do you want some music or something in the background?"

"If you like," she replied, then requested he put on a playlist he liked, giving her a better peek into his mind.

Enjoying the dance music Archer put on Faith thanked God it wasn't country. She found it excruciatingly painful. Not all of it, though. Just . . . most. Even though she'd learned some country tunes, it wasn't the old kind of country. The newer stuff with current beats, she didn't stray far from there in terms of country, barely tolerating the whining, as she put it.

Indie was her thing and often enjoyed rap and pop. Classical was good in her books too, along with some blues or swing. Really, she was all over the place.

Using her app, Faith let it go and she'd find obscure and delightful music. Every now and then, though, she'd listen to the radio to find new songs. November and December being those peak times. Maybe some in the summer coming home late in the evening from cleaning cottages on the weekend.

The radio always played things to death and would get sick of them fast. As soon as Faith heard the first few notes of a song, and made the country connection, she knew she was on the wrong side of the app. New Year's Eve was great as well. She could hear all the hits from the whole year in one night, pick what she wanted, then add them to her playlist.

Archer, still standing, held out his hand for her. Moving to get up, he leaned in and pulled her right up and to him. Her feet looked like a dancer's, he thought, the way they came from under her dress and moved her across the floor. Her delicate fingers draped over his strong hand. The other on her back.

Faith thought he was really good. She hadn't danced much. A few times before Jonsie. He hated dancing and never let her dance with anyone else either. Or even *look* in her general direction.

He'd never say anything to the guy, only to her once they got in the car. After a while he didn't even wait till then. Jonsie would shoot her a dirty look and Faith would keep her head down. Then he'd skulk around for days making her life hell, to the point where she didn't even want to go out anymore.

Thinking maybe Archer took lessons, he dipped and twirled her around his finger and as he did all she could think was *damn* . . . even his *armpits* smelled amazing. All in all, he led, and she followed.

Sultry but bluesy music came from the speakers and filled the patio. Pulling Faith closer, he made sure to keep a little space between them. Respectfully. His hand holding hers in the air, the other he had placed on his shoulder. Such a gentleman . . . and Faith could tell he needed a good rub. His neck was as hard as a rock. "Archer?"

"Hm? What's that?" he said in an attentive tone.

"Well. I just wanted to say thank you for this evening. It's been so very nice." She smiled and looked into his chocolate-brown eyes. He, into those *goddamn green eyes!*

Struggling to stay focused, Archer heard her well as she said, "You are an amazing man. You've been so polite and charming."

Then proud he had not given in to his primal urges he replied, "As any man should have treated you."

Faith started to tear up when he said that, and he stopped them dancing. Looking hard into her now, a soul, a decent human being. Someone he might care for.

"Are you okay? Did I say something?" he asked concerned.

"No. No. You didn't do anything. Well, you did," Faith stuttered. "I'm just not used to this. Being treated like a lady. Usually, men grope me, or they just ogle me across the room making me feel like an object . . . and the rest . . . well . . . they say some nasty things. Like that will get them somewhere. Not really boyfriend material. So crude."

The last thing Faith wanted right now was to be emotional. *Don't cry, don't cry,* she kept saying in her head, but she was gonna.

"Aww!" he cooed, looking over her face. "I'm sorry life has given that to you. You deserve respect and I'll show it to you for as long as we're together. Even if you only ever allow me to be a friend or acquaintance, I'd like to get to know you more . . . as a person. You're a sweet woman. Maybe I can show you how you should expect to be treated. Not just by me, but any man. There are some pigs in this world, and you should expect more from a man. He's supposed to take care of you. Be gentle, but strong when it's needed. These days men have forgotten to be considerate and gentlemanly. They don't court women anymore and women don't expect it. It's confusing and a long, serious discussion. When you're with me you can expect my best behaviour. I promise."

Faith knew he meant it and felt called out treating her this way. Why? Why had she not expected it? Was there something wrong with her? Maybe it was because her father had gone so early. Surely, he'd have shown her what to expect. A father should do that, Faith thought, as a tear ran down her cheek.

Before she could wipe it, though, Archer already had his hand on her face and wiping her cheek with the back of his hand. She felt cared for. Then he hugged her close, still keeping space between them and kissed her forehead. His sweet breath flooded across her skin as it came out from his nose and down over her face, giving her goosebumps.

Archer didn't look at her directly as he wasn't sure if being emotional made her uncomfortable. He also didn't want her to stop if she felt she needed a cry, so just took the back of her neck with his hand and gently pulled her head to his chest, squeezing her in gently.

"It's okay if you want to cry. Sometimes we need to let things out. I won't embarrass you, though, and make a big deal out of it. If it's uncomfortable I can be whatever you need. Stay in my arms as long as you like. I'll stop talking."

Swaying with her, he'd just played her heart like a fiddle. "I don't want you to stop talking," she said almost begging. He'd already made her feel better with the soft hug and not being dramatic about her crying a little.

Pulling his head away, his mouth motioning like he was saying loud, big words and seemed he was talking like a thousand miles a minute, but nothing came out. Faith laughed and buried her face in his chest for support.

Archer smiled and spun Froth around. Then twirling her under his arm again it spun her whole demeanour with it. She felt so much better.

"You're quite a man, Mr. Agenta," she laughed.

Stopping her, he held her out, pulling away at their whole arm's length and with a Spanish accent he bowed then put his hand to his chest. "Please! senorita . . . Archer to you."

"You're silly!"

How he loved that smile. Moving his head, he gestured to her. "Come let's sit more."

On the sofa he moved for her to put her feet back up and they did together.

"Life has enough serious moments. I just wanted you to smile again. I didn't mean to steal anything you were going through from you. If you feel emotional, you're allowed, and you should if you so please. It's part of who we are as humans. If you ever want to talk about it, I'm all ears. I don't judge and I won't pry at you. I just take people and moments for what they are and any lessons to be learned. Good or bad . . . I mean, I don't tolerate bad behaviour, there's other ways to express yourself. I understand, though. It happens," he told her with a very serious face.

"You're allowed to feel bad. We all do sometimes. I do like to understand people and where they're coming from. We all feel the need to be understood and accepted, to have others know us deeply and form trusting bonds. Feeling a connection is part of it all. It's one of the best parts. Laughter and joking around is great, but it's not the only medicine. When someone is hurting it can help to joke a bit, but sometimes, what they need is to have that deep understanding from someone. Either way I'm here. Relationships are all kinds of things. Whether in a work environment, home life, friendships, love, or even neighbours. I like to listen, and I'll try to understand. My heart is big, and I'll never hide that."

Faith listened intently, taking her from the issue she was struggling with. Being taken advantage of and being taken for granted hurt, never mind the mental abuse and wasn't sure she'd get used to being treated like this. *Like what?* her mind asked. *Respected?* Frankly, it was a bit scary, but she'd love to have the chance to try to condition herself to it.

"I've never met anyone like you, Archer. So bold and colourful. So down to earth and caring. It's offsetting to be honest. But . . ." Faith paused.

"Yes?"

Keeping a distance to not make her more uncomfortable, she continued, "I just . . . ugh . . . why is this so hard?!" Faith groaned.

Archer just sat back and crossed his legs, continuing to hold her hand and leaned on his elbow playing with his earlobe. Like he was tuning in to her. Touching his ear to hear better, listening. Relaxed and open.

Shaking her head in disbelief of what she was witnessing, Faith sighed. He just patiently waited. "Well..." she finally began. "Annnnnd... I may be a little bit drunk right now, but I'm just gonna go with it. I find you incredibly attractive and to be honest, I couldn't stop thinking about you. I barely slept after I got home last night. I found your site and read some of what was there, but I actually just wanted to know who'd wiped my bill clean." Then after a nervous giggle said. "Funny thing it was you. I got a *wee* bit excited, which is why I didn't sleep. Now here you are... drying my tears after realizing I've been played for a fool my whole life and making me see there's so much more to life. I didn't expect this. Like, at all."

Still listening intently and quiet, Archer wanted to hear more. Not just because it's part of who he is, but knew there was more, and she was stalling to tell him the whole issue. It was in her tone.

Though not pressing, Archer would just take what she offered. It told him more about her than she knew or would even understand. Maybe with time she would. If he had that.

Time... how he wanted her time, but just nodded for her to continue if she wished.

Faith looked into his eyes, which were fixed on her. She stalled because it was usually at this point Jonsie would be done listening. He didn't give a shit. Archer did, even though they barely knew each other. Who was this she was talking to? An *angel*?

Sighing again she went for it all. "Part of why I'm here is because I wanted to thank you for last night. The other is that... I wanted to see you. I would've been totally happy to sing your graces and leave, but this evening has been the highlight of my life," she confessed.

Shit, shit, shit... she just said that... like... out loud. Faith groaned in her head, then attempted to recover. "I haven't had the best relationships and hadn't realized how bad until tonight. It's been enlightening for sure. You've gone and made me realize how much I've been missing. I mean, I knew but I didn't know... You know?"

"I get you!" Archer told her with a smile to one side, then breathed in as he was going to say something more.

Sitting up and putting his other hand on the one he was already holding he went on. "You know, it's okay to be fragile. We all have our things. I want you to know, though, you're amazing and loved, and even though that may not mean anything to you, because I don't know where you are with that, it's true. Everything here. The gardens, the cafe, the island, its fields, shores and waters are a creation. My beliefs suggest that you created it, really. Your desire put you where you needed to be, and I believe you were drawn here for whatever relief you'd been seeking. Answers to the questions in your heart. All of life is. It only requires attention and for it to reach a tipping point. Something urgent. Through your experience you asked for more. Inspiration overcame you as you allowed and here you are. You're also a creation. Maybe one of my making. Albeit a magnificent one."

"Thank you. As are you. I've never heard anyone say anything like that. Quite fascinating. Maybe you could tell me more sometime?"

Fuckin rights! Archer heard Trevor say in his head and smiled. "Whatever you wish. I'd love that actually," he answered in his calmest voice.

"I've never met anyone so beautiful."

Archer blushing now, didn't know what to say about that.

It was as if she saw his soul. No one had ever done that. So superficial and always with the verbal diarrhea and arguments. Everyone wanting to play the victim of circumstances. Faith may have been a victim so far, but possibly she wanted to understand how to make that stop happening. She'd actually listened.

Maybe she'd try to understand. The implications of it. Faith was no dummy and Archer liked that. Not sure where she was, he also knew it would take time. It was a very long road though. It might take the rest of his life to help her see what he saw. Fine with it, he felt disgusted she'd be leaving at the end of the tourist season and wanted his mind of the track of her leaving.

"We're all here learning. If, somehow, I provoked something in you and it helped shed light on a part of your life that needs mending or attention, then I'm doing my job. Which is my top priority."

Archer had vowed to himself a long time ago to pay forward the ease with which life came to him. Maybe Faith was teaching him a thing or two. Knowing he wouldn't like the outcome of her leaving; he'd have to deal with it. Growth. Not right now, though.

"I'd also be here to help you figure it out if you needed to or wanted. It's a process that's meant for you to heal and overcome. I just wanted you to know. People do things to us. Yes, some are terrible. It's ourselves who give them the power, when we feel negativity to it. Self imposed suffering. Then we tend to blame them. The only blame they have is their behaviour. You can absorb it, reject it or simply make a mental note that they are not your tribe."

Taking his hands back Archer clasped them together, trying not to be too touchy-feely, though what he truly wanted was to just pull her to him and let her babble on about everything and anything that went through her head . . . and *wow*! Did he just think that? It was a good sign indeed.

"Now that I've completely embarrassed myself, I'll get to the point," Faith giggled. "I've never been seen as anything more than an object and possession. Tonight, I felt wanted. Like I did something for you. Contributed somehow to your day. Something noble. Though, I don't understand how. It's a nice feeling. Like . . . I was invaluable. Suddenly not invisible."

That's when Faith started to really cry and that's when Archer knew she'd found the bottom of it, having said it out loud, making it real. Tangible. Something with substance she could remould and reshape. It was in the open now with no place left to hide. No doubt the roots would run deep, but one step is all it takes to start a journey. How could she ever have felt invisible? She was so . . . Faith. Nothing to be sneered at. What had happened to this gorgeous creature?

Archer was going to find out. No doubt about that. If he could help, he surely would. If it turned out badly, then so be it. His first charge was to be of service. All else, after that.

"Wow. I didn't realize how big a thing that was. The more I look now the more I see how I've let things control me, how it tainted everything in my life to some degree. It's like . . . a weight was just lifted from me."

Faith sighed lifted her gaze up to him, searching in her mind for the words to express herself. Looking to him, it seemed as though he was proud that she'd said that out loud.

Not finding the sympathy that she was accustomed to seeing, just a quiet "well done," kind of look, and she felt stronger because of it. Most men wanted to *take* her strength or *be* her strength, but Archer had helped her to see her own. Or at least shown her where it was.

How could a person be so strong by being so tender. Such a contradiction. Faith's mind racing with thoughts about it, now had a million questions.

"Faith. You're a beautiful woman. *Very* beautiful. But, what's inside is what I cherish the most. That is more valuable than I can ever explain or express. I can only ever be on the outside looking in. A mere witness to the enigma that is you. The softness that came over your face, though, the way the heaviness in your heart shifted. The freeing of your mind in part, even if only for a moment, was a stunning sight to behold. Your face is brighter."

"Yeah?" she asked.

"Yeah," Archer answered then said, "Sometimes these things can be tiresome when you see how deep it runs. If you need to talk, I'll be right here and all ears. A shoulder if you need."

Then Archer did what he had longed to do for so long. Reaching out, he brushed that strand of hair behind her tiny, delicate ear, and it felt as good as he'd imagined.

In her mind Faith was begging him to just kiss her. Instead, she said. "Thank you for listening to me and seeing my value."

"Those who don't see you as valuable are fools and not worth your presence in their life," he came back. "They hold you back from your dreams. They've none of their own."

Feeling bad that she'd seen things that, no doubt, would break his heart, Archer hoped to be around long enough to hear about them. Just the other morning he was Archer, today he was a man with hope. With *faith* . . . oh, the questions he had, of how or why they had met, now seeing more of the picture. the synchronicities.

His obsessions didn't matter at that moment. Pushed to the wayside as they had a heart-to-heart. Soul to soul. Human to human. Not so much the sexuality and physical attraction.

That was icing on the cake, and it may have been the initial attraction, but now her demeanour, knowledge and openness, being candid and honest, that was what he'd truly longed for.

Why? Why? Why? Did she have to go? Really?

"Listen, missy! You stop that now. I want you to have a good time, though, I believe my time is getting short with you for tonight and I'm sure we could go on for hours about it. I'm super happy that you got that off your chest and any time you want to talk I'd be delighted . . . but . . . may I?" he asked with open arms.

Faith wanted to leap into them and bury herself in his chest but slid over slowly and let him hug her as he wanted to.

CHAPTER NINE
A Whole Lotta Lovin' Goin' On

Archer let Faith stay in his arms and would keep her until she felt uncomfortable. It never happened so he soaked it all in. Her hair smelled amazing, and he couldn't help but touch.

"Your hair is amazing, and I love how you did it tonight. It's very Viking," he mentioned, then ran his finger across her forehead to catch any loose strands and brushed them from her face making Faith shudder.

Sitting up to change the subject, though not really wanting to, she told him about how she'd found the style and chattered away like a schoolgirl about it.

Archer liked it . . . a lot . . .

So much so, that he smiled the whole time she talked, feeling himself becoming more and more intrigued with her. She had so many sides that he found himself captivated and had never felt the urge to look at his watch. Not even once. Nor had he considered flipping his phone over from when it laid it face down after setting the music. His obsession with time had taken a back seat. One of the very few times, actually, since Archer was very young.

Now and then he'd tried to figure out why, fighting it for a while only to find himself back at it within five minutes. Distracting sometimes. Right now, though, he was content to just be with her, knowing at some point he'd have to get her home.

She could've stayed the night. He'd have given her the bed in the loft and slept on the sofa. Hopping right into bed with her might have seemed fun at first, he'd certainly regret it now that he'd gotten to know her more. Faith meant more than that to him than just that. Besides, he'd promised himself he wouldn't do that anymore after the other women, basically celibate at this point. Regret was rather unattractive to him and had made his mind up a long time ago that taking a woman to bed would be for the right reason. Love.

After their time tonight Archer was certain that he wasn't just attracted to her physically. It was something more he couldn't explain. Plus, she had deep things to say and weird ideas about life, space, and time. All harmless to anyone else. To him, fascinating.

The afterthoughts would be enough for him to kill time until he could see her again.

Archer supposed she hadn't a mean bone in her body, though definitely had had some broken with callous words and trifling men. It's why his open heart had made her cry. It was something she'd longed for but hadn't received. They both knew it.

Faith talked for an hour about "stuff." She was all over the place. He could tell she was just nervous and suspected she'd spent a lot of time alone, along with having a lifetime to explain to him.

While she spoke of her life, Archer took her feet from the coffee table and put them beside his leg. She paused and stopped talking a moment but gave them up after a second. Not even thinking about it, he began rubbing them a bit.

It felt very good. Faith never had anyone do that to her ever. Realizing what was happening she said, "Really?", to herself and did her best not to go into it with him.

Pushing for her to continue, Archer liked that she'd let him do as he wished. Cautious but adventurous. Interesting. He enjoyed every . . . single . . . second . . . and so did she.

After some time Faith stopped talking briefly.

"More wine?"

"Oh, I think I've had enough. I just talked your ear off," she laughed.

"Wouldn't change a thing," he told her then with a crinkled nose.

"Maybe one more if Greg is still okay."

He loved that she thought of others and their needs. *Checking off a lot of boxes*, he thought.

"Maybe call him and check?"

Though not particularly wanting to let go of her skin, he knew she was right and so got up and took his earpiece. "Hey, Greg."

"Yes, sir."

"What are your plans for tonight? We don't want to hold you up."

"I'm good for whatever you need, sir. It's nice to see you having a good time."

Archer knew what he meant. "Yer awesome."

"Yer awesomer, sir."

Chuckling Archer asked, "I'm awesomer?" That was a new one for him.

"Yes, sir. Awesomer. Go have your fun. Let me know when you're ready to go."

Archer repeated to Faith that Greg was good, but they should finish the night after this glass. She pouted a bit, and he pouted back. Pouring their last, they clinked glasses. Before he could say a thing, Faith spoke first.

"To you and a thoroughly wonderful evening."

"Yes, here, here."

He'd never had a woman do that to him, unless it was business. Those women were sharks in a tank, though. They'd take chunks and if you didn't complain they'd eat you alive. They were just testing the waters and it fed their egos to have everyone listening to them in the spotlight. Faith was different, and full of surprises.

Archer didn't drink as she took a sip and with a puzzled look she had to ask, "Why didn't you have a drink?"

"It's not proper etiquette to drink when you are toasted to. Habit. Would you prefer I did? I would for you, if it made you happy."

It went against everything Archer knew and felt awkward about having to take a drink, hoping she didn't ask him to.

"You do whatever you want," Faith said smiling . . . evilly? Was that a devilish grin he just caught?

Holding out his hand for her, she didn't hesitate.

"Come . . . see the gardens."

He didn't let go of her hand this time and Faith's heart soared as they went to the balcony. It was lit up now. The sun was still up when they'd looked out before.

"WOOOOOWWWWWWowwowww . . ." she whispered, trying to take it all in.

"Ya. Kinda stunning. I thought the same the first time I lit it up. It was a lot of work. I went home filthy and exhausted *and* very burnt," he laughed.

Archer was cute and funny to her and Faith was thankful she'd braved coming to see him now. He wasn't at all what she thought.

"I can't imagine how much this took to finish."

"Well, I tore down the barn myself. That took a few months. In the beginning I had put a lot of the return from my investing to buy the land and have the floors done. The septic and plumbing were moderately costly, never mind the kitchen." he said talking with his hands. "The flooring itself I was able to get a decent price on. Just before the returns became epic, I did whatever I could do myself. When it got to a point where I was of no help, I retired to the greenhouse to get the plants ready. I watched them grow slowly waiting for this place to be ready. It was painful," Archer told her rubbing his forehead.

"Oh?"

"Yeah. Li'l brats took forever to break the surface. I worried like an expecting father at childbirth, to be quite honest."

Faith laughed hard. His face was super serious when he said that, but his tone was excited.

"Can you point to the ladies' room, please?"

The laughing was too much, and she'd meant to ask before but got tied up in her emotions.

Taking her there himself, as the staff had with the elevator, Acher clicked on the light and left Faith to her business. She was beginning to see a little of him splashed into every person she'd had the pleasure to speak to at the gallery.

Washing her hands she checked herself in the mirror. Other than being a little drunk she still looked smashing then made the sound, "Tsss," after licking a finger and touching her hip.

Once back into the office area again, Faith just watched a minute as Archer leaned over the balcony with his chin rested on his hands over the rail.

His back was wide, and his shirt was tight. It looked fantastic on him, though. She'd spent so much time looking into his eyes that she hadn't really noticed. Also, she didn't want to get caught eyeballing his body, but took a hard long look when he went for the tablet. Enough. He excited her, made her feel alive and cherished.

A dreamboat at her fingertips, he was so much more now. Not needing to have to justify the reasons that he drove her into a frenzy. Physicality is only a part of the attraction. Sometimes the initial attraction . . . and Archer's ass was, well . . . Slapable! Nothing wrong with appreciating those things too.

Maybe in the beginning on the beach it was the physical, but now he had earned and deserved her respect. He was so attentive in his offerings, with words of kindness. Real ones. Heartfelt ones. Indismissable and appreciated.

Letting go of the idea that a summer fling was a good idea, Faith considered it inappropriate now and felt guilty for seeing him that way. He wasn't an object, like the way men had treated her. Hard to resist, but wrong, nonetheless. Archer had opened up to her and she wouldn't betray him for that. She'd be the lady he deserved. The lady he saw her as. Respected. The tenderness he'd shown her, the way held her... He obviously had physical needs, but his hands never strayed. No one had ever done that. Always wandering.

She didn't even know how to feel about it. It left her with more questions than she'd come with. He did say she was beautiful and that he wanted to know her better, wanting to ask, Faith decided to wait it out and just let things be what they would be.

Surely if he wanted to, he'd kiss her. How had he not even tried yet. It had been over six hours together. Most men would barely get to the first hour and she could tell they weren't even listening. She couldn't imagine he was one to snooze. Nor was he someone who pounced at every opportunity, though. He was going to drive her right round the bend.

If they ended up spending some time getting to know each other, she would love to see more of his intentions *and* his patience. To let him have his way. Have her!

Back in the gutter. Only one thing for her to do. Lay the foundation and let it rest.

Taking all of him in that she could, Faith walked over quietly and ran her hand over his back.

He hadn't been touched in so long and couldn't help but moan. Faith could feel it rumble through his back under her hand and she tipped her head back praying he'd do it again. *God, please?* echoed in her head.

Then taking the deepest breath, she was sure his shirt would tear, Archer breathed out the longest sigh, until his lungs were emptied, and his head lowered down as far as it would in a relaxed way.

She'd lost her cool a few times that evening and was fine with losing it again. She could hold out longer, she supposed. Rubbing his back more, he stayed there for her.

Asking him if he wanted his wine, Archer grumbled, "No thanks," into his chest as let her do all she wanted to.

When she squeezed the muscles between his neck and shoulders, his body seemed to melt into the rail. Muffled in his arm he groaned, "Oh, goddddd."

She'd be a sopping mess before the night was over if he kept that up. *I'm such a pig,* Faith thought and chuckled to herself.

There was no give to his muscles . . . at all.

"Poor guy," she said softly, then leaned in and hugged him.

Archer tried to move, attempting to hug her back, but she pushed gently on his neck, then stroked the back of his hair and hugged him. Leaning into his back, he succumbed to her touch.

"Just take me," he groaned.

He felt the breath come from her nose quickly and heard the crack of her cheek pulling from teeth on the inside of her mouth.

Her hands felt good, but thought, he should probably tend to her. She was his guest, after all, but then maybe . . . just for a minute . . . so he stayed there. She had insisted in a way.

Attempting to get himself together Archer mumbled, "Sooooo relaaaxed."

Feeling as though he were floating, his head felt huge. All kinds of things were going on inside of him right then. All he could do though was feel.

"Well, come and sit," Faith said taking his hand. "Just a little rub. Okay?"

Thinking she could rub anything she wanted to, at that point, he waited on her. Leading him to the patio chairs she told him to sit. *Ordered* him to sit.

"Li'l pipsqueak telling me what to do," Archer muttered as he glanced at her face.

Folding, like a house of cards into the seat, Faith laughed until he said, "I feel kind of guilty."

"Yer so silly. Just let me for a minute. I won't hurt you."

"I hope not."

"Aww . . ." she said out loud this time.

Did he meant his hear? That made Faith second-guess her intentions and motives for a minute. "It's dawned on me just now that maybe people see you as a big tough, rich, successful, powerful man . . . and I'm getting to see you as someone who has been burdened some. Maybe taken for granted and used. It must be a big load."

"Yeah. It can be *much* sometimes."

His choice of words was interesting. It seemed he had a way of speaking that was different than the rest. Maybe in his travels he'd picked things up. He must have seen some things that would make a person cringe. Whatever it was, he hadn't let it make him become cold and selfish. Or maybe he was just opened to her.

Time would tell more. If it was right, then it was right. She'd give it to him if he wanted. Not very thrilled about going back to Vermont, at all, Archer became another reason to consider staying. Again. Time would tell.

Putting his head down, he let Faith have her way with him. If he got his chance, he'd expect her to do the same. She wouldn't regret it, for sure. The knots began to come out of him and she felt it too. They popped under her thumbs.

"Theeeerrrrre," Faith whispered as his muscles seemed to flow under her touch, then all of her work came undone. She didn't feel it, but *he* sure did. Tense again, in a good way, though.

Reaching over his shoulders, Archer took her hands in his. Pulling them down in front of him, the rest of her with them, her breasts pushed into his back, and he imagined how she'd have looked bent over behind him.

Luckiest man in the world right now, he thought and kissed the palms of both her hands.

Faith could feel the suction of his mouth, making her chirp sound.

He heard, but pretended not to. "We'd better get you home."

"Yes. Home."

She'd had enough torture for one evening but imagined she'd definitely take more another time. The wine had her dizzy. Or maybe it was those palm kisses. Either way. It was good.

Archer called to Greg telling him they'd be ready in a few minutes and Greg said he'd bring the car. Archer asked Faith if she wanted him to stay behind or come with.

She said for him to come.

"Are you sure?" Archer asked, standing up to face her.

"Never been so sure of anything in my life. I believe you are a man of your word and I trust you."

"Of that you can be sure," he said most definitely, but would continue to earn her.

Reaching, Faith ran her fingers down the back of his jaw, making him take a deep breath looking down his nose at her. Couldn't be helped. His body was as straight as an arrow, but he worked to loosen it, bringing his face back down to her.

"Archer, I've never felt more like a lady than I have tonight."

"And I have had a part of me awakened that I thought had died."

Again, Faith felt bad for him but happy she may have the chance to bring that part of him back, the way he'd helped her to lift the weight off her heart.

Holding out his arm for her to take, the way Greg had done, she wrapped hers in and they walked into the office.

"Shoes!" he shouted in surprise and darting out to get them from the patio, as she sat on the side of his desk for some balance and laughed. He'd startled her too.

"*That's some good bubbly*!" she hollered to him.

"*Ha ha! Yeah, right*?!" he yelled back before coming in from the deck and closing the door.

Passing her clutch, and one shoe, Faith looked at him puzzled but took it anyway. "One shoe?" she asked as he bent down and took her ankle. "I feel like Cinderella," she giggled as she gave it to him, resting all of her weight on the desk now.

"And rightly you should."

Putting on one shoe, Archer then opened his hand for the other, never looking at her.

Faith stopped smiling then. He was seriously taking her breath away and as he put on the other shoe, he told her a story.

"My father treats my mother like a queen, and she treats him like her king. No one gets along all the time. If he's upset with her, he still puts on her coat, opens her door, and loosens all the jars." Standing up then he looked into Faith's eyes and took her hands. "If she's upset with him, she still makes and brings him coffee while he watches the evening news. You don't just suddenly fall out of love with someone. That's not love. That's a choice. True love is unconditional, and you have no choice about how you feel about them. Like people who rub you the wrong way, though you don't even know them, or why you get that feeling. It's something on the inside," Archer said touching his chest.

"In my humble opinion, it's not a physical thing, even though science would tell us it's just a chemical in your brain. If you really love them, though, you don't stop doing nice things for them because they aren't pleasing you at the time. Selfishness does that. Feelings of anger fade. You don't withhold your love because they won't bend to make you happy."

Faith understood this. More than he knew. She'd let people walk all over her and loved them anyway. Even though they deserved love, they didn't deserve her loyalty.

Archer put his hands on her arms and rubbed slowly up and down. Her skin was like silk, and he admired it a minute before giving a smile then finished his thought.

"They can't make you happy. You do all that on your own. They can please you, for sure, but true happiness is an inside job. When you give, it's a gift. Not a purchase, transaction, an account where you make a deposit for future withdrawals or with expectations. You give out of the goodness of your heart. Like with your shoes. I freely offered. You freely accepted. I'd have been just as happy if you'd taken them and done it yourself. I was happy to do so or not. It wasn't dependant on you accepting my offer to please. It was simply a gift. As was the entire evening . . . and last night."

Holding out his hand for hers, Faith rose and stepped in closer to look at him.

"You're tall," she giggled "And very, very wise. I'm going to have to think on that. It makes sense but I'm not that deep."

"You, are delightful. I'm sure there's things about yourself you haven't noticed. I have, though, and I've had the most wonderful time with you tonight. I hope to see more of you. No pressure, though. I'll come for the drive, as long as, you're sure. I don't want you to feel obligated to me. There's a distinct difference between doing something out of obligation and doing it out of respect. Which was solely the point I was making about my parents and their love. One you do begrudgingly and end up having resentment. The other you do with joy. You don't owe me anything. Ever. I'm a grown man and I have patience to spare. Although, I must say I've had them thoroughly tested with you tonight . . . for two days actually. Whatever you wish, though, is my pleasure."

"Please come . . ." she whispered, and he'd never heard anything more tempting.

With a raised brow Archer said, "Very well." It was all he could muster then.

Faith moved in closer still and he nearly leapt from his skin. She had a power over him he couldn't describe and felt no need to. Happy to just be feeling it, Archer inhaled deeply. Her scent was amazing, and he was trying to continue to be a gentleman. Like she'd reached into his head and plucked the thought from him, said, "A gentleman would know when she wants to be kissed."

He'd reached his limits long ago, and now didn't hesitate to run his fingers across the back of her neck, the other down her side . . . oh, so slowly . . . making her breathe out hard and closed her eyes. Waiting to feel his lips, Faith's head tilted back expectantly.

Archer tipped her back slightly and just a little closer. So, so, so very close to his lips, but not quite touching as he towered over her tiny frame and keeping his mouth, just there. Lingering long. He wanted her to come and get it . . . beg for it . . . to know her desire.

Faith felt his breath on her skin, and he was just . . . staying there. He didn't kiss her! Why hadn't he kissed her yet?

Opening her eyes to see he was staring right into hers, piercing her soul Archer said, "There," before running his eyes across her face watching a single finger trace the line of her jaw from back to front.

Then, sliding it under her chin, tilting her mouth closer to his, still not touching, he surveyed her, watching muscles move in her cheek as she kissed him in her mind. Archer wanted to hear her say it, though, and with no more eye contact, he stared at her mouth, running his hand over her cheek.

"Please . . ." she stuttered.

Swiftly picking her feet from the floor, tightly wrapped in his arm. Archer owned her and she knew it.

Trying to figure it all out, Faith kissed him softly. A bit too quickly, he smiled as if he were about to teach her a hard lesson, then drew her in just a little tighter and planted a very long, but soft kiss on her and she buckled like a bridge.

He had her right where he wanted her. Right where she wanted him to have her. Having led the way for her now, Faith wrapped her arms around him and matched his passion.

When he'd relaxed his grip on her, Faith felt the floor come under her feet. Back to earth but her head still floating in the clouds.

Opening her eyes, she saw him staring into them again, with a most satisfied look about him. There was much more going on inside and she knew it. A little breathless, Faith softly muttered, "Oh, sir. I have surely been deprived."

"Then I will continue?" Archer asked seductively.

Nearly begging she answered, "Please."

Sliding his hand from behind her back, and across her belly, Archer slide to the side and put out his other arm for her to take.

"For now, then, shall we go?"

"Yes," she replied but wanted to say no.

Now Faith didn't want to leave. He'd made her curious about what he knew. She'd have given him anything that very second but felt she should continue to let him lead the way. She'd let him have it. Everything! He obviously had more restraint than her.

"Are you ready?"

"Oh, I'm ready."

Taking her then to the elevator Archer played with her braid while they waited. She looked at him like a puppy. He knew because he could see her out of the corner of his eye and he'd wait, like he had done with the little hummingbird he'd tamed.

It would come nearly the same time every day. He'd sit near the feeder, getting a little closer every day. Until one day he kept the feeder in his hand.

That day the hummingbird didn't drink. Nor the next day. For three days he waited. Then finally it did, and the next, and the next.

Until one day it landed right on his hand and drank nervously. Day after day it became more and more comfortable. Until it was relaxed while it drank. He would do the same to her if he needed to. With no words for how the hummingbird had made him feel. She was the same to him.

Touch and understanding. Patience and respect. It's universal. Everyone gets it. Some take longer than others and that was fine with him. It's what he'd always used to earn trust. A type of currency. An emotional and mental one.

Whether it was given immediately or needed to be earned. No difference. He'd never hurt her, and he knew she'd been scarred when she cried. He needed her to know she could trust him fully. There would be no intimacy until then.

Maybe some wonderful affection and sensuality. It didn't require intercourse. That's where people get confused sometimes. Rubbing feet. Giving a massage. Cleaning the house or doing it together. Intimacy can take many forms. He'd use all the things he'd learned over the years and be as she needed.

The elevator door opened, then putting Faith ahead of him, they went down in silence.

"Are you together?" he asked, when the door opened on the ground floor.

"I think so," she sighed.

"Good. Then you're better off than me." He smiled to lighten her a little.

Faith was tense looking, and Archer didn't want her to be embarrassed in front of Greg. His delicate flower and he'd keep her that way. Protect her.

When they stepped outside Greg wasn't driving his usual car.

"Sir," he nodded and opened the door.

"Miss Leone," Greg said then to usher her in first.

Holding Archer's hand, she climbed in, and Greg closed the door.

"I'm good," Archer told Greg, nodding, and got in the other side himself. Then, with the doors closed, they were on their way.

"The address?" Archer asked.

"Oh, god, yes. It's 111 Memory Lane. Sorry it's not paved," she apologized.

"We'll get you home safe. No worrying."

Greg typed in the address and brought it up on maps.

The drive home was quiet. Faith was much more drunk than she realized, and the hum of the tires was soothing. She reached over and tickled the back of Archer's hand with her fingers, and he moved to lace his between hers, then taking it to his lips, he kissed every single one. Slowly and as quiet as a mouse.

His inhale like the stabbing winds of the Yukon. His exhale as hot as the fires of hell. Giant fingers took hers like he'd done to the sea glass. Index and thumb. Faith imagined him covering every part of her body those kisses. How could she not?

Isolating every finger, he wanted her to feel them one by one. Each a gift. To wait for the next. Faith hanging in the balance of expectations and dreams come true.

How everything in life seemed to be that way. Making her aware, not only of his intentions, but to bring her mind to the possibilities it held. Not only in a sexual way, but in terms of how to view life. With gratitude when you were graced with a hope coming true. Someday he may use it as an example while they spoke. A metaphor. Maybe she'd tell him all about it.

Expectantly, he'd wait for her to recap her thoughts to him. She definitely was honest. Not gobbling up, what he'd said earlier, as true. Nor did she dismiss it. Impressing him the whole night.

Every bone in her body ached now to feel him . . . *All* of him. But somehow right now, she was also satisfied, having the wondering about them answered.

The wine had quieted most of Faith's mind, and questions faded, while just enjoying being with him. This was a new level of comfort and so leaned into his shoulder and rested her head in his neck.

Her hair tickled, and Archer loved every twitch of his muscles that wanted to scratch where they had annoyed skin exercising his patience. A challenge in his mind. One he loved. He'd need more than that to not ravage her.

Feeling her body relaxed, he noticed she'd fallen asleep after a minute. A needed a break from his mind. Putting his arm around her, to keep her to him, she felt nice, and slid back so she'd be comfortable, holding her head to him.

Pleased with the evening, she'd come in and saved him. Maybe someday he'd be able to tell her that.

Just then, Greg informed Archer they were a kilometre away.

Kissing Faith's head Archer whispered "Faith" onto her skin. She didn't move but said, "Mmmm."

"Faith," he repeated a little more loudly, waking her as Greg turned onto the long path to the cottage. He held her close, so she'd not slide.

Archer was impressed. She must be enjoying the silence. It was beautiful.

When they'd stopped, Archer asked if she wanted to be walked in. Faith just nodded sleepily.

Getting out of his side, Greg opened Faith's door for Archer to take over. "We'll be but a minute," he mentioned to Greg.

Happy that Archer and Faith had found each other, though he didn't know the whole story, Greg suspected she'd be around a long time to come. He'd had a vision, though would never admit it. Maybe to Ada though.

Archer deserved a good woman. Greg had heard about Johanna; she was not his calibre and couldn't see another who would be better for him than Faith. The others Greg had seen would never have done, and not knowing how to tell Archer, it wasn't his place to say, though his uncanny sense about people was never wrong.

"I'll refrain from kissing you again. I've not much control left and the last thing I want is to put you in a position." Archer admitted as they strolled up the walk. In his head, though, he could see himself putting her in lots of positions . . . compromising ones.

Still drowsy, she fumbled with her keys at the door. Offered his help, he kissed her hand when she passed the keys, and let her in. Faith was very tipsy.

"Please," he nodded, and swooped her up.

"Oh!" Faith said surprisingly, then giggled.

Making sure she'd be alright to get to bed, he didn't want her falling and hurting herself. He'd feel horribly responsible then.

The sofa was as far as she was going. "It's as comfy as the bed and closer," Faith joked.

Carrying her over and setting her down gently, he pulled her shoes off and spread a throw over her, then asked if she needed anything. Faith responded that she'd be okay.

"I'll get you water and then leave you to sleep. Call me in the morning and we'll get you to your car," he said, kissing her forehead.

Thanking him as he went to get water, Archer set it on the coffee table. She'd fallen asleep again before he'd gotten back to her and looked peaceful, so he watched her a minute. How lucky was he?

Moving the glass, a little further, so she'd not knock it over, Archer went out quietly and pressed the button on the door to lock it.

Back to the car he got in the front with Greg.

"Nice spot."

"Yeah, I bet the view is amazing," Archer replied, as they started down the drive.

They talked all the way back to town and Archer asked Greg to help him plan a party for the next month, saying he wanted to show his gratitude to all the staff for doing such a fantastic job every single year.

The day before he'd put the raise on their paycheques, which he kept to himself.

When they'd arrived back to the gallery, Archer informed Greg, he'd sleep at the gallery. Too much wine. Then, patting Greg on the back Archer thanked him.

Greg said it was nothing as he got into his car. If it made Archer happy, he'd do anything to help, then told him how much he admired him and loved working for him. Greg had learned so much.

On the drive to the gallery, Greg had confided in Archer, how his dad had left when he was very young, leaving him without a father figure. Which explained to Archer how he seemed so feminine. Lots of time with mom. Part nature, part nurture.

Now knowing more of his life, Archer had more reasons to respect Greg as he was also very close to his mother and a mild-mannered man.

Greg spent a lot of time with her because his brothers were so rough. It's why he'd gotten into bodybuilding, so they'd leave him alone. He had his fair share of fights, though. It wasn't just to protect himself from his brothers. He left out the part about his ability to see visions of the future and that his mother had passed it down to him genetically. It was too big and risky a discussion. Greg had stayed close to his mom to learn to be good at it. His brothers would tease about what he could do.

At one time he'd had a bully. For weeks he'd been tormenting Greg, and he was under a lot of stress. About to turn eleven, his mother never saying anything hoping it would pass him by, he went into a trance. With no clue what was happening, Greg saw the bully's life and said it out loud.

About how his uncle had touched him and how ashamed he felt. The guy went into a rage and kicked the hell out of Greg.

Teasing was one thing, hitting him was another. Even his brothers weren't that bad, so that was hard for Greg. He really was a gentle person and he'd had enough.

Other kids had heard him say it and when questioned his bully admitted it. The uncle was arrested and sent to prison. As painful as it was, Greg had saved him. He learned to take the good with the bad.

When he'd told his mother she apologized for not telling saying it could happen, and that it was way too early for that to develop. She'd never heard tell of a soul as old as his.

Still living at home with no girlfriend, though he tried, Greg rarely went out with anyone. He wanted to be there for his mother after an accident at work and it would be a while before she'd be out of the wheelchair. Then she'd need to continue with physio to get to using a cane.

Chances were good she'd walk again, and Greg wanted to help any way he could. He wouldn't be leaving home anytime soon. The other reason was so that she could keep teaching him. His ability was very complex, and he needed guidance. Some things she didn't know about and they'd have to learn as it progressed. Greg was powerful and untrained would have driven him crazy.

To Archer it seemed Greg had opened up and that was great. He always was a little closed off, and respecting that, Archer never pushed him. Greg just always let others have centre stage and comforted them.

Always seeing the bright side, he'd remind others, there always *was* one, and that sometimes it just took a while to see or show itself, but it *would* show. His confidence would bring down the toughest of situations. Which was why Archer had hired him. Huge man, huge heart. A peacemaker, like himself.

Greg tried hard to do all that was asked of him, even though he was incredibly shy. Having grown so much in the last few years, Archer, seeing his potential, gave him increasingly more public positions. Starting as janitor, he went to door greeter.

When it was really busy Archer would send him out to the gardens to walk and if he saw anyone alone, to ask them how they were. If wanting to talk, keep them company a bit, be cheery and wish them to enjoy their day. The possibility it was the only kindness they'd received in awhile. You never know.

Archer knew how to get people to open up, so did Greg. Wanting to bring out the best in him, Greg knew what he was doing. Trusting his boss, Greg followed Archer's instructions, though it was hard. He was conditioned to keep away from people.

Archer knew the security position was best for Greg and he blossomed before Archer's eyes. For Greg, he was filled with hope that he could be "normal," though Archer had no idea.

No one had ever really started trouble at the gallery but that one guy. Still, it seemed like a good idea, just in case. That one issue, Greg handled incredibly.

Sara told him when he came in the next day how amazing it was, so Archer checked the recording from the monitors. She wasn't kidding. It's like the man was overcome with some force. He was irate, and when Greg touched his shoulder, he stopped immediately.

Archer watched Greg say a few words, then the man patted his shoulder as Greg walked him out, the best of friends.

Archer asked what he'd said to him, and Greg explained that he just reasoned with him and the guy saw his point quickly. There was no better place for Greg at the gallery then and so worked him in.

For most, though, it only took one look at his size for the trouble to die down. He sure was good at what he did. Phenomenal, really, now that Archer thought about it.

"Well, sir. I gotta get home. Mom needs me to run errands for her tomorrow. I need to get a little sleep."

"Thanks again, Greg. You didn't have to stay so late. I appreciate it more than I can say. The sun is coming up now so just come in when you're ready. Your mom needs you so don't worry about the time. Take what you need. If you need some sleep, it's fine to take the day with pay. You earned it."

This made him feel good and always loved how Archer gave credit to him. It made him want to do more. To do better.

As Greg pulled out, Archer went inside and up to the loft, then went to the bathroom to brush his teeth and wash up a little. Thinking a cool shower would be good, he enjoyed it, then crawled into bed, feeling refreshed. Faith had gotten him worked up and no doubt he was in for more.

Setting his alarm, Archer thought of all he and Faith had talked about. How she'd also opened up to him and impressed him the way she'd articulated her feelings. "An opportunity to grow," as she put it.

He just laid there thinking about the entire day and sleep soon took him.

CHAPTER TEN
A Great Day to Be Alive

When the alarm went off, Archer quickly got out of bed. In his loft bedroom he could see the sun was about to come over the bushes in the back of the gardens.

Having a good stretch before going down the spiral stairs to freshen up, Archer remembered the evening with Faith. Splashing water on his face, he drew his hands down his cheeks and across his jaw, the stubble scraping under his hands. It grew fast and he'd have a five o'clock shadow at three in the afternoon.

Looking at it now, he thought maybe he'd grow a beard. It *was* the hottest trend.

Standing there a few minutes, water dripping into the sink, he pondered. It *was* full and he knew it'd be nice if he let it go. If Faith didn't like it, he'd shave it off. Right now, though, he needed life juice.

"Coffee," he groaned.

Pulling out grey sweats from the cabinet beside the sink, Archer slid off his shorts and into the pants, then went to start coffee. Grabbing Greta's twisted mug that barely fit into the machine, he pressed go, then strolled to the patio barefoot to listen to the birds chirping.

Elbows across the rail and resting his chin on his hands, as he had done when Faith was there, Archer listened with his eyes closed. Other than the chirping it was perfectly quiet.

BEEP! Silence interrupted. Dancing his way to get it as if Faith were in his arms, he dropped them a moment later, disappointingly that she wasn't. What he'd have given to share the view with her right now.

Imagining her baggy eyes and crumpled hair, he'd smile at her, and she might say, "Don't look at me, I'm hideous," and he'd tell her she was gorgeous and silly. "One day I hope to," he sighed out, then took his mug.

Steam appeared like magic when he turned back to the gardens, as the sun caught it just right, it swirled through the air, only to disappear again. Blowing it gently, watching the curls straighten into a steady stream carried by his breath, then watched as it curled back up again when he stopped.

Observing his kingdom and pretending to be a powerful emperor; tiny subjects sang his praises from the gardens as flowers began to open, wishing he could watch every movement.

Checking his phone to see if Faith had messaged at all, there was nothing. It was still very early, and he didn't know her sleep schedule. Archer, only needing three or four hours to function, even at that he was full of energy.

Not wanting to seem desperate or overly eager, he decided to let her message when she was ready, then remembered the music they'd listened to. Knowing it was saved in his playlist history, he put it on in the background. A little fast for him for the morning but, "Meh. What ya gonna do?" Archer spoke in an Italian accent. "Just go with it."

Hips swaying to the beat as he drank his coffee, he turned the music up just a little and it wafted across the gardens.

Then doing a dance down the stairs like he'd seen on the black-and-white movies, Archer rounded the corner into the gardens. Singing to his flowers and putting the coffee on the steps to do more stretching, he noticed someone watching. Oh, god, an early riser.

A little old lady gave a tiny wave, with a huge grin, almost flirting. He waved back with a smile and took his coffee, putting his hand in the pocket with his phone, then went behind the rose bushes whistling.

Embarrassed now, he sipped coffee, went to the fountains, and sat on the edge listening to the trickling.

His phone went off just then and checking, it was Trevor asking, *When will you be by? Your car isn't at the house.*

Archer texted back, *Be there in a half hour or so, bro. Just having coffee. Got news for ya.* Then put it back in his pocket to finish his coffee.

The morning was beautiful. He'd slept there often when Johanna was away and thought maybe, during the summer months, he should do it more to enjoy the morning view.

After coffee, all he had to do was put the swim trunks on under the sweats, throw on a shirt, and grab a towel.

Trevor grilled him before he'd even sat in the seat. "Spill the tea!" he shouted, and they talked all the way to the beach ... or ... Archer talked.

When Trevor heard Faith had shown up at the office he shouted, "*Shut yer mouth!*" in a deep tone and got excited for him, then listened as Archer went on about dinner, their talks, and that she stayed late.

Trevor having done some shitty things in his days as a drunk, Archer never told anyone. Not that he could have ruined Trevor's reputation. He'd done a fine job of that himself.

There to listen, he didn't pry as Archer told him about the night. Only what was needed, never anything he thought was private. Trevor liked the sounds of her and was happy Archer had had such a good night. Finally!

Now at their spot, Trevor left to run as Archer took to the sea. Running into the waves, they crashed over his legs and once in to his thighs, he dove and pushed against the tide, swimming as far as he could under the waves. When his lungs screamed for air, he arched his back and burst through the surface to lay back and float.

Listening to the water slap against his ears, Archer closed his eyes to focus on the sound. His heartbeat soon drowned them out and they muddled together. Moving his arms slowly he pushed, then floated, pushed, then floated. The weightlessness came and went. Which way didn't matter. He'd never let the waves take him far, somehow tuned with the shore and knowing which direction he was going.

If even a tingle of doubt, he'd just headed back in. No point taking unnecessary risks. A thrill-seeker of sorts, Archer was still particularly fond of staying alive and in good health.

Crossing his arms to let himself sink to the bottom, Archer thought of Johanna and that awful last conversation. The shock of her words. She'd been so selfish, the way she'd expressed concern about their possible child. And angry. He'd have been a good dad and loved their child no matter what.

Her callousness had broken his heart that day. It's why he didn't make an effort to bond with any of the other women and had become hypersensitive to selfishness.

Listening to them carefully, if he thought they were shallow, he'd find a reason to end it peacefully and blame himself, not wanting to have discussions about it, and never thinking twice after he left them. Nor feeing wrong for doing so.

Considering the fact that there was no difference between the person he was when he'd parted ways with Johanna and who he was now, Archer wondered how he'd allowed Johanna to rob him of his faith in women.

Thinking a minute, he realized how that sounded. *Faith restored*, he thought then as the ocean floor came up under him and he sat. Not feeling the tears, he cried, they'd be forever mixed with the sea, never to be separated. Then he prayed.

"Great ocean, great water,
  take these tears from me.
  Cleanse my heart, fill it with love,
  and let my soul be free.
  Wash my body, wash my mind,
  I lay my worries to the sea floor.
  Take the anguish from my heart,
  I don't need it anymore."

Archer sat until his lungs felt as though they would surely burst, then sprang up and the sand whirled around under him as he left his worries to be buried by it as it settled.

Breathing deep as he surfaced, Archer floated a minute more, and once relaxed, he looked to the shore. Finding Trevor was still far off, there was time for a round of breast strokes until, exhaustion took him in, then swam lazily to the shore.

On the way in he made the decision to let all of Johanna go. Her words, selfishness, and how it made him feel. The way he'd used her as a benchmark for judging others. He *needed* to let it go. It was making him crazy and maybe jaded.

The realization that he was still angry about the whole thing, even after all these years, it was time to say goodbye and stop carrying her around, like the story of the Guru monk and the student he'd heard.

Once on the shore, Archer grabbed the towel and dried his hair, sighing. Swimming was a great way for to relax. excellent exercise too. Winter was difficult for him, and he'd had no choice but to suffer the pool with that nasty chlorine in his eyes. He really should just get his own pool; it made more sense.

Making a note in his phone to look into that, he'd try to have it done by the fall. Those infinity pools looked amazing too. He could definitely do with one of those.

Maybe build a pool house at the back of the yard, he thought, as he sat on his towel to get some sun before getting in the car seat to go home.

Checking his phone, there was no call or text yet from Faith. Trevor still quite a piece away, he sat and dug his heels into the sand. It was always so cool this time of day. It wouldn't last long, though, and he could see that Trevor was on his way back. Close enough that he could wave, and Trevor could see. He'd waved back. Archer would have about ten minutes to kill.

Laying down to relax a minute, it wasn't long before Faith flooded his mind again. Which was fine with him. She wasn't the ghost in his mind that she'd been the morning before, and he hoped she never would be again.

The sounds from the shore all around him, he hummed a bit. He hadn't been *this* relaxed in a *long* time. Or *completely* content.

Taking a big sigh, Archer settled into the idea. He could get used to this. Maybe there was a chance he could *keep* it. For now, though, he'd try to enjoy the summer. With her, if he could, then began to feel anxiety about it and was grateful to have his thoughts interrupted by Trevor's feet hitting the sand.

"Let's go, man!" Trevor said breathless. "You have a date coming up!" and then ran to head up the dune.

Archer got up, grabbed his things, and went after him. When they hopped into the Camaro, Trevor commented, "I can never get over how good you've kept this car. It's such a sweet ride."

"It was a big project. I liken it to life. If you let things go too far downhill, it's a lot of work to restore. If you just maintain it along the way, it will always get you where you need to be. Maybe with a few speed bumps, but it'll get you there."

"So true. That's how Dora and I have looked at our relationship since I smartened the hell up. I remember seeing your parents together and love that they didn't hide things that were going on. Like repair from the rupture. It taught me a lot."

"It was good. They didn't believe in shielding us from the world. They prepared us for it. Which I'm grateful for."

Starting it up, the car wasn't loud, but you could feel its power when he stepped on the gas. The muffler gurgled quietly, and it would lift to one side. Archer revved it some before turning off the dirt road. Once on the highway, it would suck you into your seat and make your stomach sick.

"If I had this car, I'd be dead."

"Good thing you didn't, I'd have lost my mind," Archer replied back, as he rubbed Trevor's shoulder.

Making Trevor feel mushy, he said, "Well, *go, man!*"

Just before he was about to hit the pavement his phone went off. "One sec," he told Trevor.

It was Faith. *I didn't call in case you're busy. I'm in no rush. Just woke up. Call when you can.*

Texting her back he said, *Just taking Trevor home. Will call in fifteen or so. Hope you slept well!*

"That was Faith. She's ready to be picked up anytime."

"Well, giddy up those horses, then!"

Pulling onto the pavement now, Archer stepped on it to give Trevor a good run.

"*WEEEHAWWW!*" Trevor shouted and Archer drove fast all the way to the house. Not too fast. But . . . fast enough!

When they pulled in, Dora was on the front porch enjoying the sun with a cup of tea. That was her thing. Archer waved to her as Trevor slammed the door.

"That was sick, dude. Under six minutes!! You *kidding me*? Lemme know if you wanna skip any days. I'll forgive a few," he told Archer, winking.

Trevor stood and slapped the hood of the car, then whinnied like a horse shouting, "Take it easy, stud," while running to the house.

"Morning, Dora," Archer greeted getting out of the car.

He hadn't seen her in a few days and wanted to give her the usual hug and peck on the cheek. How he loved her. She was so good to, and for, Trevor.

"Mornin', dawlin'," she greeted back in her usual way. "How was the beach?"

"Little chilly, but we're getting into the best part of the season," he said, rocking her in his arms, then let her go. "I have to go but wanted to give you a hug. Haven't talked in awhile."

As she thanked him for coming out to her, Archer remembered she'd said before, it almost felt like one a brother would give when the world has been cruel.

"Kind of sticks the broken pieces back in where they belong," she'd said. Which made Archer feel good and chose to make sure to do it often. He did love her like a sister.

Dora waved as he was leaving and told him to come by some evening for supper. Which reminded him.

"Will you be over to the house for family dinner?"

"I believe so. Waiting to hear on my shift at work."

"Oh, good. The kids will love to see you!" he smiled, then turned to get back in the car. "Enjoy your day, dear."

"You too."

Archer called Faith when immediately getting home.

"Mmmm. Good morning, handsome."

"Good morning to you, beautiful. How'd you sleep?"

"I slept great! You?"

"Great sleep! Could have used more but I'll be okay," he laughed. "What time would you like to be picked up to grab your car?"

"I was just going to have breakfast. If you're not in a hurry maybe you'd join me?"

"*Yes!*" he said quickly, nearly cutting her off.

Faith laughed to herself as she pulled fruit from the fridge and kicked it shut. "Okay. I'll see you soon then?"

"Yes. You will. I'll be there with bells on," he said excitedly, not wanting to hide his feelings about her anymore. "I need a quick shower. Then I'll be on my way. I'll text first."

"Awesome. Fair warning. I'm not Devon in the kitchen, just so you know, but I won't kill you," she laughed.

"Oh, god . . ." Archer groaned.

"I'm joking. I'll make my special. It's all downhill from there," she joked further.

"I hope so. It's been an uphill climb getting here to find you. I could use the break."

"You're hilarious. Just get here already."

"As you wish." he chimed back in a soft tone.

"See you soon then," Faith said back and immediately hung up the phone.

Archer looked at the phone confused and thinking that was a bit rude. She hadn't even said goodbye or give him a chance to. The second he thought it, though, his phone went off. It was Faith saying, *Sorry. I don't say goodbye. I didn't mean to be rude. It so . . . final. I'll explain why when you're here . . . see you soon*, with a smiley face.

Fair enough, he messaged back, on his way to the shower.

Going quickly to finish up, Archer fixed his hair and picked up his razor. Looking at his beard again he asked Faith: *What do you think of beards?*

SEXY AF! she answered.

Cutting sharp lines around his neck and cheeks then put on his favourite cologne. It was smoky and woodsy. It didn't have a single hint of that sickeningly sweet and flowery scent.

Archer chose a flattering white cotton shirt, matching soft, white cotton pants, a black belt and sandals. Something comfy but not sloppy, then hopped in the car. Before leaving he thought, Faith was right about the finality of saying goodbye, and put the playlist from their evening together back on through the Bluetooth connection he had installed in his car. It might be old, but he'd had it updated a few years before.

Reaching Faith's cottage road, Archer stopped a minute and called his mother before heading up the long drive.

Telling her that he'd talked to Trevor, that he and Dora were trying to make the dinner on Friday, then mentioned he'd met someone, and asked if she'd mind if he took her along.

Debbie inquired where they'd met and after saying, she expressed that he should most *definitely* bring his friend over for supper, she'd put on extra. Like she needed to. Debbie *always* made more than three families could eat, but never wasted a scrap.

"I haven't asked her yet. So, I'm not sure she'll come. I wanted to clear it with you first."

He knew she'd say yes but was always respectful. Debbie was someone who always welcomed her children's friends in. They had sleepovers all the time and Roger would set up the tent with them in the yard during the summer.

They'd laugh all night long, if Roger had let them. He'd come out the back door and yell, "That's enough!" and they'd all cringe, then giggle quietly.

Archer heard her shuffle on the mouthpiece of the phone. Then voices.

"Dad needs to call the garage, honey. I'll have to let you go. I can't wait to see you and your lovely guest."

"Okay, Mom. Love you and see you soon."

"Love you too, dear. Bye bye," she said back, and Archer ended the call with a kiss instead of saying goodbye. It felt bizarre and oddly satisfying. Making a "go figure" face he started up the lane.

Thinking about Roger, Archer recalled the fishing trips, where he and Trevor would tag along. Roger trying to make them keep quiet as not to scare the fish and they did their best, but Trevor liked to talk. Archer always just fine listening.

Roger using it as an excuse to listen like a dad but maintained the manly distance his father had done.

Deciding what he wanted to do with his life, quite early on, Archer made the choice to be deliberately dedicated to *anything* he took on. If he was struggling with an issue, he'd ask his Roger to spend time fishing. Very much enjoying just sitting with him when he needed to decide on something, and Roger was happy one of his boys wanted to hang out with him.

Archer would sit and listen to him breathing. Watching him whittle away at a stick. Sometimes he'd make a whistle out of it, and they'd try to play music. Roger whistling and whittling while Archer tried the tree branch whistle to join in. *After* they were done fishing.

Derek and Brett were hardly ever home, and once they turned thirteen or so, they didn't identify much with Roger anymore, and thinking they knew everything, would argue with him. A lot.

Archer, though, was always pleasant to be around. Helpful and thoughtful. Mild-mannered and attentive. He'd ask Roger for help when he needed to. Working on his car, they had long discussions about life, women, careers, and cars. *All* the stuff boys tended to enjoy.

Once, when Archer was very young, Derek had gotten nose to nose with Roger. Debbie tried to get them to stop, but neither of them would back down. Archer was only eight then, but he managed to talk some sense into Derek.

Archer knew Roger would take Derek's his head off, as easily as he'd cut his last "first-slice of birthday cake." Roger was a brute of a man. Archer now just like him.

Derek and Brett got a bit chunky as they grew into their twenties. Taking to beers and eating out way too often. Debbie stills growls at them now and then. Saying she doesn't want them dead of heart attacks before the kids can get a chance to grow up. "It's not right," she'd say.

Proud and impressed with Archer's common sense and how he'd used logic to get into Derek's head that day, Debbie bonded with him on a new level. She *knew* he was smart, but that day he'd shown it outwardly for the first time.

Derek thought he'd take on his old man that day, but ended up taking on Archer's mind, and it really was no match to begin with. Derek a bit of a neanderthal and Archer an avid reader of theology and psychology, there was no way but to throw hands or walk away. Both, risky for Derek. Archer might be small, but he had skills.

Archer the peacemaker, Debbie called him from then on.

After visiting India with Johanna, Archer discovered meditation. Realizing quickly, it was what he was finally after all those times he'd asked Roger to take him fishing.

Now with all the information he could ever want, he dove in deeper.

It ended up unravelling all his parents had taught him about Christianity. He'd already left the church and Debbie became fearful he would surely go to hell now.

He tried to explain to her that her own bible told him to meditate. That he wasn't a Buddhist now and wasn't worshipping false gods. Wanting to believe him, the fear instilled through religion had its grips in her and she couldn't help pleading for his return.

Roger on the other hand left it alone. He knew Archer wasn't dumb and if he saw value in something it was probably more than he could understand himself.

He was a simple, old-fashioned man and Archer took after him there, but his mind was just a little more open. Travelling did him a world of wonders. Literally. Things really took off for him then.

Roger would always impart wisdom to Archer, his brothers, and Trevor, before they left their fishing spots. It was a ritual of sorts as Roger's father had done for him when he was growing up, and his father before.

Brett and Derek never got most of it, but Archer hung on every word. Trevor tried to understand and got the gist most times. He'd always talked with Archer about it when they were hanging out. Eventually the planted seeds sunk in after he stopped drinking, and they had amazing talks then.

Trevor's dad didn't do much for him or with him and left when he was young. Roger took him under his wing, and they got to be pretty close.

Archer was never jealous of their relationship. He was taught to share and be kind to others, to turn the other cheek and did his best with it, but now and then, made it a point to put a tough guy in his place when they tried to make him upset. Or someone else. There was no excuse to be a bully or to just be plain hurtful.

Roger and Debbie taught him to keep the secrets others told him, unless they were going to harm themselves or someone else. Roger would say, "Show respect to others even if their beliefs don't match your own. Never raise your voice to anyone. Especially those you care for and love. Be kind. If you can't, keep your mouth shut."

Now coming over the top of the hill to Faith's cottage Archer found himself getting excited, and a little nervous. The drive was good and slow, his car was low to the ground and there was no point dragging bottom and having the muffler ripped off. Haste makes waste. Reminding himself of his high priority philosophies. He put them to the front of his mind. As excited as he was to see her again, he exercised a little more patience. A dedicated man, he felt she would be his undoing or make him more powerful than he could imagine. In his mind, at least. Time would be the teller of which.

CHAPTER ELEVEN
Weekend Escape

After Faith had hung up with Archer, she turned on some music. "Can't get you out of my head" came through the speakers. "*Oh, yeah, sista. Tell it*!" she whooped knowing the feeling and began to dance a bit with her whisk.

All the tools ready to go to work, Faith diced some pineapple, apples, and mango, then arranged them in a pretty way on the hand-carved plate she'd bought from the gallery. *A gift*, she corrected herself.

Popping a piece of pineapple into her mouth and squirming, with arms in tight to her body, Faith danced in a tiny circle before going back to chopping.

Blending the pancake mix with milk and eggs then setting it to one side, some time ago she'd discovered by accident, that if it sat for a few minutes, bubbles would show on their own. To her surprise they were so much fluffier and lighter. That and not over mixing. Slowly, the pancakes progressed in complexity.

Back to the fruit, Faith took a banana and sliced it on the angle to make them long and pointed like flower petals.

The music was loud and so was Faith. Now and then she'd look out the window above the sink to see if Archer had pulled up yet. Though not knowing his car, she was sure it would be a nice one.

A strong breeze came down through the field. Tractors had been there earlier. She'd seen the dust. No doubt he'd stir some up himself. Or she sure hoped he would. "*Out of the gutter!*" she yelled to herself and kept with the bananas and slicing them neatly, then got milk from the fridge to pour into a smaller container. Standing up from the fridge something dark flashed by the window. Startled, she jumped and threw the milk container at it.

Not seeing what it was, she thought maybe it was just a bird. It'd happened before.

Waiting a moment, nothing else happened, so stood on the tips of her toes and looked through the window across the yard. Nothing but birds. *It must have been one of them*, she thought and went back to the task at hand.

The pan of oil ready for the burner and pancakes prepped to put together; Archer was all that was missing. Giving the mix another stir to check the bubbles, it looked perfect, so she tidied up any mess and washed the dishes for a head start.

The coffee pot made its gurgling sound and pleased her ear and she wanted a cup so badly. Decidedly, she'd wait for him. He shouldn't be too much longer.

Looking over everything to double-check; Faith took the fruit dish to the part of the deck that was screened in. After setting it down she covered it with a bowl to keep any bugs away and went back to the kitchen.

Pulling up Jack Johnson, Faith collected a playlist to show Archer some of her music. Jack was so mellow; she'd named him the "king of calm."

Peeking out the window, he hadn't arrived yet and continued gathering songs. With two hours filled up, she hit play and then went to the hall closet for the trolley.

The cottage had the most beautiful blue mugs with seashells embossed in silver. Taking two, she set them on the trolley, then the cutlery and plates.

Peeking out the window one more time, the flash from the polish Archer had on his car as he came over the hill, made her a little nauseous. Also instantly excited. Not scared like before, she reminded herself. It was a beauty!

Going to the front porch to greet him, hardly able to contain herself, Faith made a pathetic attempt to pull herself together opening the front door, as Archer parked the car and got out.

"Nice car!" she said with an excitement.

"Yeah. I love her. It was a labour of love," Archer agreed in a cool voice, having as much trouble as her to stay calm.

Both of them not understanding they should just explode with pleasure and revel in each other. Customs. There might be a purpose for the charade, but it was still dumb though. To them both. With nothing said about it either. Just playing the game.

Walking over to Archer with her arms open wide, he'd never seen a more lovely sight. Taking her in, he hugged her close, resting his cheek on her head and breathing her in quietly, until till he felt her move. It was a long few minutes, but so satisfying. Taking her arms from his shoulders, Faith slid them down his and right into his hands.

Pulling away, she looked deeply into his eyes. In the sun, the brown looked more like milk chocolate. Not the dark colour she'd seen the night before.

Wanting to attack him on the spot, the blood rushed to her face, so she quickly turned from him to hide it, with his hand in hers, she escorted him inside.

She had the sweetest little summer dress that flicked in the gentle breeze when she walked. Legs toned and tanned, with nails painted to match the dress, along with her soft eye shadow. Such a delight to his senses.

The smell of his cologne on the breeze, caused her to breathe deep and wrapped her up as it had the night before, making her do a little skip, though she hadn't noticed . . .

Archer did.

Does this woman get cuter? he thought to himself. He'd explode if she did, and wanted to tell her, but said, "How is your morning?" instead.

"*Oh!*" Faith exclaimed. "It's funny you ask. I was watching to see if you'd arrived. I had my tunes up kinda loud and had to keep checking," she giggled putting her hand over her mouth.

Archer could have eaten her up! "Oh?"

"Yeah, and it was funny." She exclaimed, then went forwards and informed him of what had happened in the window, then, holding her hand to her chest she excitedly expressed, "It scared the crap out of me, and I just *threw the milk at it*!" motioning as if to show him how it happened, then laughed hard. "I can imagine how that might have looked. I'm glad I got the plastic container. It would have been everywhere."

"What was it?" he asked as they continued walking inside.

"I think just a bird. I've seen them crash into the windows now and then. I think the sun blinds them. Once, I heard a crash, and went out to see what it was, then saw the bird. The poor thing just laid there on the patio. I felt so bad. I thought he was dead or maybe broke its neck. I searched the internet for information, and it said that sometimes they knock themselves out and to put a basket or something over them, so another animal won't eat them while they recover. So, I did that, then kept checking and checking. He was out a long time."

"So, it got better then?"

"Yeah. I was so glad too, I'd have had to bury it. I wouldn't have been able to just put it in the bushes or trash. I'd feel so bad. The guilt would eat me up."

She kept saying all the right things, showing Archer her heart. Inside the cottage now, he took off his sandals and they went into the kitchen.

"*Wow!*" he exclaimed looking around. It was so bright and fresh looking. "Now I see what you meant when the sun comes in."

"I just love it here," Faith said hugging herself. "Come right in. I'm just about to make the pancakes. I'll get you a coffee."

Archer went to the patio windows and looked out as she poured them each a cup. It was a beautiful view, and he couldn't help inquiring about the pillar rock just off the edge of the cliff.

"What's that?" he asked squinting and trying to figure it out himself.

"Oh, it's something! It's a rock, that somehow, has separated from the cliff. I'll take you down later if I can keep you awhile."

"You can have whatever you want from me."

Putting the pan on the burner, Faith asked what Archer took in his coffee and he answered he'd take it black, so she instantly brought him the steaming mug.

Thanking her he gripped the mug, and her hands.

Softly and slowly, Faith took them from the mug, and felt him let her go gently. A very tender moment in her eyes, Faith counted her blessings.

Sharing the story of his favourite mug, that he and Greta had made in the pottery room and how it was twisted like Trevor, Faith listened and crooned over Archer's voice. Dark and musky.

The story about it made her laugh and she kept from speaking as to not interrupt his train of thought. The way he had with her, so many times. Plus, he hadn't talked a whole lot the night before and now that he was sharing, Faith wanted more.

Letting him babble on while making the pancakes. Finally. He'd spent so much time last night letting her go on and on, she'd hoped he wasn't the closed-off type and felt relieved.

Archer asked if he could help and Faith replied, "Please! Let me treat you. You've done so much for me already. It's the least I can do."

This warmed his heart even more and let her go on but left the offer open. It was awkward. All the men in his family helped their women when chores were to be done . . . *My woman*, he thought, *Wouldn't that be nice?*

Archer wanted to do more than just help her with that sweet dress on and how it hugged her body perfectly.

Or help her off with it, the voice remarked loudly in Archer's head, making him smirk, then, mentally slapped his own face!

Don't be a pig, his heart scorned.

Turning away, Archer sipped coffee and asked what she was making.

"Oh, banana pancakes 2.0," she replied, flopping them onto each of the plates.

Going to the fridge, Faith took the chocolate and butterscotch, warmed them in the microwave, then pulled the trolley next to the stove. Putting the plates down, the microwave beeped, and she took the sauces out.

Topping the pancakes with bananas, all the points in the centre and flowering out to the edges, Fait then swirled the warm chocolate and butterscotch neatly on top and drizzled it messily around the plate to decorate it and topped it with coconut milk whipped cream and a few sprinkles of walnut.

"Dear lord! That is too pretty eat."

"Once you have a bite, you'll want more . . . trust me," Faith commented then glared into his eyes a moment before pouring juice and pulling the trolley to the edge of the island.

Getting as far as he could, fighting with his mind wanting to *really* help, himself, Archer stood and said, "Please . . ." motioning with his hand for her to give the cart to him.

Faith nodded and let it go and he stood with it as she put the juice glasses on and led the way to the deck. Sliding the doors open wide, sea air filled the cottage, with a blend of wood.

Archer got lost in it as he followed and couldn't help remarking on it. "What is that heavenly smell?" he asked breathing it in again.

"To be honest I have no idea. I've smelled everything in this area, and I can't pin it down. I thought it was the furniture. Then maybe the flooring or the curtains. I smelled the cushions and everything. So, I'm thinking it must be a mixture of all that's in the room."

"Strange, it could be cedar. It's a very warm and comforting scent."

So distracted by it he didn't notice as Faith took the cart from him, then admired the look of the screened in and roofed part of the patio that kept it shaded and a little dark. Like mood lighting in the middle of the day, it made him feel like taking a nap.

As Faith tended to the table, Archer took a minute to take in the surroundings more. Drapes were drawn into the corners that could be pulled for privacy and they twiddled in the light breeze.

It was such a nice touch along with the cozy, deep blue chairs with large, metal rings hanging from the back, which were slightly untucked under the edges of a very rustic, and stately, live edge wooden table that dawned the centre of the patio.

There was sea glass everywhere! In jars all along the ledges and a few in the corner, at the bottom of the curtains, lights tucked inside those on the floor. Noticing the thin silver wire winding along, he thought, *In between the glass and the glass.*

Faith had decorated around the jars on the floor with some driftwood. Seashells adorned the floor in front of them.

"You've got a lovely place here, Faith."

"Oh. We'll eat, have more coffee, and I'll show you around. It's just one treasure after another in here," she sighed, then waved her hand. "Please sit."

He did and let her serve him and enjoying it a great deal now, he mentioned. "I haven't been treated in forever. It's both awkward and very, very nice."

Smiling Faith put the plates down on the table and after she'd placed everything, Archer took her hand and kissed it, thanking her for the lovely breakfast and the wonderful company. The atmosphere was so relaxing that he let go of everything outside of being there with her.

Faith had never been so flattered as when she was with him. Wanting to hear more about his life, she asked and he briefly told her the important things as she went to sit.

Wanting more of her, his story was old news to him, and he was so taken by her.

Faith picked up her fork and cut into the pancakes. The whipped cream now a white lake on the hot pancakes.

"You don't talk much about yourself."

Beginning to eat, Archer followed her lead, as she had done the night before, and commented about how crispy the pancakes sounded as he dug into them.

"I'm sorry. I don't mean to be rude or guarded or anything. I'll tell you all you want to know. I just find you so interesting I don't want to miss anything," Archer responded then popped some pancake into his mouth. He'd try to converse more set the right impression.

All at once the flavours hit him. It was incredible! Rolling his eyes, Archer sat back in the chair, putting his fingers to his mouth, kissed them into the air.

Faith nodded. "Told ya."

Washing it down with coffee he had to know. "Where did you ever learn to make this?"

Faith explained about the Jack Johnson and how much she felt at peace listening to him and his music, and that her favourite song was about having banana pancakes on a rainy morning. How inspired she felt to try and make them and that they were really good but needed more.

Recipes had said to blend the banana into them before cooking, but they were heavy and seemed to be less fluffy than she wanted and over the years, modified the recipe, then tried different ways of cutting the banana. Eventually finding if she turned them sideways, she could cut them like flower petals.

Thinking about the banana splits her mother would get them on Sundays, she started adding the same toppings, but left out the pineapple and strawberry, just using butterscotch and chocolate. The other toppings were good, but it seemed too much and overpowered the banana.

Faith loved to cook and bake. She'd watch chefs make beautiful meals and desserts and loved how they used the toppings to decorate the plate when they made desserts, so she began swirling them too.

"This is 2.0."

"You're a creator for sure," he complimented, before taking another bite, nearly finishing them while she told the story of the pancakes. "I'd love to see your jewellery sometime."

"Oh, yes. I can show you anytime. You'll have to remind me. I've been so preoccupied with this book and been writing up a storm, plus the beaches are so nice. And you . . . have been a bit distracting. It's possible I may forget. It's a lot to take in and I'm a bit overwhelmed," Faith admitted, a little embarrassed.

Never much for talking about her emotions, Faith used many other ways to let them out. Like boxing and a few sports. It *did* let out energy but kept them inside her at the same time. Such a contradiction . . . and Jonsie never cared. He never asked how she . . . cutting herself off said "*So!*"

"Yes?"

"Do you have to be at the gallery at a certain time?" she asked, and prayed, he'd be free for awhile.

"I spoke with Carla this morning. If there's anything I can do it remotely. She takes care of most things around there. Including the staff and their schedules. I'm not sure what I'd do without her."

"That's super," Faith cheered then smiled. "I found her charming and professional."

"Yes. She sure is those. I have to push her some, she can be a bit of a workaholic. Not that I have room to talk. I've been known to disappear into the office for days on end," Archer confesses to her with a serious face was. She knew he wasn't kidding and hoped it wouldn't become and issue for them.

"How long can I have you for?" Faith asked hastily.

"As long as you want."

"*Yay!*" she clapped. "I have so much to share with you, I don't know where to begin. I don't want to intrude on your time. It's hard deciding which to share with you first. Is there anything you'd like to do, though?"

"Let's enjoy our coffee and let those amazing pancakes settle. I'm down for whatever you want. I hadn't thought of anything really other than breakfast and getting your car. I'm happy just to be with you is all, really," he admitted.

Then rubbing his belly, added, "That breakfast was delicious. I've had an elegant sufficiency. What a delight this all is."

Happy she had pleased him and given something he'd never had, Faith felt great satisfaction. He'd probably seen it all, she thought, after reading his bio and about the gallery. He'd been everywhere.

Could she even have a first anything with him? It had bothered her all last evening listening to some of his stories and assuming.

"I'm glad you liked them," she smiled and did a "smol viktory dance" . . . inside. Not wanting to seem immature.

He would have loved her silliness, though. It was one of the things he also loved about Trevor. So animated and the way he was able to just let go and not care what anyone thought. Suspecting she was similar. Archer figured they'd love each other.

She could play her matching game for awhile. If she only knew how taken he was, she'd just let go. But he'd wait.

Someday, she'd tell him about the dance and try to relax, thinking it best to try and be at his level and on her best "mature" behaviour, he'd seen her skip though.

To break the silence Faith said, "I don't usually make this if it's not Sunday. If you wanted, though, I'd make them for you anytime."

"I'm honoured." Archer smiled, driving her nuts. "While you definitely hit the target with the pancakes, your company would have been enough,"

"You're so sweet. Your company is also more than enough . . ." she responded shyly.

His glow made her cringe a little. He was so forward, honest and wise. What was he doing with her?

They sat awkwardly staring into each others' eyes. Just smiling away like two children, who'd just gotten away with stealing a cookie from the jar Mom had put on top of the fridge, after being told no. Each trying to read the other and not knowing a damn thing other than how happy they were.

"I thought maybe after I show you around, we could go down to the beach. I wanna show you the rock you commented on. It's quite spectacular. In fact, I can't believe it's not a tourist attraction. It must still be a secret," she whispered like someone may hear.

"Oh. That sounds like a fantastic idea. Can I help you clear the table?"

"Oh, no. You don't have to."

"I know," he said sweetly, leaving it at that.

"Well, then, if you insist. That would be nice."

They cleared the table together. He took the trolley to the kitchen then helped her rinse the dishes, load the dishwasher, and wipe the counters. When they'd finished, Faith showed him around the cottage.

It was big and bright. All the rooms had a king-sized bed over-stuffed with pillows and soft blankets. Sea shanty decorations, and fine potpourri, kissed all the rooms. The bathroom had amazing acoustics and she mentioned it.

"It does have a great echo."

"Well. Actually, I play guitar and sing some. Sometimes in here because of how it rings out. Almost better than adding reverb."

He didn't know about that and hoped she'd to teach him some things. "Nice!" Archer chimed in and let her go on showing him around more.

"I've done open mic a few times, and don't really admit that. I haven't sung much around others." Faith admitted, then wished she hadn't.

Only Jonsie and Lacey knew she was a musician, really. Right now, she hated them both and left it at that.

"Musician then, you say. How long have you played for?"

"About seven years," she said shyly. "I couldn't sing in front of anyone until just a few years ago. I was really insecure. Mom loved my voice, so I'd sing for her. I always had a passion for music, but it never dawned on me to try an instrument. My music teacher drove me crazy in elementary school, but I wouldn't join the choir."

Hoping he wouldn't ask why, Faith thought she shouldn't have even said that. Now she'd have to tell him about the bullies and the teasing and wanted to be the woman of his dreams. Not the insecure and fragile Faith she knew, trying to change and leave her old life behind. *Fuck*, she thought and continued to change the subject some.

In her recovery, Faith formulated, "The first time at open mic, though. People would say they liked my voice and choice of music, but I thought they were just being considerate. It didn't seem like anything special to me. Then getting to know other musicians, they admitted it takes guts to get up. Some love the limelight. Some can hardly stand it. I'm one of the latter."

"Oh! Maybe sometime you can show me some of your music? If you're not too shy. I don't want to make you uncomfortable."

Leaving it at that, not wanting to ask what kind she liked to play on purpose, the surprise of what she showed him, when more secure, would be fun. Plus, it seemed she was struggling in a way.

"Oh, I would for you in a heartbeat. You make me feel . . . very comfortable," she said, then took him to the master bedroom.

He'd made her feel so welcome. The mental battles might very well tear her apart but vowed to be vigilant. Keep them on a short leash. A very, *very* short one. She'd been so emotional the last few days.

"What kind of music would you like to hear?" she asked then, as they went down the hall.

"Your favourite one to play. The one that makes you feel the best. Fast or slow. I don't care."

She'd never heard anything so sweet and touched her heart. *First battle*, trying to keep cool.

"I can definitely do that for sure. Come. Let me show you the rest and we'll get to that beach."

"Yes. I'm right behi— OH! *Look at that bed*!" he exclaimed when seeing it.

The bed was stately with its four posts made of huge slabs of wood that nearly went to the ceiling. Surrounded by drapes that reached the floor and out some.

"Those eight by eights!?" Archer exclaimed, reaching to touch them.

They were connected with heavy wrought iron joints and secured with huge bolts. The wood was burned to a char, scraped, then stained a bright blue green, then coated with a thick layer of varnish. It was rugged and rustic like the rest of the cottage.

"Shou-sugi-ban . . . That wouldn't have been cheap," he said, feeling the wood now. "The finish is stunning . . ."

"Sure is gorgeous! It's comfy too. I've never slept so well. In fact, I'm not sure I've ever slept at all once I'd woken up the first morning here," she remarked, then took his hand. Walking him to the patio that came from the master bedroom Archer could see the rock more clearly now. "What's this shushigi whatever you said?"

"It's the art of burning Sugi. Japanese Cypress in English. Usually for exterior siding. It's burned about seven minutes then extinguished with water. Like firewood not totally burned. Then they wire-brush it off. The different layers burn at different rates, leaving the highs and lows exposed. It's usually finished with oil," he told her matter-of-factly. "These guys stained and varnished it, though. Gorgeous! It's a fairly new thing for most. It's no wonder you haven't heard of it. I happened to stumbled on it once."

"Oh! I don't feel so stupid now. I'll take you down to the beach now if that's okay?"

"Yes. Yes. I'm quite curious about this."

He wasn't about to let her go that easily, though. Stopping before they went out the bedroom door that led to the patio, he spun her back to him and took her face in his hand looking deeply into her eyes. "I don't want to hear you talking about my friend like that anymore or we're going to have words," he said sternly.

"Okay. I understand."

"You shouldn't say things like that about yourself. That hurt my heart." Archer said with a hug and rubbing her back.

Almost crumbled into tears, Faith hadn't thought of it that way, and realized there was so much to learn. That wouldn't be a mistake she'd make again, though.

Taking his hand, they walked to the patio then down from the tiny steps. The yard wasn't very big, and it was a sheer drop down to the shore. As soon as they'd reached the top of the stairs, he could see *all* of the rock. Not just the tippy top. It was stunning. The needly, jagged pillar stood there like the last warrior on the battlefield before an enemy that the rest of the cliff had surrendered to.

"The stairs are steep," she warned.

He stopped her at the top and went ahead of her. Faith thought it was bizarre behaviour and made her wince, then just stood there at the top of the stairs trying to figure out *What the actual fuck?*

Archer didn't feel her step onto the stairs. They jiggled when he'd taken the first step on them. Turning around, he saw she was just standing there with a look on her face he didn't like.

"Did I do or say something wrong?"

Being a straight shooter, Archer wasn't much for letting things slide.

"Well. I was wondering why you stopped me and went first," she confessed.

Chuckling softly, he said, "Oh. I'm sorry," and held out his hand and was happy she accepted it, then came to where he was.

"I was taught to go ahead of a lady going downstairs and stay behind her going up. If you fall, I'll catch you. I can't have you broken. 'Cause broken Faiths are no good."

He'd made her laugh again. It even crossed her mind, then, that maybe he was too good for her.

So collected and intelligent. Strong and brave. Outspoken and successful. All the things she wasn't. Maybe she should let him go to find a strong woman. She might get on his nerves and end up feeling like a burden to him.

Within a second, Faith remembered what he'd just said, and crossed it out like it's never been thought.

"I've never heard of anything like that. That's so sweet!"

Putting her arms around Archer's neck and kissing him, as if to apologize, took all she was willing to offer.

Stroking his hair and running her nails across his scalp, Faith watched goosebumps rise on his skin, and felt his neck relax. "Mmmmm," she muttered and kissed him again. Slowly. He was reaching her . . . and she to him.

She'd cast a spell on him, and he prayed to be at her beck and call forever.

Pulling back, looking down on him for a change, Archer's eyes still closed, she couldn't help but take the opportunity to take in all of his features, then put her forehead to his and their noses touched. Faith released him, it forced him to come back to reality. "Let's go get a look at that rock, shall we?"

"Mmmm . . . Yes," was all he could say.

"When it storms, I can see the waves crash over the top and spray into the air." She explained while moving her hands and fingers like the dancing of the mist she'd seen. "I sit and wonder what it would sound like if it ever fell. I bet it would be like thunder!"

Archer loved how she talked with her body and knew she'd fit right in with Trevor, who was also an animated speaker.

Listening as Faith spoke about how much she loved all the different places she'd seen as they admired the pillar from the sand, and commenting about how each place she'd been, had its own little nugget of treasure, Archer thought of all the places Trevor had shown him. Which to start with was the question.

The sun was now high in the sky. "It's gotten quite hot," she huffed, and fanned her face.

Archer loved it, though, a bit of a sun worshipper, he suggested they should maybe go for ice cream. Take her for a ride in the car to cool off. They had to get her to the car anyways, and the parlour was en route.

Faith agreed and they tackled the steep stairs again, him behind her, and a great view he thought, to get their things.

Faith asked if they had blueberry and Archer told her about the flavour bursts they served, and that although they used to have three flavours at once, it was always broken. She'd have to settle for two.

"The colours look like jelly on the pointed edges of the soft serve," he said happily as if to be more positive.

"Sounds delish!"

Now in the car, they went down the long lane to the highway. It was a very slow drive, and Faith noted the way the cold air intake whistled. Once they got on pavement, though, he stepped on it a little and made her giggle.

"Just wanted to see your face," Archer said with a big smile, then pinched her chin while keeping his eyes on the road. Faith stroked his hand a second then put it on her leg, with hers rested on top. "Cutest thing ever."

Archer his hand there all the way to the parlour, watching her hair flicker in his peripheral vision. They didn't speak and just enjoyed being together.

The parlour was cute, with flags everywhere. Faith chose straight-up blueberry. Archer got banana and strawberry and they talked about their lives a little more.

Mentioning school, they got on the subject of popularity. Faith knew he had to be popular.

Archer offered nothing more than he wasn't interested in most girls. His interests were for hockey and baseball. When he'd met Johanna at sixteen, they just clicked, and he was always true to her. Once flexible, and a bit of a pushover for her, he matured and became understanding. Johanna never grew up. Like she wanted to be sixteen forever.

After ten years he'd resigned himself to the fact, but still wanted to get married and have children. He didn't "know" anyone else, as he put it, and it never occurred to him to leave. He truly was faithful.

Often, she'd tease about someone based on their clothes or hairstyles. He'd gotten angry once and told her it was mean and she just stopped saying it to him, but he'd still catch her yakking with her friends about it.

Archer always stuck up for the underdogs. Gracefully pointing out their ignorance with the thought in the back of his head of something the bible said: "Why do you point out the splinter in your brother's eye, while not noticing the log in your own?"

Faith asked what was proper in that situation and about righteous anger?"

"That's tough," Archer admitted. "In Buddhism it teaches to 'see their suffering' and for the victims of their callous behaviour to find a mantra that empowers them. Which, in turn, takes away the power of the tormentor and that usually when they are approached with kindness they tend to stop."

"But Johanna didn't? How did you treat that?"

"Well. I tried to understand her. You can't force people to see their own ways. Then there's the bible contradictions of turn the other cheek and the righteous anger you mentioned. It's really hard to decide what to do in those cases. You have to use your judgment."

"How do you judge? Some say we have no right to but then we have lawyers, courts, and law enforcement. Who are we to do that? What defines morals?"

Her question was valid to Archer. He'd thought the same things.

"Morals are based on whether something is beneficial or not. Does it sustain life? Would you like it done to you? Does it cause suffering? What has the ability to suffer? Such intense and deep theological repercussions can happen when not fully considered or realized. Some lines are blurry," he sighed.

"Yes. I see what you mean. For instance, and I want to say first that I'm not looking for sympathy," she asserted firstly, staring up over her shades, "but I had my share of bullying. I chose to take boxing and work out my frustrations that way. I couldn't say exactly what I wanted, and I was scared I'd just find more trouble if I spoke up. Or end up losing my temper. Was my not speaking up and projecting my emotions into the ring the right thing to do?"

How could anyone have bullied this amazing and sweet person? And a *boxer*? Archer wanted to hug her but heard when she said she wasn't looking for sympathy. Taking it as a cue to ignore how it broke his heart, he kept it to himself.

"You did what was right for you. Some people would do it to another to find their sense of power. Doing to others what had been done to them. Essentially stealing their power back."

"Yes, but what if I could have stopped them? Maybe they'd kept doing it to others. Mates and children. Other family members or strangers in a bar."

"Right. The possibilities are endless and there's no way to know for sure unless you're them. Like I said. I can only see from my perspective. You see from yours. We do what we know and try to make good decisions. Some think about it. Some don't. Primal nature can be very powerful, and people can be blinded by it. Look at those who stay in abusive relationships. Primal nature and conditioning being the cause of them not walking away. I'm here on my first round I assume. I don't know about reincarnation and the whole time-space thing is a huge topic." Archer's mind bending now, he continued, "I'm still finding my way. I assume you can agree with that from your own experience, and I would love to talk more about this. Can I ask, though?"

"Yes," Faith questioningly. She was curious now.

"How long did you suffer before you did something about it?" he asked caringly, placing his hand on her.

"From as far back as I can remember in school. I only became aware of myself on orientation day. Before then I was just a kid in the park, playing with chalk and skipping ropes. I wasn't sure why I was even in school or what it was," she said back with a puzzled look on her face imitating how she felt then. "It was like I was just 'dumped' there and left alone, then being told about math and English, without knowing what it was even for. I was quite stunned actually. I'd never really been scared before, and it hit me like a ton of bricks. I never asked why nor said anything about it. I just sat blankly in my chair, looking out the window, wanting to leave. I dared not, though. So, when the teasing began, I just curled up in a ball inside I suppose," Faith finished with her hands in a fist tucked into her chest. "It was junior high before I started taking boxing. I thought it would help. For the most part it did."

"Did you ever tell anyone about the bullying?"

"Not really. I got upset one day and my mother heard me cry. I tried to spare her from it. I knew it would break her heart. She cried when I was sad after being left out of a trip once. The park had counsellors that brought balls and things. The city hired teens to play with kids in the parks then. I missed the cut-off date, and they couldn't get me on the bus. I swore I'd never see my mother that way because of me ever again," Faith said a little teary-eyed remembering Linda.

"That's sad to hear. What do you suppose the right thing to have done would be? Do you see it differently now?"

"I do actually. I should have told my mother. I didn't want her to feel helpless if it kept up, though."

"Do you remember the thoughts you had at the time this occurred?"

"Yes. All of it."

"If you could talk to your younger self, what would you say?"

"I'd tell her there was nothing wrong with her. That sometimes people can be cruel and maybe don't know how much it hurts. To ask them to stop. Or just ignore them," Faith said confidently.

"But you turned the other cheek. That's the peaceful way."

"Yes, but . . . it felt like shit," she responded then with a bit of a chuckle.

"It does. It taught you something about yourself, though. You're stronger than you know. The other work, to find a calm place in the midst, is the trick."

"But I hurt others in the ring."

"Yes. One they chose to be in."

He was right. "I see your point," Faith agreed, as she thought more about it. "I could have done so many things."

"When you called yourself stupid, it hurt me a bit. It only takes once for those things to seep into your subconscious and sprout. Best be careful, the subconscious doesn't have the ability to choose. The gatekeeper is the frontal lobe. After some studying, I've come to realize; life is what you make of it. You can lift yourself or beat yourself up. I promise you that I'll be as gentle as I can, but I can't let you say things like that about yourself and keep silent. Okay? That's one thing about me you'll have to understand. I actually care and I want to help."

"Okay. I understand. It's nice to know someone is actually looking out for me," she said with a genuine smile. "It's been a really long time since I felt cared for. I'll take your reprimands."

Ice cream gone long ago, Archer took her napkin, and they went back to the car. Remembering dinner that Friday coming, he asked if she'd like to come to his family's place to gather for dinner.

Faith agreed on the condition that he come for a relaxing weekend at the cottage afterwards and that he show her the "hidey havens". Also, she'd felt his tension and wanted to give him a thorough rub down, have a fire, cook some good food, maybe some snuggles, a swim, and just have him relax. Wanting the company, she said nothing of the other plans.

"Deal!" Archer said happily.

No doubt it was lonely there after being on the island for a whole two months., not knowing anyone It was the least he could do was hang out for a few days. He'd enjoy it anyway.

"Let's get you to your car."

"Can you come back for awhile longer? It's only near lunchtime and I'm really enjoying your company."

"Yes, I can certainly do that," he said . . . then thought, "How about we eat at the gallery since we'll be there anyhow. Maybe watch a movie later? Or you could play me some of your music?"

"Sounds like you struck another deal."

Then standing from the picnic bench, they strolled lazily to the car. She held his hand. He held his faith.

CHAPTER TWELVE
One Long Ass Week

Faith insisted she book them a table and called the gallery while they drove through town.

"Sara said it would be twenty minutes before there was a table."

"That's fine. We'll stroll the gardens, maybe?"

"Perfect. You can tell me more about your flowers."

When they pulled into the gallery parking lot, Greg was standing outside. No doubt getting some air. He'd break a sweat just drinking a coffee. Popping in and out to cool off but always keeping the door open to keep his ears out. Seeing them pull up he waved with a big smile.

Archer took off his belt and so did Faih, then put her hand on the door to open it. Archer touched her leg and said, "You're not learning. Close the door," and Faith immediately let it go.

"Please. Let me. You'll have to get used to it if you're gonna roll with me."

Having never been with such a person, Faith wondered in her mind why she hadn't expected to be treated this way. Something as simple as opening her door and taking her hand to leave the car . . . or get in. The thing on the stairs to the beach. Taking her napkin.

Looking out the window while she waited for the door to open, Greg waved excitedly to her as Archer said hi to him, then cheerfully waved back before opening her door.

"Ah! Miss Leone!"

"Hi, Greg. Good to see you again," she said, as Archer closed the door and put out his arm for her to take.

Greg held the café door for them to go inside.

"Casuals?"

Archer looked down. "Ummmmm. Ya. I'd kinda forgotten," he said, as he pulled at the cotton pants.

"Were we supposed to change?"

"No. I just never come in like this," he told her quietly, then asked Greg. "Probably startling?".

"Truthfully, sir, it's refreshing. It's nice to see you relaxed." He smiled, then winked at Faith.

Archer thanked him for caring and they went inside as Greg patted his back. Sara greeted Faith saying her table for two was ready early.

"What a great surprise."

Archer went in behind her, as Sara asked if her guest was with her now, or if they would join her later.

It took her a minute, but she realized, it was Mr. Agenta who was the other party.

"Afternoon, Sara."

"Sir. It's good to see you out and about."

"Yes. How is the day?"

"It was good but now it's even greater. Come, your table is ready."

The music was splendid as usual. It got Archer asking about her being a musician.

Faith told him about how she'd always wanted to play and that she'd hung out with the boys in the neighbourhood. One kid's father would cut them electric guitars from plywood. The other kid played buckets and pans. They'd had a band. Not real, of course, but to them it was. It was the best time of her life until now.

Then telling him about how and when she'd decided to finally give it a try, she'd posted on a social media page that if someone wanted to trade her services for a guitar, she was desperate.

With no idea where to start, her old friend Barry said his mother was coming to visit and that if she'd clean the bathroom, he'd give her a guitar, calling it "driftwood" and that it wasn't the greatest but would do the job.

Not caring either way, the fact that she was making a true effort was enough to hook her, after getting her hands on it.

Barry sat with Faith day in and day out, just talking about the old days, and their new ideas. Sitting several hours, for days on end, they laughed a lot, had deep conversations, and drank a lot of coffee.

She'd play till her fingers hurt to have water run over them. Relentless and working hard to make her hands coordinated, she was writing music in no time at all.

"One day he said, "Dude. You learned in six months what took me six years." Then he stopped calling or responding after he found a girlfriend. I don't know why people do that? We were just friends. It wasn't romantic at all."

"When I moved to the little country house, I focused harder to get better. I spent a lot of time alone and actually liked it. I sort of needed it; I think. It's how I ended up here to be honest."

She'd never really jammed with anyone, but a few times. It was hard. They talked so much about the original versions and the players themselves, where they were born, who they were related to, it accomplished nothing. It just filled her head with junk as far as Faith was concerned and didn't hear a word they said, just wanting to play.

Once she'd made an ad to get people over to give another try at jam sessions and it seemed like one wanted to play for them all. Then the next guy and then the next guy. It wasn't a group effort like she'd imagined. Might as well have been open mic. Which she'd done a few times.

Remembering the sweat rolling down her side under her loose top, Faith said she thought her performance was wretched but got lots of compliments anyway. It wasn't like when she was home alone and never thought she'd get that far.

"I judged myself based on what I knew I could do. Them, on what they knew. So, I let them have their opinion. No point arguing from such a different perspective. They didn't have a clue and after awhile I gave it all up and preferred to play alone."

"Interesting how you got to the conclusion of perspectives and stopped arguing with people. That's very wise. At one point in my life, I found myself sitting with a billionaire. I asked him what he found most helpful, as I was on my way to where he was financially, and he told me. Some people aren't as serious or as dedicated as you. Don't expect anyone else to meet you where you are. Go where they're to and have some talks. Take what you can from it and walk away."

"That's a really good point."

"Sounds like that's what you did."

"Yeah. It was brutal. Stunted my growth for a bit actually. I had lots of quiet time in the tiny house, though. It was so cute and cozy. I actually liked the scared feeling I had. It gave me a charge in the right direction."

More memories showing as she spoke. Faith began to laugh.

"What's so funny?"

"I met this guy. My rental house was heated by a wood furnace in the dirt basement. Everyone told me how good wood heat is, but I thought they were nuts. It didn't seem so great to me. The fire kept going out and it was constant maintenance, until I noticed the dial on the stove wasn't opening the draft damper door."

Stopping to catch herself from laughing to much, Faith continued. "The fire was just suffocating. I actually had to learn how to build one, cut my own logs and kindling."

"Oh, yeah?"

"Mm hm! I got wood from that guy. Tom is his name, but anyways, he had land across the road, dropped off a load and said I'd need a better axe. I didn't know and said I was gonna try it. He was laughing when he left the driveway. Later on, I went to try splitting wood, even though I was scared. I always am when I try new things," she smiled, then waving, dismissed the comment. "Anyway. I hit the wood, and it bounced so I tried again. It went in some but didn't crack open like I knew it should. So, I whacked harder, and it slid off the side, taking a chunk from the driveway and sparks flew!"

Faith took into laughing then. So hard she almost snorted. Archer laughed with her, thinking of the sight.

"He called me the next morning," she giggled still and with a deeper manly kind of voice, she repeated the conversation pretending to be both of them.

"'Ya . . . How's the wood?' he asked. I said, 'Not too good. I took a chunk out of the drive.' He laughed hard and said, 'You have the wrong axe. I left one on your step this morning.'"

Archer chuckled knowing exactly what she was talking about.

Faith told him about how she'd gone into town to buy new strings for the "driftwood" guitar. As she spoke, she used her fingers to air quote Barry about it being driftwood.

While waiting at the counter for the person ahead of her to finish a purchase, Faith looked around and saw a bright yellow ukulele with a happy face on it. The sound holes were the eyes. To her it looked like a "don't worry, be happy" instrument , so bought it, then went home to put on a fire as it was beginning to get colder at night.

The house also had oil heat, but still wanted to figure out what was going on with the stove.

Barry called a short while later and said his friend was impressed with what she'd done in his bathroom and that she should give him a call, mentioning his buddy had a violin he'd trade for some services. He'd seen how clean she'd gotten Barry's bathroom.

Hanging out with him in the beginning of her music, Faith waited while he smoked in there, and the walls were yellow. When she scrubbed it, her hands stuck together at the knuckles where they bent and now it was snow white.

Faith figured it couldn't be better timing and did his friend's place, took the fiddle, then called a guy for some lessons.

She'd eventually settled on guitar and shortly after hit a plateau. The uke was much easier than fiddle. Playing it for a year she hardly touched the guitar.

One day, picking up the driftwood, Faith was pleasantly surprised that her playing was much better. Her strum styles had changed, and guitar suddenly made a lot more sense, eventually picking up the mandolin. Guitar was what she wanted to master, though.

The next year she bought an electric guitar too. It was at a flea market, and cost her $1,400 for it, second hand. It made some sweet sounds, so she invested in some amps and other gear. Mostly it was for fun but dreamt of using it at a gig. It was just a dream, though. It set her heart ablaze to think about it now. As if it wasn't already on fire sitting there with him in his gallery.

Archer's eyes fixated on all her movements, facial expressions, hands gesturing her playing the instruments. he saw her pain and desires, dreams and accomplishments as they washed over her face the entire time she spoke. He was falling for her hard.

The music behind them was soothing and it was as though he was listening to her recite the poem of her life. Or narrating the book of Faith. "I can't believe how you took to all those instruments so fast. You must have a talent there!"

"I suppose maybe I do. I appreciate when people say that to me, but I also find it irritating at the same time. I may have a talent, but I worked really hard to do what I do now," she said then paused. "I've never told anyone that. I thought it might be insulting or make me seem immature. It's the truth, though. Jonsie was never home so I put in twelve hours a day most days. I barely slept. I know now that he was gone so much because he was cheating on me with my friend Lacey . . . or my so-called friend I should say. But it's all good. I love my music and it brought me peace. She did me a favour stabbing me in the back."

Archer felt that Lacey had also done *him* a favor. Ater all, he'd probably never have met Faith at all. Gratitude overcame him.

"You're really something, Faith. I'm proud of you and you should be too. What you did isn't easy. I tried a time or two and found it frustrating. You have drive, desire, and dedication. I admire you for that. Among other things. Don't ever let go of that. If it makes you happy you should never stop."

Pausing to take a bite of dessert, looking like he had more to say, Faith waited.

"I wish I could put my feelings into words, but I can't, that's the best I can do," he laughed. "Your life has been a lot of ups and downs. It must have been challenging. I do, however, look forward to maybe having the time to be able to try and express to you better."

Faith was full. Of food and pride. No one had ever said they were proud of her but her mother and her boxing coach. She'd won a few medals in tournaments. What he'd just said made her feel good about herself inside. Certain she'd stand a little bit taller that day.

"Let's duck outta here and go to the beach? You can show me how you find sea glass. I'm really curious about that. Everything about you, really. I am willing to be your humble student," he whispered across the table and took her hand.

"Even to learn to play guitar? I can teach you some if you really want!"

"That would be fantastic! I'd like that. Even if I never get good at it, I'd get your time and attention."

Like he needed to vie for it at all. She was wrapped around his finger.

"Okay. Let's go," she whispered. "Can we pretend to dine and dash?"

"Let's," he whispered back.

They left the cafe snickering and poking each other. Sara watched them with a puzzled expression and Archer put his finger to his mouth to *shhh* and left laughing. She'd never seen him like that. So . . . playful.

Going back to her work, Sara shook her head and smiled as they ran out laughing with no idea what about.

Archer let Faith get her own door for a fast getaway. "Hurry! They'll catch us. The cops will be on their way already. We gotta bolt. *Get in! Get in!*"

Slamming his door then talking about the getaway, Faith kept looking over her shoulder, "I think I just saw the lights. It's hard to tell in the day," then pretended to listen hard. "Step on it. I hear the sirens. They're on to us and not far behind," she yelled as Archer moved his mirror around.

"Did they get my plate number?"

"I don't know but, in this car, we shook them fast enough, I think," she said, pulled her hair to her front and dragged her hands down it as if worried.

Racing through the turns and up over the hill, Archer pulled into a dirt road and then into a lane for a field.

"We better lay low for a bit," Archer suggested, turned off the engine and they sat very quietly, still pretending.

Faith could hear every sound around them. Cars in the distance, birds chirping, trees rustling, and the chilling silence. It made her wonder how a person would feel if they'd run from the police. For real. How acute your senses would be. Then, she lunged forward at Archer and kissed him hard.

"*Woooo!*" she yelled in his face.

It took him back a second but then laughed hard as he got the joke. That was the Faith he knew was in there somewhere. Tipping his head over the back of the seat Archer held his belly in laughter. When he came back to meet her eyes, she had a very serious look about her, took his jaw in her hand, and climbed over the console right on top of him. Kissing him in a frenzy, he kissed her back. They'd gotten quite heated and started to grope at each other.

His hands were stronger than she'd imagined, pulling her into him that way. It made her moan, loudly, and it brought his attention back to reality. Taking her face into his hands gently and pulling back, he said, "Please."

Wanting to take her as badly as he did, Archer's heart took him over. "This is nice, Faith, and some guys would slap me right now, but I like you. I'm not here to treat you like an object or some sex kitten. You've had enough of that in your life. I don't want to be one of those guys and I don't want you to think I am . . ."

Faith held off and looked a little embarrassed.

"I very well may kick myself for this later, but it has to be said. You are a lady. I want to treat you as such. Romance is not dead, and I would like to show it to you." Pulling his shirt back together hastily around his body, in a silly voice Archer said, "Before you ravage me."

He just kept touching her heart. She couldn't figure this guy out. The pang of shame loomed around, but he'd banished it with his words. She'd have to forget all the training Jonsie had given her over the eight years they were together, and it wasn't going to be easy. She'd already had several battles just setting foot on the island. "Fair enough, I got carried away. I apologize for taking advantage of you, sir."

Archer squirmed a bit in his now uncomfortable pants and Faith climbed back over the console into her seat.

"I enjoyed every second. I would just prefer to show you how much you mean to me. We can always come back, and you can finish what you started, if you like. I'm totes down with it. It was really hot . . ." he admitted a little breathless at this woman's forcefulness.

"I'm not pushing you away. I'd just prefer better timing over a simple opportunity. Most guys would take that. I see you as so much more. A beautiful, deep woman who has overcome challenges and knows what she wants, and I can see that you go after what you want. Another admirable trait."

Impressed by this handsome man wanting her to enjoy what he offered *her*, not what *she* offered him, Faith took his face in her hands and kissed him softly, then leaned back out saying, "Imma hold you to that offer."

He wasn't trying to buy her attention. All he wanted was a proper courting. She'd been told no before. By Jonsie. It made her feel unattractive and insignificant. Like her desires meant nothing to him.

Archer made her feel like something to be valued and appreciated for who she was inside. Faith digressed and Archer caught his breath. It made her want him even more.

Wanting her to bloom for him, the same way the flowers of his gardens opened to greet the sun in the morning after the dark night. It was a beautiful thing to watch them open up when the sun shone its rays onto them in the morning dew. It was the best metaphor to describe her. A delicate flower in bloom. How he would make her bloom too when the time was right.

"That was super fun, though, and you did a great acting job. But let's hit that beach. The walk will do us good. I'm pretty full."

Faith agreed. She was full too.

Down a snaky narrow winding road they went, until it came to the T intersection. Moving forward he drove them up the dirt road ahead of them.

"Nice! I wouldn't have thought to leave the pavement." Faith said as she watched the dust fly behind them.

The dirt road was long but smooth. Four fields long, actually, she counted them before it ended into a small clearing for about two cars. Or enough room to turn, really.

Getting out they started the daunting task of climbing a huge dune. Partway up Archer took her hand and helped pull her up it. It was getting so steep her legs burned.

At the top was a crater. It had to be thirty degrees warmer in there than the rest of the beach. Faith almost instantly broke into sweat and there wasn't even a breeze.

At the top, he took her along the edge most of the way, but they'd slid down some as the sand came out from under their feet.

Archer warned her it would be a quick trek down and he'd get her to go ahead of him to keep her from tumbling down. And she would have.

Faith started laughing. First a chuckle, then giggling until she found herself not being able to get a grip, then laughed hysterically all the way down, once trying to stop briefly and get her strength back, it was too steep. It kept pulling, making her laugh harder.

"What's gotten into you?" he asked when they got to the bottom.

Try as she might to get the words out, not able to stop laughing, she finally had to sit. Archer sat with her patiently waiting until the bug got him too.

Piece by piece she told him. "I could feel how I would surely have tilted forward, and I doubt my legs would have gone as fast!" getting that much out before laughing again, Faith kept trying to finish. "I could see myself falling and rolling down the hill. Hair, feet, hair, feet, hair, feet!" cut off again by laughing, Arche was getting the picture now. Her laughing the best part.

"And then getting up with a mouthful of sand! *Ha ha ha ha*!!" she laughed, barely able to tell him the last before he caught her giggles.

"I suppose that would be hilarious. In a cartoon kind of way," Archer said, getting himself together more.

Still beside herself, Faith laid in the sand trying to breathe. "*Riiight?*"

Finally, in check and standing now, she brushed herself off as they walked to the edge of the water. Faith squealed.

"What?" he asked looking around.

"The tide is out! Wooo!" she danced happily.

"What's that mean?"

"More beach means more places to hunt."

"Oh! Where would you like to start?".

Telling him she'd check the tide chart, Faith informed him, "If it's coming in, we'll do the water first. If it's going out, then the shore first."

Typing in the address on her browser, it took forever to load. Archer pulled gently, guiding her into him, and wrapped her in his arms while they waited.

Smiling, Faith sank into his embrace, and he stroked her hair while she leaned into him. Catching it, he pulled it together as it whipped around. Faith felt wanted *and* adored.

"It's going out still," she said finally. "We'll do the sand first."

"Let's get at it then."

Taking her hand, they walked some and she asked about his past relationships, though knew a bit about Johanna. Surely there was more.

He told her about how Johanna was superficial and self absorbed. She'd never asked how his day was. Didn't care about his dreams and that he watched it fall apart so very slowly, trying to be patient and understanding. Always being supportive, until that fateful day, when he put his foot down. That was the end.

"I can't think of anyone but you now, though, Faith. You make me happy. You continue to surprise and delight me with your stories. None of the others seem to matter to me anymore. You overshadow them. They'd never even come close to you and all I have discovered just in a few days."

"You're a good man, Archer. You deserve the best," she smiled, squeezing his hand, pointing with the other. "Oohhhhh. Found one."

"Where?" he asked, as his eyes darted around.

"I'll see if you can spot it. Sometimes it's hard. Personally, I can't not see them anymore. I'm always on alert. Experience is the best teacher, see if you can spy it."

Looking harder Archer exclaimed, "Oh, there?" as he bent to pick it up.

It was a rock, so he stood and kept looking. "Oh, wait, there! How do you see that? It's the same colour as the sand . . ."

Faith asked to see it and showed him the side where it had cracked, said it wasn't ready, then tossed it underhand out to the water.

"Nice arm!" he commented with a surprised look.

"I used to be on a women's baseball team. I can hit pretty good too."

A dream come true for him. Baseball? Was she serious?!

"There's no end to you, is there?" he asked smiling and shaking his head.

"I just am what I am. If you find it pleasing, then I'll take that. I can be a little fanatical about things. Just so you know. I take on big projects and some never get finished. I can hyper focus on things too. This book is the one thing I have *chosen* to work on to the completion, knowing from the beginning it was going to be work. I just need to feel that feeling of success. The way you do. My self-esteem needs it. Something else I've struggled with my whole life."

He knew that. He'd listened and heard the way she phrased things.

"Well. At least you started. Some just spend their lives wishing until their deathbed. You should be very proud of yourself, and you look amazing, but then that's what I see from where I perceive in my mind. If I could show it to you, you may change your mind quickly. I respect your viewpoint. I will, however, continue to see you in the regards that I do if that's okay. Don't stop telling me everything about you."

Wanting to shore up what he'd just said, Archer continued. "I won't see you differently for expressing yourself or think what you say is stupid. You're still amazing even if you make errors in judgment. When we had dinner and you let go of that pain, I felt honoured to be able to witness that. I'd be honoured to continue to see you grow and I'd hold your hand through any fire you need to face, doing what I can to push you towards your own personal freedom, but I would never tell you what you *should* think or that you're wrong for thinking it. Except that part earlier when you said you felt stupid. Embarrassed, yes. That's cool. Stupid is not and words matter. I've seen people who are stupid. You, my dear, are not one of them. I may disagree with you on any given subject, but your mind is just that. Yours."

"You just keep flooring me, Archer. I don't even know what to say to that."

Taking his hands to her head Archer looked around it like he was seeing something or doing a survey.

"What are you doing?" Faith laughed.

"Why I'm straightening your crown," he smiled and bopped her nose. "You *are* a queen."

"Archer . . ." she whispered with an embarrassed smirk.

"It's okay. You'll catch on eventually. I'll keep on leaving you breadcrumbs to follow me," he encouraged and kissed her forehead.

Faith hugged hi then. Tight. So *very, very* tight! He knew he'd reached her.

"How is it that you can make me feel so wonderful? I instantly felt confidence," she said into his chest. For him, she was speaking to his heart.

"I wanted to argue with you when you complimented me so many times, having to fight it. I heard the conversation in my head. It was bizarre. I'd never noticed till you said. The more I listened the more I saw inside of myself. It's like you came in and pulled out weeds that were suffocating me. Not letting me grow. In fact. I feel like I owe you something."

"You do," he replied with a very serious face and Faith looked at him with a puzzled look.

"I do?"

Taking her face he said, "Gimme a smile."

When she did, he replied, "Debt paid," and kissed her.

Jesus, he was good! She'd never felt freer to be herself. Looking back now, Faith realized how she'd grown with him over the last few days and wondered. If she had a lifetime with him, what could she become?

"I am but a looking glass, for you to see yourself more clearly. The more spotless I am, the better you see yourself through me. I will always be tending to that. My job here is to be the best person I can be and give from the overflow. We can't have a half-empty cup and give from there. It is literally draining you." he said in a by-the-way tone and squeezed her hand,

"That's when people tend to get sick or depressed. They start losing their temper at almost nothing. Addictions could follow. Toxic relationships. It feels like there's a hole. Trying to fill it with food or shopping, belittling people or trying to control someone else, when it's themselves who are out of control. Life becomes one of misery. That's what it means when they say, 'misery loves company.' It's a lonely place to be and they're only wanting to find relief or have someone share their position. So, for myself, I work on this. That when I give, it's from a place of satisfaction and pleasure. Whether I ever get to have you or not, and I know, you're going to have to go back home. Either way I just want you to feel all the freedom that you can have with me, and that I offer you insight, to help you be all you can, until you leave me. However long or short that is. I'm good with it, I don't want you to feel guilty for hurting me. I'm a grown and I'm here for you. Not to say I wouldn't miss you. I've learned how to let go, a lifetime ago. Let's have some fun." Archer's heart hurt as he said it and felt a bit of panic strike a good blow at him. "Let's find some more glass, though! Let me help you fill your cup."

"That was the most selfless thing I've ever heard."

Taking her hand, they continued up the beach. Archer pointed out the sand to her then slid on his feet across it makng it whistle.

"*Wow*! That is so cool!" Faith announced happily.

"They call it singing sands. Tourism says it's in certain places, so tourists pay the toll booth to get to it, but it's across the entire north shore. If the sand is white, you can do that. When it's really hot and dry it gets louder. Try it!"

She did, and it didn't work. Looking to him, Faith shushed her hand to show her again and crossed her brows, looking like a caveman might. Showing again, raising his toes a bit, Archer told her to use the ball of her foot.

Trying a hundred times until finally, it happened!

Looking Archer, proud she'd figured it out, Faith kicked sand everywhere, zooming along in front of him as he followed.

Back and forth across the beach now a few times, he smiled watching. Her energy was free and fun-loving. Like a child. Feeling uptight, then Archer thought he should loosen up more. Like when they left the gallery. How could he dull her shine?

Maybe his meditation, the will to overcome, had taken that from him at some point, not fully realizing until now. Sure, he had fun and laughed. What Faith had, though, was an innocence he'd forgotten.

Stopping in her tracks, Faith shrieked, bending to pick something up.

The wind caught her dress and exposed most of her thighs, Archer stopped dead in his tracks. How was he to get himself together if she kept looking like that?

"Come see," she called, and he went forward with difficulty, feeling frozen to his spot.

Getting up to where she was, Faith turned and showed him a pile of glass. There were all sorts. Some green, dark and light. Some brown, dark and light. Whites and a tiny blue piece.

Still amazed at how he'd never noticed them before Archer watched as she rolled them under her finger. Surely, he'd been blind.

"Someone lost their treasure. They found these here and left them."

Then rubbing them lovingly Faith sighed saying. "They must have lost the spot where they put them or forgot to pick them up."

Taking out the blue one, all of her worries seemed to disappear, and she passed it to him. "Blue?" he asked.

Obviously, it was blue, he thought. He just didn't think that would be a sea glass colour. The greens, whites, and browns he could see. People drank on the beach.

"Yeah. Probably a wine bottle."

Archer admired it a moment. Passing it back to her, Faith said, "I'd be pretty miffed if I'd done that and came back to look, but never found them because someone took them. Hopefully they come before someone else takes them. It's not their treasure!"

Dear god this woman is gonna make me tie her up and never let her leave. He was worse off now than he was a few minutes ago. "You're a good person, Faith," Archer commented rubbing her back before she laid them gently to the sand. "The world needs more people like you. It'd be better off for it."

Faith poked him jokingly as if to say, "*Go on!*", dismissing her honesty.

She did her best to be kind to herself then, and the work she'd have to do sunk in a bit deeper. This was going to be a lifetime thing.

He knew it too but wanted to be around for all of it. They both dropped the subject and kept walking.

Archer had so much to learn with her. "So how many colours can you find?" he asked, not knowing what he was in for.

"Brown, white, and green is the most common. Blue is pretty common. Then there's milk glass."

"What's that? Milk glass?"

"In short, it was first made in Venice in the late thirteenth century. In Italian it's called *lattimo*. Murano also makes a glass which is so colourful. Which is obviously called Murano glass. I should really get some."

"This is very interesting. Please. Go on?" Archer asked as they walked.

Faith smiled. Big!

Knowing she was enjoying this, Archer was too. As they walked, he heard all about *everything* Faith knew and was getting more and more impressed. She could be so silly but when she talked about the glass, she became . . . Educated.

"That was quite a spiel. And that's for short?"

"Oh, ya. Sorry. I've studied this a lot. There's so much to tell you. Like I said. Wait till you see the uranium glass, which is also called Depression glass, or Vaseline glass," she giggled, looking excited. "It glows under black light. That's a whole other thing for me. I can show you the uranium sea glass sometime. Maybe we can go hunting. It's better when it's dark, though."

"Oh, god. I'm gonna get schooled."

"I don't have to tell you," Faith said, as if she'd spare him.

"No! No! I love this. It's even cooler than I thought before. I love that you know so much. Even the technical terms. If there more, go for it. Just *shoot*!" Archer said excitedly and smiled. "I'm all ears."

"Okay," Faith said back almost warning him she may go off the deep end. And she could!

Studying glass since she was small, only her mother had ever dove in this deep. Archer wanted to hear it all and she loved that.

"Where did you come from?" she asked with her eyes squinted suspiciously. "Did my mother send you?"

Archer smiled. "No, dear. It was you who has been sent to me," he responded kissing her forehead. "Tell me a bit more?"

Her face took on a whole new look.

Faith continued to educate him on her passion. "Well, okay, then. You're asking for it, though," she warned him, for the last time, then went on for another ten minutes about the glass.

"That's so interesting. You know a lot," he complimented as they kept walking the beach. "What do they use to make it white? Or the other colours?"

Faith now felt she was most definitely in a dream. If he wanted it all she'd give it to him, then went on about the milk glass some more.

"For example, the original marquee of the Chicago theatre, famous for the four faces of the information booth clock at the Grand Central Terminal in New York City. They donated it to the Smithsonian actually," she finished.

"Hm. You have a vast knowledge of this. I assume you could go on and on, from the sounds of it."

"Oh, you have no idea," Faith said in a funny voice and face.

"I've been to the Smithsonian and Grand Central. Now I have a whole new experience of them, being here with you. Do you get that? When you see something and find out more about it later, you remember being there and now looking at it from a whole new way. Like, you're right there, as someone is telling you about it. Or maybe you were passed a pamphlet and are reading it as you stand there?"

Faith loved that Archer was joining her in a great two-way exchange. It seemed he wanted to listen more than talk but was opening up more. She loved his mind. He was adoring hers.

She stimulated him and he made her feel valuable and that her passions were interesting.

Jonsie was such an ass, she thought, and was happy she hadn't let him ruin that for her. Archer, more than happy to listen, also engaged with her.

"I do kind of get what you mean. I haven't seen much really. It's why I came here. One of the reasons anyway. I wanted to get more life experience. See something different. The sea glass was the ultimate factor for me. It's working backwards for me with glass. I read about it and then find them. I have to know what I'm looking at. There one piece I really want though. Actually two," she replied.

"That's too bad you haven't seen the world. It's so amazing. Maybe you could take a trip with me sometime. I mean we'll see how it all goes, but I'd love to take you someplace. My treat."

"God. I don't know. I mean. That would be hard for me to swallow. That's a lot of money."

"Well, see, here's the thing. I don't want to brag at all, I just want you to understand. A thousand dollars to me, may be like a dollar to you. I don't know your income. So, if I say that, what I mean is I'd like to take you out for a burger. You wouldn't stress about that, would you?"

"Well. No. I suppose not," she answered, not quite understanding how much money he actually made.

"You think on it awhile. I can see by your face you aren't convinced it not a big deal. Maybe when you know me better, I'll ask again. Tell me about the uranium glass?"

"Deal," she agreed. To both things. The trip and the uranium.

Continuing, Faith told him more about the glass. "Uranium glass, or Vaseline glass, is glass which has had uranium added to it. Obviously . . ." she said giving that look and went on again with specifics about the glass, knowing the chemical composition names and all.

"Interesting. Continue."

"England's James Powell started the Whitefriars glass company. One of the first to introduce uranium to glassware, then marketed the glowing glass. Others soon followed when they realized its sales potential. Then it was produced right across Europe, then later in Canada. Once made into dishes and other household items, it bottomed out during the Cold War in the 1940s up into the 1990s. Until it became unavailable. Most items now are considered antiques or retro-era collectibles. I have a small collection myself. I've read there's been a revival in the glassware art. Mainly being used for small objects like beads or marbles, I believe. Just decorative novelties," she mentioned in a matter-of-fact way on her face, waving her hand the whole time.

"Is that safe?"

"Well, with a sensitive Geiger counter, it can be measured above background radiation, but most pieces are harmless. Just a teeny bit radioactive," she told him and moved her fingers as to almost touch.

"Oh, well that's good. Do you have much?"

"Just a tiny jar with fragments, really. I did find a few that are a decent size. Not big enough for jewellery."

"Yes, I need to see that!" Archer reminded her.

"For sure. I actually thought of going to see a local artist. If you care to join, we could do that maybe on Tuesday. Or when it works for you. That way I won't forget to take my pieces out to show you. That would be amazing if you could."

"Deal!"

"I do collect the full pieces. Vases, bowls and whatnot. I have some unique ones. There are many colours for *that* too. I had no idea till I shopped online. I've found some at flea markets and yard sales and as for the other two beauties, I hope to find on the beach. One is a bottle stopper, the other, a marble. If either of them was uranium I'd probably get a lot fussier about which pieces I pick up then," Faith laughed. "I used to take every single one, but now look for colour and size. It got overwhelming quickly. I heard there's a good spot here on the island. There was an online group I connected with before leaving Vermont. I needed plans to fill my time and do some things I love. Without being judged for them. I have the coordinates."

"Uranium marble and bottle stopper. Hm. That's interesting. Are those rare?"

"Pretty much, though some have lucked out by doing it twice a day. There are some die hard fans. You can't even imagine. I'm mild compared to them."

"Hm! For sure I'd love to go to the shop with you. Maybe accompany you on a field trip where you're going for sea glass. I definitely don't want to intrude, though," Archer smiled.

Faith was overjoyed. How could she leave him now?

"You said you were judged? For your sea glass and passions? Why? Who would even do that? It's so . . . cruel," he said disbelievingly.

"Ya," she sighed. "My ex was kind of nasty."

"How long were you together?"

Faith sighed. "Going on eight years. Almost married him until he cheated, and I caught him. Like I said before."

"Good lord, Faith. I'm glad you found out. I understand staying with someone like that. I mean, not the same people or experience, but nasty just the same. Being single the last six years, I had to look at that. Have you done the same?"

"I have. Especially since I've been here. It's helped to clear the fog from my brain, though, I have to admit. It still makes me angry and emotional. You've been such a change for me. I mean, I don't know where it's going, and I hadn't expected anyone like you to exist anyplace other than a comic book or romance novel. Earlier today I'd considered letting you go, I felt like I wasn't good enough for you. Then I remembered how you took my face at the cottage before we went down to see the rock. That was powerful. I used that to push it down and chose to keep seeing you. If that's what you still want now that I've admitted to my dark thoughts. I was hiding them this whole time, but I respect you and think you deserve the truth."

Faith's head was hung when she said that, and Archer's heart nearly came from his chest. He'd nearly lost her, had no idea, so stopped her there and then. And he wasn't happy.

"*Look*! That's not your call to make. I, only, will be the judge of that, missy. Please don't keep those things from me. I won't be upset. We can talk about anything. I will, however, be very upset if I find out you are making life choices for me without my knowledge. It's one thing if you feel you can't live up to what you think I expect from you. Which is also something that needs to be discussed if it's an issue. It's quite another for you to cancel me because of something you assume."

Faith sighed feeling humiliated. "I hadn't thought of it that way."

Should she tell him? Yes. If this became something that lasted, she didn't want any baggage or to have to confess anything late and see his ire.

Deciding to tell him she kept quiet a moment. "I have something to say and I'm not sure how to say it."

"Well, we're approaching the cottage I wanted to show you. Take some time and think about it. We can walk in silence till we get there, but I expect it to be said before we leave. No matter how it sounds to you," he said commandingly, but there was an element of concern for her.

Walking together hand in hand Archer rubbed his thumb across her skin the whole time. Now and then kissing her forehead.

Faith tumbled the words in her mind over and over. Looking for the best way to say it and trying to summon the courage that was nowhere to be found.

"Great hidey haven," she commented, and Archer smiled knowingly.

He knew she'd love it. Not many would brave the dune and the intense heat to get to the other side.

It must have been fifty metres across, and it burned the soles of her feet even with her sandals on.

It was far enough across that Faith dreaded having to do it again, and how she was going to tell him that she'd felt humiliated. But felt both would be worth it.

They must have been at least a kilometre from where they'd gone in. There was a peak that came out from the shelf, and a roof could be made out from the top of the dune, but now was out of sight.

The cliff was high and straight. Archer mentioned that Gene McLellan had built the cottage for Anne Murray and wanted to show her. Not knowing who either of them were, Faith felt as though she should the way he talked.

With very little rocks and a lot of sand, the beach wasn't good for finding any glass. One part had tiny bubbling springs coming up through the surface in little pools. Archer said it would be spectacular when they came back but wouldn't tell her what they'd see, making her quite excited. Now mixed with nervousness.

At the peak of a cliff, there were large rocks that had fallen in some storms over the winter. Faith remembered reading how The Island lost about twelve inches a year and wondered how long the cottage would last on that ledge where she was staying. She supposed they could move it if need be.

They climbed over a few rocks and around the corner before starting up the cliff. Archer helped her up the cliff after asking if she was tired or if it looked too scary, then went forward.

It was red and stained her bare feet. How could that be red and the sand white? It made no sense. It was more like soft clay, really. Muddy even.

The sand on the other side of The Island was likened to the cliffs that lined it. Red and almost itty, bitty, scratchy rocks, really.

Up and through the tall sharp grass, then around the cottage, they peeked in. No one had been there in forever. It was something right out of the seventies. The furniture and layout, frozen in time.

They sat on the deck for a bit to get a break from all the walking and climbing. There was more to come yet. They had to get back to civilization soon. They'd need water. Neither of them even thought of it, they were so full and dashed from the cafe so fast. He promised it wouldn't happen again.

Archer sat and Faith crawled between his legs and rested her head on his chest. She wanted to listen to how it rumbled when he spoke. Right now, he was quiet, though, and the sound of the air coming in and out of his lungs, the beat of his heart, with his arms around her and her long hair floating in the air, she felt safe. Safe enough to tell him now.

Two seconds ago, her heart was pounding and now felt she was in a shelter where nothing could hurt her.

"Archer," she said plainly.

"Mm hm?"

There was the rumble she wanted. A deeper sense of comfort swept over her.

"What I wanted to say wasn't all that important, the reason behind it is, though," she said with confidence now.

"I see. Continue when you're ready. I'm listening."

She was listening too. To his body and the soul that used it to talk, laugh, work, and play. The mind that expressed, no doubt, less than the soul could.

"When you scolded me for what I'd said about leaving you to go on your way, I actually felt humiliation."

"Oh?" Archer asked and kissed the top of her head, knowing there was more.

"Ya, well, and . . . It wasn't so much the humiliation that bothered me. It was the fight I had with myself that I wanted to tell you about."

Sighing again Faith's hair spun in the wind some and tickled his face, arm, and legs. It was so long! It smelled so good, and he wanted to tell her how much he adored those little things about her but didn't want to interrupt her heartfelt admission, so just kept brushing it from her face.

"I just want to tell you that the reason I'm even mentioning it, is because I get what you said, and I don't want to carry any guilt about what I was thinking, then have to battle it myself for no reason. What you mean when you speak, is more profound than I can collect at one time. I appreciate you not pushing me to tell you also. It gave me time to find what I meant."

Saying it better was always the name of the game for him. Others had the right to do the same, so Archer gave them time to do so. Heated arguments and words said from reaction rather than response usually came with apologies and he hated having to apologize.

"So, the most I meant after all of that, is, that your kindness makes me feel unworthy. Not that you're too kind. I am just having trouble accepting it. I have a lot of unwinding to do and don't want to come off as some broken trollop. I've come a long way. I don't want to hide anything from you, but I was. Thank you for making me say it. I feel so much better. You can choose to walk away now if you want. I wouldn't blame you at all."

Archer was so proud of her for saying that.

"You, my dear, have been no trouble at all. I understand where you are. In time you'll come to see that I will draw the best from you. Like right now," he smiled.

"That wasn't my best," Faith sighed. "I admitted I'm a bit broken and fragile."

"But you told me. That was brave. You risked losing me. Right now, you told me the truth about where you are. We can't fix that if you don't tell me. You thought in your head, and out of your own fear, you'd have decided for me again, if you hadn't said it. I get to choose if I leave you and you have to be honest no matter what happens. That is respect and true love. I will always let you choose and tell you everything in my mind. Whether you leave me or not."

Did he just say *we* can't fix that? Was he going to continue?

"You don't think I'm weak minded? You're so strong. I don't see what you see in me," she confessed with sadness. "I wish I did."

"Like I said, we can't fix anything until we admit it's broken. There's no strength in denial. That's where your power gets taken away. You're a lovely woman, Faith, and some have made you believe otherwise. The woman I saw kicking up sand and talking with her hands is the woman you are. You have so many sides. *So* many levels of depth. It will take a lifetime to see them all."

Faith heard that. "I don't understand you."

"Am I being vague?"

"No. You're loud and clear. I just can't wrap my mind around all that you are."

"Exactly. It will take a lifetime to discover all the layers. Maybe we can peel them from each other together."

Faith was shocked. Not knowing what to say, she sat up and kissed him. So many times, Archer lost track. Stroking his face, hair, all of his shoulders and arms, Archer was happy to have all she gave. He'd waited so long for her to come to him and wasn't going to let her go that easily.

When she stopped kissing him, Faith leaned her forehead on his and their noses touched. Archer brushed the hair from her face and took it all in his hand and stared right into her eyes.

"My little hummingbird," he whispered.

They just stayed there awhile and appreciated the moment and sentiment. Sensually running fingers over each other. Tickling bare flesh wherever it was exposed. Not sexually either, like Faith was used to.

Finally, she leaned out and felt the best feeling she'd ever had run through her body. Was it contentment? Thrill? Peace? What was it? What wassss itttt?

Her heart offered the word and she said, *No! It's too soon. Go back to sleep. Let me catch my breath. I don't even know him.*

Yesss, you doooo, it replied back, and Faith kept her denial, even after what Archer had just said.

Some things take time. Love at first sight only happens in the movies. She was lusting him. Nothing more. He was helping her repair all the damage a lifetime brings. Wounds being tended to, Faith sat back down and snuggled back into him.

.

CHAPTER THIRTEEN
Oh, Those Summer Nights

Archer suggested they go soon. The sun was getting low, and the sky was as fiery as her hair.

"Just a few more minutes," she whined. "I'm not ready to part with you yet."

That was it. He was done. He *knew* this was going to be the end of him, one way or another. There was no escaping it now. She'd drive him insane. There was no two ways about it. Fighting between his desire for her or to be a gentleman and show her respect, the voice said, *But she can't just walk around like that being all . . .*

Adorable . . . his heart finished for him.

And sexy! The voice added.

Archer just sighed and pulled her in.

"You're going to be the death of me," he whispered and snuggled her face.

His facial hair scratched a little, as Archer suggested they cuddle back at the cottage if she liked. Faith loved it though and did a "smol viktory dance" in her head again.

"What do you mean, I'll be the death of you?" she asked knowing full well she'd driven him near past the point of no return on the dirtroad earlier.

"I want you so badly. That episode in the car. *Phew!* It was hot. On the other hand, I know you're going to leave. Sure, it's two months away but it'll fly. I'm trying not to think about it to enjoy our time and . . . whatever it is we have together. I'm not asking for much. Just to be with you. You make it very hard to not to just want it all at once," he confessed shaking his head in disbelief. "I've never been so crazy about someone in my whole life."

"I find that hard to believe. There has to be other women who have captured your attention. The way you are? You could have anyone you want I suspect."

"Well, yes, they have. I wasn't all that attracted. I was trying to have a life and see now that I was settling for just anything. They couldn't keep it going and I had to admit they weren't right for me to begin with and didn't cross my mind much when I wasn't near them."

Archer wanted it all. Smart, funny, loving, family oriented, beautiful, sexy. He wasn't looking for perfection. Just perfect for him.

"You? I can hardly stop. It's difficult to focus on anything for very long really. It's so . . . bittersweet."

"Aww, honey," Faith cooed with a pout and kissed his chin. Then his cheek. Then his nose.

"*See*? That right there! That's what's killing me . . ." Archer groaned in agony. "*Whyyyyyy*!?"

Faith laughed at his way of making everything ligh. Such an optimist. It made her feel bad for letting him think she'd leave after considering moving there. "Let's get going. You're coming to my place?"

No secrets, she thought and promised she never would again. Except just this one time . . . and maybe the other thing her heart had said that she was ignoring.

"I'm taking every second you'll spare for me."

Any one of them could be the last, he thought to himself.

They crawled down the cliff. The tide had come several feet now but there was still a lot of sand exposed. On the way down they waded through the water. No need for talking. Just to be.

Faith sighed . . . a lot . . . just feeling the stress leave. The beach always did it to her. To Archer as well so he let her enjoy it just holding hands. All of sudden she froze and stared into the water.

"*What*? What is it?"

Faith couldn't even speak as she reached in and took something out, quickly holding it to the sun. "Holy *shit*!" she whispered loudly.

"*What*?" he asked again as she passed him the item. "What is it?" his face glowed with suspense.

"It's . . . a . . . *bottle stopper*!" she yelled, danced around then grabbed it back from him. "Lemme see . . . lemme seeeeeee," she squealed impatiently. Like she'd just found the biggest diamond in the entire world.

"That was something you desired."

"Oh My Gooooddddd!" Faith responded then in a deep tone then switching to a very high funny voice Faith squeaked. "It's . . . *precious*!"

Laughing while she put it to his face again, dancing a little with her feet after he took it from her. "That's pretty cool! So . . . it's from a bottle?"

"Yep! And an old one. This beach isn't the greatest for sea glass. It's almost full too. Like the sand has just done enough that it's officially sea glass. It's the best thing I've ever found!" Faith told him.

Almost crying, then jumping and wrapping herself around him, she calmy said. "And you brought me right to it!"

Faith immediately though that maybe *he* was actually the best thing she'd ever found. Time would tell.

"Well, you're welcome but . . ."

"But what?"

"I hate to tell you this but . . . You led yourself. In your joy you left yourself open to the intuitive nudges. It led you all the way here," he said with a look on his face like 'splendid job'.

"You're sweet. Do you ever take credit for being amazing?"

"When credit is due."

"You . . ." she said and stepped back into the water.

"Fine. We both followed your intuition."

"*Don't patronize me!*" she squinted at him jokingly.

"You're such a cute li'l fireball when you're angry," he teased squeezing her cheek. "No time for that, though. We gotta go. The sun is near down. I may have to use the light on my phone before we get out of here."

"Yes! We should leave then."

He'd put the glass in his pocket, so they didn't lose it and they walked down the beach, and Faith did this little skip now and then when she thought of the glass.

Archer said nothing about it. No point making her self-conscious. He didn't want her to stop . . . ever . . .

He was right about the light too. The drive through the lane, with the headlights on the blue spruce trees, was phenomenal to her.

"What's that smell?" she asked sniffing the air.

"Oh. It's bayberry. The island is covered in it," he answered and stopped the car, ran out, and back in quickly, after grabbing some leaves.

After slapping a few mosquitos from his arms, Archer crumpled them between his fingers.

"Smell."

"Slightly musky, a little like tea, and a background bottom note that is slightly flowery."

"You know a lot, eh?"

"I make soap. Kinda have to know that to blend scents."

"Of course, you do. How silly of me. What don't you do?"

"Oh, lots!" she said back, and with a sort of laugh, added, "Like get a clue people are using me."

"Where did you come from?"

"Oh, you know. Places," she said, waving her hand around in no particular direction.

"Well. Let's get you to your car and you can lead me to places."

Putting the car in drive, the sound of the engine bounced off the tightly grown trees. Now that they were moving, Archer opened the windows a crack and Faith continued inhaling the air. Then the leaves he'd given her. Then the air.

When they arrived at the gallery, he parked beside her car, held both doors for her, with the hand-hold escort. Out of his and into hers.

Telling her to drive safe and stay in front of him, she did as asked. He always seemed to have a motive and, from what she could tell, it was for protection.

When they'd gotten to the straightaway, just before the cottage, Archer saw she'd put on her brakes and drove slower, then turned on her hazard lights. There was a car on the side of the road with its blinker on too.

Looking in the car, as she drove by slowly, no one was in it. Faith thought maybe they'd needed help. *I'm becoming an islander*, she thought to herself.

Getting past the car, she saw two flashes. Someone had walked past the headlights. She then felt like a creep. It was probably someone taking a leak in the bushes, so scrunched down in her seat with a funny "Yikes" face and put on the blinker to turn into the cottage lane.

Archer stopped on the road and Faith heard him talking, then they both laughed and he drove up behind her. Once at the cottage they went in together. Sand went all over the floor when they took off their shoes.

"You grab a shower and show me where the vacuum is. I'll clean this up," he ordered. Not in a barking tone but a very commanding one.

That's his "insisting tone"? He'd be hard to say no to.

When she scooted off to get the vacuum, he followed behind.

"I'll be brief," she said.

"Take your time. Would you like me to get you anything?"

Answering that wine would be nice, he replied, "Very good" and took the vacuum, then patted her behind. "Off with you then."

After doing the floors where they'd walked, Archer got her wine, then put a towel in the dryer. He wouldn't have snooped, but they were right there in the closet with the vacuum.

He didn't mind sharing the housework. Gender roles were dumb to him. Actually, he'd do it all. As long as he wasn't taken for granted or taken advantage of. Someone leaving mess behind all the time would drive him nuts. Otherwise, it was all good.

Leaving the towel for ten minutes he took it out, rolled it tightly and neatly, then folded the ends around itself to keep it snug and warm, knocked on the bathroom door and cracked it enough to talk.

"Yes? Is everything alright?"

"It is. I have your wine. I'll set it there by the sink. Wanted to say so you don't knock it over. Don't rush, I'm good. Enjoy your shower."

Faith thanked him as he closed the door. He hadn't tried sneaking a peek, just keeping his eyes to the floor, and where the glass was to be set.

Opening the patio doors wide, Archer stepped onto the deck with his wine and leaned on the balcony. Listening to the waves crashing and lapping the shore, it was truly a heaven.

Faith came from the shower, stepped onto the soft mat, and saw the wine, also, the towel he'd left. It was warm inside as she unravelled it, with the same care he'd used folding it. *That would be so nice in the winter*, she thought.

Heading to the closet she noticed the patio light on and went over. Watching Archer there, Faith took in the view of him admiring the atmosphere. So handsome, and the way he leaned over the deck, that wide back, silky black hair and the moon beaming on his face. She didn't dare make a peep and just watched a minute.

Archer heard a crack and stood up straight. Faith bolted to the closet for something to wear and as he looked out over the yard, a fox ran through. "Fuck. That scared me," he whispered, leaning back on the rail.

He'd finally gotten his heart to stop pounding, when Faith came out through the bedroom door. "You should take one too. Have you got clothes in the car?"

"Thank you. Yes," he smiled as she crawled under his arm. "Never know when you'll need them. Always prepare for the worst but expect the best." He winked, pulled her hair back, kissed her head and said he'd be right back.

Grabbing his keys, and got the bag he had in the trunk.

Crack!

He jumped this time, then scanned the yard.

Crack! came from the woods again and then a large thunk.

"Jesus, I'm edgy . . . It's just a tree," he mumbled, laughing a little, but not really.

That was three times now and he became somewhat upset. *Shake it off, big guy, shake it off*, he thought, walking back in.

Faith was cutting up some fruit for them at the island and humming. "We didn't have supper. I'm still full but we should have a snack."

Archer looked distant when she said that.

"What?"

"Ya. A tree broke outside, and it scared the ever-lovin' god out of me," he laughed, a little embarrassed.

"Oh! Are you alright?"

"Yeah. I was a little on edge. I'd heard a noise while you were showering. Gave me a start too. It was just a fox."

Putting his arms around her waist from the back Archer kissed her shoulder.

"I found the towel you left. So sweet. There's one the same for you in the bathroom." Faith mentioned.

"Bad," he said and took a strawberry from her that she'd held up to her shoulder. "From the hand of a goddess, who could resist?" he whispered, then went to the shower.

Faith sat on the patio sipping wine and listened to him singing in the shower.

His voice was truly amazing. A bass for sure. Of course, he sang Italian. *Sheesh*, she thought. *What am I getting myself into? He's so cultured and I'm so not!*

Hearing him come from the shower, she refreshed his wine and took the snack to the coffee table. Soft lights and candles, atmosphere meant a lot to her, rarely having lights on unless it was necessary. Cozy was best for her.

"That feels soooo much better," he groaned, taking the glass she offered.

"Thank you, sweetheart, but just one more. I gotta hit the road shortly. I'm gonna sleep like a rock. That was a great day. Lots of exercise."

"Yes. It was amazing," she said back, as he sat down with her. "Would you like some music?"

"Maybe you want to play me a song? If you're comfortable enough. I don't mind waiting. I admit, though, I'm very curious," he told her, rubbing her back.

"Okay. I'll be right back. I gotta get Sophia."

"Is that your guitar?"

"Yes. I'll tell you her story sometime." she smiled back, and walked to the bedroom, appearing briefly with a huge case and a large smile. "What do you want to hear?"

"Do you have an original?"

"I do, actually. I've never sung it for anyone before, though."

As Faith opened the case and pulled out a snow-white full-bodied guitar with gold trim all around the edges Archer became very curious.

"It's gorgeous! I can't wait for this now . . . my heart."

Faith beamed from ear to ear. She really was proud of that guitar after working so hard to pay for it. It was way out her price range but . . . she had to. Taking her position, Faith giggled nervously.

"Before you begin, why haven't you sung it for anyone before?"

"I'm not sure how well I write. I mean. To me it sounds good. Knowing you now,

I know what you'll say when I tell you the reason. I'll say first I'm probably going to agree with you, though, and I'll choose my words carefully here . . ." Faith sighed, and Archer waited giving her all the time she needed. Like on the beach.

"In the *past*," she said, with a finger up. "I've been very judgmental about myself and things I do. The reasons for them don't matter really. I need to work them out in my head. It will be a job, you understand?"

Just this short time had taught her so much. Understanding more fully every day now, she'd been hard on herself, but was already doing better at being more mindful and choosing her words well. A fast learner.

The guitar showed her that. Now she had confidence. It would be shaky, and she had a long way to go, but welcomed the challenge. To be a better person. For herself, and Archer if they lasted.

Even if they didn't, Faith had a newfound self-esteem to build, which appeared to be delightful and daunting. Either way, her new path was set, and she'd walk it.

With him it would have been glorious. Without him, though, she could see it now and when she found the words to tell him, she'd express it and drive home how deep it was for her, though she suspected he already knew.

Archer was something else, and Faith did want to peel back his layers to find out who he was. Fully. Maybe tell him just how much he'd done; then confess she wasn't leaving. Some day through the week.

To her, there was no hurry now. Unless something happened, and somehow, was forced to tell him. Maybe one of the first surprises for him. Now to watch it unfold.

"I do understand doubting yourself. I went through it myself. I think everyone does throughout their life. You can't let it stifle you, though. Drown out potential growth. It takes a whole life to accomplish even the smallest things for some. Don't let your critic hold you back. It's not worth it."

Archer wanted to let her know he didn't think he was better than her. She was his equal. He'd protect her fiercely, though. It was the man in him. It had nothing to with her being a woman and being fragile.

She was a boxer, and no doubt could handle herself. Her getting hurt by someone, though, would drive him over the deep end.

"I see what you mean. That's the reason it gives me anxiety. I'll work on that. For real. You make me feel comfortable, where in the past I'd crawl out of my skin to leave. Just gone. Skin still there distracting them while I get in my car and leave," Faith laughed, with a silly look on her face.

Archer roared laughing as he got the picture. After a second it really gelled, and

Faith had to sit a minute to get a straight face.

"Mental image showed up?"

"Yep."

Rubbing her leg, he told her to go on. "I know it'll be beautiful."

He was confident about what Faith could do, and it oozed into her mind, making her feel empowered. Watching her get settled, Archer noted the size of the body on her guitar. It made her look like a pipsqueak.

He thought it was adorable and couldn't wait to hear, then, she strummed. The bass notes filled the air, as the high ones danced all around it.

Smiling he leaned back surprised at the sound, knowing now why she'd bought it, and looked forward to the whole story. For now, though, he wanted to hear the tale she would sing.

Crossing his knees, Archer sat back then closed his eyes. Relaxed now, she began, feeling he was ready.

Faith took on a proper pose, then started the melody, humming the first four barres a Capella.

He found it enchanting as she began the notes, softly plucking the strings. They fell right in tune, complimenting her coo, then developed into a full-bodied siren's song. Luring him in.

Archer found himself whisked away in his mind to a shore, in what looked like Ireland. His brows furrowed as he tried to focus on it all. It carried him away, as she plucked a few more strings, then was taken with the winds, as though he were a feather floating through the breeze and over the landscape. Faith hummed again and he fell deeper into the vision.

A very thick note wafted from the hollows of her throat, in a richness that he could almost taste, and his whole body came to attention.

She sang a song of longing. Of pain. And as she did, an image of a boat on the ocean in the moonlight, became visible through a fog.

A man stood looking at the stars, his face salted with sea spray and tears, and Archer felt the man's loneliness, as though it was his own. The heartache began to sear in his chest, and he clung to Faith's words as she told the story.

The man had been away for years, his wife pregnant when he left, he was desperately trying to get home to her and his child.

A baby no more, he'd missed that and worried about them so, as violent storms raged on the waters, yet small in comparison to the fire that burned in his soul to see them. At times he'd clung to the boat as waves threatened to end his life before he'd see them, laughing like a madman he screamed to the sea. "Is that the best ye can do?!"

Never giving up hope, he'd reached the shores of his fishing village. Sunburnt and parched, he left the boat floating then splashed through the shallow water of his homeland. Kissing his hands, he then held them to the sky. The victor.

All challenges behind him now, he ran. Through the fields and down roads. Waving he continued to pass by anyone he met. There was *no* time to talk, and his body was weary, but that wouldn't slow him. His mind centred and focused, his body must do as he commanded.

Tears streaming down his face, finally see the smoke as it rose from the chimney he and his wife had built with their own two hands. His heart leapt out from his chest.

"I'm here, love. Aisling. I'm here baby. Daddy is home," he called, as tears covered his face.

Tears ran down Archer's face too. Faith wanted to check and see if he was okay, but continued, assuming and hoping it was just her music making him feel that way. It was not a time to fall on him now. She'd see it through. Like the sailor coming home.

The man ran through the field leading to his home. The house coming into view, closer and closer. Then the fence and the animals. He was filthy and stank, his body now very thin and tired. Hearing voices, his heart raced.

Archer's heart raced, his face contorting as emotions took him over.

Running faster now, the man called his wife's name! Then again as if desperate, and when she didn't turn from going into the barn, he let out a horrible scream as

She came out the door wiping her hands on her apron and pulled her hat back from her hair, tied into huge braids. A child clung to her puffed dress, and she tucked it behind her, not knowing what the matter was.

He screamed her name again and the sound pierced her ears. "*Aisling*! *Aisling*!!" he cried.

Recognizing his voice saying her name, she grabbed the child, and ran to him frantically, he, to her, stumbling once . . . then twice. He'd not go down and she ran to him crying until they met and embraced. All three of them. The child crying in fear. His little girl didn't know what was happening.

Aisling wiped the child's face as he held on to them both for dear life.

Archer could see her mouth moving and the man touched the child's face.

The man was so happy, thinking he was in heaven, but thanking the gods anyway just to see them. Aisling introduced them. "This is your father . . . Cathal."

As Faith eased in the humming melody again the vision faded. Archer looked hard, trying to see more but it was taken over by the chiming of the guitar. Faith softly hummed, then, whispered something.

It brought him back to her. The humming. The bass of the guitar. The dancing high notes. The wine. The sofa. Where had he been? His face was soaked. So was his shirt.

Opening his eyes slowly, he looked at Faith as she was humming the last of the melody with a single chime of guitar.

With the vision gone now he still heard Aisling say "Shhhh" in his mind, then Archer erupted into sobs of pain.

Faith put her guitar down and took him to her chest. He leaned into her hard as she held him.

"Shhh . . . shhh" she kept saying, like he'd heard the wife say to the man when he grabbed her at last.

"Oh, my god!" he sobbed into her chest and held her tight.

Faith was stricken with concern.

"It's okay. I'm here. I'm here," she cooed, as he struggled to regain composure. "It's okay," she continued to whisper, stroking his hair.

What was wrong with him? Had she done this?

Wiping his face, Faith kissed his forehead, each of his eyes and then each cheek.

"I'm so sorry," he breathed softly, barely able to speak. "I didn't know."

Faith wasn't sure what he meant by "He didn't know."

"What, honey? What?"

"I didn't know you were going to touch my soulll," he cried into her chest. "How did that even happen?"

Faith smiled. She knew he had pain for sure now, but he hid it so well.

"It's alright, Archer. You're allowed to feel."

Stroking his hair more, Archer was in a sweat now and she didn't know what to say.

Sometimes there's nothing that needs to be said. Only the arms of someone's embrace could say it, so she laid back on the sofa and took him with her. Still clinging to her as he slid down her body, he laid on her hip and refused to let her go. She didn't mind. At all.

Finally, sighing a few times, Faith felt his body relax some, so just kept quiet and tickled his back.

"I've never felt so *good*!" he yelled, into her belly, finally letting go of all his pain from Johanna, and it tickled her.

Faith laughed and squirmed, but he took her and lifted her over to his lap, kissing her a million times. "My little *siren*! You, are a dream in the flesh."

Wiping his tears, he then went back to stroking her, as he sighed heavily. Finally pulling himself together. "You, my dear, are making me think I've died and am in heaven."

Faith giggled. "That was quite a reaction."

"Your music is powerful," he told her, making her blush.

"Really? It was that good?"

"It was that good. How many songs do you know?"

He'd tell her everything but not today. There was no way he wanted her to think he was coming with emotional baggage.

Would he ever have a child? He knew they were waiting for him too. His wife and child in the ether for years as Johanna denied him, time and time again. Where was she then? Where was the woman who would hear his screams? He was calling for them. How loud did he have to be?

Faith took him to the book cabinet and showed him four large binders.

"You write them out yourself?" he asked flipping through.

"Yes. I also have a pen obsession . . . I do calligraphy."

Archer slammed the book shut and kissed her. "You are a full-bodied wine that I'm desperately trying to get the rich flavour of, but it keeps escaping description. I want to know more about you, but I think you would have me here for days."

"That would be bad how?"

"You stop now. Those eyes are hypnotizing, and I really need to go."

Faith pouted and said, "I know, and I hate it."

"Let's make plans to go to some other hidey havens during the week and you can show me your sea glass art, please?" he requested. "After my parents' dinner, you'll have me for a weekend, can show me all about you. A willing, captive audience."

"Yes, let's. We should make plans."

Walking Archer to the door, they kissed gently but kept it short. Faith asked him to drive safe and text when he got home.

Archer agreed and when he did get home, he could see most of his lights were on. Had he forgotten it? It wasn't like him to do that. He was very regimented and remembering Roger yelling about the lights.

Puzzled now, he went into the house, and began turning off lights.

Dropping his bag of clothes, from after his shower, in the laundry room, he texted Faith. *Home, beautiful.*

Awesome. You make sure to get a good sleep for the beach tomorrow. I have to do some writing in the morning. Should we say around lunch? she responded.

Perfect. Trevor and I have our morning exercise and I need to sign some papers at the gallery. Then I'm all yours to do as you wish, he texted back.

I'm glad I'm not disrupting your work and thrilled you have the freedom to spend time with me. A normal job would have left us longing for more, she texted back.

Yes. Freedom was what I was working for the most when I chose what I do for a living. You get your fine self off to bed. We both have errands to finish tomorrow so we can have our time. I'm excited to be with you again XOXO, he texted.

XOXO sweet dreams, she messaged back.

Faith went around the cottage locking up, turning off all the lights, and blowing out candles, then crawled into the gorgeous bed.

Taking out a book, she put on her reading glasses. "Just a little."

CHAPTER FOURTEEN
The Invite

After such a great day, Archer was ready for bed. Just a few things to do first. Texting Trevor about the morning, then took the bag of clothes to the laundry room and threw it on the floor.

Trevor responded with, *Yep! Be there with bells on.*

Everything in order, Archer took a few minutes to read what Carla had on the schedule for the upcoming week. The typical and regular tasks, like signing off on orders and, *oh, yes*, the new artist would be sending boxes for the gallery. He couldn't wait to get a good look at them.

Clicking the memo, to refresh his memory that her name was Dana. Carla had written it in red so it would stand out. Though Archer was great with names, she always did that just in case. These days with Faith, he was lucky to remember his *own* name.

Now that everything was straight, he went to the bathroom and looked in the mirror. "Ya big baby . . ." he grumbled to himself. "Crying over a song."

It had gotten him right in the feels, though. After battling his emotions with Faith for so long, he must have gotten weak. Obsessing on Friday when she was in the gallery and wanting to talk to her, the surprise of her walking in the next day, finally bowling him over.

How they'd had such a nice night but tempted to strip her down and show her how he really felt. The way her skirt had lifted on the beach. The way she snuggled in and kissed his chin.

Thinking, she's probably just going to leave anyway and how much he'd miss her, Archer dreamt of all that could be lost. It must have just gotten him emotionally worn down and tired. *Besides*, he reasoned. *When music overtakes you like that, it should be enjoyed.* Still feeling as though he had just been overly sappy.

Cathal man, him. The little girl, his dreams. Aisling, mother figure. The desperation, which Archer felt was his. Who was he kidding? Everything before that was ego not letting him feel his pain and he wanted to have it all now.

Faith was taking care of him in the romance department. Maybe she was there preparing him to receive what he'd been wishing for all these years, but hoped *she* was it.

It had to be something significant. There was too much synchronicity. The biggest question in his mind had been, what was he about to endure to get that?

Pushing thirty-three now, time was ticking away and trying not to regret the ten years he'd wasted with Johanna, waiting for an answer. To not feel gypped, knowing she never would have, but strung him along anyway.

Eyes still a bit red, Archer rinsed his face, smiling inside about tomorrow. At some point, though, he'd have to tell her what had really happened to him.

All Faith knew was that the song had touched his soul. He'd tell her how deeply after finding the words, knowing he'd get emotional again explain the full depth of the impact.

Everything was going so well. Both of them had opened up and been honest with each other. Like the proverbial iceberg, though, there was so much more underneath.

Getting into bed Archer thought, maybe some meditation would help, and so let his mind wander with no real direction. It was less intrusive for him to let them run wild sometimes. Like a kid in a park. Easier to get to sleep at the end of the day.

Images and words roamed around in his head remembering the music. The atmosphere in the cottage, breakfast, the lovely lunch. The car ride . . . Oh, the car ride! His body responding as he became stuck in the loop of the back road in the field.

Visions of her danced through his mind. The way she laughed. Her excitement over the glass. Them in the car with his hand on her leg and how her hair seemed to float in the air coming in the window as they drove.

That skirt, those legs . . . the way the skirt flipped up on the beach. Her skin like silk, the smell of her hair invading him as she snuggled under his chin. How she'd kissed him in the car. She definitely wanted him and now he knew it.

If she kept enticing, he wouldn't be able to hold out much longer and he'd give it to her good. He *would* have in the car if he weren't being on his best behaviour, but who was he kidding?

Archer had held back on her . . . for the first time. If she kept tempting, he doubted that he'd let it slide again. Intentionally, he'd wanted to only let her have his mind. All going well, his heart. Lastly his body and hoped for all the right reasons. Wanting them in that order he'd done his best to maintain the plan.

Thoughts escalating and carrying him away, Archer put the meditation aside and let his body go where it wanted. His mind filled with her, eyes closed, he could almost feel her under his hands, and he sweetly remembered her kisses.

Her scent, how every part of her was a little different. Hair, perfume, skin, and mouth. The way her locks ran around on his body at the beach.

With the scene rolling through his head, Archer pleasured himself and it seemed to go on forever. In the end, his mind had done him in. What of her in reality?

Content for now, Archer laid relaxed. It would be enough to hold the beast awhile longer, though he knew, it would come for him again the second he saw her.

That was okay, though, just a small break. Maybe he could keep his dignity awhile longer.

■ ■ ■

Faith woke up from the sweetest dream about Archer, and he had her right where he wanted her. Right where she also wanted him to have her

Feeling her hair, it was tangled horrible, as though someone had been roughly running their hand through it. Her head tingled. Weird. Setting the book on the bedside table, her head was swimming.

Delighted with what she'd seen and felt, his voice seemed to ring in her ear as though he were right there. A little panicked, Faith had to look around, unsure if what she'd seen had happened or not.

The reality was, though, it was all just in her head and she felt disappointed about being alone. Her time with him was not only welcomed but desired intensely. Loneliness had had its way with her on a few occasions since she'd left Jonsie.

Archer had taught her so much about herself now too, so eager to listen. It was like she'd been silenced for most of her life. Like no one cared what she had to say. Him, though? He wanted all of her. Barely knowing where to start, Faith found herself all over the place. She'd try to do better from here on out.

Completely relaxed now, Faith couldn't help but smile. Life was very good now and it was all that mattered. There was no need to be dreaming about any futures. In a type of limbo, however bizarre and strange it was to her, Faith felt she could definitely get used to it.

The thought of him lingered in her head as she laid in the bed a wreck, but also unsatisfied. She'd constantly been thinking about how she'd sat on him in the car. The passion that filled her, as it came up on her like a surprise attack, she paid forward to him.

The way Archer had laughed hard when she yelled in his face after kissing him trying to be funny, though not knowing if he'd appreciate her humour.

The way his clothes looked. The soft, crisp white. How she wished he'd have taken off that shirt so she could see how the waist hung from his hips. The day they'd had was still nice. Even if she didn't see his "hip dips."

Archer maintained being a gentleman and it all rolled through her mind like an avalanche. Buried by it all, Faith's mind, unmonitored for a moment, her animal nature came running full tilt, howling to her with teeth bared.

She saw it to be a massive wolf. Wild, untamed and savage, starving, and she, its prey. It took her over and he'd seen it in her eyes. For a second. It's why he stopped laughing. She knew, he knew, and there was no time to waste.

Wishing he'd have shown her, a thing or two, about what it was like to underestimate something. How she wished he just would. Maybe she should try again.

Not sure how to call upon it at will, Faith laid thinking of how it had happened. Going through the thought process to recall it, sure, it'd happen again if he kept holding out on her.

She longed for him now and almost wished she hadn't jumped him in the car, knowing what his body felt like with her legs straddling him and the way he held her. Oh, the way he held her.

Faith missed him now, knowing so much more of what there was to miss.

Maybe it would have been better for her to not know him, than to know him and not feel every single inch of him. The depths of what he had under that cool exterior.

Dreaming of it all again, thinking that she couldn't wait to get him in her hands fully, Faith eventually just fell back to sleep. She'd show him what he does to her soon. That was for sure . . . and he *would* know her.

■   ■   ■

Archer slept well that night. The short amount he had was enough. Jumping right up out of bed that morning, hoping the morning would pass like the summers seemed to, he started the laundry and messaged Trevor that he'd be ready to be picked up anytime. Then texted Faith.

Morning, sunshine, he said in the message, then went off to make coffee.

While it brewed, Archer did some stretches and breathing. Needing to relax, his energy was super high today, a good swim would help.

With coffee ready, he sat on the sofa going over the list again, refreshing his memory and saw the note to call his mother.

Best to get that out of the way before anything. Dialling the number, it barely rang once. "Morning!" Roger's gruff voice answered.

"Morning, Dad. How's things?"

"Good, boy, good! What's on for the day? Mom says you have a woman."

"Well. Not really. I did meet someone amazing. We're just getting to know one another though." Archer laughed.

Roger would have been proud how he had been treating her. Archer knew his dad and his dad knew men. If he'd seen Faith, he'd know the hell Archer was fighting off.

Roger had always pushed him to move on from Johanna. Even before he'd ended it with her, explaining to Archer how he still felt a need to protect him, even though he was grown.

"That woman is trash," Roger always told him. Followed by, "She's not right in the head," in a whisper, but loud enough that Archer could hear him, though, then growl, "What's wrong with people? Always so selfish," before changing the subject.

Archer respected his father and so didn't argue. Now and then, agreeing with him.

He *was* right about her. At the time, Archer thought Roger just didn't know her, the way he did. Which is why he should have listened to his dad. After all. He had nothing invested or nor had benefits if Archer stayed with her or not.

Either way, Roger saw her for what she really was.

Archer, being in love, had ignored the red flags with the hope she'd come around. Roger chalked it up to Archer being young and thought "love is blind".

That wasn't it, though. Archer loved her for their tender times, as few as they were, but he just took people as they were.

Archer's opinion of love was that "love sees all and chooses to do it anyway." Lust is blind and no one is perfect. His lines were just further than Roger's. Painfully, he discovered, she just wanted what she wanted.

"Oh, okay," Roger replied almost disappointed. "I'll get Mom. See you both Friday," he said, then mumbled with the phone on his chest.

"Morning, dear," Debbie chimed. She was much kinder answering the phone.

His dad meant well, and Archer learned a lot from him. Roger was only tender with his mother, though. With others, he had a gruff, manly way about him, and said few words. When his children had been hurt, though, he almost cried. Archer knew hiding his emotions was his way of being manly, but it really was just a show.

"Morning, Mother. I just wanted to let you know that Faith said she'd love to come on Friday," he informed her, nonchalantly.

"Oh, lovely! I heard a little about her from Trevor. I ran into him at the grocery store. I reminded him about dinner on Friday and he said they'd come."

"Oh, nice! He hasn't met Faith yet either. He'll love her, I know. That saves us some time."

"Yes, dear. You're always worried about time," she giggled. Similar to Betty Rubble. "Did you ever find out why?"

"Not really. I've just learned to live with it. Drives me nuts sometimes still."

"So, tell me a little about her."

"Well, she's from Vermont, here on vacation. She had a cleaning business there and is trying to switch over to becoming a published author."

"Oh. What type of book?"

"Science fiction. She had a dream one night and it felt so real, her tears woke her up hitting the pillow. It's a bit of a romance also."

"That sounds interesting. What's a plot?" Debbie asked, more interested.

"It's a bit of disaster movie. Humans had destroyed the planet and created AI to help them, this evil genius starts messing with time, thinking he knows what's best for everyone. The main characters are looking for a foretold hero, not knowing who it is. The main characters are in love, of course."

"I see, I see. Do tell her I'd like a copy when it's released. You know how I love to read. Sci-fi isn't really my thing, but I'd give it a read if there's love in it. Also, it helps her sales. *Oh!* Maybe I should have the whole book club read it and we can analyze it. They could use some new material. They're always stuck on the westerns."

Archer could see Debbie's eyes rolling as she said it, loving the ones with war and soldiers more than anything, being a bit of a history buff.

"So where is she staying? You said she's here for the summer?"

"You know those cottages on the North Shore? The luxury ones?"

"Yes. Brilliant young lady started those from scratch. Harding, I believe. It's so great to see people rise up like that. Especially women."

Archer agreed.

"Now I'm not saying anything about gender roles, but women have to fight hard to get what they want. Unless they want to sleep with someone or have rich parents."

At Debbie's age, she'd seen and been through the battle women have had to get equal rights, and it was still a battle. "Those ones she has aren't cheap. How did she get into one of those for the entire summer? Is her business large?"

"Well, actually, her mother died when she was young and left her the house. After meeting a guy, they moved in together there. Her business was doing well and one day there was a storm. She came home early to find him cheating with her best friend then kicked him out. With too many memories in the house she sold it and decided to come here for the summer."

"Oh, my. That sounds rough. She must be a strong woman."

"She is, Mum. Funny, kind, smart, caring," he added, before going into more details. "She is very wise and has interesting opinions too. She's here to spoil herself a bit, find some peace, and a little sea glass. It's actually how we met. Her hat blew off while I was in the water, so I took it back for her. She's well into the book and has regular calls with her publisher. I'm not sure on the release date. If she's still here, maybe we can throw a surprise congratulations party, she's very alone here. With us here to celebrate, I know it would touch her heart. She's had so little in her life for encouragement since her mother passed. Ultimately, she wants to change careers and is hoping her book sells enough, so she can build her dream house and travel the world. She has dreams and she's chasing them. I really admire her."

Happy about all he had just told her, Debbie knew he was very taken. He'd never offered so much about a woman before. Maybe because they were shallow and he wasn't truly happy with them, she'd suspected.

"I can't imagine you taking anyone short for yourself now," Debbie said then.

"Mom . . ." Archer spoke disappointingly.

She wasn't making a dig at Johanna, but Debbie never liked her either. Being civil, she'd just tell Archer what he deserved, knowing Johanna wasn't that. A little passive-aggressive, really, but she meant well.

"We all need to learn our lessons."

"I know, dear. I wasn't trying to be rude. It's just. You're so successful and good-looking. All the women want a crack at you. I hear them talking. You take after your father. I've had a few fist fights myself with them flirting."

"*What? Mom*!"

"Yes. I was young once too," she giggled. "Your father would tell them he was taken, but some kept at it and he was too polite to tell them to stop, I think maybe even embarrassed. I had to put a few in their place. It's a small town and I'd have been seen as a pushover."

"I . . . did not *know* that about you."

"We all have our secrets, dear. That was another lifetime ago now. So has Faith got family?"

"No. It's sad. Her dad committed suicide when she was between three or four years old and doesn't remember much. Just that she missed him, and the memories faded. Her mom never wanted anyone else and raised her alone. Growing up, she was teased for her red hair and her mother let her go into boxing to let off steam. She can throw a punch, and can she ever throw a stone!"

"Oh? Is she a pitcher or something? Maybe she should join the women's league since she's here," she asked, intrigued by this woman that had caught her boy's eye.

"She *did* say she was on a women's league team back home. I hadn't asked if she still does it. She's been throwing *me* a lot of curve balls. There's no end to her talents and feel I get lost in it all actually."

"Well. Now. Isn't that something," Debbie said cheerfully.

"To be honest, Mum. She's had me so preoccupied with tales I haven't even looked at the clock while I'm with her. We're having a blast. I'm actually taking time out of work for awhile to be free to hang out and get to know her better. I still stay in touch with Carla, though," he said, getting his things ready for the day. "The staff is so amazing; they can handle me gone a bit. I've decided to have a party for them all and hand out raises on their cheques the morning before. Greg will help me coordinate it."

"Oh, my. That all sounds lovely! So much happening. It's good to see you living more than working," Debbie said, and then Archer heard a shuffle on the mouthpiece of the phone. Then voices. "Dad needs to call the garage, honey. I'll have to let you go. I can't wait to see you and your lovely guest."

"Okay, Mom. We'll see you Friday. Love you!"

"Okay, dear, I love you more," she giggled. "Bye now."

"Yes. I love you too," he simply said and ended the call.

It was awkward not saying goodbye. Also satisfying, though. Like suspending the conversation with a bizarre sense of continuity, which made him feel as though his mother was closer to him when they weren't together or talking.

Archer found his thoughts roaming to them more often and had more appreciation for their relationship. If that were even possible. Higher respect even . . . and he . . . rather liked it. There must be a better way to end the conversation. He was still struggling with that.

Archer was especially close to his mother. She loved *all* the boys and was always there for anything they needed, but Archer she'd taken to the most.

He'd modelled himself after his Roger, but looked to Debbie for the definition of what a woman should be like. Of course, he had his own ideas and there were things you didn't tell anyone, definitely things you don't tell your parents. Some he'd never even told Trevor.

Debbie's feminine side was superb in his opinion. Demure and mild. She could strike a verbal blow if needed, but rarely did. Except for the boys. Then she'd have long discussions about their behaviour. It could carry on for days.

Brett and Greg would make faces and sigh. Archer just listened and asked more questions. Debbie loved that about him. His thirst for knowledge. Leaving the church was hard on her, though but Archer had so many questions. Every time she'd answer them, he'd say it was a circular argument and didn't see the logic in it, so went searching elsewhere.

Archer's phone lit up and dinged before setting it down. *Mmmm, Faith*, he said in his head as he clicked the message open.

Morning, handsome. I dreamed of you, she texted.

Is that right? DO tell!

Oh NO! Lolol

Yer no fun! XD, he texted, then called.

"*Hi*!" Faith answered, cheerfully.

"Morning. I don't mind texting. It's fine to make a quick plan but I'm kind of old-fashioned. I like to talk directly to people when there is the opportunity. How'd you sleep?"

"Slept amaaaazingly," she said pouring water into the coffee maker. "What's on for today?"

"Well. I thought I'd check in with the gallery and make sure everyone has what they need. Just got off the phone with Mom and told her you'd be there on Friday. Trevor and Dora are coming. You'll only feel the awkwardness of meeting new people once."

"*Oh, fantastic*! I can't wait to meet Trevor. He sounds like a card."

Archer grinned from ear to ear, excited for them to meet also. "He'll probably behave himself with my parents around, though. Dads cracked his ass a time or two," he mentioned. "Trevor's father left when he was really young, and Dad kind of assumed the role, until his mom remarried. Then he gave him advice more than anything," Archer told her and made his heart heavy for Trevor.

"Aww. I know how that feels."

Archer heard the warmth in her voice.

"I'm sorry your dad wasn't around for you, Faith. We can share mine, though. They wouldn't have it any other way. Everyone is taken in as family when we bring someone into their home. Just so you know."

"Roger and Debbie, isn't it?"

"Yes, ma'am!"

Faith was tickled by that and raised her eyebrows. *Please say it again*, she thought.

"What time is good for you today to hang out?" Archer asked then.

"Oh! You're probably meeting Trevor soon for the beach," she said, briefly looking at the clock. "Well. I have to write for a bit. Coffee is on, so my brain starts working. I'll have a light breakfast, a shower, and then get right to the book. If I could have till late afternoon or so that would be great. I can get a lot done in a short time. I took some online courses for typing. Needed to get the hands going like the brain. It's taking longer than I realized. *So* much editing and rereading, I thought I'd do it as I go, every two chapters. I still need to do it from the start again after that."

"Good stuff! I'll go in and check on the gallery and I'll see you after that."

"Awesome. That sounds like a plan. I was thinking maybe we could go and see the sea glass shop."

"That sounds excellent to me. Should I pick you up?" he asked while getting things ready for the day.

"No. I can come in and meet you. The shop is off on the other side of the gallery. I can leave my car there and we can take yours to the shop?"

"We sure can. I doubt I'd fit in your car anyway. My knees would be under my chin," he laughed. "Text when you're on your way, though I'm sure we'll be in touch anyway. Get your book done and whatever else you need. Enjoy your day. I'm happy to be seeing you again and this sea glass thing is really interesting. Can't wait to see what's there."

"Me either. I make the stuff and I get blown away by the creativity. Even if it's simple wire work, I still find the glass itself amazing," Faith said and paused. "Okay. Let's get to work and help the day fly. I hope yours is wonderful," she wished to Archer, and did a kiss kiss over the phone.

Maybe it *was* true what they said about choosing someone like your mother. Archer kiss kissed her back before ending the call.

Throwing grey sweatpants over his shorts Archer made coffee. As it brewed, he did some yoga. A little sidetracked, having spent so much time with Faith, it'd been a few days.

It'd been so long since he'd felt truly distracted. We wasn't even like this with Johanna. They'd spent a lot of time together at school, and around other people, Archer felt like they were part of a group thing and seemed apparent they should be together. Maybe he hadn't completely thought it through.

When they moved in together, she was always gone, or they were both away. She was so caught up in her looks and taking forever to do her hair and makeup, Archer had plenty of time for yoga and exercise.

When finished, he texted Trevor again.

About to have coffee. Let me know when you're heading out.

Probably be twenty minutes, Trevor responded.

That was perfect. He could check the news and stock market investments. The day was supposed to be a little overcast and the humidity was down. The last week had been brutally hot and humid, and he looked forward to maybe a little rain. The weather app said maybe after supper they'd get some.

Finishing the coffee, Archer started the washing machine, so it'd be ready for the dryer when he got home. Throwing in the clothes, there was a loud clank. Checking pockets, he found the glass stopper. Grateful it was still in one piece, he put it on the bed next to the pants he'd laid out.

Archer had no longer pressed the button on the washer and heard Trevor beep the horn, so grabbed his towel, T-shirt, hat, and phone. Out the door and into the truck Trevor stared at him.

"What?" Archer asked as he settled in and clicked his seat belt.

Trevor didn't know what to say. "*What?*" Archer asked again, looking at himself all over. The floor and the dash too.

"You look different . . ."

"Must be the beard?" Archer smiled, as he stroked his chin. "What do ya think?"

"I like it. Looks rugged. It's something else, though," he squinted looking Archer over more, then put the truck in drive.

"Is it a good thing or bad thing?" Archer asked. After all he didn't get much sleep.

"It's good. I think you just look . . . more relaxed."

Archer had to agree. He *was* more relaxed.

"Hm. Well then. That's very perceptive of you. I feel relaxed. And content."

"How's Faith? I'm excited to meet this amazing lady who took your sanity briefly. You were a bit nuts, eh?" he chuckled.

"Ya. Right round the bend. It was so weird. I didn't know what to say or do. *So* not like me. I at least have a clue and feel my way through. She completely crippled my mind."

Talking all the way to the beach, Archer told Trevor what they'd been up to and a bit about her and their upcoming plans.

Trevor was impressed she kept up with him on the subject of his deep thoughts. He'd spin Trevor's head with that talk. Though he tried to understand, he caught the basics, and it usually made his life better. No where close to Archer there, Trevor couldn't even imagine the benefits Archer got from his own wisdom.

The beach was calm, and Trevor went right off for his run. Archer admired the ocean for a little bit before getting in.

Hoping a new chapter of his life had begun, he swam lazily. There was time to pound the waves another day. Relaxed, like he said, Trevor had noticed, and the water was warm. It was definitely going to rain later.

After swimming, Archer sat on the beach to dry some while waiting for Trevor. For the first time in a very, very long time, nothing went through his head. Nothing but the water and sand. The incoming clouds drifted in slowly. The sun had a layer over it, and he could see the ball of fire's edge. Sighing, Archer wrapped his arms around his knees and tucked in. Life was good.

When Trevor returned, they started for home. The cool and fresh air felt nice. Once back, Archer finished the laundry while he showered. A quick trip to the office and he could go to Faith's.

Texting her he mentioned, *Thinking boutchu. Hope your morning is going nice.*

Faith texted right back. *Thinkin boutchu 2. The morning is great. Had breakfast and did enough on the book. About to do some crafting. Can't wait to see you. XOXO talk soon,* she sent. He loved that she wasn't needy and left him to do his work.

Ada popped into his head then, and so considered going to the diner soon with Faith, actually wondering what Ada she'd say. She had a way about her and was always bang-on. It was possibly him just wanting Ada's approval. Knowing when Ada had said she worried about him, she actually *did* worry about him.

Thing was, though, Ada and Greg had already had some conversations about them both and she was just waiting for Archer to show up with Faith.

CHAPTER FIFTEEN
A Wonderful Afternoon

Archer walked into the office from the patio entrance and messaged Carla that he was in doing some work, and that when Greg came in to send him up.

Opening his browser, Archer typed in decorating styles, then searched the images saving what he wanted to show to Greg. One stood out as he scrolled, a man and a woman who'd gotten married. The cameraman had done a most excellent job. The tones were slightly blackened and blurred in the back and the couple were sharp. The emotions shined through.

Wow, Archer thought, hunting for the name of the photographer. Hoping someday soon he'd *definitely* need it. Sitting there he couldn't help thinking of Faith. That possibly he'd have that with her. *One day at a time, bud*, he thought. Just then Greg knocked on the door. "Enter," Archer hollered loud enough to hear, and Greg came in.

"So, we're planning a party, eh?"

"Ya. I was going through some pictures of themes and decorations. You know how I like the atmosphere to be nice," he said, clicking on his computer to get it on the big screen, then stood to shake Greg's hand. "Good to see ya."

"You seem to be a little absent these days. Preoccupied?"

Archer smiled and Greg nodded. He already knew, but his secret would never be told, unless it was absolutely necessary.

"Ya. She's something." Archer replied, but now that Greg had opened up to him, he felt closer and didn't mind sharing a bit more. Like a little brother. "We've just been hanging out and enjoying the summer days. A beach walk and ice cream."

"You need that, sir. You can't work yourself into an early grave. You'll be on your deathbed regretting not taking enough time to spend frolicking."

Archer didn't realize how wise this kid was. "That's a good point. Maybe I should re-evaluate things a little. Come sit. Would you care for a drink? Cold glass of wine maybe?"

"I have to go back to work."

"If you like, one won't hurt you. I'm not gonna tell the boss," Archer laughed.

Greg couldn't argue with that. Putting up a hand and tilting his head sideways, Greg asked "What do you suggest then?".

"Whatever you like. I'm well stocked, and it will just be narrowing it down to something specific. You like a low or high SC?" he asked Greg.

"I don't even know what that means," he laughed.

Archer informed him about residual sugars and how some wines are sweeter than others. "What's your preference. Dry or wet? Sweet or tart?"

"If you have something sweet and fruity, I'll take that. I'm usually a whisky drinker when I do have alcohol, though, it's not often. Wine isn't really my thing, so I'm not sure how to answer that entirely."

"Well, I can certainly help there. I have a scotch whisky I save for special occasions. Would you like to try?"

"Maybe another day. I think people would smell that. Doesn't look very good."

"Good enough. Sweet fruit it is," Archer chimed as he poured them both a glass, "Really? Frolicking? Not word commonly used by kids your age."

Greg accepted the glass and answered, "Yeah. I listen to motivational speakers. One of them uses it often. I think it's adorable and appropriate."

Sipping the wine, he agreed. It was particularly refreshing now that he thought about it.

"Hm. That's interesting. Maybe you can forward me some of their work. Can't get enough wisdom. Or sometimes be reminded to frolic," Archer chuckled softly, then pulled up some pictures.

They bantered back and forth about the decorations, food, and drinks. Archer suggested entertainment and Greg suggested that Archer let everyone take their spouses and children. Maybe have a face painter, balloon sculptor, and magician.

"See? That's why I asked for your help," he said, writing everything down. "Good thinking."

Greg felt proud and looked forward to the day. It was going to be a lot of fun and got excited for his co-workers. "You're very generous, sir. Is there a special occasion?"

"Well, in a way, yes, but it's a surprise. The full reason is I just want to thank you all for doing such a great job around here. I wouldn't have been able to have the time with Faith, that I'd like, having to babysit employees. I can't say how thrilled I am to be able to take this time off."

Greg pretended to try to "not understand fully," but he could see into Archer. More than he'd ever know.

"I'd cover for you anytime I could. I can't help in the office but there's things I can do if you need. I want you to have fun. It's good you have a new friend. She's really pretty and sweet, by the way."

"That she is. Speaking of which, I need to get over there soon. Can I get you to take the notes and find out prices and availability? Whatever you can get done by Friday? Ready two weekends from now?"

"Yes, sir. That's not a problem. I have a lot of spare time during the day. I'll spread it out if needed. Customers first."

Nodding, Archer commented, "Excellent approach, and thank you for keeping them first."

Archer knew he could trust Greg with it and respected that he'd do his job first. Greg was turning out quite fine and giving him the task would help open him up more.

"Good stuff then. I'll call to Sara and let her know you'll be having lunch on me this week. Take the time to sit and enjoy. You deserve that," Archer said, and slapped Greg's arm.

"Enjoy your day, sir." Greg smiled and shook Archer's hand. "Don't worry about a thing. If I have an issue, I'll let you know."

"Very good. If Josh is around, have him cover for you. I want most of your attention on this, in case anything has to be tweaked."

Greg nodded, then left Archer to his business.

Alone now, he sighed and went back to the computer and flipped through the images once again. Coming to the wedding scene, he sighed saying, "Please," before closing out the page.

■ ■ ■

Faith pulled out her jar of sea glass and went searching for the lavender piece she found as her hat went tumbling, ushering in this dream that she was now living.
"Ahh. There you are. Let's make you into something pretty, shall we?"

Setting it on the coffee table, she went for her tote of wire. Starting out with craft wire until getting better with it, Faith went bigger and ordered sterling silver. Every kind. Round, half round, flat and square, every gauge she could get. Plus, all the hand tools she'd ever need.

Sitting on the sofa, with soft music on, Faith took the glass and held it to the light, choosing which way it looked best, if it were to dangle.

Pendant or suncatcher? she thought, then flipping it around and holding it to the sun.

The craft wire, which was easy to bend and cheap, she didn't care if it went wonky. After getting into the silver, she was more particular and after some time, bought a soldering iron with the end goal being quality rings and pendants. Maybe make a chandelier.

Remembering having done a simple one with wire, Faith thought hard but didn't remember packing it. She must have, though, there was nothing left nothing in her mother's house.

Faith sighed. "Poor Mom . . ." she whispered.

Thoughts swimming in her head, Faith realized how far she'd come.

Figuring suncatcher, she took the wire needed to get it started. It took several hours to do the edges and she wanted it to be perfect. Maybe show to Archer and give it to his mother at dinner on Friday. If it turned out nice.

Grabbing her tools, she began. Getting the outside done, in what she considered, record time, this one was becoming particularly intricate. It was the embellishments that took the real time to do. Deciding which way to go and what wire to use, Faith sat and looked at it, letting it tell her how it wanted to be dressed.

Watching videos on the internet, when she'd started, they were all really simple. Then, she found masters of the craft, fell in love and couldn't imagine how they even created the designs.

So neat and glamorous, like something from a fantasy movie, she watched for months before making an attempt. The wire was all knotted and wrinkled from making corrections and her hands had blisters on them. Not to mention a few stab wounds.

Not anymore, though. She was getting good enough to actually consider making some to sell online.

Tucking it all away, Faith felt proud at how it was coming along, and thought maybe it would be done by the next afternoon. Then restated, it *would* be done by Thursday.

She knew better than that. Always starting projects expecting a quick turnover then finding it took way longer than she'd imagined, except for the soap making.

Wanting it to take hours and be able to play with the design, it happened way too fast and then it was time to clean up the mess she'd made. The oil was hard to get off and, if the soap splashed, it just smeared when wiping it up, always wondering if she'd gotten it all.

There *was* that time she'd gone to clean the stove and found it all underneath the burners, not even knowing how it had gotten there.

Where had the time gone, though? It was getting late, and she still needed to do her hair and makeup, so bounced off the sofa and put the crafting things under the coffee table.

Getting prepared for meeting up with Archer to go to the jewellers, Faith got lost in her mind. It reeled about her past, her possible future on PEI and Archer.

All of time collapsing into one place, like a time traveller, Faith rushed back and forth, and it jarred her memory of her mother and a particular day.

Faith was so frustrated. She'd done so well to keep herself engaged with her boxing, but that day, the daily teasing had gotten to her. Never telling on them that first time, she thought it was a joke until one kid pointed at her and laughed.

"Look!" he laughed in that bully way, his fat finger pointing at her. "She's so stupid she thinks it's funny!"

Then, it seemed, all the kids laughed at her as Faith slumped in her seat. Refusing to cry, as the teacher came in telling them all to calm down and sit, so she could start the class, Faith heard nothing the teacher said that day.

Linda had heard her crying walking by her bedroom, and Faith tried so hard not to make a sound. Upsetting her mother was not on her to-do list, never wanted to drag Linda into any more of her episodes, after how sad she'd gotten the day Faith was left out of the trip with the park counsellors.

Knocking lightly, Linda called her name. When Faith didn't answer she creaked the door some and said it again.

"Not right now, Mom," Faith answered, with the straightest voice she could. That wouldn't be enough, and she knew it.

Not even a second later Linda came in as Faith was punching her pillows. "Honey. What's all this? Did someone do this to you? Did I do something?" she asked, and came to the edge of her bed, sitting down as Faith turned away and wiped her tears angrily.

She wasn't so much sad, as filled with rage, and Linda wanted to see what the matter was. Touching Faith's arm to gently ask her to open up, Faith slapped her hand and Linda pulled it back quickly.

"Faith! What is going on? This is not the sweet girl I know. Are you okay? I've never seen this side of you, and I don't understand what's going on. Tell me or not, that's your choice, but I will not put up with this treatment," Linda scorned.

Faith never would never have hit her mother, but it was done before she even realized it had happened.

As hastily as she'd slapped her, Faith pulled her hands back and shoved them under her armpits. Might as well have slapped her in the face. Knowing her mother meant business, Faith apologized.

"I'm sorry, Mom," then shook her head as if to put her mind straight. "I don't even know why I did that."

Faith weeping now, Linda pulled her in hard and hugged her so tight. "You know you can talk to me about anything. I made sure of that." Linda said, then snuggling Faith so close, she was sure no one could see her, Linda continued.

"I wanted you to know that my heart was always an open door for you to hide away in if you needed. It's up to you to walk through it, though."

Linda kissed her head stroking her hair.

The hair she'd come to despise!

"I know there are some things we don't share with our parents. I've had my things also. If you need a counsellor, we can get you one. You can't keep things locked up. They'll eat you from the inside out," Linda said and tried to look into Faith's eyes.

Sobbing now, she just tucked into Linda tighter, as she began to rock, until she opened up about what the matter was. Faith sighed and shook the whole time.

"Do I need to protect you?" she asked then, and Faith still said nothing. "Has a boy done something to you? I'll kill him myself, if so."

Faith had to let it go. She wasn't taking her mother with her.

"No, Mom. It's my stupid hair. Why can't it just be normal. Like everyone else?"

"Darling. No one is normal. Everyone is an individual. We all have things that are unique to us," she comforted. "If you were like the others, then you wouldn't be you. No one can take your place and your unique position in the universe, and you are most certainly here to do something no one else can do. To see the way no one else can see. To love the way no one else can. It's a gift."

Not telling her what the kids had said, and Linda never said she knew, she reasoned more, "Faith, dear, on the inside we all look the same. This body, its shape, size, or funny smells. Yes, are all different, but it's not to divide you from others in a bad way. If everything was the same, it'd be pretty boring, and if there was nothing else to desire, what fun would it all be?"

Faith just kept listening. She hadn't thought of that.

"We're all connected but have different vantage points and perspectives that we contribute to the whole. We're all one, I believe, and only have the perception of individuality," Linda smiled and wiped Faith's tears away, continuing to explain. "You don't see your toes making fun of your nose for not being toes . . . and your ears don't laugh at your belly because it can't hear," she kept on in a silly way, twisting her face and poking Faith's belly.

"*Mom*! You know I'm ticklish!" Faith squealed, and Linda poked her a few more times. "*Mom*!" she yelled again and hid her ribs with her arms.

"Okay, okay," Linda laughed, then lovingly said, "I just wanted to see you smile."

"Thanks, Mom. I miss Papa."

"Me too, sweetheart," Linda sighed hugging Faith more. "Tomorrow we'll get flowers and bring them to the cemetery. Okay? It *has* been a while."

"Ya. That would be nice. Can we get some for Gramma too?" Faith asked as Linda felt her relax.

"Sure. Then maybe we can do some shopping too and get some ice cream afterwards."

"*Yay, shopping*!" Faith cheered and bounced on the bed.

"There's my girl." Linda smiled. "But Faith?"

"Ya?"

She knew Linda wanted to make sure she understood.

"You know . . . the other girl is also my girl. I won't always be able to fix things for you, but I can get you help or give you advice. You have to make your own way through life. We connect with others, but we are, ultimately, all alone here. Every one of us. Respect that. Life can throw you things sometimes that are hard to understand why they're happening, and it's okay to be angry. It's not okay, though, to take it out on others who haven't done anything to you," she explained sternly.

Faith knew what she'd done and apologized again.

"Apology accepted. You are never to say 'that's okay' after someone gives an apology. It's not okay nor acceptable. But being human, it's okay to make a mistake. I'm sorry means you or they will do their best to never let it happen again."

"I understand."

"You know when we go looking for sea glass and just walk the beach not talking?"

"Yes."

"That peaceful feeling is where you can connect when life gets rough, and it will get rough, but you always have that . . . Look for glass, read a book, colour, or whatever you can do to find that still place. You'll get the answers you need. We're spirits having a human experience. Spirit is wise and whole. If you listen, it will guide you. You'll always be okay."

Smiling, Linda got up to leave the room. Closing the door behind her, most of the way, just as she'd found it.

It was one of the last times Faith saw her mother before the accident. It happened within weeks of their talk, and she was glad they'd had it.

Faith's grandmother would take her to church on Sundays. Linda didn't believe in supporting something that had such dirty hands, but let Faith make up her own mind, and reinforced, how she didn't believe that a loving god would let someone, as good as her father, be tormented by mental illness.

That and the thought of him burning in hell for taking his own life didn't settle well with her. Nor that some chick eating an apple was the fall of man and all their grief. The struggles of all mankind and the suffering of animals was too much for her to swallow.

Believing in a loving god figure, a creator and holder of all forms of spirit, had to exist, for her. It just wasn't the god found in books. He was nasty and cruel in her opinion and didn't take the "his ways are not our ways" statement everyone gave, so to not have to see their god for what he was. A controlling ego maniac.

Linda's mother was a fundamental Christian, her ways were very strict and believed she should pray for Jesus to intercede and spare her father's soul. That suicide was a sin. That his life was for god to decide to end. Not himself.

Linda was outraged. What she had said was cruel and they hardly ever spoke after that but let her take Faith to church and then discuss any questions she had after the service.

Linda wanted her to have both sides of the argument. It was a tough question to answer, and she thought that any god would want Faith to make up her own mind out of the information she got. Not to love out of fear.

Faith suspected that was what made her stay with Jonsie. A jealous and self-righteous boyfriend. Had the church conditioned her to stay with him out of a healthy fear? A sick kind of twisted and demented love?

Remembering that her mother had also said that misery loves company. That those who are miserable will say and do things to make you feel the same way. To join them. It's a very lonely place to be. Most don't know the way out is inward.

Suddenly Faith had no care to want to love such a god, and it made her shudder to think of the penalty for turning away.

Until remembering her mother saying, "Your spirit is unconditional love that resides in your physical form. When you follow your heart, you'll find your way." Which made her feel a bit better. Like there was time for her to find her way.

Makeup and hair done now, Faith collected her things and got into her car, then off to town she went. The air was cooler now and the sky was a purple grey.

Glad she left a bit early; Faith stopped a few times to take pictures of the fields. All the while thinking of moving again and where to live if she did. The countryside was gorgeous, and she loved the silence, but the town was so cute and convenient.

Moving to the tiny country house from her birth home, Faith remembered her mother and how frail she was when they let her go, once a vibrant woman full of life, now dependant on life support.

For weeks, Faith kept her hopes up. Each day bringing her closer to having to make a choice, it wasn't long before her mother's face had begun to sink in and become a sickly pale colour and wasn't responding to their tests.

When they scraped her feet or pinched her, she didn't even flinch and now on organ support, the doctors declared her brain dead after doing more scans.

If she did get better, Linda would probably need a lot of physiotherapy to recover. The possibility she would be bound to a wheelchair, not able to even feed herself, was high. It would be a lot of work for Faith and the bills would keep growing.

Faith waited awhile, with no improvements. Thinking hard, she didn't know what to do. Still so young and not even out of school, she went home to a lonely house, day in, day out, almost losing track of time itself, if not for school.

The morning she had to choose whether to take the life support from her mother or not, the doctor was waiting for her to have the talk. As he explained the situation, Faith sat there devastated, and hardly heard a word but for the important things. Then was shown the bill.

It wasn't to force her, but for her to understand how this was racking up, and the doctors explained the rules behind whether a person gets surgery. It's about risk and chances of recovery, he informed her and suggested that Faith let her mother go. "Qaly" the doctor called it. Short for quality-adjusted life year.

"Worth it or not" was never something Faith would have considered. To her, everyone was worth it. The world was not what she thought it was. Shattered and exhausted, Faith was just watching Linda's body slowly die. Her mother wasn't there anymore, really. Just a shell being kept alive by machines.

She hadn't said goodbye before the accident as it was a school holiday, and Linda had let her sleep in. Faith wasn't about to tell a body goodbye. It was just meat and bones at that point, and she wanted to remember her mother in the kitchen singing as she did the dishes or cooked supper.

Saying goodbye, she'd truly be alone. It was all Faoth could bare, and told them to do it, then quickly left the room.

The doctors asked if she wanted to be there, and Faith declined. As far as she was concerned, her mother would be home any minute, so she'd better get home. It kept her from going completely insane.

Scheduling cremation with no service Faith took the ashes to the beach. Spreading her on the coast to mingle with the mermaids, brave sailors and tending to the sea glass, Faith spent the rest of the day hunting for some.

"Have a great time, Mom!" Faith said out loud before leaving. "I'll be waiting for your stories in my dreams."

Faith would come to the beach at least once a week. Even in the winter she'd still find sea glass and when it was a mermaid tear piece she whispered, "Thank you, Mom," with a smile.

Linda was still alive in Faith's mind . . . and heart . . . her mother wasn't gone, just busy. Faith felt she'd see her again.

Never crying, counsellors tried to get her to open up, but there was nothing to tell them. Thinking she was in denial, they attempted to get her to have a stay at the hospital, even in an outpatient program so they could watch her.

Faith thought they could take a long walk off a short pier but politely declined their gracious offers. She'd be fine taking care of the house till her mother returned, knowing it was going to be forever. Still, it made her feel better to think of it as a vacation.

Now in town and feeling sombre, Faith looked forward to meeting Archer. He took her so far away from the life she'd lived, and right now, she never wanted to look back.

Pulling into the diner, Faith took tissues from the glovebox and wiped her eyes. She just missed Linda so much, now and then she'd shed a tear, but never thought of her as "gone." Even now.

Her mascara hadn't even run, just red eyes. "They'll be snow white in no time," Faith cheered to herself out loud.

Walking into the diner she was greeted by Ada. With her bummed hip she shuffled to the front with a big smile. "Hi, darlin', would you like a seat?"

"Yes, please."

"You can sit at the counter or a booth. Is it just for yourself?"

"Yes. It's just me. I'd like a booth, if I could, please."

"Come then, dear. This way," Ada agreed leading her to a booth for two along the window and set a menu on the table. "Would you like something to drink while you decide?"

"No. I'm good, thank you."

"I'll give you a few minutes and I'll be right back."

Shuffling back to the counter, Ada left her to look over the specials. Choosing the fish and chips Faith sat and watched the scenes of the town play out while waiting for Ada to return. She'd done so good today not thinking of Archer every five seconds and felt proud.

Even with her insecurities, Faith felt as though she were really wanted. That he had no eyes for anyone else, that she could get used to it, and so sat in peace.

Noticing the books at the back of her booth when being seated, slipping over taking one to read while the food was being prepared, she sat back down just as Ada came with her pad to take Faith's order. "All set?"

"Yes. I'll have the fish."

"That's a good choice. Straight from the harbour today. Would you like that in batter or pan seared?"

"*Oh*! Pan seared please! With black pepper."

"You can choose fries, rice, or mashed potatoes as a side. Which would you like?" Ada asked caringly, like a grandmother would.

"The potatoes please. With lots of butter on the side and gravy too, if you can."

"Very good, dear. What will you have to drink?"

"I'll have a strawberry shake, please," Faith said, double-checking the menu, in case she changed her mind. Chocolate and vanilla were also nice. Depending on her mood.

"Okay. I'll be right back with your milkshake."

Faith flipped through the pages of the paper and read a few small articles on local news. There was a funnies page and crosswords. The usual. Then a blurb about the gallery. Curious, Faith flipped through and read about how Archer had donated a small fortune to a seniors' home to install air conditioning and a garden for the back. He'd purchased a decrepit house behind it, had the land dozed, and planted trees.

Some comments from the seniors said they'd missed their gardening so much after having to move into assisted living and were thrilled to have a place to grow some flowers and vegetables.

Awww. That's so sweet, she thought and read on.

The milkshake blender went in the background and Faith found herself surrounded by it. Then the people talking and the sounds of their cutlery on the plates.

Ada hobbled to her table with the milkshake and set it down saying, "There you go, love. Enjoy. Your dinner will be up shortly. It's quite thick so you should give it a minute."

Coming in the metal cup Ada used to blend it, the frost was thick, with Ada's warm fingerprints melted into the sides where she'd held it.

Giving it a stir, Faith realized she wasn't kidding, actually having to use force to give it a mix. She tried to take a sip and it nearly turned her cheeks inside out and smiled about it, when she failed to get any, then slid it to the side to read more. Plays and events, music, concerts, and markets.

Thinking to take in some of the music, Faith tucked the small magazine in her purse to refer to later. Just then her phone went off. It was Archer.

Hi, gorgeous. Looking forward to seeing that shop with you. Hope you're having a great day. I'm just making some rounds to make sure everyone is good then I'm free to go anytime you're ready, with a smiley face.

I'm just having a bite at the diner. I should be ready in about 45 minutes. Day has been good. Got lots done and look forward to seeing you too, handsome, she texted back.

You can come here when you're done, and we can go from there. Enjoy dinner, he informed her, so she'd know not to rush.

Faith texted that she'd let him know before she was done and only having just put the phone down, her food came. It smelled amazing.

"Oh, thank you," Faith smiled, as she shuffled the plate a little.

"You're quite welcome. If you need anything else just let me know."

The fish was massive, and the potatoes came in huge scoops. Three of them actually. Enough for a whole football team, Faith thought. The top was dented in and there were pools of gravy in them which ran down the sides like lava.

Putting the butter on top, she watched it melt and join the gravy, then took a sip of the shake. It was melted enough that for a few good mouthfuls, and it cooled her right down.

The fish didn't last long. It was delicious and she bet the potatoes and coleslaw were the same.

A dash of salt and pepper, Faith flattened the potatoes some to spread the gravy more evenly, then took a bite. Just as she suspected they were creamy and just as delicious as the fish.

Her favourite part of any meal with coleslaw, was the coleslaw itself. That would be the end judge of it all. Sometimes disappointing, she'd take a bite and it would be barely mixed together or oily.

Sometimes it would be more like some soupy thing with the cabbage chopped into the smallest bits, which just floated in the sauce. This one looked perfect. Thin strips with a little carrot for colour. Saucy but not like soup and didn't look oily at all, plus it came in a teacup.

Excited now to try it, Faith had a bite, and it was very creamy. Just how she liked it. It made her just a little bit too full, but that was fine, it was worth it.

Ada seeing that Faith was done, asked if she wanted to take the leftover potatoes home and offered to put her milkshake in a take-out cup, having barely touched it.

"Yes, please. That would be a nice snack for later."

"No dessert then?"

"Actually, yes. I'll take two of your caramelized rose apple tarts?"

"Oh, yes, dear. You're going to like those. Your meal was okay?"

"Yes, ma'am, it was amazing. I'll definitely be back for sure."

Ada took her plate and milkshake telling her the bill would be ready at the register.

Excited to see Archer now, Faith followed right behind her.

Ada punched her bill into the debit machine. Faith took it and entered a tip. Passing it back, Ada had the milkshake ready and gave it to her, then put the tarts in a paper bag while the man behind the kitchen counter put her potatoes in a container and rang the bell.

Ada passed her the container and a small box with the tarts saying it was lovely to see her and wished her safe travels.

Faith thanked her, then went out the door. *What a sweet little old lady*, she thought going to the car.

Having to a look at those tarts she opened the tiny box. They were so cute. Just like a rose with icing sugar along the edges of the petals like frost. Impressed, she closed the box and put them on the floor of the car.

Remembering saying she'd give Archer notice, Faith texted saying she'd be there soon and that he didn't need to rush, then headed for the gallery.

Pulling in, he was waiting for her outside, then started for the car, so she waited, knowing he was coming to open her door. As he did, Faith said, "Hi, handsome," from the open window, just as he took the handle. Opening the door, Archer pressed the button to wind up her window.

Faith heard the crunch of his shirt as he reached out to take her hand, it was very welcoming. Familiar.

"You look smashing as usual," he complimented and kissed her hand as she rose from the car. "I just have a few more things to do. Should only be ten minutes."

"That's fine. I can take a stroll in the gardens and finish my shake. You can let me know when you're ready."

"Very good," Archer nodded and walked her to the tiny bridge with the fountain. "Enjoy," he added, letting her go.

Quickly, he went into the gallery with the look that he was on a mission. So professional. But for her? A mysterious box. He was *so* many things to her, and he'd only begun to open up. She then felt like she'd been talking too much, although he kept saying it's what he wanted.

If it were true, she' let go of it and be herself. If not, Faith had some thing's to fix. Her mind went to dark places. The critic and the skeptic have been plotting. Self sabotage they say I counselling offices.

Deep inside she didn't think he was love bombing her. She may do well keep things cool until some time passed. It would become obvious.

CHAPTER SIXTEEN
Falling Walls

Archer went into the gallery café to check on Sara and make sure she had all that was needed. "Good day, Sara," he said and touched her shoulder in a friendly way.

"Hi, sir. You've been somewhat absent the last while."

"Yes. New ventures. How's everything?"

"Most excellent!" Sara answered. Meaning both the days work and him being with Faith. "It's been nonstop."

"Oh, good. If it's too much, please tell me. I can get you a hand," he said, as if to suggest.

"Oh, no. Don't be silly. You know me. I love staying on my toes. The challenge is fun."

"Yes, I know. Can't have my best hostess tiring herself out, though."

"I'm fine. Really, sir. It's great that it's so busy. The winter really makes me nuts."

Archer had the luxury of travelling the world on a whim if he was bored. The staff didn't have that kind of flow.

Looking around to see where her husband was, Jim was just setting his guitar down on the stage and quietly Sara said, "I miss it here in the winter. Don't tell Jim, though, hey?"

"Mum's the word," Archer said as Jim sidled up.

"Hey, big mama. What's the scoop?"

"Archer was just checking if everything is alright. Do you need anything?" she asked trying to stay professional.

Jim was a bit of a hippy and pretty loose in his lingo. Sara found it a bit irritating when they were both at the cafe at the same time. "I think I'm good. How's things Archer, me man?"

Jim wasn't considered an employee and Sara had asked him to be more professional, but he didn't care.

Sara rubbed her forehead in frustration and Archer just smiled. "Checking on my best server. She has a lot on her plate right now," he joked, and Jim chuckled.

"Good one." Jim laughed; his face shaped as though a sound should have come out but didn't. All that did was a lispy kind of a sound.

"Dear. I'm going out to have a spliff. Can you make sure I have some water on stage? The air conditioning makes my throat dry, and I don't want to start coughing during my next set," Jim asked Sara.

"Ya. The air conditioning . . ." Sara replied and rolled her eyes. "You got it."

Archer tried not to laugh. Jim having a joint didn't bother him. He just didn't want Sara to getting cranky. "Good woman you have there."

"Ya. She's a good girl," Jim said awkwardly. "I wish she'd relax a bit, though," he sighed.

"I like her as she is. Even though she runs a tight ship, I wouldn't have her any other way."

Jim sighed. "Ya. I suppose I wouldn't either. My place would be a *pigsty*!" he said as his eyes opened wide. Usually all you saw was his bushy overgrown eyebrows and lashes, then with the same lispy laugh, he tapped Archer's arm and went outside. "Take it easy, bro."

"You too, Jim. We'll see you again soon. Nice tunes," Archer complimented as Jim gave him the peace sign and sauntered out the door.

Sara apologized for his loose ways and with a stressed look on her face said, "I love him, but he drives me sometimes. Anyway. Sir. The place is running smooth. If I need anything I'll give you a holler," she said and stepped behind the podium to greet people. "Have a wonderful evening," then smiled slyly knowing exactly what was going on.

"Thanks. I will. You take it easy," Archer suggested as he gun pointed, leaving her to work.

That was it. All done. Faith was so patient to wait. Picking up his phone Archer asked where she was in the gardens.

On the far side by the marble Buddhist monk and wind chimes, she texted back.

Be right there, he replied.

Faith loved that spot. After the wish she'd made it seemed as though her dreams were being realized finally. Pondering it all, maybe there was something to all this manifesting your desires.

Her shake was nearly gone, and she didn't feel quite so full. Glad he needed a few more minutes.

What did the universe have for her that she'd put into her pouch of dreams? How deliberate had she been? Now knowing, Faith thought, maybe she'd been a bit sloppy. Her mind had been everywhere the last few days and she worried that maybe things were in motion that needed to have the power supply cut.

Not fully understanding how it all worked really, Faith was feeling her way through. It seemed to be working in her favour.

Knowing Archer was a meditator, she thought maybe it would be good to ask him some about that It would get him talking too, and she sure loved to listen to him.

Faith standing there looking at the statue, Acher watched a moment her.

Arms folded in a relaxed way. Hip to the side and a little bit of a sway with her head tilted. Like in deep thought.

Going to her Archer wrapped his arms around her and snuggled her neck as Faith laid her hands on his arms.

It was so automatic. Like they'd been together forever, and he didn't care if anyone saw nor what anyone thought of it.

"Let's go see that shop, eh?"

With a little bounce Faith replied, "Yes. Let's," and they walked off.

As usual, he did as always at the car. She was getting better at in not phasing her, and he liked the confident way she waited and held her hand for him to take. Playing right into his hands, Archer thought, *my little hummingbird.*

Faith gave him directions to the shop using her GPS and Archer kept his hand on her lap the whole time. When not scrolling, she'd lace her fingers into his, with no cares in the world but being right there.

Saying to look for the sign, Archer saw the place, they pulled into the yard with a little orange barn. Chandeliers hung from the ceilings and lit up the windows, shaded by massive oak trees. "What a neat place. I didn't know we had this."

Archer sized up the building when they drove along to the side into a parking spot. Out of the car they could hear a spring trickling down over some rocks. It was serene.

Walking across the deck, the boards creaked, and their footsteps were heavy. Soft music came from the farmhouse-style screen door and a man was humming.

Passing by the window, they looked in. A man inside was warped and twisted from the original glass. Probably Victorian era. Waving at them and rising from his seat to great them in a cheery voice. "Hellllooo!"

Dressed like in the style of the 1600s, he looked cool under the clothes, his long moustache was curled at the ends and the round glasses set off the whole outfit.

Hand extended, he introduced himself. "I'm Bobby and this is my shop. If you're looking for something in particular you just mention it and we'll see what we can do to outfit you," he informed them with a large toothy smile then asked, "Where y'all from?" in a southern accent.

Faith answered that she was from Vermont and that Archer was born and raised here.

"Oh. Nice. Nice. How is the visit?" he asked, then he and Faith had a little chat as Bobby had been in her town and knew it very well.

Archer had never seen him before, so asked where he was from and how long he'd been on PEI.

Bobby knew what was expected of him. People from town all knew each other and they were questioning of people who weren't familiar. Not suspicious or anything. Just wary.

"I came up here some years ago," he said, with his wrist flicking and added that he lived in Halifax awhile, talking very briefly about it.

"I was told I should see the island and after being shown a few pictures I took a trip over, when I saw how charming everything was, I just had to come to live." Bobby mentioned, clasping his hands and twiddling his fingers together.

Feminine and sweet, Faith really took to him.

"You're a fortunate man to be born and raised here," he smiled to Archer in a flirting way.

Archer smiled awkwardly back and Faith felt he was uncomfortable, so put her arm in Bobby's and said, "Please. Show me some things."

Archer was impressed with how Faith just took over the situation. Very thankful, he noted the grace she'd used. Especially the compassionate way she did.

As Bobby took them for a tour and told them about his favourite pieces. Faith knew exactly what he was saying, and Archer listened intently taking in the rest of the shop.

From the hand-hewn beams to the tree branch supports, several chandeliers hung from the old beams and lit the entire ceiling up, showing the antiquity of the building.

Impressed at the work, Archer asked about the building and what he'd done to it, and as Bobby talked all about it, Faith continued holding his arm like he was her new best friend. If Jonsie had let her, she'd have rocked the room and been the belle of the ball. That would never do.

Feeling like she'd discovered her true self, Faith stood proud, but in her mind, thanked Archer for coaxing her out of the comfy shell she'd been in. He'd made her feel comfortable in her own skin.

Somehow, showing Faith her own value by valuing her as he did. Maybe he *was* the looking glass she needed to see herself more clearly. Really, Faith was taken aback, as much as Archer had expressed *he* was.

Bobby, now feeling like he'd said enough, returned Faith to Archer. Taking his arm, together they walked through the shop.

Archer asked what she liked, and digging in her purse, she whispered "One second."

What was she doing? It was like she was digging for gold in her bag. Just then, pulling something out and concealing it with her hand wrapped around it, Faith checked over her shoulder. Bobby was back to humming music and weaving wires, so moving Archer along with her arms, Faith showed him.

"A flashlight? I thought you were taking out a gun," he laughed.

"No, silly. It's a black light. We're gonna go uranium hunting. If we find one, you'll see."

Motioning for him to hush, he wasn't even saying anything!

"Silly girl. What are you up to?"

Faith just took him along and clicked the light now and then. Whispering, she said what she was looking for and the light went on in Archer's head. He knew what she meant now and watched intently.

Moving around the shop, they saw some beautiful pieces. Faith talked about the weaves and the glass like he knew what she meant, which he thought was adorable and just went along on the ride.

All through the building they went, and not one piece of uranium was found. A little disappointed, Archer suggested they find other shops and do more hunting.

Faith told him of a place in Souris that had a great beach, having talked about it with one of the social media friends she'd met online. Archer agreed Faith should go and that he'd love to join in, then suggested they should go on the weekend.

Faith had many, many plans for him, though. Juggling them in her mind, she figured they could squeeze in a late-night trip.

Before leaving the shop, Faith bought a small piece. Archer had tried to take out his card, but she slapped his hand gently. Bobby hadn't seen, so that was fine. No trouble. He liked her fire and independence, but she'd have to learn.

Leaving the shop, Faith gave a tiny hug and off they went. The night was quite cool.

"*So!* Why did you stop me buying that?"

"Well. I'm sorry. It was an automatic response. I didn't mean to be rude. I just . . . haven't had many things bought for me and I've been fighting the urge to argue with you this whole time," she admitted. No secrets.

"That's fine. I appreciate that about you. Take charge kind of woman when needed?"

"Always. You have no idea."

And he didn't. Faith paid for so much. Jonsie was such a skin flint and loved having that power over her. It wasn't that he couldn't afford it. Nor could he not afford to help with the house. He just . . . didn't.

"I've learned to be self-sufficient and slaved for everything I've gotten. I'm frugal and I don't spend much outside of what's needed."

"May I make a request then?" Archer asked with his eyes on the road, holding his palm up for her to put her hand in. "If we are out, you are to leave your wallet at home. I didn't find that embarrassing or anything. I just want to treat you the way you should have been from the start. I won't go into my bank balance again. You don't need to pay for anything I can afford, and there's not much I can't. Please. It's my custom and I would appreciate it if you observed it. When you're out alone, buy all you want, but with me? Please?"

Faith was the one who was embarrassed now. Over what, though? Her bruised ego? Her defiant, independent nature? What was going on with her? Would he ever stop showing her her true self? Her faults and misconceptions? She sure hoped not. This peeling off of her layers made her feel naked on more than one occasion, though it was liberating.

"Okay. Alright. I'll do my best."

"That's all I will ever ask of you is to try your best. There's no pass or fail with me. Okay?" he asked lifting her hand to kiss.

"Okay. You'll get my best. Promise."

The thought of it scared Faith a little. What was she going to do? Arguing was such a waste of time to her now that Jonsie had worn her down and out.

Leaving Archer wasn't even a consideration. He wanted to treat her like a precious gem. That would be dumb. What concerned her was, would she grate on his nerves?

As they sat driving, the sun gone long ago from the clouds brewing, a large drop hit the windshield with a crack and scared the life out of her, making her jump and scream abruptly. They both laughed as more hit the car.

"*Holy*!" Faith yelled and held hand to her chest. "I nearly had a heart attack," she laughed.

The thought of that scene scared Archer, though. He wanted the vision out of his head. *Now*! So asked, "Are you coming in for a bit when I take you to your car? Or I could come over if you like?"

"I'm kind of worn out from my day but I'd love if you came for an hour or something. I want to talk a bit."

"Is everything okay? Did I do or not do something?" he asked concerned.

"Nope. I just want to explain the whole 'I don't say sorry' thing to you. That was kind of rude," she answered rubbing his fingers and watching the rain.

"I get why you might not say it. I've been doing it, to try and understand why and it does feel better than goodbye. Just saying I love you to mom and ending the call felt weird, but then I felt good. Like I carried her with me still."

"Yes. That's the whole point. I want to explain how I got to that point. I also wanted to know if you'd tell me why you broke down when I sang to you," she said nonchalantly. "If you don't mind. In the other case, I can wait."

"Is it bothering you?"

"Well, not really, but I am very curious, and you *did* say you'd tell me. I'm just poking a bit."

She was right and Archer loved that she'd called him out. That she waited patiently but didn't let it fester either.

Faith was learning well from him, and she thanked god that Archer had come into her life. He thanked them too. For her.

With some easy-listening music in the background that he'd put on just for her, Faith leaned on his shoulder. She was getting very attached to him.

Her heart offered the words again and she swallowed them down as before, just wanted to be touching him, feeling his warmth and his body. This soul who seemed to know her better than she knew herself. Strong. Vigilant. Outspoken and kind. A monster and a guardian, it seemed. He was like the energy of the universe captured in a soul, then squeezed into a body that, no doubt, was way too small for it. Even though he was massive.

Faith felt ... safe ... for the first time in her life. It wasn't his size or his martial arts skills. It was his honour and nobility. The best part was that her heart *and* mind felt safe, and he'd push her over like a domino now at anytime. If he so much as hinted that he wanted a future with her, she'd be hard-pressed to say no. Even if she hadn't already thought of moving there.

To go home and make a life in Vermont again? She'd struggle to get it done. In his arms was where she wanted to live and would never tell him, unless he said it first.

Guarded and skeptical that anyone would truly value her, let alone love her, Faith had built a wall, but Archer knew what loving someone meant. He'd told her about Johanna. Faith would have left. He didn't.

Knowing, after telling him about Jonsie, Archer would probably say *he*'d have left. Both of them too dedicated to give up on love. Even when it was beating you down.

If Archer said he wanted her, for a fact, and he didn't give in to whims of fancy, he'd have meant it.

She'd tear down that wall even if it meant by her fingernails. Broken and torn off, she'd not stop till it was dust. The words that just ran through her head said that maybe her heart was right all this time. Maybe she really *did* love him. But is it "in love"?

She'd die to save him if it came to that. Maybe she was just getting up to speed where he was but was also holding himself back. Who would be the first to crack?

If Archer called her to him, she'd come. The fires of hell wouldn't stop her now. Confessing it would be a challenge to let go of everything behind her, Faith was hardly accepting it in its infancy. Knowing in her heart, if she called for him, he'd come in like a beast and tear anything asunder that got in his way or tried to stop him. He'd have to be killed.

Now and then, when a car passed by, the lights would light up his face, and from the position on his shoulder, she could see his mouth and nose. Now and then he'd pull in his bottom lip and chew on it a second. Watching every move of his muscles, his cheek would dimple. Faith watched it like the rain. In silence and adoration.

Once back to the cottage, she opened the wine Archer had grabbed from the office. "Would you be a doll and light the candles, please?"

"With pleasure."

Bringing the glasses to the coffee table, Archer quickly set coasters down for them.

"Thank you, sweets," she said softly, really coming around to him. "I just wanted to tell you briefly why I hate goodbyes."

After giving him the gist of it, his heart sank. "That's sad to hear. How are you now with it?"

"I'm good but, every now and then it hits me hard. I cry for days. It's not like depression or grief. It's just sadness."

Archer couldn't imagine being left so young. Instant adulthood. He knew how he was going to feel when his parents left. He'd had them for so long, though, hoped much longer to go.

Now it was his turn. Explaining why he'd been hit so hard by Faith's song, Archer told her of how he and Johanna always had this dance around the subject of children.

How he patiently waited for the answer to his dream. The frustration of dating and how it seemed life was passing him by in that regard. That possibly the story overwhelmed him. How he identified with the man in the song, with no relief forthcoming.

Faith comforted him with soothing words about how wonderful he is and that surely his dream would soon be realized.

Finishing their wine, Archer mentioned he should get going for some sleep. Having spent the day together, they both felt no desire to cling for more and it was good.

Walking him to the door, they kissed gently, her hands on his face, his arms wrapping her up. Both not wanting it to end, there was some comfort in letting go.

"Drive safe. Text when you're home please?"

"I most certainly will, my queen."

This made Faith smile big. Just what he wanted, and hoped he could keep doing that to her forever.

Faith watched out the window as his car lit up the treeline at the top of the hill.

Home, sweetheart, came faster than she knew.

So good. I had a great day with you again, she texted back.

As did I. Sweetest of dreams and peaceful rest to you lovely, he sent.

With you in my life, that will be easy. XOXO, Faith texted, ending the conversation.

XOXO, he sent back.

Sliding deep into the bed, Faith pulled the covers and switched off the light. Ending a glorious day.

CHAPTER SEVENTEEN
I Scream, You Scream

In the morning, Faith was the first thing on Arcer's mind. Knowing her phone was off, he texted good morning and would wait for her response. It didn't take long. He hadn't even set the phone on the counter to make coffee and a small breakfast.

Good morning, handsome. Hope you slept well! Faith texted back.

Archer called right away. "Good morning, beautiful. How was your sleep?" he asked, his voice deep and gravelly.

"Slept amaaaazingly," she answered pouring water into the coffee maker. "What's on for today?"

"Just some office stuff," he responded, then started to say something else until he heard her yell. *"WHAT? Are you okay?!"* he asked loudly and leapt from the sofa.

"One minute," she whispered, and put the phone down on the counter.

Archer paced frantically. What the fuck was going on? Grabbing his keys, he started for the car.

Taking the bat from on top of the mudroom shelf, where she kept it, Faith quietly went out onto the deck. Maybe it was just an animal, but she heard what sounded like scuffling. Whatever it was, it wasn't small. She wasn't one to take chances and her instinct was to fight.

Walking around the patio with the bat high in the air, she did her best to be as silent as possible and froze when the deck squeaked. Faith took her foot back listening a minute, but only heard the trees, and her pounding heart.

Putting the bat down, she looked suspiciously then laughed at herself for being silly, then waked back inside and picked up the phone.

"Sorry! I thought I heard something."

Archer was furious now. He always got really worried when put in that position, after seeing so much in his travels. There were crazies out there. It didn't matter to him that The Island was a safe place to live, with little crime. He'd only heard of two murders in his whole life and unfortunately, couldn't say the same for New York or the other big cities he'd travelled to.

"What was it?" he asked in a very commanding voice. "Do I need to come there?"

"No. It's okay. I'm sorry if I set you off. I think it was just an animal. It just frightened me."

He'd already had the car started and in drive with his foot on the brake, ready to race over if needed, so put the gearshift back in park and turned the engine off. He'd have been there in less than ten minutes. The car would have done the drive easily. "You scared the shit out of me," Archer sighed. "My heart's pounding."

Faith winced on the other end.

"I'm so, so, *so* sorry."

Archer sighed again and got out of the car. "It's alright. Shit happens. I'm just glad it was nothing, and you're *sure* it's nothing, right?"

"Yes, I'm pretty sure," Faith returned, as the coffee maker made the sound she loved.

"I'm not convinced by your tone. I'm staying on the phone. Lock all the doors till I get there. I'm not kidding."

"Don't be sill—" she was cut off.

"Now," he ordered.

This time he was serious. Faith jumped and did as she was told.

"Tell me when you're done. Windows too. You have a/c, don't you?" he asked in a kinder voice.

"Yes, I have a/c," she confirmed for him, locking the patio doors.

Archer then heard the windows snapping shut. "Stay on with me and do a sweep. I'm not messing around. It may be nothing, but I won't rest till I know you know for certain. Closets. Under beds. Shower. Everything."

"Okay! Okay!" she grumbled.

Archer sighed on the other end frustrated with her sarcastic "okay's," and Faith thought he was being overprotective. "I'm not overreacting, Faith. I need to know it's fine. Until I can get there. I've heard horror stories. I won't compromise with anyone when it comes to safety and well-being . . . Even you. I won't be questioned on this. It's an order."

He was probably right, so Faith did as he said. "Thank you. You scared me with your tone at first, but I understand. It feels nice to be cared for."

"You go. Tell me what you're doing as you go."

Faith locked all the doors and windows, repeating it to Archer as she went, checking under beds, in all the closets, and showers as he'd told her to.

Once knowing the coast was clear he said, "Good. I feel a bit better. Now I have to get Trevor for his run. I'll see you at eleven sharp! Just leave everything as it is please till I get there?"

"Alright. You have fun and enjoy your swim. Don't worry about me. I'm going to do some things around here and get to that book. I can't wait to see you."

Faith pulled out yogurt and frozen fruits to make a smoothie for after breakfast, saying, "Can't wait to see you either."

Still feeling apprehensive, it would be hard to shake. When Trevor picked him up, Archer told him about the call. Admitting he felt better but was still worried, he became unusually quiet and wouldn't have much fun that morning at the beach.

"Message me if anything happens and you want to go," Trevor told Archer, then left for his run to not keep him waiting too long.

Archer put in his earbuds and sat on the shore. If Faith called or messaged, he wanted to hear it. *I swear to god if anyone lays a hand on her ever, they'll meet their maker sooner than they'd planned,* he thought as the soft music played in the background but wasn't soothing to him at all.

Trying to relax some, he did some tai chi, just wanting his mind to settle in the process. It only worked him up more. Taking his hands slowly together, as if in a prayer, Archer pulled them to his chest and breathed in and out in a large way, to slow his adrenaline and bring his mind to focus.

Travelling the globe had shown him what the world was really like. Before then, he'd had a small world view. With no internet and PEI always being twenty years behind everyone else, even after the internet became available, the crime rate was low. Break and enters, a few cars stolen, both usually by people they knew. No carjackings or murders. A few accidental deaths at bar fights.

When Archer left PEI to travel, he got an eye-opener. Women who carry keys in their fist or park near a curb so as not to be grabbed from under their cars. All the ones who would avoid dimly lit places walking home from work late at night, single mothers working two jobs. The violent men, the poor children, who couldn't defend themselves from adults or people they should be able to trust, abusing them their whole lives, his anger building.

There had been a time or two when Archer had had to use his training on tough guys. With a flick of the wrist, he'd twist a pinkie finger, they'd let out a wail and freeze, begging... and he'd wait for it. Humiliation was as good a teacher as a mistake, usually they did what he said then. Which was simply "go home."

Remembering the pitch of their screams made Arher laugh a bit. *Big toughies scream like a girl,* he thought and felt a bit better. Just as he sat, Trevor yelled, now that he was close enough. "*You okay?*"

"*Ya! Had a moment!*" Archer yelled back.

Trevor's feet thumped in the sand the closer he got. "S'up, bro?"

"I'm just still edgy and a bit freaked out. I was blowing off some steam."

"Well, I'd hate to be the sorry fuck that would be on the receiving end of what I just saw," he laughed. "You're going down hard, though, for this one, eh?"

"Ya. I'm losing it for sure," Archer sighed. "I don't know what I'll do when summer ends. I don't even really know what she's going back to. We talk a lot, but I feel I don't have a full picture. With the house sold and not working, she loves it here and I'd love her to stay. See what we could have. I know, but she might need convincing."

"I suppose you can only take it as it comes and hope it works out in the end?" he offered to help Archer.

"Yep. Pretty much. I want to convince her to stay awhile longer. It's hard to approach the topic. We just met, really, and I'm trying to enjoy it, but that dread of her leaving always finds its way in. The more I get to know her, the more I want to see. There's no end to her beauty for me. I can't even describe how it fills my heart."

Trevor wanted to help, knew he couldn't, but offered anyway.

"If I can do anything. You name it."

"I would, brother, thanks, but it's all up to her now," Archer replied back, slumping a bit.

"It may just be familiarity. Routine. If she has no family, her only friend backstabbing her, like you said, left her lover and quit her job too? I suppose you might ask her?"

"You're right. I'll wait until we've gotten through a little more of the summer. I don't want to scare her off. Ya know? But thanks for that. I'll mention those things and maybe ask if she's really in a hurry to get back. That maybe, she could stay at least a little longer. I may have a chance to get her to live here awhile and see what she'd miss by leaving. You have no idea what I'd do to keep her. I'd buy an apartment complex. A house. Whatever. If she insisted on paying rent, I'd let her. It would be easy for me to do." A little more hopeful, Archer slapped Trevor on the back and said, "Thanks."

"You taught me well," he retorted jokingly, knowing he'd hardly done a thing.

Archer wasn't dumb. He was just stressed out and would have figured it out easily, just needing a prod.

Archer laughed at Trevor's statement, Trevor didn't. "You've always been there for me like an older brother, Arch. Always watching out for me . . . Even when I was being a dick, and I *was* a dick. Those years I spent drinking, you always did you're best to keep me standing on my own two feet and when I couldn't? You always softened the blow and never made me feel like a piece of shit. You're a keeper!"

Always with the jokes.

"*Stop*! Yer gonna make me catch feelings," Archer teased.

Trevor leapt up as fast as his dad bod would allow and hobbled across the beach. "*Try and keep up, fucker!*" he yelled.

Laughing hard now, Archer struggled to get up from where he was sitting, eventually getting to his knees, then ran up the hill still laughing.

Trevor had gotten all the way back to the truck as Archer made it to the top of the hill. The look of Trevor hobbling along the beach and his comment had gotten him so much, he struggled with the dune.

Coming down the other side, the truck jerking as Trevor bounced up and down yelling, "*Yeehaw! Let's go!*", Archer got the giggles again.

Once in the truck, Trevor looked at him with a goofy face and revved the engine with his foot on the brake, making the truck bounce and leap forward in jerks. Like a steed ready for a good run behind the gates at the racetrack. Snapping his head back, from the look he was giving Archer, to look forward, he dropped the gear shift into drive and took off really, really slow and carrying on the character he giggled, "Hee hee heeee."

Archer cracked hard then as Trevor resumed his normal self, and they drove down the dirt lane.

"Yer an animal," Archer commented gaining composure. "Life would be boring without you."

"*Stick around, bud!*" he yelled. "I haven't even gotten *close* to going crazy. Should be quite a show, wha?"

The drive back was quiet and nice. Archer could always count on him to lighten the mood. Trevor thought he didn't have much to offer in the way of wisdom or advice and assumed he always brought others down. Archer disagreed. Trevor did more than he was even aware of. Often. Then, pulling up to Archer's house, he got out.

"AMARRAW!" Trevor yelled.

"AMARRAW!" Archer yelled back. Meaning he'd see him in the morning.

Archer went in and put the clothes in the dryer, then started the shower.

While it was getting hot, he looked in the mirror. The beard looked nice and thought to text Faith. *I'm beginning to like this facial hair.*

She texted right back with a smiley face, hearts for eyes. *It's dreeeeeamy!* she informed him.

You want it to be long rather than trimmed short? he asked.

YES PLEASE!

Very well! Show me pictures when I get there maybe? How has the morning been?

he asked.

Super quiet with all the windows closed, she responded with a tear face.

Awww. Well. If there's one that's high, go ahead and open it, he sent back with a smiley.

Thank you! There is one actually . . . but I didn't want to open it. I thought it might make you upset.

It made him feel better now knowing she'd done as he'd asked. To please him, *and,* to keep herself safe.

You're such a good girl, he texted back with a devil face and a smiley, then hopped in the shower and cleaned up. Hearing his phone go off again as he got in, Archer figured she probably had a smart remark for him for when he got out.

Stepping out, he dried off and checked the phone. Yep. She was being a brat, it was all good, though.

Putting on the cologne Faith liked, he hoped maybe she might tempt him again. Then breathing in the scent, Archer remembered her nose flared as he came beside her and knew very well which was her favourite so far. The musk and sandalwood. A certain look came over her face.

Taking the clothes from the bed where he'd laid them out, Archer got dressed. A nice crisp shirt, relaxed-fit jeans and belt.

The sea glass stopper bounced off his leg as he slid the pants on. *Oh, yeah!* he remembered. He'd tucked it in there before leaving for the beach with Trevor. *She'll be so happy to get that back.*

They might end up in the water or on the beach again and so packed shorts and a T-shirt in his bag. Might get that swim in after all.

Everything ready, Archer called Carla.

"Just a few phone calls today, sir. You can do them when you wish. Nothing is pressing, but if anything comes up, I'll call," she informed him.

"Good, Carla. You enjoy the day."

"Enjoy your day also," Carla suggested back then added. "Sir?"

"Yes?"

"It's good to see you having a good time outside of the gallery. Every one of us have hoped for you to find something, or someone pleasurable enough, that you make time for. I heard from Sara that you two were giggling when you left the gallery. It made my day to be honest," she said in a way he'd never heard from her before. Like she was proud of him. "I wish I'd seen it myself. The way Sara had told it to me, it seemed like it would have been pretty funny. You're always so serious and professional."

"Carla. That is the sweetest thing you've ever said to me. You treat me like gold, and

I couldn't have asked for a better assistant."

"It's my pleasure. This job has been rewarding and very satisfying for me. You've done amazing things for others and I'm proud to say that I work for you. Both of you have a lovely day together. I'll not interrupt unless it's an emergency, and to that I say, good day to you."

"Thank you, Carla. Good day to you also."

Slowly figuring out how to work this "no goodbye" thing into his vocabulary, it seemed that Carla was catching on to what he was doing. She was very in tune with him as an employer.

Texting Faith, Archer said he was free for the day and could come by anytime, hoping she'd say to come now.

Laundry now in the dryer, he went off to make a sandwich and checked the time. It was nine thirty and the minutes dragged on as he watched some news but didn't hear anything they said.

Checking his watch, more often than usual, ten thirty rolled around and he hadn't heard back. Thinking Faith must be deep in her book, Archer couldn't wait any longer. So what if he was a tad early.

Grabbing the bag, a little more full than usual, he'd also put extra clothes in, just in case he ended up needing them. There were a million reasons he might.

On one side of the cottage drive, was a row of trees, with a few lanes cut into them. On the other were the wide-open rolling fields of canola flowers, which wafted into the car, and taking several deep breaths of it in, he'd always associate them with her now.

Coming close to the top of the hill, Archer saw there was a car in one the short drives between the row of trees that ran the whole length of the field on the left.

It was the car from the night before. Maybe he owned the land and was checking on his fields. Probably why he was on the side of the road that night. Looking back to the drive again, Archer started whistling as he felt the relief finally come over him. Just about right where he wanted to be.

Rounding the top of the hill, the roof of the cottage came into view. Not that his stomach had settled any, having not completely shaken the feeling of butterflies she'd given him, mixed with the anxiety from early in the morning. The butterflies he'd take. The ride was nice, but the glass stopper dug into his hip under the seat belt. He'd be happy to give it back.

It was such a slow drive. Agonizing now that Faith wasn't with him and the situation this morning.

Finally arriving, Archer shut down the engine, and without hesitation, started up the white pebble walkway. It crunched under his weight and pierced his ears in the silence. There wasn't even a breeze that day and being in the group of trees was like being in a sauna. The U shape of the cottage was nice and offered shade fairly quickly. Goosebumps covered him in the temperature change with the front door nestled in the centre with a roof and small patio area.

Going to knock, he saw the door was slightly ajar. *She said she'd locked up*; he thought and got a little miffed. There's another lesson he'd have to give her. She'd make sure the next time round when Archer asked her to do something, of this magnitude, it got done.

Poking his head in and calling her name, but not too loudly, there was no answer. *Maybe she's in the shower?*

No, she said she was getting in after we got off the phone, Archer remembered, then he heard a thunk.

What was she doing?

Thunk again.

Was that the dresser drawers?

Shoes off now, Acher walked on the cold tile floors. They were so clean his feet nearly felt stuck to them. Now through the kitchen, he entered into the hall and just before he was about to call her name again, so as not to startle her, he heard a voice. A man's voice!

Heart sinking, his rage grew as he tried not to jump to conclusions.

Going more quietly, Archer's mind wanted to explode. It raced with thoughts of her with someone else. It wasn't that he felt he owned her, but she did say that she was single, so assumed it meant she wasn't with *anyone* . . . but him.

Approaching the bedroom door, it was wide open. The drapes were drawn, and the master bath light was on. Just enough for him to be able to see around the room.

Heart racing now, he paused to go in. What was he going to see? Her and some guy doing things he'd dreamed of? Not so along ago masturbated to? Feeling dirty he prayed it was just the plumber fixing a leak.

Struggling to keep cool, Archer made the move. Peeking in, he saw the bed was made, Faith's laptop was open on the spread. Maybe there *was* a plumbing problem!

Knowing if he went just inside the door, he'd be able to see into the bathroom from the stand-up mirror on the far end of the room near the bed. There were shadows as the light moved around, so he crept through, deeper into the room. If he was overreacting, he'd just slink out, try to call her or just knock, then excuse himself to save his gall. He'd just come in uninvited. So many feelings washed over him, and he felt dizzied by them.

The crisp shirt tucked in his pants, cinched by the belt, crinkled under his movement. The voice came again.

"You thought you could just walk away, bitch?" *Thunk!* "Ignore my emails?" he snarled through his teeth under heavy breathing. "Ooohhh, it took a long time to find you." *Thunk!*

Archer couldn't believe what he was hearing. Who is this guy?!

"And what do I find waiting for me when I finally catch up to you? Out whoring around with that guy like the skank you are," he chuckled. "I thought you loved me. You said you'd never leave. Guess you'll learn your lesson today."

Archer lost his mind as he walked into the frame of the door. Faith was on the floor bleeding with this guy throwing her limbs around.

"Wake *up*!" he screamed. "You picked the wrong guy to fuck around on . . . you gotta *see* what I'm gonna do to you. Better wake the fuck u—". Archer cut him off before the guy could utter another syllable.

Running in, Archer jumped in the air and brought down a heavy fist, right on the side of his head. It was solid and made the guy stumble and fall to the side staggering, while Archer took the time to look at Faith briefly.

He could see she was still breathing. Not wanting to move her, in case there was a neck injury or something else unapparent, he checked to see where the guy was.

Was he an intruder? Had Faith let him in? He still didn't know what was going on, but he wasn't taking any chances.

Regardless of whatever had been done or said, she didn't deserve this. No one did. If Archer moved her and she were crippled by him trying to help, he'd never forgive himself.

The man got to his feet, holding his head where Archer had struck a decent blow. He should have been knocked out. Maybe he was on drugs or something. Possibly in the wrong place. Could be just a weirdo.

After checking for blood, he screamed and came at Archer, but caught a swift uppercut instead.

Staggering back into the glass shower door, it buckled from his weight and shattered. Him falling into the shower with it.

As he laid there, Archer went to Faith and felt her neck. Nothing moved around, so checked her over more. He had to see where the blood was coming from, in case it was severe, then sighed when he found a large lump with a tiny cut. He'd had worse cuts on his finger from the copy machine paper, really.

Hearing the sound of glass scraping the shower floor, the man was starting to get back on his feet, so Archer chose to take the risk of picking Faith up from the bathroom floor. Hands under her arms, he pulled her body out. He could have lifted her but didn't want to leave himself vulnerable and unable to protect her.

Sliding Faith's limp body near the bed, Archer set her head down lovingly, while keeping his eyes on this pathetic waste of skin.

The lanky man came at Archer again. With a *bat*! Seeing the blood he knew what had happened then, the picture was crystal clear.

Pretending to not notice, Archer watched from the corner of his eye. Lanky dude wasn't leaving there unscathed, and when he'd gotten close enough, Archer balled his hand again from his position on the floor, then punched him right in his mid section. As he did, Archer felt ribs crack under his fist. It went deep into the man's stomach and he staggered back, falling to the floor trying to catch his breath.

Picking Faith up, Archer set her carefully on the bed and looked her over quickly. Nothing was broken, her breathing was steady, pulse too. He kissed her forehead and said, "I'll be back briefly, princess," then went to the man.

Taking a good look at lanky dude's face while he struggled to breathe, it was the man who owned the car who he'd seen that night on the side of the road.

Reaching down, Archer grabbed his leg and started dragging him from the room and into the kitchen by his ankle.

"It's not her who's made a mistake. It's *you* who picked the wrong guy to fuck with," Archer informed him.

Lanky dude tried to argue with him, but all he could muster was a gurgle, then passed out.

Archer put him on the floor beside the kitchen table and went to the drawers to hunt for rope or something to secure that guys hands. All he found was an apron and pulling the long strings out, he snapped them. It would do, he thought, as he went back and put the guy in a chair then secured him by tying his arms along the sides of the chair.

Archer then went to the cupboards and found two short pots to put under the front legs. Tipping the chair back, he set the front legs down on top of them. If he even flinched, the chair would fall over, and Archer would hear, then tend to this idiot if need be. Faith was his main concern now.

Double-checking that he'd tied lanky dude well, Archer went to tend to her. Sitting beside her on the bed, he checked more thoroughly.

"Faith?" he said, watching to see if she'd wake but nothing, so repeated more loudly. "Faith!" and tapped her cheeks. "C'mon, baby girl . . . Wake up . . ."

"Faith!" Archer poked more aggressively than checking all her limbs, joints, ribs, neck again and head, everything seemed fine. Even taking to pinching her skin now and then, he wasn't getting a reaction. This wasn't good.

A volunteer firefighter in his late teens and early twenties, Archer watched paramedics when they came to the scene, studying their responses. He knew exactly what to look for and she seemed okay.

Finally groaning, Archer knew she'd come to. "Thank *god*!" he sighed and tapped her cheeks again quickly and didn't stop. Faith's eyes rolled around like she'd pass out again.

"Faith. Come!" he commanded, his voice causing her realize what was happening.

Still confused, she looked at him and pulled away. "It's Archer," he told Faith tenderly.

Then sitting, Faith surveyed the room, and remembering the danger, she yelled, "We have to go!" as she attempted to get them out, but he'd gripped her shoulders tight by then.

"You're safe. Everything is under control," he assured her.

Still confused from her bump, she felt it. "Oooh, that's not nice."

Archer asked if she had anything for the headache that he knew was going to come soon. Trauma is like that. You don't feel the pain at first. When the adrenaline wears off, it screams back into your life like a banshee.

Faith pointed him towards the bathroom, and he told her to stay there, glass was everywhere. No telling where it had slid to, he hoped he hadn't cut her while dragging her out, trying his best to make sure it was just her feet on the floor.

Taking a thick towel from the closet inside the door, he laid it out on the floor to get to the drawer of the cabinet. "Who is that?"

"It's Jonsie. He found me somehow. I didn't tell anyone where I went. For the last year he'd been sending emails wanting to make up, but I wasn't interested. I told him no a million times and he wouldn't stop. After awhile I quit reading them and just put them in the trash," she answered, giving him more than he'd asked for. Which was good. She was being open and honest with him.

With a bottle of ibuprofen, Archer said he'd get water from the kitchen, and for her to stay put. Wanting to know more details of how it went down, he poked slowly. "When did he get here?"

"All I know is, I was on the phone with you, and I did as you asked. Everything was locked as far as I know. I'm not even sure how, or when, he got in. I went to go and take my shower, like I said I was going to, and he approached me, grabbing my arms and I spit in his face. He pushed me down, and when I stood up, he was swearing things at me that didn't make any sense. He called me a whore and I backhanded him."

Starting to cry, she was so angry, Faith pulled herself together enough to continue.

"I told him he had to leave, and he started out of the bathroom, but then turned around and hit me with my own bat!"

Sobbing, she laid back onto the pillow. Archer sat beside her to comfort, and she turned from him, embarrassed she hadn't handled it. Reaching for her again, Faith pulled from under his touch.

Sighing, Archer tried again saying, "Faith. I know it's hard," which made her cry harder, so he laid behind her pulling her into him.

After all, she'd spent so many years being ignored and mistreated, no doubt used to having to lick wounds on her own with no one to care, he let her stay with her back to him. His hummingbird.

It wasn't long before Faith turned and hugged him back, and in a softer tone Archer said, "You're such a strong woman. That was dangerous, but I'm so proud of you. You don't take no smack, eh? I'll be sure to take note of that."

Faith snorted at that, knowing he was trying to lift her spirits. Taking in a deep sigh, she tried to sit up.

Giving his hand to help, Archer asked if the light was okay, and she nodded yes, then assured her he'd be right back, leaving to get water and ice for her head.

Looking around hastily, Faith yelled, "*Wait*! Where is he?"

Leaping from the bed and darting to check the bathroom, until she saw the mess, Faith then turned to Archer as if to repeat her question, which he wasn't answering.

Bolting for the door and down the short hall, with him right behind her, Faith stopped dead in the kitchen. There was Jonsie, broken, bleeding, and tied to the chair. Archer sighed and rubbed his forehead.

"See now. You were supposed to stay in your room."

Faith went over to Jonsie to inspect. "Jesus, Archer. Did you do this?"

He'd have to give her the details now and Faith listened to his explanation and looked Jonsie over, while Archer wished she'd go back to the room as Jonsie coughed up blood and made a gurgling sound, making her gag.

Archer knew at least one of Jonie's ribs were broken and may have punctured a lung. He'd seen it before.

Still unconscious, Jonsie's head bobbed around as if it weren't attached properly. Faith threw up on the floor.

"This is why I tried to spare you. I'd hoped you'd have listened, but it's okay. You had the right to know, and I would never lie to you. This is not like me to do this to someone, but he was threatening you when I got here, and I lost my cool. He kept coming back at me, though. It had to be done. He left me no choice."

"I'm so, so sorry."

"If you've been totally honest with me, and I'm not saying you aren't, you have nothing to be sorry for, Faith. He made his own bed and he'll lie in it," Archer told her taking her by the shoulders, then said, "Come. I'll clean up all the mess. You need to rest. Trevor is on his way."

Trevor *wasn't* on his way. He hadn't called. *So* much was going on and Archer wanted to get some info from this guy before he called the police, and he *would* call them. Later.

Faith let him take her to bed and tuck her in. Archer hoped he hadn't just traumatized her forever and ruined any chance for them to continue. It was the *last* thing he wanted.

After getting her settled, he went to the kitchen and took the jug of water from the fridge and a cup. Jonsie groaned and tried to lift his head, a sorry mess now. Archer went to him, looking him over.

Jonsie opened his mouth to say something, and Archer waited a second. "Fuc—" he was about to say then *WHACK!* Archer punched him right in the face, breaking his nose.

Jonsie screamed and went back to continuing the nap Archer insisted he have. "Right back, muffin," he whispered in Jonsie's ear.

Hearing Faith's feet hit the floor, he bolted with the water and cup in hand, popping round the corner. She ran right into him, and he didn't budge. It was like running into a brick wall, but being a brave woman, she demanded to know what that noise was.

Putting an arm around her, Archer insisted, "Come. I'll explain. You need to sit."

Pouring water for her as she sat on the bed, Faith took a sip as he opened the pill bottle for her. She'd be feeling that bump any time now.

Taking the pills, Faith drank water while Archer explained what happened from where he stood. Leaving out the part where he'd just broken Jonie's nose, of course.

Hand over her mouth, as he told how it went down; Archer spared the gory details. He wasn't trying to come off as a saint nor a hero. He also didn't want her to know what he was capable of. Especially when it came to her, though had a right to know something.

"Now I'm not saying how this is gonna turn out," Archer sighed, almost wishing Jonsie would die before he got back to the kitchen. "You, though, need to see a doctor. You may have a concussion. I'll call and see where Trevor is. He'll get you to the ER."

"I feel kind of sleepy."

Archer did some vision and motor skill tests with her. "I think you'll be fine. You're not stuttering or anything. I'll let you sleep for a very little bit but may wake you often till the police come. I want to make sure you don't slip into a coma or something."

"What about Jonsie?"

"Don't worry yourself with him. The police will handle that," Archer said firmly, pulling up a light blanket for her.

After Archer was done with his own interrogation, though.

"You're an angel, Archer. You may have just saved my life."

Faith now snuggled into the blanket, all Archer could think was that it was the least he could do. She'd already saved his life, he felt. Maybe worked himself to death or an early grave the way he was going.

Kissing her gently, Archer stayed till Faith fell asleep, with a vigilant ear on the kitchen of course, she finally dozed.

Closing the door over, most of the way, he called Trevor. It went to voicemail.

"Ya, dude. I need you in a bad way. There's a situation."

Leaving few details, for evidence reasons, he knew Trevor would pick up on the seriousness. Leaving the address Archer requested "Text me back asap," then went over to Jonsie, still referring to him as 'lanky dude', in his head, with no interest in addressing him as a human being with feelings.

Still unconscious, Archer took out his phone and opened the recorder app, just then, got a text from Trevor. *On my way*, it read and Archer knew he wouldn't be long. Trevor had always been a speed demon anyway.

Taking a mug, he poured some cold coffee and put it in the microwave. At the island, one hand on the counter, the other on his hip, he thought, *What the fuck will I do with this disaster?* Meaning Jonsie.

Once the coffee was hot, Archer took it to the table and sat down, figuring he'd think of something. Until then, *Cool as a cucumber*, he told himself.

Sipping coffee, he peered out the patio doors and thought of how he was going to extract a confession from this douche bag. Just then his phone went off. "*Almost there!*" Trevor messaged.

CHAPTER EIGHTEEN
Decisions, Decisions

Calmly drinking coffee, Archer tossed scenarios around in his head about how to get Jonsie to confess to what he'd done when Trevor burst through the door. He knew by Archer's tone it wasn't a knock and wait for an answer kind of thing. Archer watched Trevor as he took it all in and having never been there before, it seemed to Trevor the house was in order except for the "broken mistake" that was tied to a chair and gurgling.

Trevor walked over to insect Jonsie and Archer was quiet as a mouse, but for the slurping of his coffee. Trevor was dumbfounded. "You did this?"

"Yeah," Archer sighed. "He left me no choice."

Trevor got right close to Jonsie and said, "Brooooooo . . . you fukt him *up*!" then kind of laughed. He, being a bit of a sadist, had broken a few guys in his days before, and after, he met Dora. It always tickled him pink to observe the aftermath.

Almost nose to nose with Jonsie now, Trevor said, "Like . . . I've never thumped someone this hard. The fuck he did anyway?" then didn't wait for an answer before he'd whipped around to look at Archer. "Where's Faith?!"

"She's in sleeping right now."

"Did she see this?"

Concerned for Faith even *his* stomach turned a little as Jonsie kept gurgling when he breathed. It sounded thick like it was clotting, with a wheezing or whistling sound too. Like the clots where flapping around as he clung to life.

"She saw him like this," Archer replied, pointing with the coffee cup still in his hand, almost like giving a toast. "It was in the beginning, though. He didn't look or sound quite this bad." Then, taking another sip, Archer sucked air through his teeth. His blood was beginning to boil again. "She was knocked out before I got here."

"SSHHHitttttt. Can we get him to stop making that gurgling sound? It's making me ill," Trevor asked as he started moving further away, leaning on the island. Then it sunk in. "What *are* we gonna do with this then, eh? Your problems, bro, are my problems. I'm not leaving you here like this."

"Well. I'd hoped I could get him to confess. I have the recorder ready and was hoping you could keep Faith company while I extract what I want from him. I will, of course, pause it if I need to apply pressure to get the confession. I'm not fond of the idea of him seeing you. I don't want you implicated. It's one thing if we say you came after the fact. He made the choice coming here and doing what he did, but I turned this episode around and now it's up to me to put an end to it."

"Ya. Sure, sure!" Trevor affirmed as Jonsie groaned and began the task of trying to open his eyes again.

They were swollen from the punch Archer had thrown that broke his nose. Realizing what had happened, Jonsie whipped his head up, as fast as he could, and the chair tipped.

Archer flew out of his seat and grabbed him by the shirt, to keep his head from hitting the floor. "No going back to sleep yet, muffin," he said as Jonsie fell within a millimetre of the hard, marble tiles and choked the way his neck was bent.

Archer sat him back up after kicking the pots away as Jonsie insisted on protesting. "You'll break my neck . . . asshole!"

Trevor put his hands to his head. No one had ever gotten away with saying that to Archer and didn't dare speak.

"That would be bad how?"

Sitting down and with a tone, that appeared to Trevor to be seemingly level-headed, Archer continued informing "broken guy," what he'd gotten himself into.

"The woman you attacked is my friend. I've put her to bed now and if you wake her up? Well . . ." He fake laughed again . . . "I can't say I know what I'll do, I mean . . . I've already crossed a line and can't go back now. If you went out horribly?" Archer paused, then leaned in to whisper in Jonsie's ear, "It'd be no skin off my nose at this point."

Trevor wished he knew what Archer had said. This was getting interesting now. Watching him play this roll caused Trevor to see Archer differently, and also realized, he'd never want to get on Archer's bad side. His ass would be kicked before he'd even realized he was in a fight.

This was not the guy he grew up with who saved bugs from spider's webs.

Sitting back down, Archer sipped coffee and watched Jonsie's face for signs of fear. He wasn't showing a lick, even if he felt it. Archer took it to the next level. "Yer gonna be doin' some talkin' I s'pose." He said, then got up, went to the counter, and rummaged through the drawers for a tool.

Taking the nutcracker he giggled and clacked them together, all the way back to the table, then ran them down Jonsie's face. He hadn't seen what Archer had but felt the cold metal.

Panicked now, Jonsie didn't hide his fear and screamed, the way those tough guys did when Archer exerted pressure on their pinky finger. Archer taught Trevor how to get someone in the right position, but he never got the chance and just pounded people. Having heard the scream before, he laughed a bit.

"Relax! I'm not gonna cut ya. I may, however, crush a few things," Archer sneered with a smile, then looked at Trevor. "Grab me a towel, will ya?"

Trevor scurried to look. Archer wanted Jonsie to know he wasn't alone now, and that he was in some serious shit. Jonsie kept quiet.

"There, there, now. No need to be like that," Archer teased, and tsk'ed at Jonsie.

"Go fuck yourself."

Archer got right in his face then, as if to inspect, while Trevor looked for the tea towels and after finding them, Trevor slammed the drawer and snapped one.

"Thanks, dude," Archer said holding his hand out for Trevor to throw it to him.

Then, folding it slowly, he wrapped it around Jonsie's head to cover his eyes. "Seems like I'm not the one in the position to be getting fucked," he laughed immaturely again. Intimidation was half the battle in Archer's opinion.

Looking to Trevor, Archer shooed him with his hand to go to Faith, as he put a finger to his lips for Trevor to stay silent.

Still having his boots on from work, they hit the floor heavy as Archer sat on the table and pulled his coffee over. There was no way Trevor wanted to see what Archer was going to do anyway. If he was bluffing, he was good. Trevor believed horrible things were about to happen. Jonsie must be even more terrified, he thought.

Going to the closed door, Trevor knocked and went right into the room with his eyes down. "I'm sorry. Are you decent?"

"Yes." Faith answered.

He looked then and she was sitting up with her legs tucked in, bouncing them and biting her nails, just watching as he closed the door.

Not knowing what else to do, Trevor wiped a sweaty hand on his pants, before offering to shake Faith's.

"*Hey*! I'm Trevor. You must be Faith," he said in the politest voice he could muster. She was as visibly shaken as he felt, taking his hand.

"Yes. Hi. What's going on out there?" she asked without hesitating. Not sure she entirely wanted to know.

"Well, as far as I can gather, someone has made a very bad choice and is regretting it right now," Trevor answered and started pacing. "I mean. I've never seen Archer so angry. Actually. I've never seen him angry."

Faith rushed and went to the door when Trevor had paced himself away from it, and before her hand could touch the handle Trevor loudly insisted, "I wouldn't do that if I were you."

"Is Archer okay? I don't really give a fuck about Jonsie."

They both jumped when they heard a blood-curdling scream come from the kitchen. Faith pulled her hand away from the door.

"Do you have ear buds? If you do, I'd put them in and turn up the volume. If that guy cooperates, and he'd do well to, things should calm down. It sounds to me, though, he may have to learn the hard way. I hope for his sake he catches on fast."

Faith went to the drawer and pulled them out, and just before putting them in, she looked at Trevor as if to say, "Really?"

He motioned for her to hurry and opened a bag of peanuts he'd taken from his pocket. Nice and loud and crunchy. Just then came another scream and Trevor looked really nervous to her. They both jumped and Faith jammed the pods into her ears.

With her phone she, hastily, clicked on the first video that popped up when the app opened. A cooking tutorial.

Great, she thought. It could play in the background while hunting for something with heavy bass, no silent parts, and sat against the headboard, feet pulled back in.

Trevor chewed peanuts and hummed to try and muffle the sounds.

■ ■ ■

In the kitchen after Archer had heard the bedroom door click shut, Trevor now out of earshot, and Faith assumingly busied by him. Archer began his interrogation.

"You'll leave with all your parts if you talk. Or don't and see how it goes."

"You ain't got the balls," Jonsie laughed.

Archer reached down and pulled off a one of Jonsie's shoes and dropped it on the floor heavily, then went to the deck and took the rock that he'd seen on the steps the night of the moonlight swim. Taking the towel from Jonsie's eyes, he wrapped it around the rock and put it on the floor.

Pausing the recording, Archer went to the drawer and got the meat tenderizer that he'd seen when taking out the nutcracker.

Rubbing the cold steel across Jonsie's foot, he waited a second. "Last time I'm asking. My patience is wearing thin."

Jonsie just sat there.

Leaning in, almost nose to nose, Archer screamed, "*Fucking go!*"

Jonsie tried to call his bluff, keeping his silence, so Archer hauled back and slammed the side of the tenderizer down against his baby toe from a front angle, driving the bones up into his foot. That was the scream Faith and Trevor heard.

When Jonsie stopped crying, he caved.

"Okay. Okay. I used to be engaged to her and I cheated. I tried to make it up, but she wouldn't even message me back.

Bitch wouldn't even answer my calls!" he screamed thinking Faith would hear.

She'd told him the truth. His "good girl." Archer knew his instincts about her were bang-on. Jonsie just confirmed it for him.

Pausing the recording again he said, "Wrong answer," and did the same to the next toe. That was the one that convinced Faith to put in the ear buds.

Trevor heard that one loud and clear, even through the bag crinkling and chewing of the peanuts.

Thinking of what he could do to spare Faith, Trevor tapped her arm and motioned for her to take the ear buds out. When she did, he asked. "Can we get to the beach without going through the kitchen?"

"*Yes!*"

Happily taking his hand, leading him out the door from the bedroom, across the patio, and down the steps, it wasn't as fast as Trevor would have preferred, but quick enough. Once in the yard, he dialled Archer's number.

Picking up all he said was, "Yes?"

"I'm taking her to the beach," Trevor informed Archer, crossing the lawn, Faith nearly running.

"Good, one sec, I'll be right there. Stay on the line and don't move."

Suspecting this would freak Jonsie out even more, and not wanting him to hear, Archer went out onto the deck and waved to Trevor.

"I'll call the police once I get what I want from him, I'll text ya when I'm done. They'll send an ambulance and a few cars. Don't go far."

Jonsie now feeling like he was in some Mafia shamble, he regretted everything. Even knowing her name. What had he walked into?

Trevor ended the call and gave him a thumbs-up before joining Faith. Archer went back in the house and closed the sliding door. Then the curtains.

"Can't have any witnesses," Archer laughed, as the metal grommets on the drapes scraped across the rod. Jonsie's heart had really sunk then.

Returning to the recording he said, "Go," before pressing the record button again.

"I lost my cool," Jonsie admitted crying.

"Tell me how it went," Archer demanded calmly.

"She sold the house out from underneath me, went to a place in the country, then took off here. I heard a rumour she'd moved. It took me a month to find out where she was. I had to date the travel agent and fuck that disgusting slob to get into the office and find her file."

"Have you been to my house?"

Jonsie stopped talking, so he picked up the tenderizer again and paused the recorder. "Do I need to remind you what happens when you stall? I'll keep pausing the confession if needed. I'm totes cool with it. Some things I have patience for. You I do not," he sighed.

"Fuck, man. Have some mercy, will you?" Jonsie begged.

"The mercy you showed her in the bathroom? The calls? The text? The emails?" Archer said softly. "That kind of mercy?"

"What do you give a shit about her anyway? You think she'll treat you right?" Jonsie laughed . . . for a second. The screams had loosened the clots and sank deeper into his lungs.

Archer watched as he choked and said nothing. He was entitled to feel jilted, but not to push himself into her life after having clearly said no, and, most certainly not, threaten her, or her life.

Beside himself with pain now, Jonsie prayed the police would show up. He was going tell them how he'd been tortured. Archer read his mind somehow.

"I haven't called the police yet and won't until you tell me what I want to know and say what I want you to say. We can do this all day if you prefer. I'm kind of starting to have fun."

Jonsie nodded, so Archer pressed record. Finally, he'd decided to tell everything. How he'd been watching them for days and that she was spending all "their" money on fancy shit. Telling how he'd broken in after making noises on the deck to distract Archer, then slipped in the back door and hid in her room until she went to bed then left, leaving a window unlocked for later. Archer wondered how much he'd actually seen and heard. What if he'd have stayed? They might both be dead right now.

"I went in through the window in the morning, after rehearsing what I wanted to say. I waited a long time for her to get up and wanted to talk it out. I needed to piss and went outside. She must have woken up when I was out."

Waiting for her to finish making coffee, he watched in the window. The open concept wouldn't let him go back in unseen. So, created another distraction to make her go outside, while he went back in.

That was the flash she'd seen, causing her to leave Archer on hold.

"She had no idea I was inside. I heard you both talking on the phone, and I had to sneak around as she was locking everything up like you told her to," Jonsie confessed. "When she went to the shower, I got a bite to eat. I was starving by then. I scoped out the place and found what I could use as a weapon in case you came back. So, I took the bat with me and went to the bathroom. She wouldn't let me talk. When she spit in my face, I lost it, and pushed her. I really wanted to punch her right in her selfish face," he said as he chuckled lightly, then choked a bit more. "When she backhanded me, I really lost my shit. That's when I hit her across the head with the bat. I paced around a minute feeling bad, but then I realized, she had it coming. I was going to take her out and bury her alive. She should've paid for breaking my heart and ruining my life,"

He had no shame in what he was going to do.

"Wasn't so hard now, was it?" Archer passive-aggressively spoke, then clicking his teeth, added, "Well, it didn't need to be."

In his seat across from Jonsie, Archer kicked his two crushed toes and admittedly, it was the worst scream he'd had ever heard.

"*What the fuck, man*!? I told you what you wanted to know!" Jonsie yelled.

"You did. I was making a point. It was your choice to come here. You realize that now, I think. So, here's what's going to happen. I'm gonna call 911. When they come, you're going to tell them you snapped and lost your head. I caught you in here and you ran. I chased after you and when you came round the corner you stubbed your toe on something and ran into the marble island. The fall maybe broke your rib, you don't know. It's all a blur now.'

Jonsie just laughed and Archer continued calmly. "I'll tell them when you fell, you landed on your face and that's what broke your nose and probably knocked you out. When you came to, I had you tied up and you decided it was best to fess up to help with your sentencing. You'll be grateful now that I don't bury *you* alive, you human piece of panty waste."

"Like fuck I am. You can go fuck yourself. I'm telling them all about what yo—"

He didn't finish his sentence. Archer cut him off by punching his broken ribs. Jonsie cried and spit up more blood, then passed back out. Resigned to gurgling once more.

"You shouldn't burn bridges while you're standing on them," Archer muttered as he logged the recording, then sent a copy to his storage online before calling 9-1-1.

Sounding distressed, and shaken, as best he could, Archer told them he'd walked in on an assault and the guy was nuts. He was afraid, but went after the guy, that he ran but tripped and got knocked out.

They asked who was hurt and Archer told them, but also threw in that he had training in trauma and high-stress situations in his time at the fire station. That it was under control. The guy didn't look too good, though.

They asked if he was okay, and Archer replied he was just shaken and afraid this guy might snap. The guy was already going on like a lunatic, so tied him to a chair and asked them to send the police.

Answering all their questions he told them that he'd tend to the victim, Faith, until they arrived and if anything changed, he'd call back. Archer also mentioned there was nothing he could do for the intruder.

Asking the address, he gave it to them, then listened as they relayed the info to dispatch and ended the call. He knew they'd record anything that made it through the phone. That wasn't a chance he was willing to take.

This asshole waking up and saying something Archer would regret was the reason. He had to give the story first or the recording.

Archer then called Trevor and said for them to come up from the beach. Faith needed to clean up and be ready to give her account to the officers. Not wanting to sway her statement, he wanted her to tell them only what she knew.

Which is why Archer had sent her out. Faith shouldn't know of what had happened, for fear she'd have to lie and screw them all. Trevor understood and said he'd tell her.

Wishing she'd stayed in the bedroom, Archer thought of how he was going to break it to her when asked. He wouldn't offer the information, but he also wasn't going to lie to her. Not a chance.

Archer needed to see her, to be sure she was okay, to show her that *he* was, even though he wasn't. He'd never have thought in a million years he was capable of anything like that and found it quite disturbing that his mind could be so . . . bent.

Waiting for them on the deck, Archer stood when they came over the top of the cliff, until Faith saw him. Running for him, covered in tears, he went to her slowly, like all was fine, not wanting to cause more worry than was necessary.

Opening his arms, she just jumped into them, wrapped herself around him, and covered him in kisses. Archer gave Trevor the peace sign behind her back and told him to come in and he'd make them coffee. Faith stayed attached to Archer the whole way back to the cottage, thanking god he was good.

"Are you okay? Is it all settled?" she asked quickly.

Not answer anything but 'yes' to her, there was no need to go into it unless forced.

Taking her in through the bedroom door and setting her down, or prying her off of him really, Archer mentioned that she should clean up in the other bath and not look into the kitchen on the way by. Not even a *peek*.

Trevor noticing his eyes, he was sure Archer was talking to him more, really. He'd seen it before.

Trevor promised to keep her company while Archer made them coffee. He could use one right about now. Maybe even a two-four.

Both impressed by how Archer had handled the situation, and terrified of him now, Trevor had a new level of respect for his best friend. Some would have found what Archer did a little evil, but Trevor didn't and would do whatever Archer needed from him now. With pleasure.

Trevor stayed with Faith as she wiped her face and dabbed her cuts, then threw the towel on the floor, disgusted, and held her hands out. She was still shaking.

Slapping them on her legs, she tried again. Still shaking. Tired of it, Faith wished for it to stop. It felt horrible. Like after she got out of the ring. Her mind was fine, but her body screamed adrenaline.

Trevor put his head down, feeling bad for her. "You know?" he said quietly. "Archer cares for you an awful lot. I've never seen him so volatile, but I mean he did spare us most of the details. We both know, though, that he did what was best for you and now he has to try and protect himself. We have to protect him. What he did is illegal."

"Yes. You're right. I'm prepared to throw Jonsie under the bus for what he did. Not just to me but to Archer. He doesn't need this in his life, and I feel like a sack of shit. It's all my fault."

Trevor couldn't help but hug her.

"It's not, Faith. It's that douche bag in the kitchen. No one deserves to be attacked in their own house. It's one thing if you get into a fight all of a sudden. Things escalate. You were just here peacefully, though. It's wrong. I'm right behind whatever you say. I mean. I don't even know the whole story. I'm just gonna say that Archer called and asked if I could help. He was shaken and didn't know what to do. Maybe that he had caught someone in your place and had assaulted you and he needed help getting it under control. It's really ninety-eight percent of what I know. So technically it's not a lie."

Faith already loved Trevor. He'd been so good to take care of her and make sure she was safe. All he said was that he didn't want her mixed up in any more than she already was or had to be. A good man.

"Dora is lucky to have you. Archer too . . . and me . . ."

Trevor felt that in his heart. Knowing she was right; he gave himself some long overdue credit. "Thanks for saying that."

"It's true, though. You didn't have to come. You could've wiped your hands of it at any time. You really pulled through for us."

"I guess we're family now," he nodded with a slight smile.

Trying to find a spot in her mind where she could relax a bit, Faith remembered what her mother had said, "Your spirit having a human experience," and "Misery loves company."

Breathing in deep, then out . . . in . . . then out. She began to listen to the sound of her breath, sinking into the echo in the bathroom as it bounced off the subway-tiled walls. It wasn't long before she heard the heavy boots of the officers and the tinny voices of dispatch through their walkie-talkies.

Faith began the arduous task of going to meet them and sighed before going into the kitchen with Trevor. The police were already inside and waiting for her.

Archer was between her and them with one arm tucked into his ribs and one on his chin listening. Hearing them come in, he turned and looked at Faith, tilting his head to the side, his eyebrows rose, as if to say "I thought I told you. No looking."

Faith put her head down. He *was* clear about that, but to her, it couldn't be helped, knowing if she'd done anything else, she wouldn't be able to be genuine in her description for the report. They'd see right through her. She had to act like Jonsie had tripped, that it was awful, but an accident, when he'd tried to run. No one had done anything to hurt him. They were all trying to help.

Trevor had told her what Archer wished for her to say. Jonsie couldn't object. He was a mess. Her intent to protect Archer now was priority.

One officer came alongside her to move to another room and get her statement. Faith told them everything she knew and was then interrupted by the voices in the walkie-talkies, discussing the recording Archer had made of the confession. There was no doubt he'd be there for her, no matter what. She'd do the same. Basically, she was going to have to lie a bit. He'd put himself and his whole life on the line. Everything he'd built . . . for her . . . She'd never betray that. *Ever.*

Satisfied with her statement, the officer let her go. Coming from the bedroom, Faith heard the stretcher.

Once round the corner from the hall, paramedics were lifting Jonsie onto it. Back and forth, they spoke in another language calling it in to triage at the hospital, one of them repeating what the other had said. The voice on the other end asked what their ETA was. "He's stable enough that we can move him now, but he's had quite a fall. It's about a thirty-minute drive," one of them said.

Listening to them reporting all the injuries, that they knew of, Faith put a hand over her mouth as Archer stood there very somberly.

That was a lot, and she knew he'd done it. What had actually happened? Faith couldn't imagine, but remembered the screams, plus they were alone there in the cottage for quite a long time while Trevor kept her occupied on the beach.

Going to Archer, he took her under his arm, kissed her head, and asked how she felt, and Faith said she still had a headache.

One ambulance gone now with Jonsie, the other was there for her, but said she didn't need it. They insisted on doing a few tests, to check her functions, making sure nothing was going on. Passing the same testing Archer had done, she still refused to go.

One paramedic insisted Faith come with them, or at least, be taken for a good checkup. It was his job, and he knew the repercussions if there was any damage and didn't inform her.

"The ER knows of the incident and if we can't convince you to go, at least keep an eye out. If anything should happen, get there straightaway or call and we'll come. Concussions don't always show right away, and they can be quite serious. We can't make you go. That's your choice. You're lucky there're no other injuries. That could have ended with you in Jonathan's situation . . . Or worse."

Faith thanked them for coming and led them to the door. She just wanted them all out.

Trevor knocked on the wall announcing he'd finished his statement and had to dash. Dora was losing her mind even though he said it was good.

Giving them the peace sign he left, most of the officers were right behind him, all piling towards the door at once almost. Save one.

Staying behind he told Faith, "You're a lucky woman, Faith, that Archer had come by. We listened to the recording and Jonsie was incredibly disturbed by the breakup, it seems. I mean, the injuries were horrible, and I can't imagine his pain. Seems his heart was in the worst shape, though. He must have been missing you to get in the shape his mind is, doing this. Maybe out of his right mind altogether. We'll have you in another day and we'll go over the recording. Or maybe Archer can let you have a listen before you come. It's a lot to process."

Taking off his hat and tucking it under his arm, he continue. "You're in good hands with Archer here, though. I can say that for sure. We go way back."

Leaving it at that, Archer had told him that she didn't know Jonsie was going to bury her alive. Now wasn't the time to drop that bomb.

Inside, Archer laughed about Matt saying Jonsie was broken up about her leaving. He didn't give a shit about anyone but himself. He *was* going to bury her alive. *That's so fukt*, he thought in Trevor's voice again.

"Yes, I'm very lucky," Faith agreed.

"I went to school with Archer here," he told her, trying to lighten the mood some. "He always stuck up for the little guy. We could have used him on the force. He chose to be a humanitarian instead." Then joked, "Which is fine, I suppose. It helps us in other ways. He gets kids off the streets and works to do so much for them and their communities. You can't imagine what he does. Plus, he's way too modest," he poked at Archer.

Faith smiled. "Is that right? He hadn't mentioned any of that."

"Matt. You know I like to help, but I'm big on staying from the limelight. It's not about the money or the glory. It's about the happiness. I hate braggarts."

"Yes. This is true. Some of us build bridges while others only dare to cross them. You are a godsend, to be honest."

With that, Matt looked to Faith saying, "Here's my card. Stay in touch. We'll get a report ready for the owner of the cottage. Would you like us to call for you? It's quite a difficult time. We can help ease the blow if you need."

"*Oh*! Would you? It's kind of got me scared. I'm afraid she'll end the contract."

"Yes. We can relay that to the owner," Matt assured her. "Do call us, though, if we can help with anything. We'll be in touch when we find out from Jonathan what's going on. We haven't gotten a statement from him. He can't right now and really after hearing the recording . . . he's not in his right head either. He'll need a psychiatrist."

Faith was ready for this day to end.

Putting on his hat back on, tipped it and went for the door. Like a higher power heard her, though, Matt stopped in his tracks and without looking said. "You're in good hands, Miss Leone," and quietly closed the door.

When the footsteps were gone from the deck, Archer took her into him tightly.

Sighing, Faith asked, "Do you hate me now? Is this a blemish on me?".

"No. There's nothing anyone can do that puts a blemish on you. You're beautiful in my mind. Inside and out. I respect what you did. That was horrible for you to have to go through, and you left him when you should have. You stood your ground and defended yourself, as best you could, when he came to attack. I'm just happy I made it here in time."

Kissing her forehead, trying to get rid of the vision in his head of Jonsie burying her alive, Archer hoped she wouldn't hear his heart. It filled him with rage again.

Jonsie was lucky Archer didn't give him his own medicine. He sure felt like doing it and also felt he hadn't been punished nearly enough. Regardless of what was already done. "Do you see me differently?"

"Well, yes. I didn't see what you did, but I heard some of it. It frightened me, to be honest. Part of me is touched that you put yourself in danger . . . The other part is a little afraid."

"I did, what I did, to protect you. Then I did, what I did, to protect me. And I'd do it all again if I had to."

Risking rotting in some jail cell and slowly dying not being with her, Faith thought, if she'd had any inclination on having more than some summer fling, now would be a great time to say it.

"You could've taken him down and called the police. What you did wasn't just protecting me and you. You did things I think you might regret later and if they find out, you could lose everything."

"I've seen his kind before. He'd have lied his face off and so many have walked away from domestic abuse, only to find the woman dead later. I couldn't have it. I doubt you'd want to be shackled to me day and night. I'd have not let you out of my sight."

"You think I'm worth that much, do you? Losing everything? Your freedom included?"

Looking into his eyes, she pierced his soul.

"Well. Faith. We've only known each other a few days really but I *was* filled with rage. Men think they can do whatever they want, and the law just slaps their wrists. What would've stopped him from coming back for you, really? I had to make sure he wouldn't be back, for fear of what he'd get next time."

"Would you do that for any woman?"

"I suppose not. I may beat a guy if I saw it happening but prob—" he began to say until the reality sunk in. Had he been fooling himself?

"I see your point. I do have strong feelings towards you. They overwhelm me sometimes. I don't deny that. I don't know how to explain them yet. Your leaving has me confused about my feelings. I've been trying to just enjoy you, but that nagging feeling lingers in my head constantly, reminding me that I shouldn't let my heart get involved. I so really, really, really want to let it go, but I can't. My mind says if I did give you my heart it would be destroyed when the fall arrives. I'd surely fall with it. My heart keeps telling my mind to stop, but it's very powerful. I listen to them all day long," he told her in obvious pain. "I know you planned to go back to your regular life. I worry, though, you'll forget about us, and I didn't want to bring it up. It's negative and you don't deserve that. Especially right now. Since you brought it up? That's the truth," he promised and paused a moment.

Faith waited knowing there was more. He was just finding better words.

"You're on vacation and you'll go home. I've come to accept that. My heart wishes you weren't, but whatever makes you happy, makes me happy. Okay? Don't fret about it. I won't make it hard for you to leave. Not in million years. I care too much about your happiness. In fact, I want your happiness more than I want you."

"Okay, see? That sounds like love to me. It sounds like what every girl dreams of in a man. Like you said before, it's way too soon to be saying things like that and I understand what you mean. It will break my heart, to have to leave too. I adore you so much. I've never felt more wanted and special in my life."

"Dad worries about my mother leaving him alone. That someday he'll be without her. The way I do about you. She lives with him to the fullest, every single day, and never worries about what lies ahead. She's not worried about when he goes home for good, that she'll be alone. There's too much to enjoy for today and has so much fun with him, that she just swims in the good feeling he gives her . . ." It sank in deeper. "The way you do with me . . ."

Faith just looked at him and feeling his anxiety, she had to tell him.

"I wanted to tell you that I'd considered moving here. There's nothing for me I Vermon. I had an awful time with it. Part of me said, life here would be a new start, something good, a beginning. Which was before I met you. Then, when we met and having discovering more about who you are, I'd thought about staying more seriously."

Faith paced while Archer's heart pounded, and his anxiety went through the roof. *Please. Say it. Say it*, he begged in his mind.

Staring out the bay window Faith began again.

"I tried to reason with myself that I barely knew you and that if it didn't work out, how would I be able to change my mind? I mean . . . I'm being honest with you right now. It's so hard."

Archer stood patiently but wanted to scream.

Fighting to find the words, Faith decided to just be out with it.

"After what you just said . . . I think I have my mind made up. I'd merely toyed with the idea and wasn't really serious. I was just having so much fun here. If my book sells and I do well, I probably would have been back. I didn't want to leave. Then I was lost in you . . . in me too. I still am. When I'm with you, I don't even care about tomorrow. We're here now and that's all that matters. But . . ."

Archer hung there on her words, heart in his hands as she paced the floor. "But?"

"Well, I'm thinking . . . Maybe, I should take that idea more seriously after what we've just admitted. I've never felt this way about anyone. I can't imagine not feeling this way for the rest of my life. I know it sounds crazy too."

"Neither have I, Faith. I want to take you and make you mine. I really do. And I don't regret saying that. At all."

Like she reached out and took that heart from his hands, her eyes lit up.

"I did regret saying that, but, when you said you don't regret it, my soul danced. How can I deny that? I *can't* deny that. Can I?" she stated like asking herself more than she was asking him, obviously beside herself in a battle. Faith was a strong woman but had never had the opportunity to exercise it, other than her business.

"Would you really stay?"

Faith paced a minute more then stopped on a dime. "I would really stay."

Archer saw the fear. That scared him now. Putting his arms out for her to come she hesitated. He didn't like that either.

"Faith. Come," he encouraged softly.

She did. Slowly. Like an animal that had been beaten. His heart cried for her.

"Come," he repeated softly as she stood before him.

Archer wanted her to come *all* the way. He'd thrown his heart at her feet several times and wanted it back. Not all at once. He just wanted . . . some . . .

Waiting, and standing before her, an open book, a target, he was brave. She could crush him right now.

"I want you to do what you feel is right in your heart. If you leave, I'll be a wreck. We don't have to stop talking. I can visit. You can visit. If we feel this strongly now and have this incredible bond, we don't have to let it go. Distance doesn't mean anything. I have more money than I know what to do with. I don't mean to brag. That's not me. I just want you to understand the lengths I would go to, to keep you," he whispered as, she fell into his arms. "We can go slow, so you're certain about your feelings and who I am. I won't change. Unless you just stay here. That security would bring heaven upon me, and I'd show you how my heart celebrates your name."

What he'd just said was one of the most romantic things ever. She possessed him. It was obvious. It seemed as though he possessed her also. She, denying it. It was just her wounds, the inner critic, Jonsie. Could Archer put the chip back in her shoulder? For real?

"The truth is . . . I don't even know how to begin to leave you. I'm left breathless so often. At first, I thought maybe it was to lure me in. I planned to try and get you in bed and maybe enjoy you for the summer. Then, I was swept up with you. From the minute I set foot in your office, you already had me. I can see, now, that you're just magnificent. It's not a ruse or a ploy. It's just you. Your heart. It's the most beautiful thing I've ever seen, and I was drawn to you like a moth to a flame. Anyone who doesn't see your inner beauty is blind. But I know now that I was blind until I saw you. My eyes have been opened to a world that I thought was only just a fantasy. It's not the money or the gallery or the cafe. It's not the cars and whatever else you have. It's the way you look at me . . . the way you cause me to look at myself. I had a hard time thinking you actually liked me. That was my issue. You've helped me to see that."

"I'd do that forever, Faith and cherish every single time I saw you let go of any of your pain or insecurities. Like the first night at the gallery when we ate on the patio. Anything that's mine, is yours. I ache to see you continue grow. 'Play with me' as you put it. Nothing would please me more."

Rocking her in his arms, Faith felt safe now.

"Even if the events today hadn't happened and pushed us to this conversation. If you hadn't just admitted how you feel about me. I'd eventually have to admit how much trust I gave you from the very beginning. When I saw you that first time. You felt like home and I thought it was insane. I hardly really know you, but I feel like I've always known you. I never want to be without this feeling ever again. Without *you* ever again. I want to know your joy, dreams, and fears. If you even have any."

He did have fears. It was losing her.

Opening herself to him fully, Faith kept talking. "If I can be that place of peace for you, I'd do it in a heartbeat. No questions asked. To be really honest . . . I want to be there for you, as you have been for me. I may not be as wise as you, but I can help at times."

Archer let her go and paced. "I feel very uncomfortable right now," he said, with a bit of humour behind it, but really, he meant it. "I'm sure you've noticed that I am never at a loss for words. Right now, though, I'm speechless. I want to run away with this and . . . Are you sure you feel the way you just said?"

"I'm certain. I've never been so sure of anything in my entire life."

Scooping Faith off her feet, she laughed and Archer kissed her tenderly.

"Let me show you how I truly feel. No barriers. No doubts. Give me some time. It's all I ask. I wasn't expecting you, so let's play out the summer and you can tell me, then, what you feel. I want you to be sure. Totally sure. Until then, my dear. You are going to get spoiled rotten!"

"As will you!"

Faith didn't have a ton of money, but she had a heart that would make all the hearts in New York seem like a merry-go-round, next to a suicide roller coaster.

Archer carried her back to bed and told her to pick a movie for them to watch and that he was going to make them some food. Neither of them had eaten all day except for a few bites of bread between them and the sun was beginning to set.

"What kind of movie?" she hollered, from the bedroom.

"Anything but murder or thriller!" he yelled back.

Having had enough excitement today to last a lifetime and wondered what would happen with Jonsie. What the owner was going to do with the cottage now that there was damage. He couldn't let that all go to the wind and decided to call Matt.

"Hey, Archer. Everything okay?"

"Yeah. Faith is doing alright. I'm gonna hang around a bit in case the bump on the noggin proves to be more than it seemed."

"Oh, good. You're lucky, you can just take what time you need to do that. She's pretty special to you, eh?"

"She is. Amazing woman. So kind and happy. I was wondering, though. Did you happen to get a hold of the cottage owner?"

"I thought we'd wait and get the statement from Jonathan first. If he's not awake in the morning, I'll give a call."

"Oh. Well. I'm going to pay for any damages. It wasn't her fault. So, if you can put that in the report that would be great. I don't want to see the owner's insurance take a hit or anything and there's the whole, ending the contract thing. It was just unfortunate that this all happened. How is that all going?" he asked to poke for info, hoping Matt would be straight-up.

"Well. It's good you got him to confess on your recorder. It seems he may not make it through the night. They've had to resuscitate three times already. They can't keep doing that. The body can't take the shock," Matt said seriously. "As far as I'm concerned, the case is about closed anyway. That was good decision-making you did, on her behalf. If you hadn't shown up it may be her in that bed right now and he'd be far out of our reach. We'd never have known it was him. She's lucky. I mean, he did say he was going to bury her alive."

"I don't know what I'd have done in that case. It would be horrible. Has he got family?"

"As far as we know it's just his mother and she's in a home, suffering with dementia and Alzheimer's. Even if they tell her, it's likely she wouldn't know who they're talking about. It's all a shame, really, but people snap sometimes. If he'd asked for help, we wouldn't be talking right now."

"Ooh. Sorry to hear about his mom. It may be for the best, though. It would be painful news to get," Archer replied in a way that seemed caring. He may for the mother but not for Jonsie.

"Yeah. It really is. One sec . . ." Matt said, and Archer could hear dispatch repeat codes and then Matt's muffled voice. "Gotta go. They say there's an emergency at the hospital. Jonathan has woken and is being violent and rambling. I have to head over. I'll let you know if there's anything else."

"Fuck," Archer said under his breath as Matt hung up. There was nothing he could do now, but he wasn't about to tell Faith that Jonsie was awake and talking.

Food finished and putting it all on the tray, he asked if Faith had chosen a movie.

"How about sci-fi?" she yelled. "I've been flipping through these and there's only a few I haven't seen or want to see."

"Whatever you pick is great. You want juice or water?"

"Juice, please."

Archer took the food in and asked if he could use the washer to get the stains from his clothes.

"Only if you sit with no shirt on," she grinned, peering over her glasses and wiggling her eyebrows.

"My god. You look adorable in glasses. How can I argue with you?"

Putting down the tray of veggies, fruit, and the tall glass of juice, Faith offered him the glasses.

"Here. Put those on? They're not prescription."

Doing as she asked, Faith slapped her heart. "You look even more dashing. I was hoping you might look a little nerdy. You make everything look good," she giggled.

"One sec."

Archer went down the hall to the bathroom and put his things in the sink to soak, and her towels from the bathroom in the washer. Back in the bathroom, he wet his hair and brushed it with his hands to part in the middle, then flattened it. Coming back to the bedroom, he slouched in a nerdy way.

"How's this then?" he asked her jokingly and Faith burst out laughing.

"Nice try, though!"

Taking them off, Archer gave them back and smoothed his hair back to normal. A trickle of water ran down his chest, catching Faith's eye. Not to mention her attention. Always hyper focused on him, Faith shook her head to straighten it out.

"What?"

"Nothing," she muttered, still shaking her head. "You just look amazing."

Smiling he agreed that, yes, she *did* look amazing, then told her to eat, saying he wanted to clean up the glass in the bathroom.

Faith tried to argue they could do it together later on, he wouldn't hear of it, wanting her to get some nutrition.

"I'll join you soon. It won't take long," Archer assured as he waved his finger for her to start eating.

Finishing all he'd made; Faith hadn't realized how hungry she actually was until the first bite, then watched as Archer cleaned up all the glass while he listened to trailers that played in the background.

"Can you hear those?" Faith asked.

"Yep! That last one sounded interesting."

"Ya. I thought so too. I think we should just watch that. I'm getting confused now which was good."

Dumping the last of the glass into the bin he'd taken from the kitchen, Archer pushed it under the counter. There was a lot and it was really heavy, actually. Tomorrow he'd get Trevor to come with the truck and get rid of it at the dump. Washing his hands, he heard Faith's phone ring.

Not recognizing the number, Faith answered questioningly. "Hello?" and after a minute she sat up straight in her spot. "Oh my . . . Oh my . . ."

Archer came from the bathroom and sat beside her on the bed, minding his own business, and had some of the food he'd brought in for them.

Faith covered her mouth and breathed out saying, "Ohhhh."

Archer knew it was bad news, so, reached out and touched her leg with a soft rub to comfort her.

"Okay . . . okay . . ." she spoke softly. "Thank you for calling, officer," she finished.

Looking to Archer, Faith just stared.

"What, dear?"

"Jonsie is dead," she informed him.

"How?"

"Apparently, they had to resuscitate him several times. About an hour ago they were losing him again. After they'd gotten him resuscitated, he jumped up as if he had no injuries and then went off like a maniac mumbling a bunch of things, that made no sense to the hospital staff, and had to call Matt to deal with it. When they tried to calm him down, he attacked an officer, ran, then grabbed a woman in the hall and tried to drag her off as a shield. They had a standoff outside of a room. When the woman escaped, he panicked and jumped out the window to his death."

"Jesus!"

Faith burst into tears. Archer held her and waited for her to calm down before asking if she wanted to talk.

"I thought he was going to talk and spill the beans. I don't know what happened in the kitchen with you two. I don't really want to know. I'm just relieved the statements we gave and his confession you recorded is the end of the case."

Archer sighed with relief. He was worried about the same thing. The nightmare was over. Now on to the healing. "I'm here for whatever you need, Faith."

"And I'm here for you."

Knowing what he'd done might be weighing heavy on his mind, Faith then caringly said, "If you need to talk, I'm here," then took his hand and kissed it. "I don't know if what you did was easy for you or not. I can't imagine it was. If I can do anything, please tell me?"

It wasn't that hard for him to do and would do it all again without hesitation. For her? He'd have done almost anything. Carrying a heavy load from early on in his life, what he desired was a partner who would help him hold it all. Not give it to her. It was just that she'd be his extra strength, being her king. He'd also carry her load, with complaints.

What she'd said made him emotional. No one had ever had such an impact with those words on him before. Possibly because Archer felt he actually *would* tell her his concerns and doubts. To finally be fragile.

His heart latched onto it and would never let go. Though he could handle most anything, Archer always been good alone. It was a "want" more than a "need" for him. But being with her like this . . . Archer realized he'd be *half* the man without her.

With Jonsie out of the picture they could go on. Move forward. Leaning in, he kissed her tenderly and she returned it with a heated one. Stopping her, Faith looked into is eyes and came at him again.

Archer wasn't sure now was the right time to get into that.

"Faith. Are you sure you want to do that? It's been an emotional day."

Faith kissed him softly. "I'm not confused, Archer," she asserted, then kissed him harder.

Fighting the urge to push her away, not wanting her to regret anything they did, slowly, Archer found the strength to join her. Maybe it was him who was confused. Maybe it was him who was holding back. Maybe it was him who needed comfort. Maybe it was just *her* that made him weak.

Throwing a leg over him, Faith pushed him to the bed. Actually, he *let* her do it and loved that her hair flowed over his body, as it had in his fantasy.

In that instant Archer lost all control . . . Or did he just begin to get it?

It didn't matter. He had her. The cottage would be settled in any way he had to. Ready to let this be what it was and stop analyzing it, they made love like neither of them had a care in the world. Their hearts mingled and their bodies danced like only they existed.

CHAPTER NINETEEN
The Whole Fam Damily

Both exhausted and full of each other now, and as Faith laid on his chest, Archer felt a tear hit his skin and run down his side. "Ssshhh," he comforted, the way she had done to him, then wiped her face. "What's the matter?"

"The matter is. I've never felt so taken in by another human being. Other than my mother. My heart feels so full it could explode. Like people do in a musical."

Those tender moments are what made life worth living, for him. The money was great. The gallery, his family and friends. His little hometown, the baseball diamond and the team. But this? This is what made Archer feel content. When walls came down and souls bared themselves. Naked and vulnerable. Accepting and bending to flex with the moment. No shame. No fear. Just pure positive love. After a nice breath in, Archer said he understood, from his perspective. What he'd give to see it from hers.

"I've never felt more accepted either, than I do with you. Women have thrown themselves at me. For my money, my looks, or what I could do for them and their social status. It's so ugly. You? Just take 'me', not asking me to be anything, other than I am, and I swear you came on the wings of the angels," he told her assuredly. That was what was in his heart to say. "I feel wrapped up by you and your warmth is more than I can bear sometimes, but I don't doubt it at all. I doubted myself. I doubted that I'd be enough. That you'd leave. Money can't ensure someone never leaves you and when cash doesn't matter, when it's not a factor in how a relationship stays together, it can make you feel a little naked. I asked for this, though, with all my heart. I've never been afraid to lose anyone before. You make me feel like there's nothing I couldn't do. With ease too. My only regret would be that it would take a lifetime to explain myself to you, but I would take it on in a second."

Faith just stared into the dimly lit room listening to him. Lost in his words, his voice, the way he breathed in before he spoke. His large chest rose up and bent her neck and her arm barely reached his other side. Nestled in, under his heavy arm, was the most comfortable place she'd ever been, and Faith memorized the moment.

"Archer . . ." she said almost feeling ashamed that she'd thought about leaving him not that long ago and that she wasn't good enough.

"No, Faith. I hear in your voice how that makes you feel, and you need to believe me when I say this. There are parts of ourselves we hide from others. When you find someone who you can truly be yourself with, you should tell them. I thought about our talk in the kitchen, and, as much as I thought I was pulling you into me . . . I was, in fact, pushing you away. It's why I stopped you in the car that day and earlier when you kissed me that way again. I wanted you to be sure you really felt what you thought you did. When you made that point in the kitchen as I spoke of my parents, I still kind of pushed you away. When I finally let go, I realized what I'd been doing. It will never happen again. You are priceless to me, and I need you to stop devaluing yourself."

"I don't want you to hide yourself from me, in any way, and how do you seem to know me so well?" she told him abruptly. "You read me like a book."

"Don't kid yourself. You've done the same to me. It's like we're the same person sometimes. Or maybe we're psychic?!" he joked. Then, knowing she was being serious he apologized.

"I'm sorry. I was hiding myself. I wanted to be honest with you, but I had to be honest with myself first. I didn't realize I was even doing that. You're a grown woman and you deserve the right to make your own decisions. I sort of took that from you, the way you nearly took my right to choose to be with you, no matter what you thought of yourself. I apologize. It's not my place to tell you how to be 'you,' nor how to love someone. I want you to be unapologetically Faith. It's all I truly need from you. No one wants an owner. I will still own you, though, I hope. With your permission."

"Maybe I need to be just taken now and then," she smirked and his heart skipped a beat . . . he heard what she meant, and now having admitted her truth, she assumed the game was on.

"Good then."

Faith picked up her head and squinted her eyes at him. "What?" he asked.

"I'm looking for the door to heaven that I seem to have walked in through," she laughed.

Archer tapped her forehead saying. "Heaven is in there," then winked, slid his finger down her nose, over her chin, and moved to her heart. "This is its playground."

Opening his hand, he rested it on her chest. The palm was hot and made her head tingle. Slowly she felt it fill her body on the inside, then it traveled up and down her spine.

"Good. You felt that."

"Felt what? What did I feel?"

"I sent loving thoughts to your heart. I love that you felt it. That says a lot to me. I'll tell you more as we go," he said, as he put her head back to his chest. "You really should get some rest. It's late and this day has been a hard one. Mind you, it couldn't have ended better."

Was he actually psychic? He joked about it, but . . . How did he know she felt it?

"You can say that again," she sighed. "Is this real? It feels like a dream. If it's a dream I never want to wake up."

"This is very real. I'll be here when you wake, so get some sleep," he whispered squeezing her in.

Not long after Faith dozed off. Archer was happy to be there, but laid looking at the ceiling, just listening to the clock. He was a bit of a night owl.

Realizing it had been some time since he'd last done a serious meditation, he closed his eyes. Picturing a light from above, sparkles and glitter filled the air and settled onto his skin, lighting him up. Colours flashed before his eyes as if travelling at lightspeed and he struggled to catch glimpses of images that floated past his sight.

They'd come into view then fade, barely leaving a trace before the next came. As he allowed them to come, Archer's eyes stopped darting around to see each one.

Deep in it now, everything went white, and he felt himself be wrapped in the peace that he was very familiar with. Like going to sleep, but fully aware of the transition.

Moving from his body, the weightlessness overtook him, and he drifted up and up, until high above the ground. Up and up more, the land became blobs on the blue dot he called home. The image he had, floating out, was hard to see. Everything just became a blur, like time didn't exist. Only sensations. Perceptions twisting into something nearly indefinable.

Floating through space now, passing planets, galaxies, and suns, Archer began to feel a pull and found himself swooping down onto a planet, soaring over the surface.

There were so many types of trees and animals. Like he'd never have been able to imagine. But wasn't this his imagination?

He didn't know anymore and the flight went on for miles, until he felt himself swooping again. Up he went through its purple clouds, past more planets and so many more star systems than he'd ever dreamt of. Still, more, littered the distance.

Feeling a pull take him down onto a massive planet, chrome looking he thought. It seemingly called to him. The feeling that he had little to no control, felt soothing to him in this place. Not like when he was in his body. Worries and fears became curiosity and excitement. The only wonder was, *what is it?* No thoughts of protection were needed.

Closer and closer he went, until he penetrated the atmosphere. It was very warm and smelled of melons, and, as he drew closer to the surface, Archer could see buildings. Closer still, there was roads and people.

They seemed to be on a mission of their own and didn't care to notice him, and as he came down to rest, his feet touched the chrome street. Expected it to be cold, it looked as though it was liquid, but was just a polish, and very warm.

Looking around at all the buildings, Archer saw many kinds. Humble ones, palaces, shacks, and skyscrapers lined the path. Walking until he felt drawn to one in particular, it looked like a museum or library. Large, white pillars held the entirety of the roof and it felt familiar somehow. Like . . . home . . .

Climbing the steps, Archer could hear a humming sound. Deep and rhythmic. As he opened the double front doors, it grew louder, maybe even more in unison or the depth of the voices together.

Huge cathedral walls greeted him. Not what he thought to expect from when he'd seen the outside. Stained glass windows reflected their patterns on the mirror-like, white floor and Archer's footsteps echoed all through the large hall. Like on the stairs of the gallery. Many doors lined along the sides, but he didn't feel particularly drawn to any, and so, left the large room and started down the hall.

Following the hum, it turned into a voice that said welcome, welcome, and tears filled his eyes though he wasn't sad. It was like a response to the relief he was feeling. The ease of letting all his worries disappear in defeat of love. The urge to receive enveloped him now, as the words went back into the humming sound and filled his chest, bouncing around. It lifted his feet from the floor, floating him down the rest of the hall, where scenes from his life were displayed on the walls. Good and bad.

Some were bright and vibrant, some were faded. Some dismal and distorted. Scene after scene presented itself in the long hall until, faintly at the end, he could see a pillar.

Focused on it, Archer could feel himself speed up. The more he focused the faster he went. Until he found himself right there in front of it.

A light shone down from someplace above that he couldn't get a bead on, seeming as though it were everywhere and nowhere at the same time. Just then, a tiny speck of dust floated down so slowly, he thought he'd go mad waiting for it to land. Down, down, down it came, closing the gap between the light source and the top of the pillar that was also polished to a mirror finish.

It got closer and closer and closer. Then, tilting his head sideways, Archer watched, so close now it was almost touching and seemed as one, and like time froze, he looked at them both.

The pillar, then the dust, the pillar, then the dust. An overpowering urge to blow it away came over him and he did it impulsively. Destroying the agony of torture, waiting for it to fully touch its reflection.

Ceasing all other possibilities, it floated up into the air creating a billion new possibilities. Infinite in nature. Unquantifiable.

The hum in his chest became his own voice. "I only but need to make the decision to dispel my worries, as I'd done to the speck of dust. Opening myself to all possibilities."

He'd said it out loud, though the words never came from his lips, in an instant, Archer felt himself be lowered to the floor as the coolness touched his feet. Turning around, he felt as though the message was received and it was time to go.

Walking on his own all the way down the hall, Archer took a better look at the images he'd seen on the way in, and realized the colourful scenes were ones he had held close in his heart or repeated in his mind. Some unwanted, as they made him feel a looming negativity. It was outside of him, though, not on the inside like he'd have felt in his body.

Let them go, he heard in his head and, though, not knowing entirely how, he did. The thickness in his chest disappeared.

Going the full length of the hall, Archer said his final goodbyes to the memories, and didn't feel an ounce of loss. Through the front doors he walked, and stepping onto the front steps, he was whisked away, like a bolt of lightening. *Whoosh!*

In seconds he found himself hovering above his body. Whatever the force was that had taken him, he asked for it to stop. A millimetre before entering his body, he did stop. Nose to nose, like the pillar and the dust, he thought to pull back and did.

What? he thought. *Back more,* he spoke in his thoughts, and he did.

Watching himself lay there with Faith under his arm, possibly the only chance he'd ever have to witness this, Archer wanted to see. To take it all in. All of it. Like he was branding it on his soul. Them together. Happy. Forever . . .

When satisfied, he eased back into his body, by thought alone, and felt its weight take him over. The first thing he noticed was the clock. Tick, tick, tick . . . Maybe part of his obsession with clocks. It reminded him of his mother's heartbeat when he first came into the body. The one she and his father had made together.

Tears were streaming down his face. Tick, tick, tick on the pillow. Like Faith's dream. Maybe it wasn't a dream. Maybe it was a vision!

Faith moaned and rolled over. Archer could feel she was sweating. He was always really hot, and her wild hair probably wasn't helping.

Gently, slinking his arm out from under her neck, Archer turned the fan on to low. Enough to move the air some, then took the robe from the chair.

Feeling quite euphoric now, after such an insane day, he was incredibly thirsty.

Being overwhelmed by meeting Faith. How he felt so powerfully towards her, and all they shared together in such a short time. Their connection, Jonsie, their confessions, the way Faith said she didn't even know how to begin to leave him now, and the love they'd just made.

The out-of-body experience was quite a heavy load. He'd need time to absorb it. All of it! The entire week was . . . out of this world.

What has the universe got in store for me now? he thought grabbing the water jug from the fridge. His throat felt like a desert, so downed the whole glass, then another, and still poured a third that he took to the patio.

Leaning over the rail and looking to the stars that he'd just seen in his vision, once whirling and savagely violent, all he saw now was, specks. Feeling insignificant, yet all powerful in his own strengths, he said a thank-you and walked down the stairs. The moon was high in the sky, and Archer craved to see it on the water.

Setting the glass on the bottom step of the patio, Archer thought he'd pick it up when going back in. The thirst had subsided some and water sploshed around in his belly when he walked.

The dew on the grass was cooling, as he walked through the yard, making his way for the cliff. The light of the full moon shone on the trees and the top of the pillar rock. It called to him. Like the pillar in his own temple, there on that planet, in god knows what galaxy or reality. It started to make some sense now.

The pillar. It must have been significant. He hadn't had it on his mind, and never forced the visions, always letting them come as they may.

Sometimes he knew exactly what they meant. Other times? It would take months or years before he'd see the relevance, as if they were premonitions or tools on the journey of life. Archer had heard, from psychics he'd watched online, that they were. Not believing in that hogwash, he also took his own opinion of that at face value. Until they became more.

A woman he'd dated briefly was a tea leaf reader, telling him a few tales of clients, and how she was just *so* accurate, people would come to see if anything bad would happen. She'd tell them and it *always* came true.

Archer believed that "you speak things into creation," so asked her if she felt bad for making those horrible things happen to people. She had no idea what he meant and just stormed off. Archer didn't give two shits either. Those people were ignorant and careless in his opinion. They had no idea about quantum entanglement or anything of the sort. High on themselves. Telling people things, they didn't want to happen, which was the reason they did.

Seeing into one timeline, or whatever was going on, and pulling into another possibility, maybe they were getting things mixed up with their all-knowing-ness . . .

Suggestion is very powerful.

They should have been helping people build themselves up and stop spreading doom and gloom. There were too many to count. It irritated him and so he washed his hands of it. It was junk as far as Archer was concerned.

A person's job was to elevate themselves and then give from the overflow. What she was doing was guessing she knew the answer, and setting it in stone for her client, if they believed her. That was not love and he wanted nothing to do with it.

Listening to the waves lap on the shore, Archer watched the shimmer of the moon reflecting on the ocean, like diamonds at his feet. After making his way down the steep stairs, the wood ticked under his foot.

Just like . . . the clock . . . like his tears on the pillow. *So* many things were becoming relative to him now and his body was humming with a sense of unity . . . like a song . . . uni (one), verse (song). His mind exploding with possibilities. Like the message of the dust from the vision. One thing running into the next, he drew lines in his head to make a map. Possibly find a way out.

But everything just made more sense now. How he'd built his empire, travelling the world, the synchronicity. Faith and that morning at the beach. The way she'd come to his cafe later that day. How she'd returned the next afternoon, pleasantly surprising him, after he'd been feeling dread about their appointment. The way she filled him up.

He'd asked for this and remembering Faiths words, he just prayed . . . that he wasn't the one dreaming now.

As his foot hit the sand, the robe wasn't far behind. Naked now, Archer waded into the water, feeling as though he were being baptized by it, and blessed by the moon beams. Hope in his future, with amazing new experiences, hoping a child would be his next dream realized. Certain he had Faith now; he'd walk into it all proudly. Fully aware. With deliberation. Unapologetically "Archer" and take what came as a gift, even if he couldn't see the outcome.

Don't expect from others to do that, which you, are not prepared or willing to expect from yourself, he thought. He had, in a way, expected Faith to have done that, not even knowing her struggles.

Thinking, *That was wrong of me. Expecting her to do what I hadn't thought to do myself.* He'd ask her forgiveness later.

Hopefully she'd do the same then in their journey together, *if* she chose to come. Fully. Unapologetically "Faith."

He'd guide her if needed, walk with her, and together they could grow. Not demanding her to be what he needed to feel pleased. Archer knew his happiness was his to create. It wasn't her job to please him. He'd wait for her if she needed time. He'd fight beside her if she needed him to be strong. It was all about ebb and flow and standing beside his mate. To never rush or push her, just being there. To lift her up and hold her tenderly. Lovingly.

Happiness was his to define, but now, it weighed heavily in Faith's hands. In the end, though, Archer would have no one to blame, for his pain or disappointment, but himself. Both of them were free to choose what they wished, and for the other to be okay with the choices they each made. Archer was trusting her and setting her free simultaneously. So many things existing in the same time and space. The lines were blurred yet he felt the space between them. Life was so very good.

Once in the water to his thighs, Archer sank in. With all his might he prayed. "Please. If there is a god. Please. I've waited so long, been diligent, fallen and picked myself up, hated and forgiven, I've revelled and suffered. Surely, you could see fit to bring me the love of my life, and maybe you already have. Maybe she sleeps soundly in the bed we just shared. Either way, I accept all of it, no matter the challenge. Please. A child *must* be on the horizon. I beg you . . . I'll be more patient . . . but please . . . have mercy on me."

Feeling heard; Archer rose to the surface slowly and swam. There was no tugging from the currents, so drifted lazily, keeping his position gently with his arms. The sound of the water making him feel peaceful.

Faith woke a little then and reached for him. There was nothing but bed and sat up quickly, calling him. Nothing came back so she got up and saw that the robe she'd laid out for him on the chair was gone, hoping he was at least still there. Probably naked under that robe too.

Clapping her hands and rubbing them together, her mind went quickly to the love they'd made earlier, and hoped maybe she could talk him into being that again.

Taking the other robe, Faith slipped it on and went to the kitchen. The lights were on low, and the sliding doors were open, so called to him out the open patio door. No return yet. Calling again, she still had no reply. So, walking to the edge of the patio steps, she saw the cup of water flicker in the moonlight and knew where he was now. He'd become slightly predictable to her. Familiar. It felt nice, though.

Following his footprints from the stairs, across the grass, leading to the beach, atop the stairs she looked around, then saw the splash. "Archer, you foolish man!" she shouted, loud enough for him to hear.

As Faith descended the stairs, Archer heard her and spun round. The water sprinkled through the air from his hair. Like that first day he'd saved her hat. Only this time, it was the moonlight that dazzled in the droplets. Faith felt graced to have seen both the sun and moon spray from him. He surely was both to her now. Her sun and her moon, happy and brightening her world. Day and night. "How's the water?!" she yelled out.

"*Glorious!*" he hollered. "*Whoooo!*"

Now having swam closer, Archer was standing just off the shore, Faith could see he was naked. "Come in," he asked, and she laughed. "What? Come in," he asked again.

"Stop," she giggled.

Splashing through the water towards her, he whined, "C'moooonnnnnn!" but Faith just wiggled in her robe and wrapped it tighter.

"Are you scared?" he asked, trying to provoke her, walking up, completely naked, he promised, "You'll be safe with me."

"I don't know . . . I've never done that."

"Never?"

"Never," she stated firmly.

"Me either," Archer whispered in her ear, as he held her. "C'mon. How many chances like this will we get. Life is for living," he begged.

"Well . . ." she hummed.

Pulling the tie open on her robe, she let him in. Archer pushed the sides, opening the front, his cold hands on her skin made her scream.

"See? No one can even hear you," he whispered in her ear. "I can do whatever I want to you down here," he teased. "If you let me, that is."

"Mmmm, I don't know," she said, getting cold feet after almost consenting to a moonlight skinny dip.

"Well. I'm going back in. It's beautiful. I'll have to imagine your wet naked body in the moonlight, I guess. Mmmmm," he growled.

"Mmmm," was all she could say.

Head swimming now, Faith said he was cruel.

"Okay. Well. I'm going innnnn," he sang tauntingly, and hid his package. "If you want some, you'll have to come get me. *All this and more could be yours!*" he laughed, on the way to the water.

Seeing every curve of him as he turned and went back to the water, Faith yelled, "*Argh! You suck!*" and took off her robe, running to the shore.

Hearing her steps thump on the sand, then splash in the water behind him, Archer turned around to see her leaping, and caught her . . . Barely.

With a devilish grin he said, "I'll suck whatever you want, as long as you please."

"Promises, promises," Faith giggled. "You can't threaten me with a good time and get away with it, you know."

"Say what you mean and mean what you say," he replied and kissed her as he took them to deeper water. "Right now, though, it's swim time. You'd better prepare. It's not super warm like during the day, but it's wicked once you adjust. Stay close. You can swim, but I'm keeping an eye on you. It can take you out faster than you realize. I do it every day."

"Okay. Yer the boss," she teased, taking his hand. "Lead the way."

They walked out and Faith groaned a few times before deciding to just dunk under and get it over with. "*Whooo!*" she yelled loudly.

"Right?" he laughed.

"This is actually a rush," she said, floating a bit with her feet still on the bottom.

"Don't get brave now," he said ordered.

"Sir, yes, sir," she giggled.

Swimming so long the sun had started to come up. They laughed and loved, not really wanting to get out, but they were both hungry and needed a drink, deciding that later on they'd start a fire.

On the way up from the shore they brainstormed about what would make the night better. Bring glow sticks, a blanket, food, water, and she'd play some guitar for him and maybe he'd sing with her under the moon. Paradise . . .

Faith suggested they take a shower and try to get some sleep and said, "No funny business," promising to give him whatever he wanted later.

They slept until noon with the drapes closed, keeping out the sun and heat.

Faith waking first, looked over to him, still asleep. Archer's back to her, she rolled over and put her arm around him.

"Morning, sunshine," she whispered into his back and kissed it.

"Morning, angel," he whispered back in a sleepy voice while picking up her hand. Kissing the palm of it, like that first night at the gallery, he then put it on his chest.

"Can I get you anything?" he groaned.

His sleepy voice was so cute to her. And sexy.

"I have you and it's all I need right now."

Faith kissed his back. Long, soft ones and Archer moaned every time she did.

"You feel soooo good," Archer told her as he rolled over to pull her into him.

It was slow and hard. So was his breathing. Getting lost in it, Faith nestled her head in his chest.

"That was awesome," she said, as his breath ran over her slightly bared shoulder.

"What was?" he asked, a bit groggy still.

"Waking up next to a god."

"Mmmmmmm," is what came back.

"I don't wanna get up," she retorted, like a bratty kid on a winter school day.

"Well. *We* have things to do! It's Friday. I thought we could go shopping. Maybe pick up something for Greta and Jonah. We also have wedding plans to make . . ."

Faith pushed away from him and said, "*What*?!"

"I'm teasing," he laughed.

Slapping his arm Faith grabbed his jaw in her tiny hand and saying, "Maybe so, but that's not funny. Never mention that again unless you mean it!"

"You're right, you're right. I'm sorry. That was kind of mean, now that I think about it." Archer then admitted, "I have thought about it, though."

Faith's eyes popped wide and she tried to push him away to look at his face. He'd locked his arms around her, though. Pushing a second time she said, "*Archer*!" in a serious tone.

"What?" he asked cool as a cucumber, eyes still closed.

Pushing again and he let her go, then reached for her face to touch it gently, but Faith slapped his hand. "What do you mean?"

Raising his eyebrows, Archer looked at her for a second.

"Archer. You talk . . . *right now*!" she demanded.

He liked this sassy little fireball he was holding onto. "What should I say?"

"Well. Start with what you're talking about and stop playing dumb," she growled.

"Well . . ." he said.

"Well!" she said back.

"And . . ." he said.

"*No and*! You haven't said the *well* part yet!" she charged, getting frustrated.

Archer sighed, "Well. I thought of us having a life together. How sweet you are. How we get along. It escalated . . . fast," he confessed.

"Yes. It was fast. I had merely thought of being your lady and here you have me in a dress," she said almost scolding him.

"Shhhh'yeahhhh," he winced. "Maybe I should have kept that to myself. I was just trying to joke around. You're right, though. It's not something to joke about."

"No. It's sweet," she said, finally calmed down. "Just freaked me out."

"I'm sorry, it wasn't my intention to rile you up that way."

"Did I look pretty?" she asked, poking fun back at him.

"You . . . looked . . . *stunning*!" he affirmed, taking the wind from her sails. "Except . . ."

"Except what?"

"There is only one thing that could ever be more beautiful," he sighed.

She knew what he meant. "Well, the future is there to discover and it's spotless. It's up to us to find the way. There is so much to look forward to. Most of my life I was just drifting. Until I left Jonsie. This trip I made was on a whim. I was looking for something. No idea what, at the time."

"Sometimes people do that. Throw caution to the wind," he agreed.

"I just wanted a new life. To leave the past behind me and become something greater. Feel some freedom and treat myself. Then I found you."

Archer's heart thumped hard. In his half-sleepy state, the word "welcome" flooded his head. It was the voice from his vision. Had his prayer been answered?

Faith continued. "If fate sees it fit that our future is together, I'll gladly accept it. Until then, all we have is today. We should make the most of it."

"I'd follow you anywhere."

"Archer?"

"Yes?" he responded, accepting her question but wasn't prepared for what came next. Faith was always so light-hearted and gentle, listening to his words. Intently. As if she were learning.

"I have some deep, burning questions. The kind that were never in my mind before we started talking. You speak of meditation, and I can see how you are. So together and composed. So strong and brave."

Flattered, he thanked her and let her continue.

"You're welcome," she said without hesitation. "So, here's the thing."

Searching to find the words she confessed. "I hope I say this right. If it's confusing let me know, okay?"

"I will. Go on."

Archer was very interested now.

"I heard once that you have the power to create your life by the thoughts you think. Some say it's habit that makes people successful. Like you . . . and so. Well . . . Argh," she groaned as Archer let her take the time she needed. "This is so hard."

Thinking more, they laid in the bed. Archer enjoying the moment.

"I'd like to know what you did, and I want to know your thoughts on life, and all the things in it. I know it could take a long time and I don't want a summary. I want the full version. I think we have time for that."

"Faith. It would take a lifetime to explain it, really. I'm still learning myself. Meditation speeds things up in my opinion. Or at least I think it does. It appears to. There's so very much."

"Well, I'm good with it taking a lifetime. I'll seriously do your meditations. I'll also do my best to not hold you up or slow you down."

"Whatever I can help you with, I surely would."

"Tell me a few things?"

"Was there something specific you wanted to know?"

"Yes. What do think about a person being a deliberate creator in their life. Is that possible? I mean. I know what I've lived. I know everything I've ever thought, and I think I see a correlation between them."

Then working it out in her mind, Faith continued, "Since I've been here, things have changed. I've changed, and what I mean is, is that I was always angry. Well, not always, but a lot of the time. Things seemed to just be hard. Then when I left Jonsie, and wanted something better, everything seemed to fall into place. Like magic. Do you believe that can happen?"

"I think it's quite likely to happen. I've studied this a great deal."

Laughing she said, "*Oh good*! 'Cause I felt like I might be losing my mind. Maybe I have. I don't know. Or did I just wake up from a nightmare. Is this the sweetest dream?"

"Life is what you make it. It's hard to say. Atoms have been known to be in multiple places at the same time. When the observer looks at it, it collapses into something temporarily solid."

"What? That's crazy. How does it know what to be? What's the observer?"

"That's the crazy part. No one knows. Religion calls it the soul. Some call it higher self. Others still call it Chi. Buddhism and science call it consciousness. Some say there is a universal consciousness. That we all contribute to it. That sleep is the time when you become non-physical. Meditation the same. Sex is another way to get there. Orgasm being the closest you can come without being dead."

"Good lord. That's a lot to take in. So, these atoms . . . What is going on there?"

"It seems to me like they time travel. Going forward to see what to become, then moving back into the past to be it. All existing at the exact same time. For us, time is just a construct of being human. To relate to one another. Have you ever thought of someone and remembered good times or bad. Then all of a sudden, they pop out of nowhere? Or seemingly no where?"

"Yes. I've had that happen."

"Some say you can do that for a parking space, for instance. A job or a house. Even a life partner and physical or mental healing."

Faith could use some mental healing after the life she'd lived. The abuse. The teasing. Her mother and the money problems. They all seemed to be just memories now that

Faith felt so far away from that life. They followed her like a pack of wolves, though.

"Yes, that's what I meant. Creating your reality. *So*, you believe that?" she asked.

"I can tell you this. I've tested it to my satisfaction, and I do my best to be in the right places at the right time. Mostly mentally. I did get quite negative, and the mental battle ensued about women. I really wanted . . . you . . . to be honest," Archer smiled and continued, "But all I found were superficial women, who wanted what I have. Not 'me.' Like I said. I didn't care for them either. The conversations were stale and fruitless. Verbal babbling to me. Then I'd remind myself that I created that, through my negative thinking. Back and forth it went. Noticing the gap all the time. It was so frustrating. Then I'd do my best to let it go. The absence, I mean. Slowly, it would creep on me again and then I'd argue with myself that I didn't feel it deeply enough. That maybe I wasn't specific enough. Then I'd argue that I shouldn't be. Who am I to say what a person should be. More arguments. It created the void again. It was a hell," Archer affirmed assuredly. "But I'll tell you this. If I found a place to just feel the feeling long enough . . . and really, I don't know where I was, or what I was doing, that allowed you into my life. I don't even care now. Whatever it was will never be known. Maybe I had to wait till you caught up to me. That's why I said you attracted the sea glass stopper. *Oh!*" he jumped.

Getting out of bed Archer went to his pants and dug in the pocket, then went back to lay beside her, then passed Faith the sea glass stopper.

"This belongs to you. It's the reason I came earlier than planned. Maybe you were creating more than you realize too."

Smiling, Faith just looked at the stopper, her brain exploding all over the place. The implications of it took her back. All of it held in her hand with that one piece of glass.

"I think I have to think on that. I can hardly wrap my mind around what just happened. Never mind all of the things before that. So bizarre."

"Welcome to my world," he joked.

"Is this what meditation does? Change your mind, I mean? Like. I've never had a deep thought in my life. Like, I was so basic," she admitted. "This all is overwhelming. Will it get better?"

"I don't know what it is for you. I only know what it is for myself. I'd love to hear all your ramblings, though. I'll warn you now that meditation can't hurt, it's the twisted nature of the undisciplined mind that's hell. It can really throw you off and sometimes it's hard to keep it all neatly packed," he laughed. "But it gets better. Don't let time pile up on you. Even if you feel you need to process it, another session might clear it up. Do as you feel. You may find yourself doing things out of the ordinary. Like a program update. You'll get used to it."

"Hm," was all Faith could say.

Looking forward to it somehow, Faith needed to have her mind filled. Feeling now, like she'd been starving her whole life, and never even knew it.

"We can talk more about that?"

"Anytime. Day or night. If you find yourself feeling lost. You call me," Archer said with a smile.

"Whether it's with me or not. I want to tell you that you'd be a great dad, Archer," she said hugging him.

"And you would be the most beautiful, lovely and wonderful mother."

CHAPTER TWENTY
It Is Decided

Archer hugged Faith tight and asked if she'd like coffee or something to eat.

"Coffee would be amazing. There are probably some biscuits left in the fridge too, I think. Warmed with butter, please, and the blueberry spread is in there too. It's from just up the road. Feel free to make yourself anything. There's eggs and bacon if you like," Faith suggested.

"You got it, cupcake. Stay right there, unless you need the bathroom or something. K?" Archer insisted cheerily.

"Yes, sir."

No man had ever made her breakfast in bed before.

Only her mother had. She'd done it a thousand times too. It's just how she was. Motherly and loving.

Rising from the bed, Archer strode the length of the room for the robe. Faith wondered again how she'd gotten so lucky then thought, *just* look *at him*!

"Can I put on some music?" Faith asked from the bedroom. "Something easy?"

"Yes, *god*, yes!" he yelled.

Going to the doorway, to not have to yell so loud, she said, "I wanted to make sure. I'm connected to all the speakers in the place and didn't want to freak you out," as she laughed.

"All good, baby girl."

That sounded so good to her, "baby girl."

Keeping it soft at first, Faith slowly turned it up, then set the phone down. In a minute she heard him whistling. How did he know that artist? They didn't have many followers on their web page yet. Maybe she and Archer had more in common than either of them had thought.

Smelling the coffee, Faith closed her eyes. Flashes from the day before ran through her mind. It was so insane. Like the death throws of her old life dying, Jonsie sat gurgling in the kitchen chair, broken.

Feeling bad for him, he *did* bring it on himself. *If there is a god up there*, she thought. *Give him peace, please.*

No feelings for him anymore, Faith wouldn't wish hell on anyone, if there even *was* one.

Like things were complete, Faith put her hands behind her head and hummed with Archer. Dishes clinked and she loved the sound. His soul, so close she could hear its energy.

Wow. She was getting the hang of this some. Listening, Faith found herself at peace, sinking deeper and deeper into the sounds he made, and dreamt of hearing Archer every single day. The thought of losing him now was unbearable.

Thinking then of her loose ends at home, the book nearly done, she wondered what the next year would bring. The hopes that the book would be popular, made her feel excitement and a sense of pride. The critic in her mind rattled around making noise, trying to distract.

"Not this time," Faith said aloud and went back to daydreaming.

The house she wanted to build, the travelling, nice cars, beautiful clothes, fancy restaurants too. All the things Archer could give her in a heartbeat, she wanted to earn them herself. The lavish homes she'd cleaned. That's what started her dreaming.

"*Hun*!" Archer yelled. "What do you take in your coffee?"

"Honey in the cupboard, coconut milk in the fridge. Most of all I'd like it with '*you*'!" she yelled back.

"Roger," he said, making her chuckle.

Faith heard him putting things on the tray, so sat up. Checking her phone, she noticed her publisher had sent an email and clicked it open.

Dear Miss Leone,

We are very excited to receive your first novel publication transcript. We hope everything is well and still on track for you. If you need assistance, please feel free to call.

If we don't hear from you soon, your agent will be in touch.

Congratulations on your achievement!

Faith set a reminder in her phone to call after the weekend as Archer came in.

"Everything okay?"

"Oh, yes. Just reading an email from the publisher. Had to make a note in the calendar," she said, typing in the agenda. "You sounded so cute out there. I have to say."

"Awww. Cute?"

"*Mmm hm*!" she replied cheerfully and put her phone away. "The sound made me feel happy."

"Now that's cute," he told her, placing the tray down on the nightstand. "How is the book coming anyway? Will you take a break after what happened?"

"Nope. My dreams won't be on hold for anything, but you," Faith answered then winked.

"Well, the way *you* won't hold *me* up, I'll give the same respect," he winked back, "I may pause you briefly, though, if that's okay."

"Oh, yes," she smiled, "Smells so good!"

"Here, madam."

"*Ooohee*. I'm starved!"

Taking the plate, Faith smiled and thanked him.

"Coffee," Archer said passing it like an offering.

The first sip always the best, she closed her eyes and tasted every molecule. Especially after the talk they had about the atoms. Everything seemed . . . different.

Coming to his side of the bed Archer sat, saying, "I have the same. I wanted to see why this is so good for you. I didn't make a big breakfast. Maybe we can hit the diner today if you would."

"Yes, sounds good," she said back then took another sip. "Hope you like the dessert breakfast."

With his mug in hand, Archer brought it up for a cheer. Faith took her cup as he said.
"To you and I, to dreams and blue skies,
To heaven and earth, and all that it's worth,
To hills and valleys, to trees and seas,
To all the wonders, to all that be,
To all the things I dare not dream,
To all that is, and all that seems."

She'd never heard anything like that and with her green eyes in amazement, Faith said, "Archer. That was beautiful!" then took another sip of coffee to help gulp down her emotions. "Is that a poem you read?"

"No. It came from a vision."

"How long ago was that?"

"About 10 years ago I think."

"You remembered it? How did you remember that?" she asked astonished.

"Ya. My mind is like that. There're things I desperately want to unsee," he laughed.

"Good grief. Your brain is unreal. What was the vision?"

Archer took a bite of the biscuit, his face scrunched up and enjoying the flavour, Faith waited for him to swallow before answering her.

"How have I not had this before? It's delicious."

"Right?"

Swallowing another bite, he washed it down with a few sips of coffee, then began to tell the tale of the vision.

"After a trip to India, I learned that I'd been meditating my whole life, just not that seriously. I took a hike up the side of a mountain, while Johanna had a photo shoot. There was this really, really sketchy bridge that I felt drawn to cross. It scared the crap out of me, and I knew I had to do it again to get to where I was staying. I delayed a bit and took a walk around and found a site that had some digging done on it but seemed to be halted. There were massive stones all around. Cubed. I climbed on one and sat. It was so peaceful. The view was amazing. Thinking about what I had learned while I was there, I sat to do a meditation. A good and serious one, hoping to calm myself down for the walk back over that damn bridge," he laughed.

Faith hung on tensely, eating her biscuit. Archer had another bite and a sip of coffee before returning to the story. "*So*! Anyway. As I sat there, a feeling that the site was sacred somehow, I was shoved right into a vision. Someone had taken me to the shore and as we sat in the car on the cliff, and kids were running around. I don't even know who drove me there. It's fuzzy. Probably not relevant anyway," Archer said shrugging, then had another bite.

He was leaving *her* on a cliff with how he was telling the story. *A real cliffhanger*, Faith giggled to herself, fascinated with this story. Done of the biscuit, Faith drank more coffee and watched him as he continued.

"I'm not sure, either, how I got out of the car, but I went down the steps and onto the beach. This old guy was standing there polishing bottles, all of them were different. They were bent and stretched. Every colour I could imagine. I wasn't sure why he was polishing them. He was really old. I could tell by his hair and eyes, though his body was very young. He reminded me of a surfer dude. Ratty cut-off jeans and a faded tank top with stains. His hands were dirty and his brown leather sandals were very, very worn. Passing me the bottle he was polishing, I looked over the beach, and I could see glass *everywhere*! So I yelled to the kids that they would get cut and to stop running. The old guy touched me, and I had to tear my eyes away from the danger on the beach. In another respect, I couldn't stop it. When I looked at him finally, he told me those words."

"And you never forgot them?" she asked.

"No. They burned into my soul," he replied. "So, I'm there, holding this bottle, and all of the stress I had disappeared when he spoke. It was so bizarre!"

"Yeah. That is. What do you think it meant?" Faith asked then.

Popping the last bite in his mouth he muttered, "I'm not certain. It was profound, though. I thought maybe it was telling me to leave Johanna. That she wouldn't give me what I so badly wanted. That I was wasting my time, maybe the creator had a better idea for me, and I should pay attention. Hindsight is 20/20, though." Then smirked.

After telling Faith the story, Archer thought, maybe it was god telling him that Faith was coming and that he should free himself up and be more perfect. As to enjoy her more deeply.

It seemed obvious now. The sea glass, the bottle, the kids and his worry. Not knowing how he arrived on the cliff. Tuning back into their conversation, he kept it to himself. For now.

"Live and learn, I suppose."

"True. What's the alternative?"

"I suppose what we discussed earlier?" she said, as if wanting to talk more. "What if the bottle was a symbolic gift? As if to say, not there, here," she suggested.

"That's kind of deep, eh? Maybe you're not as broken as you think."

How did Archer know that she felt broken? Did she tell him? Use those words? Faith suspected Archer knew more than he was letting on.

"What made you pick those words?"

"Don't know. Popped into my head. I did listen to everything you've said. You need to believe in yourself more. You're brighter than you realize."

"It's weird you chose those particular words. That's what I actually thought, though I didn't use that terminology. You may be right, though," she sighed, having been hard on herself.

"Faith. You are a beautiful woman. Inside and out. You're strong and self-reliant. Very smart. Look what you've taken on by turning to become an author. Without even having a plan? Do you know how brave that is?"

"Seems stupid to me now," Faith answered and hung her head.

Setting his mug down, then taking hers, Archer sat up. Taking her hands, he squeezed just a bit. "Hey! You listen, missy. You're following your heart, and you have no idea what kind of guts that takes. Even when the world would whip you into submission of a daily grind, you asked for something better. Divinely inspired ideas struck you and you're going for it! Doubt will kill your dream. Please, don't do that. You're a powerful creator and I have your back," he assured her.

"I don't want your money, Archer." Fait said a bit upset.

"I wasn't suggesting that. I meant moral support. Someone in your corner cheering you on and watching you step into the fullness of yourself. You can't imagine how proud it makes me to be able to stand by you now. When you step right into the fullness of that, I can say, *'Ya, baby girl! Woooo! You did it! Look at you go!'*" Pointing out into the room, as if at her gala, Archer had a huge smile on his face, then said, "That's my girl. You see that? *Mine*!" he laughed and pretended to push people aside, so she could walk proudly. "Your courage has, is, and will be noticed."

"I'm sorry. I have more things to work on, I guess," Faith admitted.

"No problem. We all do. No one's perfect. Just different battles at different times. You'll find your way. Maybe I can help or at least keep you company," he said and kissed her.

"I'd like that."

"Let's get ready and get something at the diner. Okay?" he suggested, then slapped her leg and squeezed.

"Yes. Let's go!"

Once ready they got in Archer's car and went off to town.

At the diner, Ada was happy to see Faith again. "Hi, dear!" she said coming to serve her, when Archer walked in behind her. "Oh! And Archer too."

Giving a slight giggle Ada tried to hide the smile. Oh, she knew. Long before they ever walked in together. "Would you like a booth or the counter?"

"Hi, Ada darling. We'll take the counter?" Archer said as a question to Faith, while rubbing the small of her back.

No problem with public displays of affection, Faith thought to herself. Very good.

"Counter, please." Faith answered.

Ada took them right over from her side of the counter, after grabbing mugs. Placing them down she asked, "How were the tarts, dear?"

"Oh, god. I forgot about them with all the things that went on," she said to Archer.

"Yes. I heard about it all. That was so sad. Are you alright, dear?"

Wow, Faith thought. Things travel fast in small towns. "Was it on the news?"

"Oh, no, dear. My daughter, Mary, is a nurse at the hospital. She told me about it all after getting home from work. It really shook her up," Ada said pouring their coffee.

"You really should have gotten a checkup. How do you feel? I could get her to run over and see you."

"Oh, no, no. I'm fine Ada. Really. Archer's been keeping an eye on me." Faith smiled, rubbing Archer's arm.

"Well, couldn't be much better than a doctor himself."

"Ada, stop." Archer smiled.

"What will you have, or do you want a few minutes?" she asked to change the subject.

"I know what I want. We'll let Faith have a minute, though?" Archer said.

"Sure, dear. Let me know when you're ready," Ada said and went into the kitchen.

Archer drank coffee, while Faith read the menu. He knew the comment about the incident upset her and just rubbed her back. After deciding what she wanted, Archer checked to see if she was alright. With his eyes. Faith just nodded and smiled.

"So. Would you like me to drop you off and maybe see you tomorrow? I can stay, though, if you'd like. I don't mind."

Faith thought a minute. "Well. You know. I have the book to get done and I'm sure you have things you need to do, so, how about we call it a night. After a moonlight swim?"

"That sounds like a great idea, actually. I totally loved that. It's not perfectly full anymore. Officially. But we won't tell," he winked.

Faith was about to say something, but Ada came back. "So, lovelies. What will you have?"

With their orders taken, Ada went to the kitchen and Archer heard Birt say hi to him while scraping the grill. Archer's burger was always specific and Birt growled the first time, but now he knew. It wasn't complicated. It just wasn't "farmer's style." Slap it together and slam it on the plate.

"Hey, Birt," Archer hollered, then asked Ada to bring some water.

When she returned, Archer then asked Ada about the family. Faith listened in to get to know her. Ada was brief and asked more about Faith. Where she was from, if she had family. All the usual questions an old lady would be interested in.

Before they'd finished eating, Ada thought about what Faith had said and felt bad for her. She really had nobody, and that incident must have been horrifying.

"Well, dear. It's good you have Archer keeping you company," Ada said directly Faith. "Can I get you dessert?" she asked then with an air about her that Faith found charming and powerful.

"Yes. Dessert would be good," she responded. Her meal wasn't big and she certainly wasn't full yet.

"How about a tart since you didn't get to them?" Ada asked and Faith thought that was a great plan.

Setting them each down a tart, with a small scoop of ice cream, Ada said sweetly, "On the house, dears."

Thanking her, Archer and Faith had the tarts. Both of them agreed, they were wonderful. Before leaving, Ada had put a few more in a little box to take home for later. Then, just like that, they were off. Back to her cottage.

Getting into the car, Faith mentioned they should stop and get some glow sticks in case anything happened. It was a quick stop to the gas station.

Chatting on the drive, Archer asked about the book. How much she had done and when she'd be finished, and Faidh stated that she'd hoped to have it completed on Monday. Now, after that episode, it would likely be one more week.

"I wanted to publish to get wealthy and spend my days doing whatever I wanted. Maybe write more. In my mind it sounds so good, then my critical side starts at me, I get frustrated and find it hard to get any of it done. Like it's work. After reading a bit, for editing, I get my motivation back as thoughts brew in my mind."

"That can be troublesome. We all have that critic I think, though some would never admit it."

"It's so funny how I'd just come to live with it. Like there was nothing I could do about it. It's held me back so much," Faith sighed and corrected herself. "Or I've *let* it hold me back."

"Wow. That was awesome. Do you see what you just did there? You took your power back. I'm so happy for you. And don't worry, it's okay, you're still young. Some never get successful till they are in their fifties."

"God. Don't tell me that. Fifty is a long way away. If the book doesn't fly by then, I don't know what I'll do."

Looking out the window, Faith feared the worst.

"Don't be afraid. That'll put a wrench in. Plug through. Have fun. You're doing a great job. Besides. You're a survivor. You'll do just fine no matter what you take on, I believe, and really, either way I'll make sure you're okay. Wealthy from your book or not."

Faith had always financially struggled but couldn't imagine living off of her man. It just wouldn't sit right. She didn't say that, but did say, "That's sweet of you. I think the book is gonna do great, though."

"I hope it does. You'll be so proud of yourself. I'm already proud of you. Without the book sales."

Now back at the cottage, Faith put the tarts in the fridge, on top of the other ones she'd forgotten about.

"Can I ask a favour?" Archer asked.

"You can ask, but I suspend saying yes until I hear it."

"Can you play some guitar and sing more for me?"

"Oh, yes. I can do that for sure.'

"We should've gotten some wood on the way," he said disappointingly. "We could've had a bonfire."

"There's wood under the back stairs. Three piles, I think," Faith informed him, before going to the mudroom and taking keys off the high shelf.

"*Yes!*" he exclaimed excitedly as she passed him a key. "Is there a cupboard? This unlocks it?"

"No, it's just under the steps. That's for the cottage. I want you to come and go as you please."

"Are you serious?"

"Very," she simply said.

Just beginning to say, "You don't hav—" she cut him off this time.

"I know," she said back as Archer hugged and kissed her. "Get your clothes from the car and put them in the drawer of the dresser? On your side."

His side, he thought, and spun her around excitedly. "Go, go, my little muse. I need my siren," then set her down and patted her behind to scoot.

"Once I get things together, I'll get us some wine?"

"I think, because we'll swim later, I'll want to be sober. Can't protect you if I'm half buzzed. You have some, though, if you like."

"Fair enough," Faith agreed. "I love how you're so responsible. I also love your playful side," she said, patting *his* behind now as he turned to go to the car.

"Mmmmissy. You'd better stop."

"Good. Glad I can make you squirm the way you do to me."

"Oh, you'll be squirming later," he whispered.

"What?" she asked.

"What?" he asked back. "Watch yourself. You'll stir the beast in me," Archer informed her, as he closed the door.

That would be fine with her, after the other night. She'd take all of the beast he'd give.

When Archer came back in, Faith had blankets, pillows, and water for them both, as she'd decided wine was certainly *not* the best idea.

Archer took the bag to the bedroom to do as Faith had asked. She followed while brushing her hair some as he unpacked his bag.

"I'll get Sophia. You grab the wood?"

"I'm already getting wood," Archer replied.

"What?" she asked.

"What?" he asked back.

Faith sneered at him then laughed.

"I'm already getting wood!" he repeated, and Faith couldn't help laughing more that he didn't get the joke. Her mind in the gutter, she immediately heard that perversely.

"What?" Archer asked, then two seconds later understood. "Stop! I meant I'll *get* the wood. I'm out there now. Can't you see me? Get yer mind out of the gutter, bad girl," he said as if he were innocent.

Reaching over, Faith slapped his behind again and Archer squealed dramatically, stood, turned to face her staring, then continued putting clothes in the drawer. When she did it again, he jumped away, squealing once more and jokingly stated. "Stop harassing me!"

Faith grabbed him and pushed her body into his as Archer backed away. "What? What? Madam!" he cried, in a girly kind of way.

It was hilarious, but Faith felt naughty then, becoming more serious. Pawing at his and kissing his bare chest that poked from his button-up shirt. For a minute Archer enjoyed it, but really, wanting to behave for now, he then carried on the game.

"Stawwwwpppp!" he whined, as he left the bedroom through the patio door with his arms flopping and hands waving.

"Yer no fun," Faith grumbled.

Turning to look at her with a funny scowl, Archer stuck his tongue out. "I'm getting out of here before I don't let you out of here," he said dramatically again and closed the door fast with another squeal as she lunged for him.

It reminded her of a funny cartoon character she'd seen. Archer could hear her laughing hysterically as he ran down the steps to get the wood.

Taking a bag of it to the pit, he found a hatchet on top of the pile. Both in hand, he stacked it neatly beside the fire for quick feeding. Some he split for kindling, then lit the fire. Boy Scouts had served him in that department. It was going within seconds.

Faith came out with a tray of water, the two tarts, chips, and cookies. Neither of them ate much junk food, but today was special.

Running over, Archer met her at the bottom of the stairs and took them.

"Thank you." Faith smiled and he bowed, "you're welcome".

Faith went back in for blankets and pillows. He came for those as well. When she'd come back with her guitar case, Archer took it from her, and they walked together to the fire. Paired with the full moon, the flames were lighting the yard nicely. The blanket already spread, Archer held Faith's hand as she sat, and put the case beside her.

Pausing her, with a finger in the air, Archer said, "Oh. One sec," then went to the patio and took big fluffy cushions from the chairs. "*Idea*!"

"Lean up?"

"Oh. That *is* a good idea," she complimented as he pushed it under her.

"There now," he said, as if to say she could sit.

"Oh, so much better. You think of everything."

"Well, not everything. I have my days," Archer said as he sat across from her by the logs as she opened the case.

"What do you want to hear?"

"Something contemporary," he suggested.

Faith put her fingers to her chin to think as Archer poked the fire, added more kindling, then piled on a few logs. There was a decent bed of coals now.

Staggering the logs to let the air flow, the flames grew and the crackle that came from them, as the wind blew through, was sweet to his ears. Catching the wood just so, glowing bits of ash rose into the air. With a big sigh, Archer sat on his cushion with his poker stick.

Watching he dreamed of a future with her, then let it go. All of it. It would be what it would be.

There was no need to protect his heart anymore, feeling he had her, Archer would do whatever it took to keep her, *and* keep her pleased. Whatever it meant.

Faith named a bunch of musicians and Archer "Yepped" every one, as he poked at the fire.

Faith could see his white teeth between the flickering and the dark. The rise and fall of the flames as he stoked the fire. As he so graciously had done to her not that long ago.

"If you'd sing with me, I'd love that. You can tell me what song. If I don't know it, I can probably fake it."

"OMG! Yer sooo gooood," he said, like Faith was a star, and he was her valley girl groupie, then smiled to himself.

Laughing, Faith told him he was silly. Then snorted.

"*Ha!*" he hollered, pointing at her, and they both laughed then.

"Stop! I can't laugh and sing at the same time," she complained, but not complaining at all. "Which reminds me."

"Okay. Okay. I'll stop," he said and pretended to zip his lips.

Still giggling, Faith started to play and finished her thought. "If you don't mind swearing, there's one I'd like to do for you. I laughed so hard when I found it."

"Fuck ya. Do it!"

"Okay. The other one's first. I have to remember the lyrics. It'll come to me, though."

She then played all the ones he'd suggested, then began to play one of her favorites. Archer laid back on the blanket and put the cushion under his head, saying, "*Yes!*" then clapped along.

He sang with her in the chorus. Just softly, though. Really just letting loose, it seemed he glowed. She'd have played all night to keep him like that.

"Damn, baby girl. That was *wicked*! Do 'the thing.'"

"The thing?"

"Yaaaaa. The thing you said. That tune you suggested. Doooo ittttt!" he said in a kind of a whisper.

"Okay," she giggled, remembering the words.

The melody was upbeat, and Archer kept time with his snaps. Doing one turnaround, he waited for the words to begin.

The lyrics were clever, and he listened sharply as Faith maintained a decent composure to pronounce them all. When she'd finished it, he was laughing uncontrollably. "See? That's what happened to me when I heard it," she howled.

"That was *fucking hilarious*!"

Crawling over, Archer took her face, kissed her with a tiny peck, then sat back down. "How did you ever find that?"

"It was in an app I have on my phone. Sometimes I put it on and let it ride. I've found some great material that way," Faith said with a big smile. "That one I just *had* to learn!"

"*That* is a *keeper*!"

"I wasn't sure I would remember all the words to do it for you, but they came . . . In pieces, but they came. Phew!" she said and wiped her brow. "Is there something you want to hear?"

Trying to think, nothing was coming. "Hmmmm . . . Can I think on it? Maybe play your favourite one?"

Plucking on the strings, Faith said, "Sure."

While she picked, Archer began to recognize the song. Chasing Cars.

"Oooh, good one."

Laying back, he was silent and let her play, staring at the moon. So many sounds came from the guitar. It was a nice instrument.

Softly and slowly her face became very serious. One of the best and touching songs, in his opinion.

"If I lay here . . ." he sang with her, and Faith felt her soul dancing.

Archer harmonized with her perfectly, letting her sing the verse, then joined her again for the chorus. Letting her go on her own again.

Faith continued. Archer laid there looking at the moon, lost in the music, and in her. At the end of the song, Faith rang a chime that went out across the yard and bounced back from the trees and with a surprised face, she looked at him. "Oh! Did you hear that?" she asked and tilted her head.

That was it . . . he'd decided . . . He'd marry this woman. How could he not?

"That was so beautiful, I nearly cried," Archer admitted.

"I know how you feel . . ."

Faith didn't understand how deeply she'd touched him. "I'd heard someone do it at open mic and I did cry. I vowed to learn it, and couldn't find the chords anywhere, so I had to figure it out myself. It was hard, but realized my drive, when I finally got it."

"You did a wonderful job," Archer complimented.

"Thank you, doll," she smiled then exclaimed, "Oh!"

Asking if he knew a few songs she'd thought of at the last minute archer said, "Hells ya. Sweet tunes. Give'r. Then we'll have a tiny snack and go for a swim."

"Deal!"

Archer took everything in when she finished. Faith followed to get towels and their robes. The fire was dying down, so they just let it go. The trees and cottage were a good distance from it, so there was no harm.

Swimming for hours, they splashed and hollered. Floated and talked.

Not being able to help it, they made love. In his arms she was nearly weightless in the water as it splashed over their bodies. The moonlight flashing on the ripples.

Faith felt as though life couldn't get any better than this. If it could, she thought her heart would explode.

CHAPTER TWENTY-ONE
A Fine Day, Indeed

Friday morning Archer woke with Faith's head on his arm and her arms around him. Slowly she woke, so he just laid there holding her. As far as he was concerned, the whole world was in his arms. Kissing her forehead, Archer ran his hands over her face gently. Appreciating, adoring, and yes, loving her. Not many days ago having fought with his heart, saying, it's too soon. So had she. Both of them so very wrong.

Groggy with a still half-asleep mind, Faith felt how his weight made her roll into him. Sighing a hundred times, every time Archer gave her his lips. Gentle kisses on the forehead, and she felt the warmth of them as she'd never been woken up so softly. This was sensuality.

Silently they laid, just feeling the room and each other. An intimate moment, until Archer's phone rang. He'd taken the day off from having a swim as it was a big day for them. Supper with the family.

Archer asked Faith to make her pancakes and they had breakfast on the screened-in patio. A sign of more days to come like this.

After breakfast Archer told Faith she needed to get some work done on the book as he wanted her attention for the weekend, but that after that, they'd resume their normal schedule. Like before they met.

It had all been such a whirlwind and was nice to be seeing each other so much. Since Faith said she was going to stay, Archer didn't worry about missing time her now. It was as simple as a drive.

As she typed, he sat on the deck and watched the birds fly and swoop around the tops of the cliff. He meditated awhile, her typing in the background from where he sat. That would be his new tick, tick, tick. He felt it in his bones. Having seen much of the world, all he'd done for people and the legacy he'd built, Archer thought this would be his greatest work. Keeping her.

Relaxed and peaceful, he found himself brought back, with a kiss on his forehead and the smell of fresh coffee that Faith brought to him. They sat together talking about what needing to be done. She was serious.

How life could change in the blink of an eye. His future sitting before him, speaking of her dreams, which would become theirs. Never having a day that Archer had been more satisfied, the coffee tasted better than usual.

The air fresher than he could ever remember, the sounds around him crisp and clear, surely, he'd been half the man he thought he was. Seeing it all now Archer couldn't imagine life without her.

"I need to get the sea glass piece I am making for your mother finished. It shouldn't take long," Faith told him, getting up from the chair.

"Yes. I've no problem keeping busy. What would you like for lunch. I'll cook this time."

Faith thought that sounded lovely, so going to the kitchen she looked, settling on meatballs and spaghetti.

Weaving wires round the glass, she'd look up now and then, watching him move around the kitchen and humming. He was happy and looked amazing. There were a million moments she just stared. Admiring him, just being "him." Archer was a spot of comfort, floating around her to capture any time she pleased.

He'd made the most amazing spaghetti she'd ever eaten. The kitchen stocked well with spices, fresh from Kate the Spice Lady, Archer sure did know how to use them.

After lunch, Faith wanted to get ready to go to his family dinner. Archer insisted on clearing the table and doing the dishes, and that she let him take care of it all, wanting her to feel comfortable meeting them, and to take her time getting ready. She, the light of his life, her comfort came before his own. He wanted to ravish her, but there was plenty of time on the weekend for that. For the rest of their lives, he hoped.

The next thing Archer knew, she was back in the main area. As Faith walked through the kitchen, it seemed slow motion to him. Taking in all she was, he told her how amazing she looked and to give a spin for him.

Faith giggled awkwardly and gave him a turn. Her navy-blue pants had a high waist, with super wide legs, which looked like a skirt. It matched well with her white top, with a tie just under her breasts. The rope dangled in the back down past her waist.

Moving to the material, Archer commented, "Ohh. Nicccce. You have fantastic taste!"

"Oh, thank you," Faith said kissing him and putting her arms around his neck. "You have a way with words."

Archer hugged her back.

"We should go. Like . . . right now! Before I strip you out of those clothes and have my way with you again. Good grief, woman. You'll have me sideways."

With that, they got in the car and went to his parents. On the way he asked if she was nervous and Faith replied with a cheerful, "Nope."

Smiling to her, Archer decided to let her be for awhile. She was enjoying the ride. "I'll show you where I live. We're passing it anyway. You're welcome to come there anytime you like."

"Thank you, sweetheart," she smiled, then put her hand on his leg. "It's so nice that you're all so close to each other. I find it very charming. You're very lucky."

Moving to take her hand back, he grabbed it and put it back. "Please. I like you doing that. It's nice to be touched and feel wanted by someone that I want just as much."

Faith just kept smiling and looked out the window. "I'm going to need to give you a full rub down soon. I quite enjoyed watching you melt under my hands that first night, knowing I was making you feel better. You're pretty hard on it," Faith giggled.

"I can't even help myself. My mind doesn't let me stop for long. You'll enjoy the benefits, though," he informed her shifting his weight, said, "Oh, I didn't really tell you about Dora and Trevor. With his rough upbringing, plus his dad leaving when he was so young, never mind his stepdad and *his* daughter, Trevor had a lot of trouble processing his anger. He took to drinking and then met Dora. She was quite a party animal too, until they got married, deciding she wanted them to have better things, stopped. Money and having a home were more important to her. Trevor kept at it awhile. He was bad for fighting too. It was like he waited for someone to say the wrong thing. He socked them good too. Spent some time in jail for it. She stuck with him all the way through."

Stopping the story, a second, he looked out the driver's side window and beeped the horn. A farmer on a tractor waved back, then Archer continued, "So, yeah, he lost his job over it a few times. He'd been working there since he was in his mid teens, so they kept taking him back." Looking over his sunglasses then, Archer mentioned, "He *is* great at his job. I must say."

"What does he do again?"

"Electrician. HVAC".

"Oh, yes, and Dora?"

"Nurse."

"Right out of high school she started. After taking the candy-striper course early on, she loved it. Trevor wouldn't let me help when they were struggling, financially. Her in college and him out of work. So, he let me buy some land. I paid a nice price, and he wasn't in a position to argue. He needed it and refused to take a loan. I really wouldn't have wanted the money back. He's just too proud. Cleaned right up shortly after that, though, and says he thanks god every day, though he's not a believer, that she didn't leave him. Still can't get rid of the guilt."

"Wow. He's fortunate. Some people go right under," Fath responded.

"Yes, it's sad. Can't make them want better . . . You're going to get a warm welcome. Just wanted to let you know, in case you're not much for hugging with meeting new people."

"All good," she assured him.

Getting close to the house, Faith commented on the gorgeous day and how it seemed to almost never rain.

"It's not like that in the fall or the spring. Winter is nice, though. Seems it's almost always cloudy. I adore the snow. It brings silence and life to otherwise dead-looking things. We're in a weird part of the jet stream and the weather can be torrential. In the morning it's winter. Mid-afternoon can feel like the middle of the summer then back to near freezing temperatures by four in the afternoon," he laughed. "Storm days are the best. Curled up at the fireplace and having hot chocolate. It's so beautiful when it comes down softly under the streetlights at night and everything is quiet. I had a pole installed at the house, so I can sit at the window and just watch it. It sucks me right in. The tree branches get heavy with snow, and they droop until it can't hold the weight. When it slides off, the branch flings snow into the air. Sometimes I can't wait and go to get a drink or something. When I come back it's already happened."

"It must be nice having money like that where you can do those things. So many say it's the root of all evil, but I never believed that. Yes, people do evil things with money and for money. The money itself is just an object. I don't think people are evil either. For me it seems there is a stream of wellness and love that is ever flowing. Some people just get distracted from it," she stated.

"That's an interesting idea. How did you get to that conclusion?" Archer asked, wanting to know more. It had consumed him for most of his life and he'd never heard anyone describe it that way.

"My life experience. We didn't have much growing up. I had some anger issues and I fell to drinking myself," she confessed. "I didn't know where the bottom was. When I became self-employed, I eased off. I can handle a few now. It's what I meant when I had dinner with you the first time."

"Did I push you that night? I really didn't mean to," Archer asked, concerned he'd made her slip.

"No. No. I'd told you I didn't drink often. That's why. I was afraid I may fall back in the first few years, so drank nothing. Now that I've dealt with my issues, it's okay for me now and then, to indulge," she admitted.

"Oh. Good. I was worried for a minute. Does my drinking bother you?" he asked then.

"No. You don't get stupid. You just get a little giggly. It's cute, actually. I don't expect others to not have fun. If it's an issue for me, I just leave. It's the attitudes people get when they drink that sets me off."

With that, Archer vowed to watch himself from here on out. He didn't tell her, though. Pointing to his house, when they went by, Faith commented how beautiful it was. Then pointing Trevor's house out, it was much more moderate and not very big, but still nice.

Archer's place was modern-looking with a seventies feel to it. Quite large too. "That's a big place for one person," Faith commented.

"Well, I like open space and I have a gym. It's on a slab, so there's no basement. The garage has all the tools I need, so that part had to be big. It's basically a shop inside. Hydraulic lifts and welding things. Dad and I have always worked on cars. It's bonding time for us."

"Oh. Well, that makes more sense then."

"Just a few hills and we'll be at my parents. Are you nervous?"

"Nope!"

Happy to hear that, Archer mentioned he was considering adding to the house. "I was thinking I may put an infinity pool in the backyard off the deck and maybe a pool house. I'm dreading the gym pool this winter."

"Ooh. That sounds dreamy!"

"Of course, you're welcome to my place anytime. Maybe next weekend you can come stay with me? A vacay on yer vacay?" he joked.

"Yes! We can do that," she smiled as Archer slowed down coming to the top of a hill.

"Here we are," he told Faith as they pulled into the long lane.

A stately white farmhouse stood at the top of the hill. Mature maple trees dawned the entire driveway on both sides.

The lawn was perfect, and, as they got closer, Faith saw they had a full deck that went around both corners of the house and all along the side.

"Does that deck go right the way round?"

Archer hadn't heard anyone say it that way before, making him giggle a bit. "Yeah. It took the four of us the entire summer to build it. Dad, Brett, Derek, and I, but Trevor came over to help us most days, though. Mom had her ideas about what she wanted the house to look like. She'd have Dad put in walls and take some out. Move doors. Put in bigger windows. Mum didn't like that the windows weren't even when they bought it."

"Holy!"

"Ya! Dad would grumble when she asked him to make changes, but always did as asked. She could get quite cranky," Archer told her matter-of-factly and then with a very serious face he added, "She can't stand socks and shoes, but also hates dirt under her feet. I can remember telling my friends to get their shoes off. If she felt even one tiny bit of dirt the whole of the house would have to be done."

Faith knew what he meant. She was the same.

"I swear! She'd be in our rooms vacuuming the curtains once a week while we tried to play games or talk. It was sometimes easier to just go to their house," he laughed.

They pulled into a wide part of the drive where cars were to be parked. Roger was seated on the deck, enjoying a beer and reading a book. Getting up to greet them, he stopped at the screen door to call Debbie.

"Kids are here," he yelled and went down the stairs to them.

Archer got out, opened her door, and took her hand. Walking her over to Roger, he let out a big, "*Hi, dawlin'!*"

Passing her hand to Roger, he kissed it and pulled her in for a hug. "Roger, Faith. Faith, Roger," Archer said formally.

"Call me dad," Roger insisted hugging her close. It was warm and Faith knew then that the apples never fell far from the trees.

Roger slid Faith under his arm and turned saying, "Archer, me boy!"

They hugged with Faith still under Roger's arm. "Come in. Mum's waiting on you. Anything you need help with taking in?"

"Just some stuff for Greta and Jonah. We can get them after. Thanks, though." Archer answered.

Roger put Faith ahead of him, staying one step behind, but held her hand all the way up.

"The plants are lovely," Faith complimented as she looked the length of the deck. "Who has the green thumb?"

"That would be Deb," Roger said just as she came out through the squeaking screen door.

Debbie tucked potholders into her apron as she greeted Faith with arms outstretched.

"Debbie, Faith. Faith, Debbie," Roger said introducing them.

Letting Faith go, Debbie looked her up and down, taking in her outfit. "Lovely . . . Just lovely . . ." she whispered. "So good to finally meet you," then slapped her arm gently like a mother would. "Come in from the heat. I thought you were going to grease that," she mentioned to Roger, never looking right at him as he held the door for them both.

Following Debbie, Faith smelled patchouli. No doubt a hippie in her younger days. Archer followed behind them, then Roger slapped his back as he passed. They talked softly and then Faith heard Roger give a rough laugh. He was still quite strong and able looking, she thought, and must have been quite a brute in his younger years. Turning to watch them, Archer came into the house and Roger left to the get grease from the garage.

"Would you like tea, coffee? Maybe lemonade or a cold glass of wine?" Debbie asked as they walked into the living room. It was pristine.

"Lemonade would be nice actually, please."

Archer showed Faith to the sofa, then went straightaway to get the lemonade, while Debbie chatted with her.

"I'd heard there was an incident at the cottage?"

Archer came in then and took over the conversation as Faith had done in Bobby's shop. Knowing his mother, she'd grill Faith.

"Faith had a jealous ex who was trying to get back into her life. I don't blame him. She's a sweet woman with her head on straight. Apparently, he'd snapped from the stress and tracked her down here, broke in at some point, and tried to force his way."

"Oh!" Debbie exclaimed covering her heart. "That must have been frightening. Are you okay?"

"Yes. I'm fine. Bump on the noggin is all and a little cut. Archer came in and saved me."

Archer kept the fact that Jonsie was going to bury her alive, to himself. If Matt told her, that would be fine.

"Ya. He tried to run and tripped on the corner of the door frame, taking quite a spill and hurt himself badly. I called the police, and they came straightaway," he explained to Debbie.

"Oh. He's lucky Archer didn't get his hands on him," she breathed to Faith, and took a sip of her tea. "The news said he'd suffered a fatal accident and that after a battle through the night he succumbed to the injuries. Then I heard, he had a battle with police. He even took a hostage then committed suicide?"

"Yes. He'd cracked a rib on the island of the kitchen, I believe. May have punctured his lung. He was in bad shape when the ambulance came." Archer stated as Roger came in.

The door squeaked a few times, and they could hear the grease gun. The door squeaked again . . . and then the grease gun. "Thank you, love," Debbie said loud enough for him to hear.

Faith understood Archer better now and how he paid attention. Making a note to watch Debbie and Roger more through the evening, she passed Debbie the flowers.

"Oh, so nice. You didn't have to."

"I know. I wanted to."

"Roger . . . Faith brought flowers. Would you put them in the nice vase and on the dining table? It's in the China cabinet."

Roger came and took them right away. "Thank you, handsome," she cooed with her nose crinkled.

"No problem, babe," Roger replied, which made Faith smile big. So cute he used that word for her.

Archer stood up saying, "I'm gonna help Dad in the kitchen a minute. Be right back," then followed Roger.

Faith heard their deep voices and laughter. Pot lids clanked, which made Debbie get right up. Faith smiled to herself. They were all so adorable and she could read them like a book.

"Excuse me," Debbie said.

"Sure."

Listening in Faith heard Debbie growl at them, and they skulked back into the living room. Obviously scolded.

Just then she heard the sound of footsteps on the deck, Trevor and Dora walked right in. Everyone said their hellos and Faith stood to meet them.

Trevor bolted right for Faith with his hand out. "It's good to see you again," he cheered, with arms open to hug her. Dora next.

"And you too," Faith said. "Nice to meet you finally, Dora. Archer says wonderful things about you."

"All lies!" Trevor teased.

They'd barely sat down, and the kids ran across the deck. Roger took after them like he was twenty again and whistled a tune three times. Like a call. Greta in first, she jumped into his arms, with Jonah close behind.

He was a little older and still had his soccer gear on. Much shyer than Greta, seeing Faith, Jonah hid behind Roger. Bobbi Jo came in behind them, saying to Jonah, "Here. Take your clothes and go change in the bathroom."

Jonah ran with the bag as Brett came in. Roger introduced them to Faith. More hugs and when Greta saw Archer, she ran right to him.

"Munchkin!!" he roared happily.

Scooping her right up, Archer garbled into her neck with his face. Giggling, she pulled away, her face serious now, ran her hands over his beard.

"You like it?"

Nodding, she put her hand under his chin and rubbed it back and forth, as he chatted with Brett, briefly, about work. Greta stared for the longest time.

"Be right back," Archer said to Faith again, and took Greta to the kitchen.

Debbie hollered and Faith heard her say, "Hi, sweetie!" then it all settled a minute.

Bobbi Jo was quiet, and she could tell that Jonah took after her. Brett on the other hand gabbed up a storm with Roger.

"Derek and Shelley will be by shortly. They had an errand to run so we took Greta for them." Brett mentioned.

Bobbi Jo looked uncomfortable, then got up and quietly excused herself before going to the kitchen.

The ladies laughed and Archer came back out, Greta on his heels with a sucker.

Going right to Faith, Greta jumped on her lap, pushed the sucker in her face, crinkling the wrapper, frustrated. Passing it to Faith, she looked to Archer for permission.

Nodding it was okay, Faith pulled the wrapper off for her. Greta turned and sat comfortably in her lap and leaned in on her chest.

"She loves everyone. Jonah, not so much. He'll come around, though," Archer mentioned to Faith.

A few minutes later Derek and Shelley came in. When Derek came through, he whacked Brett off the back of the head and his hat fell off.

Brett just put it back on and said, "Hey, jerk. How's things?"

It was just their way.

All introduced now with the whole family together, it was noisy with little conversations going on about the room. Shelley told Faith to come to the kitchen and sat her down at the far end of the island of the kitchen.

"Those guys will bore you to death."

Checking on the pots, Bobbi Jo then pulled out a stack of plates while Debbie made the gravy.

"Can I help?" Faith asked.

"Maybe next time, dear. You're a guest. Thank you just the same. How's your drink?"

"Delicious."

Jonah came in to hug Debbie and after kissing his head she asked. "Did you meet Faith?"

"No," he simply said.

Faith just waved and let him do as he felt comfortable with.

Mashing the potatoes, Shelley talked to Jonah about the game, telling him what a good job he'd done. Seeming to prefer to hang out with the women, maybe scoping Faith out, Jonah hung around Debbie while she did the potatoes.

"Can you tell the boys dinner is ready, Faith?" Debbie asked.

"Sure," she answered, then went to the living room.

They all jumped to get food. Faith waited for Archer.

"Mum's a great cook. Let's eat," he smiled then took her with him.

All lined up with plates, they talked amongst themselves. Archer took Faith to her seat and asked if she needed another drink. She was beginning to feel apprehensive and said, "Maybe I'll take that wine."

"Red or white?" Archer asked.

"White, please."

The kids were served first to get them sitting. Greta shuffled her food around on the plate. She didn't like it touching and it was a bit too close. Using a butter knife to measure their distance, she was happy when the peas stayed where she'd put them.

Jonah whined about the veggies and Bobbi Jo tried to hush him. Once Brett and Derek were out of the way, Archer told Faith to come get some food.

Roger in front of her making a plate for Debbie, who was sitting with the kids at the table whispered. "Take all you want, dear, there's tons. Deb always thinks she's feeding the whole NFL," he laughed.

Taking a little of each thing, Faith filled her plate. Archer too, and after all seated the room got quiet. Taking each others' hands, they spanned the length of the table around, then bowed their heads. Faith followed them.

Debbie gave thanks for the food and Roger said a few prayers. When he'd finished, they all said amen and the noise resumed. Glasses clinking, they toasted to Faith and welcomed her formally into the fold.

After dinner, the men took all the plates.

"That's their job," Debbie said taking Faith's hand from the plate, then asked. "What would you like with dessert?"

"Coffee would be great," Faith answered, hoping she'd get it the way she liked it.

"Mum, where's the honey?" Archer asked before she'd finished the thought.

A moment later, Archer brought the dessert and coffee. Derek to Bobbi Jo. Brett to Shelley. Then the kids came with their own. Several kinds of dessert splayed the table. Bobbi Jo had a bakery of her own in town and had made her specialty pie, just for Faith.

The kids bounced around while they ate. Archer told them to sit quiet and that Faith had a treat for them in the car, after they finished dinner.

Jonah pumped a fist as he shoved an entire brownie in his mouth, while Debbie rolled her eyes. Greta just sat there smiling at Faith.

"She reeeallllly likes you. More than usual."

Poking Greta's side, she wiggled, and Archer turned to Faith. "I'll be right back. I'll get the thing from the car. You have your coffee."

Faith quite liked how their tightly knit family was and settled into her seat getting comfy. Bobbi Jo and Shelley were especially interested in Faith, asking where she was from and what she did for a living. Faith told them all they wanted, while they tended to the kids.

Archer came back just as the guys were taking the last round of dishes from the table. After helping them, Archer told the kids to come with him and Faith to the living room. Off they went, as the rest of them sat and talked.

Faith showed them the game and explained it a bit to them, while Archer listened in. He'd never heard of the game.

"Bocce ball. That sounds like a blast! Let's go to the yard," he suggested, and carried it out for them as it was quite heavy.

Opening the box, Archer let Faith take out the pieces and show them what to do, then said he was going back into the house to do the dishes.

Watching out the window, while he scrubbed the pots, Brett and Derek talked away, but Archer didn't even hear them. Faith was so good with them, and he took it all in. With dishpan hands, he grabbed another beer. His third now.

Everyone else was outside playing the game and laughter filled the air. The sun was just above the horizon. Shelley told Jonah, another half hour, he'd had a long day and she wanted him in bed soon. Greta was already in her jammies in the yard. She'd fall asleep on the drive home as usual.

When the evening had ended, they all hugged and said their goodbyes, and walked the kids out to the car. Faith gave them each a treat bag after they'd gotten buckled into the car.

"It's gift cards," Archer told the ladies. "For a rainy day," then winked.

Pulling out, horns beeped, and the kids waved. Archer said they'd better get going too, that he and Faith had plans for the rest of the evening. Hugging and telling each other they loved one another, Debbie and Roger returned to the house. The sky was a bit dark, and the yard lights came on for them.

"I've had a few too many. I'll have you drive?" he asked Faith.

"*Oh, yes!*" she answered excitedly.

Opening the door for her, Archer told Faith the car can be snaky if there's a wet road and that she may want to stop a little sooner too. "

"It's not fibreglass like the new vehicles. Other than that, have fun."

Faith bounced in the driver's seat as he went to the other side. Buckling up, Archer got in as she turned the ignition and revved it to check the pedal. It rumbled under her hands, making Faith even more excited.

"This is *so cool!*" Faith yelled and put it in drive.

Archer thought she looked sexy as hell in the driver's seat. Buckling up too, he said as Trevor had, "Giddy up those horses, then. Watch your speed. She's touchy," he smiled.

The yard lights went out as they pulled onto the pavement. Faith was very careful to heed his warnings but felt a rush of energy listening to the steady low rumble of the engine. Hyper aware of everything.

Pulling into the cottage road, she drove slowly, like Archer had done so may times, then pulled into the driveway next to the Cooper.

"Same rules apply even though you're driving," he told her than as she shut the engine down.

Once inside they hugged and held each other all the way the bedroom. Tonight, they were both tired, and so, just laid in bed holding each other until they fell asleep. It was nice and relaxed. They both needed that.

The excitement of everything through the week was draining and now that the future seemed to be stable, they just listened to each other breathe. Everything in the world was right just then.

CHAPTER TWENTY-TWO
Things Worth More Than Gold

The rest of the weekend was as great, to Faith, as she'd imagined. The TV hadn't been on even once. Talking about their lives, hopes, dreams, failures, triumphs, he'd let her in.

That Monday, Archer went to work, a new man. All the staff noticed. He was kind and gentle, but now had a peace about his face, and they knew his heart was content.

Archer insisted they spend a little more time in their own places and Faith agreed. Being together every minute wasn't healthy, saying absence makes the heart grow fonder Archer left Faith to her work. He was so right too. She missed him like crazy.

Throwing the party for the staff as he'd planned with Greg, Archer gave them their raises. The summer was full of romping and playing. Exploring boundaries and pushing limits, and they spent much of the time in retirement, just shutting out the world.

Faith taught him about her crafts, Archer taught her about making money and loving herself more. Also, about forgiveness and how to accept help, compliments, and Faith very much enjoyed his guided meditations, getting lost through his voice into the unknown, eventually going on her own, after he'd taught her how to reach Zen.

The final draft of the book was in, and it was in the promotions and marketing stage of the process.

Very proud of her, Archer took her to the fanciest restaurant for dinner. Faith discovered that she had been cooking steak wrong all her life.

Not seeing anything else on the menu that fancied her, she chose the steak. It melted in her mouth.

The weather was great all the rest of the summer. Rainy days, the best for Faith, though. She'd stop everything she was doing and played guitar. Even writing a few songs.

Archer surprised her by taking her to open mic, not saying where they were going, then revelled in how everyone else enjoyed her singing.

Faith had started another book, made sea glass jewellery and soap over the next few months. Helping her get a table at the market, Archer went with Faith to sell the goods. Just something fun for her and new for him. He'd learned so much about crafting, and she, so much about herself. Life truly was good.

The months flew by, and Faith packed her things to go back to Vermont, wrapping up her old life. Archer joined her a few weeks later. He also had loose ends to tie up for the season, as the gallery closed for the winter. Secretly he'd gotten her an apartment and brand-new furniture.

Actually, he bought an the entire complex and revamped the whole thing without her knowing. Faith would lose her mind if she knew she was getting special treatment.

To keep the secret, Archer hired someone to be the caretaker and collect rent, which he put into a separate savings account to invest for her. In case there was ever anything she wanted, or the book didn't do as she'd dreamed, prepared to take the scolding.

Also, he prepared for the off chance that Faith wasn't as sure as she thought. Archer would let her go, but make sure she'd never need anything, ever again.

She'd never know, and he'd never tell, unless he had to.

Faith talked so much, and Archer listened to every click of her tongue pulling from the roof of her mouth. He knew her taste well now, and wanted to give her a beautiful place, with everything taken care of as a "welcome home" gift, just wanting her to relax. She'd been through so much and eventually learned not to argue with Archer about money. It meant nothing to him.

He knew she wanted to do it on her own, though Faith let him away with furnishing her place, but told him no more. Archer promised her that, though said, he was still going to treat her in other ways. She promised to let him and do her best not to feel guilty.

Joining her in Vermont, Archer helped her pack and let her pay for the move. He did as he'd promised. It drove him *nuts*, but he *did* it.

The pool was installed over the summer and Archer cancelled his membership. Faith would come when he wasn't home, use the gym. While waiting for him to get home, she cooked supper and they'd sit by the pool to eat, until it got too cold to do it.

He taught her self-defence and Tai Chi. Faith was beside herself about how *much* it helped, and how far she'd come in such a short time.

They had many parties, and she'd sing for everyone. Archer tried to play guitar but couldn't wrap his mind around it and decided to stick with the shakers.

Faith noticed his rhythm and asked if he'd try the drums. Archer progressed quickly, and loved to pound on them when he was alone. Relaxing him, like the ticking of the clock. The boom, boom, boom wrapped him up.

Faith found some girlfriends and Archer welcomed them in as his own. They really were great people, and Faith loved them with all her heart.

They had their girls' nights out and he'd have the guys over for pool and beers. Not Trevor, though, soda for him, and Archer would only have the one.

Faith's first book hit the bestsellers list. Then the next and the next. He'd travel with her when she went for TV interviews and podcasts. Now and then did motivational speeches for people and volunteered at the addictions centre.

The next year, for the holidays, Archer gave Faith a full scholarship to get her psychology degree. She was more than intelligent enough and capable of passing. He didn't doubt it, nor felt he'd been overly ambitious, in giving that kind of gift. She could start a practice if she wanted, but, in any case, he knew it would help. Even in just the writing alone. Archer knew, also, it would help her come to terms with unresolved issues that maybe she wouldn't admit to.

Over the next few years, he dreamed of coming home to her. Their place. Not his, or hers, and waited patiently for the right time, knowing Faith was fully with him. He'd taken her to foreign lands and lavish hotels. Partly to kill time, partly to fulfill her dreams and watch her face light up in childlike wonder at it all.

One day, Archer suggested she go to town and buy something pretty. Mentioning that she always looked good, he said to "just get something new".

"Where are we going?"

"To dinner and then I have something to show you."

That was all she was getting. Knowing she'd pry it out of him, Archer made an attempt to get off the phone quickly. She had her ways now with the degree, and he couldn't resist those eyes.

"Go get something special. It goes on my card. *No kidding*!" he argued.

"Fine. Fine."

"Hey. I'm *not* joking," he repeated, knowing she was rolling her eyes. Archer knew Faith, like he knew himself. Telling her to put things on his card, the bill never showed up. "I love your independence, but I'm insisting on this!"

After a moment of silence, Archer sheepishly said "Please?" as if he were a wounded jaguar.

"Okay . . . You win. What time should I be ready?"

"For six. The table is booked. I'll be there at fifteen to. Please be ready?" he begged.

Faith was famous for not being totally ready. That mane of hers didn't always play fair.

"Actually? Maybe get your hair done?" he insisted trying not to be too bossy. "It makes you late sometimes and I can't afford it today."

"What are you up to?"

"*No! No! Not this time!* You just . . . get ready!" he exclaimed and hung up.

Laughing at his sharpness, Faith knew Archer meant business. Immediately going out the door and once in the car, she called Monica and Tamara for coffee and shopping. They all went to get her dress, then Faith sent the picture of the bill, with his card number printed on it.

Good girl. Now the hair, he texted back and Faith did as she was told.

Parting ways with the girls now, Faith suspected it was something extra special, so, asked the stylist to give her an up-do, with a few pearls in the folds, and some that cascaded from the side. Like on the dress.

It had a few sparkles on the edge where it crossed over, which she'd match with eye shadow. Nothing super fancy. Long and flat, in that green she loved with her hair.

Archer picked her up on time, in a limo of course, nothing strange. He did that sometimes saying it was for him, so Faith wouldn't complain that he was spoiling her too much, so let him have that.

After dinner they drove to the country. Halfway to where they were going, Archer gave her a blindfold and with a certain voice told her to put it on. Faith had learned not to argue with that tone.

"Do you know how much I love you?" he asked, helping to put it on her.

"Yes, and I love you. So very, very much," she answered, then asked for a kiss with her lips.

He did, then made sure her eyes were securely covered, and Faith pouted. Able see a bit before, just under one side and out the front window, she was now clueless. Trying to follow by using other senses, she soon got lost to where they might be after a few turns, then sat there feeling silly, playing with her hands.

"How was your day?" Archer asked kindly.

"It was nice actually. I had the girls come shopping to buy the dress. We had coffee and then I got my hair done. Can I at least have a hint?"

"*Nope!*" he said firmly.

The silence resumed. She'd pushed him too far that time.

"You suck," she said jokingly.

"Yep, and you'll learn to live with that."

Faith felt the car almost stop and turn. The gravel under the tires gave her no clues. Other than they drove very slowly, she couldn't imagine where they were.

"You're doing such a great job," Archer complimented, Making Faith excited then.

His silence was hell. She'd found that out early on in their relationship, his voice, sometimes a reward to her.

The limo slowed to a stop, the driver got out and Faith heard Archer slide out his side, then over to hers right after. The smell of the ocean filled the air, as Archer took her hands and helped her from the car.

"No peeks," Archer reminded her, as he helped to put her arm in his with that suit on, she loved. It was so soft.

Walking, she could hear the gravel under her shoes. Making a guess, Faith thought it must have run all the way from the road, right to the door or stairs. The tires made popping noises as they drove the length of road. Glad she'd worn her wedges; her heels would have been awkward and scratched from sinking into the gravel.

"Up the stairs. There's four." he told her, and Faith felt for them with her foot as Archer assisted her to go slowly, then told her to stop.

Faith heard beeping and his heavy breath. Everything was now very acute without her sight. Wherever they were was really quiet. So much so, that his breath seemed heavy. Hearing a door latch click, she waited.

"I'm going to take this off now," Archer told her caringly as he touched the mask. Faith heard the car leave and was now super puzzled. "The light may be bright so open slow. You've been under there nearly a half hour now."

Taking it off, Faith kept her head down. Her eyes were kind of stuck anyway. Opening them, she saw her shoes on grey boards and could smell caulking, along with fresh wood. There was another smell, similar to his cologne. Maybe cedar?

Raising her eyes slowly, Faith found herself standing in the doorway of a gorgeous home which looked familiar.

"What is this?" she asked walking inside.

Archer came behind and wrapped his arms around her waist. "Do you like it?"

"It's gorgeous! What exactly am I looking at?"

Step after step, it began to sink in. "Is this the cottage?" she asked then excitedly. Thinking back, she remembered the drive now.

Archer was smiling ear to ear. "Looks nice?"

"It looks sooo gooood. Did they do renos? Are we spending the weekend?" Faith asked excitedly, running her hand over the marble countertops.

"Not really. I bought it after your rental was done. It took a year to get it the way I wanted it. It had to be winterized first, so it'd be done on time. They needed both winters to do what I designed."

He didn't say he paid double what it was worth to get the owner to let it go. She drove a hard bargain and was a dream home to her.

"You didn't!?" Faith gasped. "I *love* what you did with it," Faith remarked, turning to him . . . on his knee with an opened box with a *very* modest ring inside!

"I knew it would be a perfect place to ask you," Archer said with tears welling in his eyes. "Would you be my wife?"

Faith burst into a joyful, "*Yes! Yes!*" and it rang through the large room.

"Yes?" Archer asked, unsure he'd heard right and wanted to hear it again.

"*Yes!*" Faith repeated shaking her hands as if they were wet.

Standing up, Archer kissed her tenderly. When putting the ring on her finger, his hands shook as much as hers, then she leapt into his arms.

"Faith. I never dreamed this. I couldn't have. You're something from the heavens to me, and I've been so patient, wanting this from the beginning. It was painstaking to let things be as they were, until I could make them what I want. I waited for you my whole life and needed this to be perfect as it could be."

Archer was extremely emotional, and Faith knew he was excited *and* relieved to let that all out.

"Just the words from your lips would have been enough." she told him.

Staring at each other for an eternity, Archer broke the silence by saying, "I'll make you the happiest woman in the world."

"That was done the day I met you, my sweet king. You saved my soul," Faith smiled. There were no more tears to shed.

"And you showed me mine, the way you've polished yourself. I see myself more clearly. It's a beautiful thing."

"Thank you honey. I couldn't have done it without you. Monica is gonna *die* when she hears. Oh! Your parents. Do they know?" she asked hurriedly.

"Only Trevor and Dora know. I had Trevor watch over this project when I couldn't be here. I didn't want you being suspicious."

"When do we tell them?"

"If it suits you, I'll plan for a party here next weekend? Shush till then?" he requested of her.

"Oooh. That'll be hard. Monica knows me so well. I'll be all weird," she answered pacing around and wiggling her fingers.

Feeling the ring turn on her finger, it jarred her about what had just happened. Taking it between her finger and thumb, Faith felt a rush of joy and a heavy calmness come over her chest.

"Mrs. Agenta . . ." Faith whispered softly with a huge smile.

"I was a wreck for the last month trying to keep it from you. In the beginning it was easy. So much distraction with your moving. The trips away helped, but I think I paced a hole in my office floor. When it was done, all I had to do was wait for the right day, knowing I was in love with you the night you sang to me by the fire. Two years ago, today."

"Archer . . ." she cooed; with no idea he'd even had the thought then. Archer had kept that from her to make the proposal even more grand.

"You'll have to find your poker face with Monica."

In her mind Faith heard "challenge" and it settled with her. "Can we stay the weekend? Since we're here now?"

"As you wish. The driver is just in the field before the yard. I can let him go and have Trevor bring the Camaro?"

"Yes. Yes. That will do," Faith said wringing her hands.

"Are you alright?"

"Um, ya. I'm good? I'm *good*! Sorry. I got lost in the details," answered and shook her head.

"Yer sure you're good?"

"Yes. Yes. So sorry, love," she replied and paced.

Archer went outside to call Trevor and give Faith a minute to process things. He'd left the door open and could hear her shoes clump through the cottage. Yep. She was checking it *all* out.

Trevor's phone rang. "SSSS'up, buuuuuuddy?!" he answered.

"Hey, yeah. She said yes."

"Was there a doubt?"

"Well. Not really. Still worked over my nerves, though. Can you bring the Camaro? We're gonna stay here for the weekend."

"For sure! I'll get Dora to drive the truck and we'll be there shortly."

Archer could hear Dora squealing in the background and laughed. He could see the scene in his head.

"Cool. Well, we'll wait here then, and I'll show her around," he told Trevor. "Thanks, man. Yer the best."

"See ya soon."

Faith had them all not saying goodbye anymore.

Rushing from the back as Archer came in, Faith told him how much she loved the changes and how perfect she thought he'd done.

"I'm so glad you like it. I listen to every word you say and had a good idea, but plans changed along the way as I got to know you better, and just so you know . . . they're gonna want to see you, eh?"

"Oh, yes. That's fine."

"So . . . for the announcement, it'll be a garden party," Archer said clapping his hands together. "Care to see the gardens?"

Faith's eyes nearly popped from her head. She could just imagine what he'd done. "Hells ya!" she yelled.

That made him laugh, and with his huge smile he said, "This way m'lady," and took her to the patio doors, turning on the lights. The whole yard lit up now as Archer led her across the larger patio and down onto a smaller one. The yard looked huge to her.

"I thought it would look smaller with the garden."

"Well. I had the building moved back. I wanted it to be here as long as possible."

Squeezing his arm, Faith affirmed, "You're so extra, but I wouldn't have you any other way. Show me your treasures."

As they walked through, Archer told her about the flowers. Faith knew that, not a single one, would be insignificant. Each of them had Archer's love poured into them and Faith adored having that kind of perspective. Also due to Archer.

Looking back, Faith wondered if she'd have ever been this enlightened if not for him. Listening as he told the tale of the gardens, Faith drifted off in her mind with his words. He *was* a great storyteller, and she could listen to him go on and on.

The fountain was lit perfectly. The entire place was all so different . . . except . . . the firepit. It hadn't been touched. He'd had large, oversized cushions made for them. Replicas of the tiny ones they'd sat on that night.

Tearing up, Faith told him how wonderful he is. *If I'm dreaming . . . please don't wake me*, she prayed in her mind.

Just then, car doors slammed. "Oh my god. I'm a mess. I have to fix my face. I'll be right back," Faith exclaimed.

"You've never looked better, but even so, the bedroom door is open if you want to freshen up," Archer said then slowly and softly wiped her tears as he adoringly looked over her entire face. Like she'd just returned to him after having thought he'd never lay eyes on her again. "Still gorgeous."

Seeing she was anxious, Archer let her go and Faith ran through to the back of the cottage and into the sliding bedroom doors.

"Helllooooo," Archer heard Trevor say through the house.

"Out here, dude. On my way," he yelled back walking closer.

Trevor had come out to meet him and stood on the deck with his eyes lit up as Archer came up the stairs.

"Damnnnn . . . It was nice in the day. I'd never seen it lit up at night, though," Without a pause, he called, "DORA!"

Rushing out, Dora instantly there. "Wha . . . ooooohhh," she exclaimed as her eyes lit up too. She *wanted* to say something, but nothing came out.

Archer dug his hands into his pockets and watched them be swept away with the works. "Looks good, eh?"

"I can't even grasp it all. It's the most beautiful thing I've ever seen . . . Where's Faith?"

"In freshening up. I'm sure she wouldn't mind seeing you."

"I'm out!" Dora said with a wave of her hand, then quickly headed back in calling Faith, so as not to startle.

Archer and Trevor let her go. They knew the sister code.

"Yep," Trevor said.

"Yep," Archer said back.

"They'll be a few minutes. Care for a pop?"

"Ya. That works. Can I go have a look-see?"

"Yes. Be my guest," Archer answered. "I'll bring your drink."

Trevor's eyes were lit like diamonds as he looked around and carefully walked down the stairs. Reaching the fountain, Trevor just stood watching it tinkle. Archer found him there.

"What ya think?"

"Even though I watched it happen, I didn't see this in my head," he responded cracking the can.

"Couldn't have done it without ya, buuudddy."

"You had it. I just babysat. Wait'll she sees the beach."

"Yep," Archer said.

"Yep," Trevor said.

Archer had them built a beautiful walkway all along the cliff, with a small deck tables and chairs, with a floating boardwalk that led to a barge with more seating, thinking they could have beach parties down there. The stairs weren't steep anymore. Archer had had them build in stages with a turn. He'd growled a few times for them to not do *anything* to that rock.

Faith came out then, dragging Dora by the hand across the yard and a huge smile.

"What are you to imps up to?"

"Tell, tell," Faith urged poking Dora.

"No. It's your big day," she said shyly.

Archer raised an eyebrow looking at them. Then at Trevor, who wouldn't make eye contact.

"Tell him, Trevor!" Faith whined.

"Trev. You can tell me anything," Archer agreed.

Dora looked at Faith, as she mouthed "tell him!" to Trevor.

Dora sighed and took Trevor's hand, telling him, "He'll be happy."

Archer took a very serous face now. Almost angry looking and crossed his arms.

"Dude..."

"We're having a baby," he finally told Archer.

Squatting down to the ground, with two fists, Archer hissed, "*YESSSS!*"

"Told ya," Faith uttered with a smirk.

"I didn't wanna say. It was an important day for you both. I didn't want to steal any light," Trevor said honestly.

"Brother. You're as important as any of us. Your part of my family." Archer reminded him, then looked at Faith. "Our family..."

"I felt it might ruin the night," Trevor admitted.

Archer gave Trevor a man hug to show his happiness for them. "Dude. You made it even more amazing."

"Thanks. We're pretty excited," Trevor confessed then, letting it show.

"*I'm* excited for you both! We should celebrate. Let's have you over for lunch tomorrow?"

"Sounds like a plan," Dora acceptingly smiled. "We should go, though. I need my rest."

"Yes. Yes," Archer agreed. "I'll see you out."

All together now, they went into the cottage and out the front door. Archer and Faith walked them to the truck, telling them to drive safe. After they'd left, Archer scooped Faith up with a *WHOOP!* and carried her inside.

"Tomorrow, you see the beach. Right now? I get to have my way with my future wife."

"I so love you," Faith said and cuddled into his neck.

"I so love you," Archer responded, lovingly looking into Faith's eyes, melting her, as he closed the door.

CHAPTER TWENTY-THREE
Darkness Into Light

The garden party was amazing, Archer and Faith spent the next year planning. She kept her apartment, for his parents' sake. Old-fashioned, she didn't want to upset them. Archer had lived with Johanna, but that didn't matter to Faith. Roger and Debbie were her parents now and she cared what they thought.

Throwing a shower for Dora, after the baby, they knew what to get her then. She'd chosen to wait for birth to discover their sex. The pregnancy was smooth, but the labour was rough. Dora said she'd do it all again, though and they'd named him Asher.

It meant blessing, but they also wanted to name him after Archer, for all the help he'd given them. Trevor was an absolute wreck during the labour, but felt he'd finally made it up to Dora for all the grief he'd put her through earlier in their relationship.

It was funny for Archer to see him all gaga over his boy. Trevor didn't really take to kids ... but now? He wanted to know all about them. Almost ignoring the adults.

The next few months seemed to fly right by for Archer and Faith, and when the big day came, she wore a flowing, emerald green coloured, dress.

Tradition meant nothing to her and didn't want a dress that was all big and fancy. Having to argue with Debbie, Faith never won her over. She'd let them have her living alone while they were engaged, but she was gonna have her green dress. White made her look wiped out, she thought.

She left her hair down with a few curls at the bottom. Archer always loved it that way.

Dora was her maid of honour, of course. Trevor, his best man. Monica and Tamara, her bridesmaids. Brett and Derek stood with Archer. Jonah was their ring bearer and Greta the flower girl. It was perfect.

"Are you nervous?" Dora asked.

"Nope. I'm actually not. The way Archer treats me, and the things we've talked about, I was pushed into learning a lot about myself. Insecurities shown to me, I had no choice but to fix them or be miserable. He compliments me so much, I have almost none left. The course was great to help too. Every time I felt awkward or insecure, I took the time to meditate on it. A minute here and there worked wonders. Once I got into it, though, I found it relaxing. Not much rattles me anymore." Faith smiled.

"Is that right?" Dora asked.

"Yeah. I have to confess that I do have butterflies. Not bad, though," Faith admitted. "It'll be hard not to run to him."

"OMG! His mother would be DED!" Dora cried out loud, emphasizing DED in a deep voice and a funny face. Faith laughed so hard she nearly lost control.

Dora checked the clock and reminded Faith. "It's almost time. A few more minutes as Miss Leone, and then? A new chapter . . . you look stunning," she complimented.

"Thank you, Dora," Faith said lovingly.

Monica and Tamara had been in their own rooms, getting ready. The second they'd finished, both scooted to Faith's room and knocked softly on her door, then came in giggling. "We're all ready when you are," Monica said barely able to contain herself.

All of them squealed at once, then laughed about how it sounded. Like a bunch of teen girls who had the most popular guy wink at them in the hall. It became a thing for them all. A cacophony.

Leaving the room, their dresses swooshed down the hall. Once at the door leading to the chapel, they went to Faith, making sure everything looked nice, and then all gave her a cuddle.

"You're going to do amazing and I'm gonna cry. I just know it," Dora told Faith, after Monica and Tamara went in, then gave her the warmest sisterly hug, Before going in herself, Dora said, "I love you, sister," then went through the door.

She'd started calling Faith that, once she'd actually moved to PEI, and spent some time together. It made Archer happy to see them get so close.

Faith had a family waiting, but right now, stood as alone as a person could be. No father to give her away, she imagined him there. Faith felt his presence throughout her life, though her memory of him had faded so much, she sensed a heaviness at major points in her life.

Like when the kids teased her, Linda's death, spreading her ashes on the beach, when she'd left Jonsie and sold the house. It gave her strength as she matured. Becoming more prevalent.

Letting it wrap her up, Faith became stronger and tried not to cry as the doors opened. Her dress was plain but also magnificent on her, everyone stared adoringly. Shelley and Bobbi Jo, the most excited to see her.

They'd wanted this for Archer, more than anyone there, knowing what a treasure he was. They'd had some trash men in their past. Brett and Derek were *very* good men . . . but, not quite like Archer. Special in their own rights. Sensitive and caring, Archer was a gem. Brilliant and shining. Always was! The overachiever . . . for his own satisfaction.

Thank you, Faith said in her mind, before taking the first step. *Now*, she was nervous as her foot touched the floor walking into her new life, alone. The first step of a wonderful world that waited.

Everyone whispering as she went down, Debbie blew kisses and Roger did a head bow, as if to say, good job.

Archer stood there, proud as any man could be. Huge toothy smile and hands clasped together. Tall, straight, square shoulders, and the best poker face she'd seen yet.

Stepping up beside him, Archer took her hand, just for a second, before the ceremony began and mouthed, "You look amazing," the way he had, that day on the patio at the gallery. Exaggerated and overly animated.

It took her stress away and the ceremony went off without a hitch. They offered their own vows, which was the poem Archer had taken from his vision. The one he recited as a toast. With the exception of one more line.

Jonah brought their rings and together they put them on. Together they quoted the poem. Two voices as one.

To you and I, to dreams and blue skies,
To heaven and earth, and all it's worth,
To hills and valleys, to trees and seas,
To all the wonders, to all that be,
To all the things I dare not dream,
To all that is, and all that seems. . . To all the new, great and wondrous things.

Debbie sobbed, *screw the colour of the dress*, she thought. Such a silly thing to nitpick about.

Now announced man and wife, Mr. and Mrs. Agenta, they kissed and went down the aisle together. Dora and Trevor behind them, then Monica and Brett, Tamara and Derek, their parents, then the rest of them flooded the aisles to meet at the gardens Archer had erected in her name. As beautiful as he saw her and made him feel.

At the cottage was music, games, and food for guests to enjoy, while they had pictures taken at the beach below. Some stood on the stairs watching. Roger especially.

Faith had written Archer a song, when they arrived up to the gardens, Archer saw a single chair, a microphone, and a stool.

"What's this?" he asked.

"Now you wait," Faith answered. "Like I did in the car the day you asked me to be your wife," she giggled.

"Well played," he agreed.

Not knowing, Archer fretted about it while dinner was served, wondering if this was how Faith had felt.

So many times he'd made her wrestle demons with his compliments and gifts. She had so many issues with self-esteem, which he never understood.

When Faith took the psychology course, she was able to explain it to him better. Archer couldn't imagine people being so mean to her, though. She was so very beautiful to him. Perfect. Kind and considerate. Loving and thoughtful. Selfless and strong.

Now, though, Archer understood her even more. There was no reason for him to be nervous right now, yet he was. He had *almost* everything he'd ever wanted.

Music softly played in the back, as people mingled after the meal, and just before they were to cut the cake, the DJ made an announcement. It was time for a special performance by Faith. Calling them both, she took Archer's hand and led him to the lone chair facing the stool, his cheeks flushed red under his amazing tan. Archer's white suit glowed in the sun, flashing, like the water from his hair. Once in the sun, once under the moon. The light that peeked through the shade of the trees that hung over the dance floor, danced on his suit.

Sitting him down, Faith kissed him as people clinked their glasses and hooted. A beaming smile on her face, she sang to him. That lullaby voice. The crooning and haunting one he'd first heard. Feeling awkward as Faith serenaded him, with the song she'd written about him. Singing her praises, about the beauty of his soul, that he bared only to her, it was beautiful and by the time she was done, Archer was crying.

The way she said so much, with just a few verses. The guitar setting the emotion. Immediately, he began to clap, everyone else followed his lead, as if they were waiting for him.

Archer couldn't help going to Faith, then taking her white guitar, he passed it to the hands they'd hired and kissed her. When he pulled her in, Faith thought he'd crush her, it was so tight.

Knowing how much it meant to him then, that was what she wanted. For Archer to see his own soul the way she did.

Before letting her go, he whispered in her ear how much he adored her, and everyone aww-ed at them, without fully knowing what she had just done.

The hired hands now had everything from the dance floor, the DJ congratulated them once again, and got the party started.

Wanting to sneak off and spend a minute alone, they made several attempts, but kept being sidetracked by guests wanting them to talk a minute. They'd have to wait. Many glasses clinked for them to kiss. Every two seconds it seemed.

Roger had the father and daughter dance and cried more than Faith did. Many times he'd prayed for a girl. All boys made him have to show his strong side and he wanted a girl to be tender with. He'd have brushed her hair and let her paint his nails, if she wanted. Right now, though, Roger let himself fall into the role. Bobbi Jo and Shelley had their own dad. Faith was special to him.

When the song had finished, he gave her hand to Archer and Debbie took Roger away, a mess. He couldn't get it together, admitting to Faith, later, that he would have loved to have a little girl, giving her away, then told her that she'd do just fine and felt as though she was his anyway.

Faith was more than he'd dreamed for Archer, feeling he was special and expected so much for him. He'd hung on to Johanna for too long. Not sure whether that saved him from marrying the wrong woman.

Archer would never cheat. Ever!

If Faith had shown up and he'd married already, he wouldn't have given her a second look, nor the time of day. Roger felt they were destined to be together.

Maybe they were. Their circumstances seemed to be fated. Fitting each other like a glove.

It'd always tortured Roger to see Archer hang onto Johanna. Now, he thanked her, for keeping him occupied, while Faith found her way to him.

They went "home" that night. It was Archer's house, but not anymore. Packing her things that week, Faith moved in with him completely, their lives continued to blossom. Faith thanked the gods for blessing her life. Whoever that might be.

Debbie and Roger insisted it was Yahweh, but she agreed with Archer. Many paths, one truth. Faith had done some research and came out still undecided.

If there was a god, and they wanted her attention, they'd have to show her something and not knowing the difference between a miracle and a rare event, how could she know for sure? There'd need to be many signs. It was as intense an idea to her, as the fact that humans didn't even have an example of nothing.

Using Archer's term, *intellectually honest*, Faith felt in her heart, there had to be more. It was all anecdotal and so suspended her opinion. Being able to attribute it all to fate or destiny or whatever. All Faith knew, for sure, was that she was happy.

The holidays rolled around again. She celebrated like everyone else around her, but it was just another day to her, really.

This year was special, though. They'd agreed no big gifts, as they had more than they needed, donating money all year long, to those less fortunate. Funding and building houses for those who'd have been, otherwise, thrown on the streets.

They built more hostels, aided in people getting educations or upgrading, to make their lives better, never asking for anything in return. Most of the time, remaining anonymous.

Archer usually got them a trip someplace, though. Which was fine with Faith. Always doing so much for others and doting on her, he needed a vacation in her opinion. When travelling for her books, Archer missed some, due to the gallery. Winter was their time.

He'd bought Faith her dream car this year and left it in his parents' garage. The Cooper was too small for Archer's legs, and sometimes, she liked to drive. The Jeep was too bouncy, and the car was too much power.

That morning they got up, made breakfast together as usual, then tackled the dishes. Then, it was gift time.

Sitting by the tree and fire, they opened their gifts from others, while holiday music played in the background. Reading cards, they set them on the mantle one by one. He. Then her. He. Then her.

With a tiny tree to the side, where their gifts were, Archer took his to her. Passing a small box, he mentioned the other gift was at his parents'. She could get it later.

Kissing him, Faith said. "Thank you, sweets," then opened the box. Tickets to Egypt. "*Ooh*. Nice!"

After that Faith then got his boxes. Passing one, Archer opened it to find a hand-carved wooden watch.

"Wow! That's so cool!" he said reading the insert. "No more stripping down now at airport security, between the watch and the belt last year."

"Yep! Every piece is wooden. There's a guarantee. If it breaks, you give it back and I'll have it replaced."

Faith smiled big then, "Now for the best."

Snuggling in with Archer, she handed him the second box. It was so small. Opening it, he took out a key chain.

"World's best dad," he read out loud. "But . . . I'm not a dad."

Looking at her confused, Archer reread it. "I don't get it. This is a joke somehow." She was always doing that to him, making him think.

Looking to her again, Archer stared, waiting for Faith to give him the answer to the joke, but she just raised her brows and said, "Really. You will be."

Jumping up excited, he asked, "AM I A DAD!?!?!?"

Faith kept smiling.

"Stop . . ." he grumbled, looking at it again. "AM I A DAD!?!"

Archer was *so* excited; she fell over laughing. "Tell meeeeeee," he cried flopping his arms down.

"You're a dad," Faith confirmed happily.

Scooping her up and kissing her a million times, he asked. "Are you serious?" then set her down so very carefully. "I'm sorry. Did I make you car sick? Shit. Oh. I mean damn. I mean poopy."

Faith laughed. "I'm not fragile, dear. Maybe nauseous these days. I won't break, though, and they can't hear you yet."

"Wait. Why didn't you tell me? How far are we?" Archer asked stressing out and rubbing his forehead.

"I'm sorry. I didn't want you to worry. I'd have told you if I'd suspected. I know how you stress about me. You're like your dad, and I thought, maybe I just had a bug or something. I just felt off. I still have my period, so I had no idea. It hadn't stopped."

"Fuck! I mean poop. Is that safe?" he asked.

"It's fine. Some women have gone into labour thinking they had gas pains. They never knew they were pregnant even, till the labour. We're all different," Faith replied. "*Imagine . . . Labour!*"

"Get out." Archer exclaimed as he sat down. "So how far along?"

"Twelve weeks, give or take some days," she answered.

Archer did the math on his hands. "That only gives me six months to get ready. I'm *so* doing everything with you. Imma spoil you rotten. I want to try that machine all the guys have been doing that I've seen on the internet. It simulates women's pains. Period and labour. I need to know what you might go through."

Faith laughed at the thought of him curled in a ball, wailing. The guys she'd seen only had it on three, which is a regular period.

"I get to record," she laughed.

"Deal!"

Faith admitted she was beside herself the last two days, keeping it all a secret and asked, "Is that how you felt planning the cottage and proposal?"

"Pretty much," Archer confessed.

"How did you handle that for months? The cottage even took a year."

"Oh, I near lost my shit. I, very well, may have. On a few occasions, I've had to apologize," he said wincing.

Archer had lost his temper at the construction guys when they didn't stay on schedule.

Faith wanted to tell him so badly, it nearly slipped out a few times, as she was mentally cracking. Glad it was over now, she admitted she'd also had time to think, while keeping it from him. Faith's mind reeled with what issues might arise.

"What if they have physical or mental problems?" Faith asked.

"We'll handle it, baby girl. Don't worry." Archer assured her, then told her about his out-of-body experience and the vision he'd had the first night together and the midnight swim. He hadn't worried a day since then.

"Thanks for that. You're so right," she smiled, seeing his point.

"There's nothing to worry about, until there's something to worry about. We got this," he reaffirmed. "My parents are gonna flip!"

Archer never mentioned how Johanna had said the same thing. The sting in his heart crushed him a little as he kept his composure. Faith saying out of concern, Johanna out of selfishness and how much work it would be.

Tossing things a bit in his head, Archer wondered, "Should we cancel Egypt?"

"Let's talk to the doctor first. I think it will be fine, though, as long as there's no complications. I won't have your whole dream threatened, and their life, because of a trip," then holding her belly, Faith said, "I wanted this too. More than you know . . ."

Archer's heart, felt as though it would surely explode now.

"You'll be the best mom ever."

"I'm a dad," Archer kept whispering to himself here and there, as they watched all their regular movies.

Miracle on 34th Street got them to noon and lunch. As they made sandwiches he giggled. "My li'l muffin, is makin' me a muffin. Hee hee hee."

After lunch they watched *The Muppets Christmas Carol* and then the original black-and-white version. That got them to supper and his parents' place. Popping out names to each other the whole afternoon, Archer looked at her with his mouth wide open.

"What?" Faith asked.

"Grace . . ." he said softly.

"Oooh," she remarked, interested in that one.

"That night at the cottage when you first sang to me. So much had happened inside. I'd kind of forgotten about it. It's been a wild ride," he said, remembering, which made him teary, all over again. The wait, done. "You saved me, Faith. This? Is Grace from the creator. I believe that . . . After the first night we made love, I found myself awake looking at the ceiling and did a meditation. I couldn't sleep and didn't want the good feeling to end, so I went for water, then went to the patio. The moon was glorious, and I couldn't help going for a swim under its glow before you came down. I felt euphoric and centered. I hadn't told you. I will now. It wasn't a secret, I, just didn't feel the need to tell you. For me, then, there was no better time, or place . . . I begged. I begged so hard!" he told her. "So, for a girl? The name Grace would be so nice, for me."

Archer was excited when she agreed. "Yes. It is a nice name, and I can't think of a better one. I think grace brought you to me. So, okay. Agreed."

Archer over the moon now, they snuggled, with the cushions from the sofa on the floor, in front of the huge bay windows. The snow drifted onto the fir tree, the branches bending as the time went on, while they ate popcorn and had juice.

Archer vowed to himself he was done with alcohol, wanting to be clean. Maybe now and then. Like today. He'd just have one celebratory one and be done till next year. It didn't bother him a bit.

"Graaaaccce," he kept saying followed by. "*Sawweeet*!" and then bounced a little.

He'd dote over Faith even more now, which to her, was fine. She was used to it and seeing it all in her head, she knew. Today would just be the beginning. "The snow, *this*. The ice, *that*. The doors were *much* too heavy". Faith laughed inside at him.

They agreed they'd do what Dora and Trevor did. Wait to see who came out.

"I gotta call Trevor," Archer said almost asking permission.

"Yes do. On speaker phone, though. I wanna hear too."

Calling Trevor and Dora, Archer was almost bouncing when he answered the call. "Happy holidays. Put Dora on speaker phone?" he asked and Trevor did.

"Hi, Archer. Faith. Happy holidays," Dora greeted.

Faith said the same and Archer followed then, saying "So!" then paused.

Trevor knew he was about to drop a bomb. He always said "so" first.

"I just sent you a pic."

"Shut yer fukkin mouth!" Trevor roared, after looking at the picture of the keychain. Dora hooted in the background. "Bro. I just got goosebumps."

They could hear Dora sobbing in the background now. "I prayed so hard for you both. I pleaded and pleaded. Your mom and dad too," Dora remarked through her tears. "I knew god would hear us. Does Mom know?"

Everyone called Debbie mom.

"We'll tell them all at dinner. I just found out myself."

"Brooooooooomygod," Trevor said. Which all came out as one word. Faith laughed under her fingers.

"Asher will have someone his age soon enough," Faith stated to Dora, which excited her. The fact that he'd have someone to be playing with.

Asher was full of energy, like Trevor. He really dragged Dora around. Just as Faith thought it, a crash come through the phone, then crying.

Dora growled. "I told you *no*! Good lord, give me the strength."

Asher got into everything. They really had their hands full with him.

"Gotta go, man. Dora says he's stuck in the rungs on the back of the chair. Fuck my life . . ." Trevor sighed. Archer did a literal face palm.

"I'm super happy for you though! Let's have coffee after the holidays?" Trevor suggested.

"For sure. Hope he's alright. Text me."

"Will do," Trevor replied, and Archer heard him groaning before he hung up and checked the time.

"We'd better get to the house. We still have gifts to load in the car."

Just then, his phone went off. Trevor sending a picture of Asher, they felt bad, but it also made them laugh.

Always going overboard with the kids, and Archer wouldn't hear otherwise, he checked with the boys to see what they needed, then asked what they were going to get, before he went shopping. Especially if it was something out of their price range. Always from Santa though.

One of his favourite things to do, Archer only really shopped now and then, but he'd go a bit nuts with the kids' gifts, when he did.

Packing everything in, he thought of the rough Jeep and was so glad he'd gotten Faith the SUV. She might be sour, but what the hell. *He was gonna be a dad*! Nothing could ruin today.

Archer helped her in the car, as always, and bounced to the music all the way to his parents'. When they'd gotten in and said their hellos to everyone, they brought in the gifts.

Roger and the boys helped after dinner, then they all exchanged cards. Gifts were saved for the young ones. It was about being together for them as adults now. Not the gifts.

After the kids had destroyed the living room with paper and they'd gotten that cleaned up, Archer told everyone they had an announcement. Helping Faith up, he said they'd be having a baby sometime in June.

Everyone hollered. Brett and Derek shook their hands, and the women hugged them both. Roger cried again. Debbie thanked god.

When everyone had left to go sit for dinner and the noise was gone, Debbie stayed behind.

"Of all the people, you deserve this. No child could be more fortunate."

Then lifting her glasses to dry her eyes, Debbie then breathed out hard. Archer went and held her a minute.

"I'd prayed for this, more than anything I've ever prayed for," she told him and hugged as tight as she could.

Like when Archer had had his first heartbreak. He'd gotten pretty tough after that, or at least hid it better.

Debbie cried as hard as he did that day. It killed her to see her boys in pain and Archer never wanted to see her that way again because of him. Just like Faith, he thought.

The day had been long for Archer with his excitement and had burned him out. "I think we'll head out. I'm kind of beat."

Hugging them both once more, Debbie said, "You guys drive safe," as she patted Archer's arm, like she was tapping out of a wrestling match.

Feelings were creeping up on her again and she didn't like being emotional. So much like Faith. Maybe it's why they'd bonded so easily. It was said that men will lean towards people like their mother. Women attracted to men like their father.

Roger knew this and thought it was so bizarre to see Archer with Johanna. She wasn't like any of the family. A shadow to him now, that led Archer right to his Faith.

"Watch the ice now, Archer," Debbie reminded them as they were going out the door.

"Oh!" Archer exclaimed. "I forgot! Your other gift."

Roger jumped up. "How did we forget that?"

Car crazy he'd had the garage heated to "keep the babies warm" he'd always joked. Freshly waxed now, Roger didn't have much left he needed to do anymore. Especially the winter. So, he carefully put a nice coat of wax on it and undercoated it. Winter was harsh and the salt would have it destroyed in no time. He couldn't have that. Opening the garage door in the hall they all went out. Shining under the bay lights, was a black-cherry red, electric SUV.

"Bouncing babies are nice, unless it means in a Jeep," Archer laughed. "Good call on my part. I know you love the Cooper, but I can't get in it, and I know you like driving. Now, it seems, it will serve an even better purpose. Keep the Cooper. We can use this with the kids."

Faith just looked at him. He at her.

Did he just say that? Kids?

"It's all inspected, registered, insured, and ready for our winters. If you want to take it home today, you can, I know the Jeep annoys you. It's okay. Can't blame you," Archer affirmed.

"I'd love to." Faith smiled to him and with a peck on the cheek she added, "Thank you for this."

Getting in, Faith pulled out of the yard. It was such a smooth ride home. She'd put the Cooper away for the winter and maybe use it if she was going out by herself. Faith thought now, she could take all her friends out for girls' night. Monica was always so cramped in the back.

Archer didn't sleep at all that night and just laid in bed looking at cribs and toys, picking colours for the baby's room. Neutral, white, clean. Faith could choose the rest. Of course, she had final say.

CHAPTER TWENTY-FOUR
Attention to Details

After their appointment with the doctor, Archer and Faith took their trip to Egypt. She'd given them the okay. There were so many things Faith said she wanted to see. The pyramids. Dinosaur museums. Elongated skulls. Ruins of ancestors, like Stonehenge and Viking settlements. Temples and sites that had to be excavated. Archer would make sure she'd see them all. Maybe some things she had no idea about too. Checking them off one by one, it would slow down with baby coming now.

On the trip to Egypt, they saw the pyramids and did some shopping, tried new foods and enjoyed music. Nothing stressful. They brought souvenirs home for family and art for their house. It was a lovely trip.

When Faith started to show, Archer bought a stethoscope to listen to her belly sometimes. Every night actually. He'd rub her feet and read books to baby about the planet. Telling them about their home. About how in love they were and the plans they'd made. Faith played guitar as much as she could, feeling the vibrations on her skin, knowing baby would too.

All in all, the pregnancy was good. The morning sickness went away quickly, and Faith was happy about that. Archer, overboard caring for her, she let him do what he wanted to. It was his experience too.

Spring came and went, and Faith ballooned in the last month, dreading summer that was coming quickly. It was already getting warm. The food cravings drove her a bit nuts.

Thinking it was an old wives' tale, Faith soon found out it was true. Debbie, and all the women in her life, made sure one of them was available every day now. In case Archer wasn't close by. The gallery was in full swing, and he struggled to get through the days.

Family helped by making food and cleaning. Faith had some trouble bending over now, but still insisted on helping. She wasn't incapacitated. Knowing they meant well, she appreciated it, but sometimes it got on her nerves.

Archer had been to all the classes and meetings he could about having a newborn.

He watched videos of childbirth and felt bad for his mother. He was a large baby and Debbie was so little. Archer just prayed their child would have mercy on the love of his life.

Baby's room all ready and several bags packed, they were ready to meet their angel. He'd booked her a private room and a personal care nurse to have all the attention she needed, with peace and quiet.

Hoping he'd be holding baby for Father's Day; it came and went. Faith got him a tiny cake just for them. As far as she was concerned, he was still a daddy.

Overdue now, they'd made an appointment for induction and had no longer gotten home from the appointment when Faith made a face as Archer unlocked the garage door.

"What?" he asked.

"Either my water just broke, or I peed myself," she laughed.

Archer just stood there with a blank look on his face as the colour drained out.

"Let me check before you panic."

Laughing at how he'd suddenly became unglued, Faith waddled to the bathroom just inside the garage door.

Archer paced outside the bathroom waiting and when Faith came out, she said, "Yep. Water is broken."

"Let's go then?" he asked hurriedly.

"We need contractions first, silly. They'll just send us home. You can call the nurse, though."

She arrived within the hour and Faith still hadn't felt anything other than pressure. The nurse said she was mostly dilated. No telling how long it could be, she wanted her in her room. It may progress quickly.

All at the hospital now, they checked her in, baby was coming either way now that the water had broken. The nurse kept an eye on Faith. Very well, Archer thought. Happy he'd done that, he thought of how crazy he'd have gone waiting for the hospital nurses to check. Sure, they were capable, but they were both special to him.

"You'd better call Mom and Dad," Faith told him.

All the classes he'd taken went right out the window and was beside himself with worry. The monitors they'd strapped to her, were a comfort, as baby's the heartbeat fill the room. A steady and fast ticking. Like the clock.

Faith groaned just then, and Archer rushed to her side to sit.

"That was a good one."

The nurse checked as it subsided and told them wouldn't be too long now. Things were well underway. Archer never left her side then.

Roger and Debbie had been in and stayed with them awhile, then went home to eat, saying they'd be back later on and for Archer to call if anything developed.

A few hours passed after that, and Faith said Archer should eat something. He couldn't, though. His stomach was in knots. There was no way he was leaving her.

The nurse gave them space earlier but insisted on staying closer now, watching the monitor closely and checking the paper that came out. Feeling Faith's belly on the contractions, she commented that she was pleased. They were nice and strong.

When Faith started groaning and having to control her breathing, the nurse asked if she wanted an epidural. "They're going to get intense now." She informed Faith.

"Intense now? This isn't intense?"

"Well, I mean you could go any second, really. We need to prepare for the worst, though. If it takes a long time, you could find yourself dealing with a lot of pain for longer than you'd prefer. There's no way to tell," the nurse affirmed.

"Then, yes, please. If it's more than this . . . I'm not sure I can take it."

Another hour passed before the anesthesiologist came with the epidural. Expressing his delight for them he excitedly introduced himself. "I'm Adam and I'll be helping you out here."

Faith, thankful now, got ready. Adam had Archer sit in a chair and let Faith lean on his shoulder for support and motioned for him to keep her there.

"Do your best not to move. It'll be a pinch and then you'll feel cold on the area,"

Archer couldn't watch. In the spine? How was she taking this?

He whispered their vows in her ear to distract her and Faith listened with all her might. The next thing she knew, he was packing his tools to leave.

"That's it?"

"Yep. You'll be right as rain now. You did a great job."

When he left, Faith said she felt much more comfortable. It was more like a muscle twitch. Another hour passed and she told Archer he'd better call Mom and Dad again. Feeling like she should push; Faith wanted them to have time to get there in case it went fast.

The nurse asked for space and Archer went to the end of the bed behind her. Asking for a push from Faith, she calmly assured her. "Okay. That's good. We need to have the room ready. I'll get the doctor. Baby is ready to come," she smiled.

Faith was excited but when she looked at Archer his mouth was hanging open and yes popping.

"If it's a boy? Name him whatever you want . . ."

Faith laughed. "C'mere, silly."

"That was more than I expected. It's cool on TV and whatever, but now that I'm here? I can't even," he said as the nurse came back.

"They'll take you in now."

Archer was ready, but not ready at all.

There was a good-sized staff in the delivery room, with lots of space, and the lights were low.

The doctor came in, cheerily saying, "Hi. This is an amazing day," and smiled before checking Faith.

Saying to push when Faith felt a contraction, she did.

The doctor felt around. "You're gonna do great," she encouraged, then said some medical terms they were familiar with from the shows they'd watched.

Nothing to freak about, but it didn't help him feel any better.

"You let us know when you want to push, and we'll be here to help. We see the crown already."

Three times Faith pushed and was told the head was out.

"One more good push now. We'll wait till you're ready. Once we get the shoulders it'll all be over."

Faith told them she was ready, and they all got in their positions, like ball players waiting for the pitch. Pushing as long as she could, they all cheered quietly to not scare baby, then did what was needed, before handing baby over.

Hearing the cry, Archer's heart slowed, and relief swept over him.

The nurse tending to Faith, took baby to her and saying, "You have a lovely baby girl," with a smile.

They both crying as Archer looked to Faith saying, "You did a great job, Big Mama," and kissed her. Then Grace.

There was more to do with Faith after Grace had finally come. It all seemed to go on in the background, though, as she laid there getting hugs from Archer while the nurses checked baby, technical things, then, took her back to Archer. With his heart as full as he'd ever felt, Archer passed her over and walked beside Faith in the stretcher, holding Grace.

Debbie and Roger met them in the hall, and they were introduced to Grace before taking Faith back to her room.

Archer placed her in Debbie's arms, while Roger cried. Snuggling her, they said prayers and cooed.

"She's an angel," Debbie smiled as Roger stroked her face so delicately with is huge hands, and hummed a tune.

Faith had never seen anything more beautiful in her life than these people, and her daughter. Coming to PEI was the best choice she'd ever made in her life. So many miracles since she came there, Faith wondered how it all had come to be. She never could have seen this coming.

Tired now, Faith enjoyed the feeling of the bed and blankets, without the huge belly. Archer held Grace as she slept, not taking his eyes from her. Completely in love.

After a few moments Archer passed Grace to Faith and they kissed her saying, "To all the wondrous things," together.

A few days later, they were home. Archer stayed as much as he could. The gallery was hopping, so he kept the nurse around for a month, just until Faith had settled in as a mother. In case she had questions or ran into an issue. Giving the nurse a room to use, while she was there, she stayed out of the way, unless she was needed.

As the years flew by, Grace and Asher became friends. Dora was around a lot more now that he'd grown out of his "get into everything" stage. Monica and Tamara weren't around as much, as they found men of their own.

They all did something together once a month, taking their men with them. It was like a side family for Archer. He liked the guys.

Roger and Debbie would come and sit with Grace in the en suite. Every two weeks he'd kick Faith out to have fun with the girls. Usually sporting their lunch or dinner.

When Grace was three, Faith got pregnant again. A boy this time. They named him Jesse.

He was very different than Grace, and she hovered over him as he grew. Protecting him, like a big sister should. Feeding him and changing his diapers, Faith was in awe of this little girl. An old soul for sure.

When Grace turned seven, Roger died a few months later. Archer was beside himself. Knowing Debbie was the strongest one, he thanked god that Roger went first. Roger would have been lost without her.

Debbie moved to a smaller place in town and sold the house. She passed away before Jesse hit high school.

One day Archer came home early. Grace and Jesse were still out with friends after school. He thought he'd sneak up on Faith and make some overdue love while the house was so quiet. The kids kept them busy with sports and clubs. Faith had done a lot of travelling lately, the gallery was about to hit peak season, and school wasn't quite out yet.

Expecting her to be in the office typing, Archer found her laptop was open, but she wasn't there. She wasn't in the kitchen or dining room either. He'd already passed through there.

Thinking she may be in the bathroom, he hoped to catch her naked. Slapping his hands together Archer rubbed them expectantly, smiling as he went. She wasn't there either, so checked the yard next.

Maybe laundry in the basement? Nope.

He even checked the closets.

Both her cars were there. Where could she be? Out with the girls? Then, sending her a text, he heard her phone go off . . . Bizarre.

Dialling the number, Archer listened as it rang on his end. Then hers. Following the sound, he found it on her desk, next to her open laptop. Worried now, he looked around for notes and checked his emails. Nothing.

Going through her phone to see what she'd been up to through the day, there was nothing since she'd texted him to have a great day at 9 a.m. and a call from each of the kids at noon.

Archer's heart sped up as he went outside, yelling through the yard. No answer came back. Monica said she hadn't heard from her. Nor did Tamara. Dora had been out all week with Asher at a tournament and Trevor hadn't heard from her either. This wasn't like Faith at all.

Pacing around, Archer waited. There was nothing else he could do, so called the police station and spoke to Matt about what he'd come home to and how strange it was. Nothing seemed out of place but his missing Faith.

When Matt insisted he come over to take a look around for some clues to help Archer calm down, Archer took it and thanked him. He couldn't even think straight.

He wanted to ask the kids but was also afraid they'd get scared. If faith didn't show, he'd have to ask. Until then he'd stay quiet about it.

Matt came straight away and looked over the yard and the house. There was no sign of a struggle or break-in and suggested Archer call the kids, but he refused.

Archer knew how sensitive Grace was. She'd be onto him in a heartbeat. It was like she was deeply connected to him. He did, however, send them each a text, asking when they were coming home and if Faith was picking them up.

They said they'd be home after supper. Their friends' parents had asked them to stay to eat, then they were going to hang out for awhile after that and get a lift home. Each of them saying "Mom knows," they'd called and told her when they were on lunch break at school.

"Well. That gets us to twelve thirty this afternoon." Taking off his hat Matt scratched his head. "We can't file a report for twenty-four hours. Is there anyone else you can think of, she might go with?"

"No. She's very regular in her ways. Almost predictable. Which is why I'm worried. This isn't like her at all," Archer sighed, rubbing his forehead.

"I hate to ask, Archer, but have you both been good? Has there been any fighting?" Matt asked with his eyes to the floor.

"We don't fight. We barely even disagree. As a matter of fact, I just let her have her way. It seems to go like that a lot. She's not irresponsible and we're very happy."

"Again, I hate to ask. It's necessary, though. Has she been depressed?"

"What? *No!*" Archer answered, insulted that he'd asked.

"Archer . . . I've seen a lot in my time on the force. People get depressed. Some too ashamed to ask for help, resort to unfavourable solutions. I wasn't meaning to imply anything."

"Yeah. I'm sorry Matt. If Faith was depressed, she'd tell me. We don't keep secrets. If she is? She's superb at hiding it. There has to be something else."

"Does she have enemies?"

"Never. She's the salt of the earth."

"Some people are unstable," Matt mentioned in a by-the-way tone. "Does she have a stalker? She's pretty famous, you know."

"She's never mentioned anything. I can check her emails. It'd take me some time, though."

"Well. For now, there's not much to be done. I'll let all the guys know to keep an eye out for her when they're on patrol. You go through her emails. If you find anything let me know. It could be a lead. Send me a list of places she may go to get away from it all," Matt suggested.

"But her cars are here."

Matt's walkie-talkie went off and codes spilled out of it. He listened closely, then turned it down and resumed their conversation. "She may have walked. Send the list. Let me know if she comes home. If not, we'll go from there. If she's seen, I'll let you know right away. I have to get going. There's been an accident. I'll check in with the hospital before I pull out. I could be caught up awhile with this."

Archer thanked Matt for all his advice and the time he'd taken to come out to look. He also apologized for snapping at him. Matt was just trying to help.

"All good, Archer. Stay in touch and we'll get to the bottom of this."

Then patting Archer's back, Matt headed out talking into his shoulder with more codes and asking for details.

The kids came home at nine that night. "Where's Mum?" they each asked when they came home.

Archer told them she was out and that they should get any homework done, grab a snack, and get their teeth brushed, doing his best not to seem off.

Grace knew something was up, though. Studying psychiatry on her own, it'd always fascinated her. Faith taught her a lot and they'd talk about it for hours. She'd watched her mother go through several courses growing up and it drew her right in.

Faith told her about people and how they can get sideways of themselves. How trauma can create a mess that takes a lifetime to correct. That some never got better. She wanted Grace to know about how people can be irrational and wanted her to make the right decisions for herself.

Faith loved that Grace's heart was so big and that she wanted to help, but also wanted her to know it could be trouble and to be very careful. People hide things and appear to be quite normal . . . until they can't anymore.

When Faith was sure Grace wanted to do it and wasn't backing down, she insisted Grace take some type of self-defence. She might need it but hoped not. Better to be safe than sorry.

Archer taught her some, but Grace needed a consistent class and to socialize. She tended to sit in her room, absorbing information. Three nights a week they took her to judo.

Faith had to grow up fast when her mom had died, barely seventeen. They wanted Grace to be prepared for the world.

Not knowing much back then, it was hard to have to just drop into adulthood, without parents to guide you. The money situation alone was difficult, let alone relationships. Jonsie played her like a fiddle.

Archer knew Faith had to have had dealt with unstable people in her seminars, ones like she'd referred to with Grace. She never said anything though, to protect him no doubt. Archer would have gone insane knowing some of her fans followed her around on the streets when she travelled. PEI was a safe enough place but it didn't mean much to him now with Faith missing. Some whack job might have made a special trip to get to her.

Jonsie had done a number on her, in their time together, and that day. Something they never mentioned, though. Nor Jonsie.

Archer knew her so well. She'd never be out this late. It was going on ten now. Pacing around, he kept checking his phone. Nothing.

Going to the cabinet, Archer pulled out a bottle of scotch that he saved for when guests came. He hadn't had a drink since Grace was born, but for the odd glass of wine with family. Faith would drink one glass with her girls' dinner every two weeks, and on special occasions. Like their anniversary.

It was better for them that way. Archer said he worried if something had happened, and they had to drive to the hospital or something but couldn't if they had been drinking. He didn't take any risks at all anymore.

Nerves rattled now, he pulled the cork out and took a glass from the cabinet. The bottle clinked on the rim as he poured, he was shaking that badly. Putting the bottle down, Archer wrung his hands nervously, as if to think twice.

Feeling his wedding band, he spun it while thinking of their lives, then rubbed his eyes with his finger and thumb, digging right in, as if to push the tears back into his body.

Smoothing out his lashes, he dried the tears that kept coming, then picked up the scotch and slammed it down. Pouring another, he drank that one too. It was rough and burned all the way down and did nothing, other than make him warm.

Sitting down in the round oversized chair by the cabinet, Archer put his face in his hands and cried quietly, so the kids wouldn't hear. Their music was loud upstairs, and he could hear thumping. Grace dancing, no doubt.

Dread loomed like death in a seniors' home now, and when his phone went off, Archer answered emphatically, "*Faith?*"

He didn't recognize the number.

"Sorry. It's Matt. I just got back to the station and wanted to check in with you. Have you heard anything?"

"No. Nothing," Archer spoke softly. "Is there some action I can take? I'm losing my mind," he wheezed.

"The boys haven't seen her anywhere. We've been to all the places you gave us in your list. They still have their eyes out, though. I'm going off duty, but you can call anytime. There's got to be an answer and we'll find it!" Matt assured him again. "Do the kids know?"

"I don't think so. I didn't tell them," Archer answered, voice cracking as he tried to keep himself together.

"Don't, unless you have to. No point worrying them too," Matt suggested.

"That's what I thought."

Matt had managed to make him feel a little better. At least able to stop the tears.

"Once you get the kids to bed, you could have someone come over. It may make you feel better to go out and look for yourself. Get your mind shifted some. It's probably nothing. If you find her or she shows up . . . I'm the one to call first. Okay?" Matt said commandingly.

"Understood."

"You're sure there's no depression?"

"God, no," Archer replied loudly but in a kinder way this time, then whispered, "Faith loves her life. She loves the kids. Her job. She doesn't do things like this. Something is terribly wrong."

"I can understand how you feel. If you're right, then she'll show up eventually. Try to stay calm and positive. Also stay in touch," he tried soothing again.

"Thanks. I appreciate all you've done, Matt. Really. Though I know you're using reason. I'm not convinced."

"We'll talk soon either way," Matt assured.

"Yes. Thank you again," Archer said ending the call.

Then looking up at the clock, he sighed. Grace was standing in the doorway, interrupting his stress.

"Daddy?"

"Gracie! You scared the life out of me," Archer said with a fake laugh. "What you need, cupcake?"

"I know what's going on."

Standing up, Archer went to the cabinet and put the scotch away to keep it from her. She'd already seen it though, he supposed.

"What? Nothing's going on," he chuckled.

Grace sat on the chair and patted it for him to sit beside her. He did.

"I heard you on the phone. I can see you've clearly been crying . . . I know Mum is missing."

"I'm probably overreacting," he responded with a chuckle to shake her off him.

Grace wasn't buying what he was trying to sell her. Climbing onto his lap, she hugged him tighter. Like when she was little. Archer broke down and sobbed into her tiny shoulders and she rocked him as he cried.

Grace was so strong and confident saying, "Sometimes people carry burdens they don't talk about. Mom is one of those. When she's upset, I can feel it. You too, Dad," Grace said confidently and rubbing her chest. "In here."

Was she an empath? Archer thought, looking into her green eyes. Like Faith's. Taking her hands, Grace wiped the tears from Archer's face, then rubbed his forehead with her thumbs and slid both her hands to his cheeks. Like Faith. Brushing them over his eyes to close them, she kissed his forehead and each eyelid, then wiped the tears again from his cheeks, kissing each one. Like Faith.

What? How could this be? Faith had done the exact same thing that night he cried to her. Archer looked at her puzzled. Did Faith tell her?

"What made you do that?" he asked suspiciously.

"I saw Mom do it to you at the cottage the time you wept when she fist sang for you."

There was no way! Was there?

"You were both so in love. Neither of you telling the other. I had hoped you'd say it, but you wouldn't admit it. I knew, though," she said with a smile. "It's why I chose you both . . . to be my parents."

"You couldn't have seen that, Gracie. Did Faith tell you that story?"

"No. I was there. You couldn't see me. I didn't have a body yet, but I saw all the times you showed love to one another. Everyone does. When they're born, though, they forget. I didn't."

"I find that a little hard to believe."

"It's okay. You don't have to believe me. I'd be skeptical too if I were in your shoes. It's not very reasonable," Grace admitted.

"How did you become so amazing?"

"Amazing Grace" popped into his mind.

"I can only be what I am, Dad."

Faith had also said that to him once.

"Right now, I'm here for you. I'm a big girl now and you don't have to hide things from me. You've always been there, Dad. Let me do this for you now."

"Gracie . . ." he spoke starting to cry again and took her tiny face in his hand, rubbing her cheeks with his thumbs.

Hugging him, she said, "We won't tell Jesse, though. He won't understand."

Archer cried as he held her, like holding onto his sanity. Grace would stay as long as he needed her to but smelling the scotch on his breath, she asked, "Did you eat, Dad?"

Seeing her for the young woman she was, not the little girl he remembered, Archer wondered how he'd not seen her grow up.

"I can't. I don't even know what to do. I feel so lost right now. I've never felt out of control, but for a few times," he confessed to her.

"Like the day I was born."

"What?"

"Yeah. The day I was born. You were so scared for Mommy and I . . . I tried to comfort you, but you couldn't hear me."

"Gracie . . . this is going too far. I don't understand what's happening here and it's scaring me a bit," Archer said sternly.

It didn't shake her though. Grace didn't care. He needed to hear what she had to say, so continued. "I asked to be born right then. It was the only way to relieve you of your worries. Only having me in your arms would be all *anyone* could have done for you."

Archer looked at her in shock and Grace just smiled.

"I said those exact words . . . In my head. I never told anyone," he whispered.

Suspicious now that she was being honest, Grace knew what no one else did about the way he'd felt that day. "I know," she stated taking his hand.

Archer's heart slowed down as a peace overtook him then looked to the sky. What was going on?

Grace took his face in one hand, then took Archer's hand, put it on his chest and said, "No. Dad. It's in here. Not 'up there' . . . Can we have some toast?"

To Archer, it seemed random to ask for toast out of nowhere.

Grace knew he didn't have an appetite, but toast wasn't heavy. Faith gave it to her when she was ill with the flu, and it always made her feel better. To this day, she adores the smell of toast. It's always so much better when someone else makes it too. She was showing care in a way she knew how to express.

"Yes. Yes," Archer answered and got up.

Grace took his hand and never let go as he got the bread. Taking it from its bag with one hand, into the toaster, then the butter, knife, and jam.

Grace clung to him watching every move he made. Like she'd never seen anyone make toast before.

"You have to let my hand go, honey, so I can finish the toast," Archer teased.

She did but latched to his body instead and stood on his feet. Like when he'd taught her to dance. Archer laughed and buttered the toast. She wasn't as light as she used to be. He'd take it though.

"Blueberry jelly too," Grace grumbled into his chest. It came out muffled, but he knew what she wanted. Apple never falls far from the tree.

"Okay," he answered going to the fridge, Grace, stayed attached on his feet and waist.

Not complaining, Archer just spread the jelly and took it to the table on her plate. "There you go, Gracie doll."

"Thank you," she said letting him go, then sat in the comfy chair. "Now you," she ordered. "Milk too, please."

Archer cocked his head sideways. "Yes, ma'am. Authoritative today."

"You know you need it," Grace retorted and bit into the toast.

She'd just saved him from self imploding and knew it too.

"Grace?"

"Yep," she answered with a mouthful of toast.

"When did you grow up?"

"I'm wired in, Dad. Always was," she explained without hesitation.

"Wired in? What's wired in?" Archer asked as he buttered a slice of toast.

"Wired in. Like. You know? To the host . . . or god. Whatever you want to call it," Grace said and paused. "Like a computer to the internet. It's always on. Just most don't use it. They could if they wanted to."

Taking two glasses and the milk, he poured Grace some and took his toast to sit with her at the table. She glared at him gently, then looked at his cup and Archer just poured the milk not needing to be told twice. She already had with her eyes, then snapped her head sideways, as if to say, "that's right."

Rolling her eyes Grace rose to get the knife and jelly, then sitting back down, she chugged her milk and pushed his plate closer, as if to say, "eat already!"

Scooping out some jelly Archer had to know, more. "Sooooo. Can you tell me about the host? Or is it a secret?"

"Nope. No secret," Grace said wiggling her feet under the chair. "Eat. I'll talk when you do."

After Archer had a bite she asked what he wanted to know.

"Where *is* the host?"

"It's all around you. Like a field," she answered, trying to find the best words. "You know that time, when you drifted off and went into the vision? With the hall and the pillar? The focused place where you shooed the dust in your personal hall of records?"

What the hell? What did she really know?

"Go on."

"That's where you're most connected. You get a kind of . . . download," Grace answered.

"Continue," he urged finishing the first slice.

"What I mean by wired in, is that I'm always there. Like I never left. Or forgot. Does that make sense?"

"Kind of. Yes. I've found the only way to truly know something is by experience itself. Anything else is just data."

"Dad, it's allll just data . . . You know how you feel for Mom? Jesse? Me?"

"Do I ever!" he answered trying to swallow the toast and not keep her waiting.

"It's that. Only infinite and unconditional," Grace stated.

All Archer could do was crunch his toast and listen now.

"That's hard to grasp, Grace. I can't even fathom it . . ." he crunched on, feeling much better now.

"When you expire, you'll know it. The way I do. Death isn't a bad thing. People cut themselves off and then hold onto things that are drowning them. Like a lifesaver. It's very backwards. Then, they point to all kinds of things outside of themselves to explain why they have a hole inside. Like fear of death. Poor excuse to be miserable."

Archer couldn't believe his ears and just stared at her over the cup of milk he was drinking and thinking she knew more than she had the ability to express.

"*Dad*! I'm *not* making this up!" Grace asserted, a little miffed at him.

"Dear. I'm not doubting you. It's just ... wayyy over my head ... I'll try to understand if you can tell me more," Archer said as he put his hands up not wanting her to stop her talking. "Doesn't have to be right now, but I'd like to hear more, though ... Over time. It's pretty heavy. You must be powerful. How do you handle knowing all of this? You haven't said anything about this before."

"It's just ..." she stuttered.

"Just what, love?" Archer asked before finishing the milk.

"People only understand to the depths of which they have looked within themselves. I listen well. When I hear the cues, I share. I only say what's needed."

"I'm so, so sorry. Have I been that shallow with you, Gracie?"

"It's okay, Dad. To you I just looked like a kid. And I was. I didn't have the vocabulary I do now. I wouldn't have been able to tell you anyway," Grace smiled, taking his guilt away.

"You are one amazing girl, I tells ya," Archer said slapping his leg.

"I know, Dad. Thanks for saying it anyway. You're the same kind of amazing. Mom too ... and Jesse ... Even though he's annoying," Grace muttered then rolled her eyes. "Can we watch a movie while we wait for Mom to get home?"

Archer didn't quite believe it all but gave her an A+ for attempt.

Leaving the dishes on the table they went to the sofa. Giving Grace the remote he told her to pick, and they curled up together.

Archer in the back and she in front of him, he played with her hair while she picked a movie, then talked all through the credits about this and that. Archer soon fell asleep. Grace with him.

CHAPTER TWENTY-FIVE
The Longest Nap

Archer was woken with an elbow to the nose. "*Oh, Jesus!*" he whispered and crunched his eyes together, shielding his face with the other arm, even though it was way too late.

Sliding out from the back part of the sofa, Grace fell in to where Archer had been and curled up as he sat rubbing his nose, then checking his finger for blood, sworn she'd broken it. He'd heard it crack.

Covering her with a throw, he sat on the end of the sofa and checked the time. It was daylight, at least!

Slinking through the room, as not to wake Grace, Archer searched the whole house and found nothing, but a sleeping Jesse. His heart sank all over again.

Grace had made him feel so much better last night, he decided to go back to the sofa and sat on the end again. Taking her feet, Archer laid them on his lap, making him feel hidden from the world, and comforted him somewhat.

Grace started mumbling and Archer smiled as he watched her face contort. How he loved her so. She mumbled a bit more and he covered his mouth with his hand, trying not to laugh, then looked out the window.

"*Mommy!*" she shouted.

Archer's heart wrenched and tears filled his eyes. Crying again now, he rubbed her tiny feet, trying to get a grip on himself.

"Who's that?" Grace asked. "Where are we? Are you okay?"

Archer watched her now and listened in.

"No . . . I can't see a way out . . . I'll look, though," she said in a way that seemed like she was having a conversation. Her eyes darted rapidly under her lids.

Archer frozen now, waited for her to say more. For one reason or another, he pulled up the recording app on his phone and set it on the back of the sofa.

"All I can see is a shed . . . trees . . . a stream . . . *Mommy!*" she cried again.

Should he wake her?

"I'm sorry . . . I can only fly. I can't untie rope or move anything."

Was she having a nightmare? Moving to wake her, Archer felt bad for laughing a minute ago, then she screamed, "*Don't!*"

It scared him near to death. Was she talking to him? If not, then who?

Archer hit the record button and Grace sobbed, then screamed, "*Mommy*!!"

It was blood-curdling and made him jump back, but he hadn't woken her.

"What can I do?" she asked, then was silent.

"Daddy wouldn't believe me," she answered.

Who was she talking to? Wanting to know more, he left her to sleep. Or whatever she was doing.

He was just about to wake her when she'd said that . . . and now? Archer wasn't sure of anything anymore. Especially after what she'd said last night, about being wired in. He'd believe just about anything at this point.

"Mmm . . . mmmmm," she groaned.

Speak, Gracie! he said in his head, needing to hear more.

"Dad?" she said out loud. "How did you get here?"

Gracie? Do you hear me? he thought. There was no way this was happening. It had to be a coincidence . . . but he couldn't help it. This was too weird.

"Yeah. But . . . I can barely make you out and I can't see you either. Can you get closer?"

Archer closed his eyes and found a still spot in his head as quickly as he could. Maybe that would help. He had no idea what he, or she, was doing, but she'd stopped talking.

Gracie, please talk to me?

"That's better," she answered out loud.

Where are you?

"In a shed, with Mom and some strange woman. She's tied her up . . . *Stop*!" she cried.

Gracie, what!? Archer thought in panic.

"Daddy, she's bleeding, and her eyes are puffy," Grace said as she started to cry harder, then screamed, "DON'T TOUCH MY FUCKING MOTHER, YOU COW!"

Archer nearly had a heart attack and opened his eyes to look at Grace. Tears streamed down her face as she lay there quietly. Her body still. Was she dreaming? Was it a vision?

Closing his eyes again, he found the still place he was just in. Trying harder to focus and not let her jar him again.

In his mind alone, Archer asked, *Gracie, can you show me where you are? Or bring me to you?*

"No, Dad, I can't. I can't leave Mom."

Tell me what you see . . . Where are you at?

"I don't know . . . You have to come somehow, Daddy."

Archer didn't want to know but one thing. Where?

Where, though, Gracie? . . . Where?? he begged.

"I don't know . . ."

Listen to me . . . my brave, strong girl . . . Can you go outside the shed?

"I can't leave Mom."

Why? Are you not allowed or because you don't want to? he asked then. If this was real or true, there had to be something she could do.

"I don't want to . . ." she answered.

You need to, though, dear. We need Mom to come home with us, he told her gently, but she'd stopped answering him again.

Grace! Archer shouted, and her body jumped.

I'm sorry I scared you. You have to tell me more. Listen to me, honey and do as I say, he asked then, but she was silent.

It felt like forever to him although it was only a second. If it was true, a second could be the difference between life and death.

Gracie? Can you hear me? he asked desperately.

"I'm sorry, Daddy. What do I do?"

Tell me what you see. The shed has trees. Is it in the woods, someone's backyard? he asked. *Can you just go outside for a minute? Find a road?*

"Yes, I can. Let me see . . ." Grace answered a little hopeful now, then was quiet for a minute as he waited impatiently. "Yes, there's a road."

Go to it, please?

"But, Mommy."

Go, Gracie. You have to. I'm coming to get you both. I need you to do this so I can help, he told her, trying in a soft way to reason with his sleeping daughter, flying on a wing and a prayer right now that it wasn't a dream.

"Okay . . . I'm on the road."

Move down and find a sign . . . Anything . . . he said gently.

"Vegetables . . ."

Good girl. Go further, he guided her.

"Two, two, five."

Such a good job . . . How far did you go?

"A long way."

Go back, then. Can you go the other way? he asked, trying not to push her.

It certainly seemed time may be of the essence for Faith, if he was right.

"Okay," she answered. "I can hear all of your thoughts, though."

Careful not to think too much, Archer waited. It was silent a minute, then Grace said, "I'm back to the lane leading to the shed . . . Mommy is screaming. Daddy, please help her . . ." Grace begged.

I know it's hard, but you have to keep going up the road. Tell me what you see. Anything that stands out, he told her commandingly this time.

Sobbing horribly now and shaking she did ask she he asked, then after a brief minute, she screamed, "HELPPPP!"

What, Gracie? Tell me, he said calmly in his head.

"It's a cop car!" she said, rather excited.

Can you talk to him? Make him go to the shed? Archer asked as hope filled him.

"I'll try."

On the 225, Matt was on the road with a car pulled over and writing them a ticket. Hearing a sound, he snapped around dropping his board on the road, then vomited. The person in the car watched in the rear-view mirror.

"Officer. Are you okay?" she asked, sticking her head out the window.

Matt waved a hand that he was okay and took a few deep breaths. His head hurt bad. "I'm losing my marbles. This job will be the death of me," he said quietly and picked up his board.

Again, hearing a sound, Matt whipped around pulling his gun out and pointing it to the road. Looking both ways, he saw nothing but him and the person in the car. Scanning the bushes and listening hard, he found nothing else.

Putting his gun back, Matt finished writing the ticket, then went to his car to do the paperwork.

"He can't hear me . . ." Grace sobbed. "It's Matt."

Archer didn't want her to be disheartened. *It's okay, honey. Go to the car. Give me the plate number, then the badge number for me good girl*, he prompted then with confidence.

"The plate number is 473 AP. His badge is 062002."

Nice job! Come back to me now. We're gonna go get her, he told Grace, not wanting her to see any more than she already had.

Opening his eyes, Archer repeated the numbers and letters in his head over and over, as he texted them to Matt, then asked if it meant anything to him.

He answered right away. *How do you know my badge number?!?!?!*

It wasn't, but a moment, after Matt took his thumb from the keypad, that his phone rang. It was Archer.

"*Matt!* You have to listen . . ." Archer said in a panic, and desperate.

His stomach was so sick, and his head pounded. Struggling not to vomit as he rubbed Grace's leg, Archer thought of what to say to Matt.

"I know this sounds insane, but please trust me. Are you on the 225?"

"Yes . . . How—" Matt tried to ask, but Archer cut him off.

"Doesn't matter. I know where Faith is . . . kind of. You're close. I need you to help," Archer begged.

"Archer this is fucked," Matt said looking into his rear-view mirror, then up the road ahead of him. "Are you following me? Where are you?"

"*Home!*" he yelled losing his patience now. "I'm sorry . . . Please, just listen."

Grace woke up then, from his yelling.

"I can't say how I know, but I do. I'll explain later . . ."

Matt sighed. "Well talk then. I feel ill."

"There's a shed in the woods, just in a short lane, near a stream on the 225. Faith is there you need to find it. She's in trouble."

"Fuck, Archer, there're fifty sheds on this road easily, and streams all over the place. It would be like looking for a needle in a haystack," he said despairingly, as he pulled up the map on the laptop he had in the car anyway.

Grace still half asleep said, "Red shed with a black tin roof."

"*Red shed, black tin roof!*" he shouted to Matt.

Archer had nearly taken his ear off screaming so Matt put him on speaker phone and sighed. "Let me look."

Matt scrolled, then zoomed. Scrolled, then zoomed.

Archer checked with Grace, that she was okay. When she nodded yes, he got up and paced on the floor waiting to hear back. It wasn't but a moment, but losing his patience, he yelled, "MATT!"

"Jesus, stop yelling. I'm looking," he growled back.

"Please, Matt . . . it may save her," Archer begged now begged now.

"Scrolling . . ."

Matt was now running out of patience for this shit. Scrolling up and down the road, he saw a shed, and a stream with a short lane. Zooming in, it was right behind him. Looked like a match. Pressing the street view, Matt saw the red peeking through the trees.

"Shit, there's one on the old Chandler residence. Civic number is 2504." Matt said amazingly. How did Archer know that? What was going on?

"Please go. Hurry. It sounds crazy, I'll tell you when I get there how I know. I know the place you mean. I'm on my way," Archer snapped and hung up the phone.

2504 Archer kept repeating to himself.

"Stay here, Grace. I have to go to the shed. I'll call Trevor and he'll be right over. Keep an eye on Jesse," he told her, thinking a task would help her.

He was the one who needed help, though, and fuck was he ever sick to his stomach.

Kissing her head and thanking her, Archer went to the car and Grace watched him lose the last of his marbles calling Trevor, as she stood in the window.

"Dude. Can you go to the house? Keep an eye on the kids for a bit? I have to run out," he asked.

"Sure, man. Dora is on her way home from the bridge. It'll keep me busy. You alright? Did Faith get home?"

"It's a super long story and I'll tell ya when I get back."

"Alrighty. I'll go now."

Trevor bolted from his chair. Archer had that tone again, like when . . . Jonsie. Worried now as he ran over to stay with the kids, getting to the door, he put on his best face and took a deep breath. "Be cool. Be cool," he told himself going in.

"Morning, Gracie. Did you eat yet?" he asked, going straight to the kitchen like nothing was wrong.

Not wanting him to know what had happened, Grace replied, "Nope. I just woke up." She was trying to seem cheery.

Trevor didn't have a clue and she wasn't gonna be the one to tell him.

On the 225, Matt put his lights on, but not the siren, and drove back down the road. Pulling into the short lane, he left the car running and turned off the lights.

Archer was on his way, so Matt left the car close to the road for him to see, and as far as he dared, in case Archer was right. He may need the car to be handy. If nothing was there, Matt was going to have a good chat with him about this wild-goose chase.

Checking the layout once more, he called in to dispatch to tell them where he was, and what he was doing there. In case he needed backup. With no idea what he was walking into Matt wanted them to be on alert.

"Copy . . . What's the code?"

"10-14," he answered, getting out of the car and silently closed the door.

"Copy . . . on standby."

Using the grass all he could, to approach quietly, he undid the holster and just then heard shouting come from the shed. Freezing to listen, Matt heard a woman swearing. As he got closer, he also heard a woman crying, so crept to hear better.

"Faith, you're such a troll," Lacey said.

Faith begged, "Lacy, please! You don't have to do this." sounding very tired.

This was crazy, Matt thought.

"Hm . . . I know . . ." she cackled as Matt peeked under the door of the shed.

It had a huge gap, and he counted four feet in total, and the end of a bat. Not sure that was all the people inside, he went slowly along the wall to the window. Footsteps came behind him and Matt whipped right around with his gun drawn. It clicked on the movement, right into Archer's face.

Archer fell to the ground and put his hands up, as Matt rolled his eyes and mouthed "Where's the kids?"

Archer pulled out his phone and holding it up, Matt saw Trevor's contact picture. "Stay back," he ordered he mouthed.

"Please. My kids . . . My husband . . ." Faith begged to Lacy.

Matt looked in the window and listened to the conversation. Lacy's back to him, he could see Faith was tied to a chair. Bloody and parched looking. Lacy had blackened Faith's eye, and it was swollen so badly, she could only see out of one. Matt thought she didn't have much luck with people and bats.

Thinking on how this could have gotten to this point, Faith tried to remember. Lacey had blindsided her in the garage after getting home from the grocery store. The food was still in the trunk. It was all she knew.

Lacey filled in the gaps for her. It seemed to Faith that the villains always liked to brag about how they'd gotten away with their perfect crime, all the while incriminating themselves, so she listened well.

"I must have sat in the garage all morning waiting . . . and waiting," she groaned, like a valley girl who didn't get her smoothie in 1.4 seconds, having to wait a full two minutes then chuckled. "It felt so good to club you over the skull with your own bat."

Picking it up, she stroked the long end, then brought it to her eyes, looking at it adoringly. "I laughed so hard when I went for the trash can to dump you in. I had you tied up, praying you'd wake up and see your fat ass get thrown in with the rest of the garbage."

Faith's blood began to boil.

"My plan took months. It was pretty hard not to just beat the fuck out of you right there and then. That would have defeated the purpose, though."

Lacey put the bat on the floor, leaning on the tip.

Faith hadn't even noticed herself being followed. Was she blind?

"You're so fucking stupid. And really, I don't give a fuck about your precious family. Maybe when I'm done with you, I'll comfort that hunk of a husband you have, work my way in and just take your place. He's pretty sexy. Sweet ass and nice big . . . Well. You know. I'm sure I could accommodate him," Lacey purred then licked her lips. "Or maybe I'll just take him and the brats out too, but . . . before any of that happens, you'll suffer. Like Jonsie did."

Archer mouthed "Go!" to Matt.

Jonsie's name had popped, and Archer figured out what was going on. He couldn't have her say another peep. They'd both be fucked . . . and the kids. What was he going to do when Matt got her to talk?

Hesitating another second, Matt wanted to hear more of the conversation to know what he was going into, or if anyone else was there but Archer pushed him to go, again.

Matt sighed and pointed for Archer to stay put, then slid along the wall again, careful not to rub his shirt on the wood. Archer hoped he hadn't put anything together about Jonsie and was sure glad he hadn't recorded any of that.

Pausing at the door, Matt took a good breath, then put his hand on the latch and it clicked.

Fuck! Matt said in his head.

Lacey heard it too and picked the bat up over her shoulder, listening. With only one thing to do now, he kicked it in and pointed the gun at Lacey. "Police!" he yelled. "Put the weapon down."

Lacey didn't move. "Put the weapon down," he repeated.

Scanning the room quickly, Matt took the walkie-talkie in his hand and reported the scene. "Dispatch . . . 10-53 in progress."

"10-4. Emergency vehicles on the way."

"Copy . . . Put the weapon down, ma'am. Slow. Hands where I can see them. We can talk about this," Matt tried to reason.

"I can't go to jail," Lacey laughed. "I'm too soft for that."

"Last time I'm asking, ma'am. Put it down, kick it away and back up."

The time for bargaining ended as Lacey swiftly brought the bat to Faith's head and whacked her onto the floor, chair and all. Matt instinctively shot and the bullet bit into her gut. Possibly non-fatal.

Archer's ears rung when the gun went off and he snapped up to run into the shed.

Lacey shot, Faith bloody on the floor, tied to a chair, and unconscious, Matt checking to see if Lacey was breathing.

"*Nooooo!*" Archer screamed as he ran to check Faith.

"10-53 suspect is down," Matt reported checking Lacy's pulse. "Unresponsive."

Archer checked Faith as his heart skipped a beat. "Please. Help."

"I'm sorry. I had to make sure she wouldn't get up for another attack. The ambulance is here. They'll get Faith," Matt told him.

They were already on their way with him reporting a weapon. Before Matt could say that Archer shouldn't move her, he had her untied and was scooping her up, heading for the door of the shed.

Ambulance doors slammed as he ran down the lane with Faith, her head bobbing around as he screamed for them to help.

Opening the back doors, Archer carried her inside as a second ambulance came. Setting her down, they pushed him out of the way to work on her, calling in all kinds of things he'd never heard of.

Pacing outside as the other team took a stretcher to the barn, Archer froze and fell to his knees. "*Please, god . . .* I can't live without her. The children."

As one paramedic treated Faith, the other called in the report. "Copy. Triage is ready. We have to go, sir. Are you family?"

"Yes, she's my wife. Please."

"Follow us in then, we'll let them know you're also on your way," he directed.

The other closed the door, went to the driver's seat, and turned the sirens on.

Archer ran to his car as the ambulance pulled onto the road.

Dirt flew as he and squealed out, racing behind them. "*Why are they so slow*?!" he screamed and punched the dash. It cracked under his fist, driving his knuckle up into his hand but didn't notice.

Pulling Matt up on his Bluetooth Archer called.

"Yes?" he answered.

"She's alive. I'm going with them."

"I'll meet you there. The suspect is in the other ambulance."

Archer pulled out around ambulance and beat them to the hospital. Rushing in, and rambling about the happenings as they pulled in. The siren and lights were off as they passed by the window. Watching them, it seemed to move in slow motion.

"NO! NO! NO! NO! NO!" Archer yelled.

The nurse came and said it was okay. It was just protocol to turn all the sounds off. "The doctor is already waiting. In the meantime, let's get your hand looked at."

"Just help my wife, please," he cried. "I'm fine."

"Sir, you are not fine. We'll do our best for your wife, but you need to be seen. Your hand is definitely broken," she said taking him by the elbow. So tired, he let her lead him to a room.

"Code red, code red," came over the speakers as the second ambulance came in.

Archer watched it go past the window, again, in slow motion. *If she's not dead already . . . I'll fucking kill her if Faith dies*, he thought. His heart pounding out of his chest, his body shook in time with it.

Hours passed and Archer had heard almost nothing. They'd put his hand in a cast and offered him something for the pain. Refusing them, the nurse insisted, but he felt fine.

Archer just sat in the waiting room they'd put him in, away from the rest of the patients. He prayed the whole time and Grace heard every word he said.

Daddy?

Yes, Gracie love? Archer answered. *Can you help her? Please help her.*

I can't, Daddy. I'm so sorry.

It's okay, honey. You did so great. I'm so proud of you. I know Mommy will be too when she comes back home, he reassured her. Though, not sure it was her he was trying to convince.

The host has her. She's fighting.

Good, my sweet girl.

It almost made him feel relief, thinking of what Grace had said in the kitchen. Unconditional love.

And you. Me and Jesse too.

How is Jesse? Archer asked.

He's good, I didn't tell him. Trevor and Dora are really scared, though. I told them it's okay, but they don't know what we did.

Her voice was cheery and helped him to take a deep breath.

Oh, honey, if it weren't for you . . . it would have been horrible . . . just horrible! . . . he told Grace and was very careful not to think about Jonsie or what had happened so long ago.

I love you, Daddy. I have to go. I can't stay long here like this. It makes me sick. It's different when I'm asleep.

I love you too, my saving Grace, Archer said laying his broken hand on his chest. Just then, the door opened, and the doctor came out.

"We got the bleeding stopped but we'll have to wait to see if she regains consciousness. We did what we could. It's up to her now. She took a few good blows."

Wanting to be realistic, he spoke in a monotone way to not make Archer feel hopeful, nor worried. He'd seen people die of less.

Matt came from the far end of the hall, and hearing what the doctor had told Archer, he hung his head. He'd seen what Lacey had done himself. The sound echoed in his head, and he was glad Archer hadn't been in the shed. He'd seen many things in his day and didn't have much hope for the situation. Taking off his hat, Matt signed a cross on his chest.

"We'll keep a close eye for the next twenty-four hours. Hopefully, we'll have some answers then," the doctor confirmed and rubbed Archer's arm.

"Can I see her?"

The doctor looked to Matt, in case it wasn't allowed, and when Matt nodded yes, the doctor told Archer the nurse will take him in, and that Officer Eddine would be outside her door. Until it gets right.

The nurse came then and took Archer and Matt both down the hall and into Faith's room. Giving her a quick check for vitals, she left them to sit with Faith. Matt told Archer he'd have to get a statement.

Archer knew it was coming and hung his head. After tapping his shoulder, Matt turned to leave them alone.

Knowing how insane it was going to sound when Archer told him that Grace found her in some dream state, or whatever had happened. He'd need to talk with her about this when he got home. Resigned to the situation at hand now, he took his phone out.

"Matt?"

"Yes, Archer?"

With the recording ready to play, he passed the phone to him and just as Matt opened his mouth to ask what he was looking at, Archer said, "*That* . . . is *all* I know . . . It's all there in the recording. You saw the rest."

Walking up to Faith's bed, he looked down, still not believing his eyes. He barely recognized her, and it took his breath away. She was so swollen. "Broken Faith is *no good* . . ." he whispered in her ear hoping she'd heard him, then kissed her head.

Matt closed the door to give them a few minutes and nodded to Officer Eddine, still stationed outside the door, then went down the hall some before he hit play on the recording.

Shaking his head, he tried to understand. He could hear a tiny voice and then silence, the tiny voice, then silence.

The sound of Archer's crying came from inside the room, making Matt feel bad for them all. As he kept listening to the recording, his heart was breaking for them.

Continuing the recording, the tiny voice said his plate and badge number. He recognized that it was Grace, and the picture came into view for him then.

"*Oh my!*" he sighed with wide eyes and turned it off to listen in a more private place. Knowing Trevor's number was in the phone, Matt took it and called from his own cell, to make sure the kids were okay. Specifically, Grace.

Trevor assured him the kids were occupied and that he and Dora would do whatever was necessary to keep things going until Archer got back. They'd go from there.

"You are both very kind. May god bless you both," Matt spoke solemnly.

Going over the recording in his car several times, trying to make sense of it, Matt was scared for them all now.

CHAPTER TWENTY-SIX
Recovering What Was Lost

Archer sat with Faith all night and she hadn't woken up and Matt had messaged saying he'd return around ten thirty in the morning for a statement and told Archer to try and get some rest, maybe eat something.

The nurse came in then to check Faith's vitals and IV again, telling him the doctor would be in shortly.

"Have you slept?" she asked Archer without looking away from her task.

"No. I can't," he answered with bloodshot eyes, not taking them off of Faith.

"Archer . . ." she said turning to him, causing him to make eye contact. It was Birt and Ada's daughter, Mary.

"I'm so sorry, Mary. I didn't recognize you."

"I know this is hard, but you have to keep your strength up. Have you even eaten anything at all today?"

He hadn't. The last bite he took was with Grace . . . How long had it been since the toast? Counting back, he thought, *This was Thursday. The incident was yesterday . . . it was the night before that.*

"You're probably right," he admitted, then put his gaze back to Faith.

She knew he'd heard her but wasn't going to do anything about it. She'd seen it a hundred times before.

"Faith will go for testing when the doctor comes, and we'll be awhile. I'll have someone bring a cot for you and get you a bite to eat. Please do your best to take advantage of it," Mary asked politely, but he knew she was being firm with him.

"I'll do my best," he promised. "Thank you, Mary."

"She seems much more stable now," she told him, to help ease his mind some. "That's good news. The doctor will know more when we finish the tests. We'll do all we can."

"I know, Mary. The only thing that can reassure me right now, is for her eyes to open and know who I am," Archer sighed.

When finishing what she was doing, Mary went out the door and closed it quietly. Archer heard her talking, then she came back in with a tray of food. "It's not much, but the idea is nourishment. I'll leave the tray here. Try and at least have a snack."

Putting it on the wheely cart they use for the beds, she rolled it beside him, pushing it down and in, just under his nose. Maybe the smell would get him to listen to his body and be rational. Zoned out, Mary took off the top.

"Archer . . ."

"Yes, Mary. Thanks so much," he responded and looked over the food to satisfy her. The toast smelled good, so asked if they had blueberry spread.

"Let me look."

Mary's pants crinkled when she walked, and her shoes squeaked on the floor taking the turn from the room. Archer heard voices again and more clinking before she came back in.

"There was only one. Here's some raspberry and strawberry in case it isn't enough."

Setting them on the tray, he thanked her, and Mary went on her way. Taking the jelly Archer spread it on half a slice, then jammed it in his mouth. *There*, he thought, trying not to cry, Gagging a bit but managing to swallowed it, his stomach growled as he took the lid from the cup of milk and chugged it. *Good enough.*

Matt had taken what he needed from Archer's phone and gave it back in case the kids needed him. Taking it from his pocket, Archer messaged that he'd have a few free hours, if Matt wanted to get his statement.

Messaging back, Matt responded he'd be there for ten thirty as planned.

Saying he'd see him then, Archer sat back in the chair feeling how tired he really was. Mary came back a moment later and got the machines ready to move with Faith, for further testing.

Closing his eyes, Archer listened to the sounds in the room. The clock steadily ticked. His eyes began to drift but then the doctor came in, asking how he was, how his hand felt, or if he was doing okay in general.

Archer answered her questions and left it at that so she could tend to Faith. To hell with him. He'd be fine. As long as she was.

Informing him, the doctor said Faith had a concussion, that there was some bleeding on the brain, but they'd caught it and figured was fixed. Wanting to be sure, though, that fluids hadn't built up, that was much of the testing.

Faith couldn't tell them if there was pain anywhere else, so they wanted to look deeper now that she was stable, then told him to try and rest some. Mary would let him know when Faith was coming back and that they were very concerned for him. Archer knew. He was too. It was the outcome that would say for sure, how he'd do.

The doctor went to the next room then, and Archer heard her cheerfully greet the man with a horrible smoker's cough.

Leaning into Faith as Mary got the papers together, spoke softly into her ear, "To you and I, to dreams and blue skies. Come back to me, please. I so love you."

Mary touched his shoulder, and Archer moved out of her way. Putting the side rails up she told him to get some sleep. It would make him feel better.

"She's strong," Mary comforted. "Mom and Dad are praying for you all. The whole church is."

His eyes filled with tears then. He didn't know what to say. Mary just rubbed his back and took his good arm, walked him to the cot, fluffed the pillow and told him to lay down. Doing as she's suggested, Archer was in no shape to be arguing now.

On his side, Archer watched every move. Two male staff came and took the bed from its locks and the wheels squeaked across the floor. He'd never heard anything so horrible in his life.

Everything hanging in the balance now, Archer let her go in his mind, as they went from sight. It seemed more to him as though, he'd let Faith take him where she was going. Comforting her, it seemed, and himself.

Rolling onto his back, everything was crunchy . . . but soft. Archer closed his eyes and found the tick of the clock. Taking deep breaths, he found a place to be still. It was very surreal. Not quite comfortable, but it would do. He took a few cat naps, still very aware of the room.

The door swished. Matt's belt jingled and his heavy boots clomped on the floor, almost seeming like music, so Archer sat up saying hi to him.

"Lay back and relax," Matt said caringly. He knew Archer had to be in pain. Not just his hand, but his heart. "I need to ask questions about the recording."

Pulling a chair over to sit, he took out his scribbler, clicked a pen, then set his hat on the floor. "Help me understand what I heard on the recording."

Archer sighed. "It's hard to explain," and attempted to clear some of the "nap fog" from his head.

"Well. Can you start by telling me why there was only one voice?" Matt began.

"That was Grace. She was sleeping and I thought she was having a nightmare. I was going to wake her up, until she screamed. I don't even know why I hit record. It was just a feeling."

"Who was she talking to?"

"Okay. That's where it gets strange," Archer laughed. "It was me."

"I didn't hear you talking at all," Matt said in that way police do when they interrogate people.

"Well . . . because I talked to her in my head," Archer confessed.

"Why was she talking out loud if you were talking in your head? It doesn't add up," he stated, seeming to not believe what Archer was telling him. His tone, also, in that police way of getting people to become emotional and confess.

"Well. I had had a thought and didn't say a word. She answered me, though. I pried further and thought it was a coincidence. Turned out it wasn't."

"Okay. That's hard to believe but tell me, how did you get the number from my plate and my badge? Did you see them before?"

"No. I never cared to look. I'd no need to."

"How did you get it then?"

"Grace told me," Archer offered hoping Matt would believe him.

"How did she get it?" he asked then, knowing Archer wasn't telling if he didn't ask.

"I asked her to get it," he laughed.

"How?"

Matt knew but wanted to hear him say it.

Archer took a deep breath and said, "In my head . . . I asked her to leave Faith, wherever she and Grace even were, and go to the road. I don't know exactly how she did it. I still have to talk to her. I got the feeling that maybe she's psychic. She'd said some amazing things the night Faith went missing and made me feel better. I didn't realize how spiritual she is."

Archer just gave up everything.

"Psychic?"

"Well. I guess that's what it is."

Putting the pad and pen down Matt said, "I'm going to tell you something off the record."

Archer looked at him puzzled as he went on to tell him about the noises he'd heard. How he'd vomited on the ground. "I didn't see anything, but heard the sounds again, and it scared the shit out of me. I've had a pounding headache ever since."

Archer didn't know what to say, other than to tell Matt he felt the same. That it probably had something to do with Grace and what she could do.

"Social services are going to be getting a hold of you. I'm sure CPS will too."

Archer's heart pounded out of his chest.

"You'll do well to say she'd had some kind of a dream and leave it at that. They'll test the fuck out of her. We don't want that," he told Archer, making him sigh.

Knowing Matt was right he asked, "What am I going to say to them?"

"It won't be right away. We'll have coffee at the house, where it's more private, and I'll give you some suggestions. They'll put her through the wringer to find out what she's got."

Matt wasn't about to let them go to the wolves. A very spiritual man, Matt believed in ghosts, heaven and hell, angels and demons, divine revelation and the whole shebang.

"Should I get a lawyer?" Archer inquired then.

"If I were you, I would. As a father, I wouldn't trust the system. I do my best in my work, but I've seen some shit that would boil your blood," he told Archer. Then said, "I need to play the recording now and get your side. I can't let it go. It's evidence and I have to do my job. I'm sorry."

"Of course. I understand," Archer told him.

Matt took out the phone and played the recording, pausing where Archer was supposedly talking, trying to piece it together on his notepad. Archer remembered every word. How could he not?

Matt wrote down everything, then told Archer he should get some more sleep and that he had to go back to the station and enter the statement into the file.

Archer walked him to the door and before leaving, Matt said, "I hope Lacey gets better, so I can slap her with every charge I can."

"How is she, by the way?"

"Not well. She isn't awake either. Everybody's sleeping, but you. I know she's connected to that Jonsie guy. I heard that much. Not sure if she's family, maybe a girlfriend. Might never know. I shouldn't have shot her, really. I could've done something else. You both are like family, though. I was pretty angry. I may lose my badge over it. We'll see."

Matt was torn between regret, concern for their families, and personal worry. Archer felt bad for him now. The one thing that bothered him was that he was so close to Faith when he'd pulled the speeder over. If Grace hadn't doe what she'd done, he'd have kept on driving and figured that god had a special purpose for Faith and prayed she'd recover to do his work.

"Try and get some more sleep. Sorry I had to wake you. The fresher the memory the better, though," he finished and shook Archer's hand. The good one . . .

Thanking Matt for everything he'd done, Archer closed the door. One more thing checked off, so went to the food tray and ate the cold eggs and rubbery bacon. The toast that remained was soggy, but his stomach thanked him anyway.

Sitting back on the cot he called Grace on Trevor's line. When he answered they talked briefly. Trevor didn't know much so there wasn't much to tell. Dora got on for a minute saying she loved them both and that the kids were fine. She'd taken Asher to her mothers for a few days. Whatever Archer needed, they'd do, then, put Grace on the line.

"Hi, cupcake," Archer said and forced a smile.

"Hi, Dad. How's Mom?"

"You don't know?"

"I can't hear her anymore," Grace told him with sadness in her voice.

Maybe it was the anesthesia, the MRI and machines. Archer was sure they had something to do with it but went on to tell her how Faith was doing. That the doctors would take care of her, and he'd be home soon.

Then, briefly telling her about Matt, the recording, and what he'd told Matt about what she'd done and that she shouldn't say anything to anyone, until they could have a private talk. Grace knew what he meant and promised to keep the secret.

"Good girl," Archer said lovingly. "I love you so much. Put Jesse on for a minute, please?"

"Love you too dad," Grace replied.

The phone hit the table as Graced yelled for him.

Jesse came out of breath. "Hey, Dad. What's going on?"

"Well, buddy," Archer said trying to make light of it. "Mom had an accident, but the doctors are taking good care of her. When she wakes up, I'll get her to call and talk. Okay?"

"Okie dokie."

Jesse had ADHD, but his patience was out of this world. Archer remembered the time Jesse had asked him to take him to the park when he was two. Archer was busy with things around the house and said he would do it in a few minutes, then forgot.

When Jesse woke in the morning, they had breakfast and lunch. Out of the blue, it seemed to him, Jesse asked, "Can we go to the park now?"

"*Yes!* Yes, we can," Archer said and jumped right up.

He'd kept him waiting a whole day, that night and half the next day. Jesse didn't even care and the memory made him laugh a bit.

"Take care of your sister and do as Dora and Trevor say. Okay? Buuuudddyyyy."

It was Archer's way of saying he loved Jesse.

When Jesse started school, he was embarrassed to have Archer say it, or say it back. They made a deal. Buuuuddddyyy meant I love you to Jesse.

Trevor got back on the phone saying he loved Archer and that he hoped Faith would come back soon. Archer thanked him, said he was the best and that he loved him too.

Ending the call, Archer felt more weight off his shoulders and fell to the pillow, listening to the clock again. It was quiet, his mind wasn't overwhelmed with so much and he fell right back asleep. A real sleep.

Mary woke him as they wheeled Faith back in. "Good. You got some sleep and finished the food. You'll be stronger now."

A subliminal suggestion that he agreed to.

"Yeah. I feel a lot better. Thank you, Mary," he said taking her hand and rubbing the top of it gently, *that* was more the Archer she knew.

"There now. The doctor will come in a few hours, before her rounds are over, and let you know the results that we have."

Putting all the cords back where they belonged, Archer sat in the window on the sill. It was a beautiful day. Mid summer. No doubt hot out. The hospital was always so cold, but the humidity seeped in somehow.

Mary chatted with him about the kids to distract him and it worked like a charm.

Looking at Faith, Archer smiled now saying, "She'll be so happy to see them again."

"Yes. No doubt. They'll be happy to have her back as well. Do let them know to be careful with her. She needs to heal. Nothings broken, but she'll be sore for awhile."

"No Broken Faith" sounded great to him!

The day ticked away, and Archer kept busy reading the paper. Mary took him dinner and having come to terms with things, now that he'd had some sleep, food, and time, Archer ate it all.

The doctor said Faith looked alright. No bleeding. No fluids. No breaks. A small fracture on her skull. Positive feedback was enough to hold Archer for now.

"She must have had an angel with her."

Everyone Archer knew was religious and really believed it. Feeling loved, but still in no mind to consider it, he let it go for now. Thinking there might be something to it, he made a mental note to search more. Maybe give it a fair chance.

Archer stayed the night and listened to the beep of Faith's heart on the machine . . . that's what made him really relax. He wished he'd thought of it sooner. Like the clock. Tick, tick, beep, beep, tick, beep, tick.

The clock faded and beep . . . beep . . . he fell asleep.

After waking, Archer opened the door to hear life move around in the halls. He supposed it would help her too. Calling the house, Archer put them on speaker phone, so she could hear.

Doing another round, the doctor told Archer he should go home. They'd call if anything changed. The kids needed their dad.

Archer agreed and texted Trevor that he'd soon be home. As he left, Archer had to pull himself away, feeling guilty, leaving her there like that. Searching his heart to find hope it would all work out, faith would be his companion. Not the one he wanted, but it would do. It was a waiting game now.

Maybe in her state, she'd finally be able to see how much he loved her, making him feel a little content.

The kids, happy to see him, and he them, Trevor and Dora stayed awhile. Archer told them all he knew.

Jesse asked to have Chinese food, and Archer said they sure could and ordered enough for them all. Later he showed Dora and Trevor the recording. They had no idea what they were listening to, and he had to explain it a few times.

Trevor was the most shocked, not believing in spirits or ghosts at all. Sometimes laughing at people who talked about aliens. A big skeptic.

Not now, though. He just sat staring into the yard. Everything he believed, was shattered.

Days and weeks passed with no sign Faith would come out of the coma. Testing her reflexes a few times a day there was no response. Archer bought all the machines he'd seen in her room and hired a private nurse to live in the house. There was an en suite anyway.

He'd read all of her books to her, hoping she'd follow his voice and know her own words. The kids would sit in bed with them and watch movies. Grace brushed her hair. It was all she could do. Faith wasn't connected to her anymore.

Grace continued her courses in psychiatry but moved onto neurology. Hoping to find a way to get into the brain.

Comatose ones, maybe reach them, figure how to take them back out. Taking computer courses Grace spent a lot of time in the garage soldering and making programs with her husband. Yes. She'd gotten married.

They had the ceremony in the gardens of the cottage with the windows opened and speakers, so Faith could hear. Grace knew she was in there somewhere.

The kids now gone from the house; Archer missed Grace typing. She'd sit in Faith's office, and it made him feel some comfort. Like she was up and well. He loved the sound and would just close his eyes, listening. Picturing Faith sitting there.

Jesse went into law. The way things had happened, he wanted to make sure those who were guilty of crimes, paid for what they'd done. He was merciless . . . and angry and seeing how fragile Archer had become without his mother, Jesse didn't want a partner, but had someone he saw now and then, not wanting to love anyone.

Archer never gave up his hope, or his Faith. He'd wait as long as it took.

CHAPTER TWENTY-SEVEN
And on That Note

Faith screamed loud as she could, but nothing came out. How could she tell them she was there? She'd heard them all talking and felt pain as the doctors checked her body. It was excruciating.

Faith also heard all of the talks Mary had with Archer, she told Faith everything she was doing when changing her clothes and bathing her. She also knew Mary was right there, when the staff changed the sheets.

She had to *do* something. "Wiggle a finger. C'mon. Flinch your nose. *Do something*!" Faith commanded her body. It did nothing.

Grace's voice was with her in the shed and also when Faith was slipping in and out of consciousness. Now, she'd called for Grace a hundred times but there was nothing. Just the silence. Except for that constant *stupid beeping*!

Sometimes, it was so loud, Faith thought her head would pop right off her shoulders, then the deafening silence again. She didn't know which was more annoying. The screech from the MRI was intense. Painful even.

How could she let this happen? Having taken boxing and self-defence with Grace, Faith could have whooped Lacey's ass with one hand tied behind her back and she'd have gone down like a wet noodle. The beeping got faster as Faith had the thoughts of what she *should* have done, losing her temper.

Frustrated and not knowing anything of time, Faith felt defeated and sighed . . . *wait*! . . . Her body just took a deep breath! She wasn't entirely helpless! A natural response, Faith had to find out how to command it.

Making attempts to move, there must have been a trick that made her body respond that one time. Eventually figuring out, it was when she gave up fighting.

Not sure how, Faith spent some time meditating. Having done that many times before, she was familiar with it, even having achieved Archers "divine mind", several times. There was barely a difference between it and the space she was in. There was no sensation of leaving her body, like when she'd gotten the hang of astral projection. This place felt like divine mind itself. It was going to be tricky.

Thinking it could take a long time to feel the differences, if there was any, she'd no definition of time at all in this space. There *were* no days and nights. Just the white. It could be but a moment, or a lifetime.

Thinking on it, her only option was to mentally picture her body. Mind was all she had, or consciousness. A million questions flooded her thoughts, about her thoughts. It was like living in them, being stuck in her head.

Eventually, though, she'd come to understand. In her head, or what felt like her head, Faith hummed, and it went on forever not having to take a breath to make it happen. It just seemed to fill the place she was in with sound. No vocal cords needed.

It baffled her, but she wasn't about to stop. Sure, if she held it long enough, the space would explode. Like a glass under the intense frequency of sound from a speaker.

Faith hummed, picturing her body in a Buddha-like posture. With no sensations, she imagined *everything*. Understanding then, who the observer is, that Archer had talked about that day on the beach, peace filled her now. The beeping was gone. The talking was gone. It was just her, the hum, and the desire to see her family again.

All of a sudden, the hum went away, and frightened her. She'd gotten so used to it. Silence again.

Losing her temper Faith screamed, and it roared of her throat, filling her ears. Then, sat bolt upright in bed! She was out! She'd done it!

The nurses all screamed in terror, then realizing what had happened, ran over and checked Faith. Realizing she could see light and feel the bed under her, Faith laughed. Loudly.

A nurse pushed her slowly to the bed with a hand on her back and one on her head, telling her to take it easy. Faith laughed hysterically but did what they said.

"Hee, hee, hee, hee, hee," she went on giggling, still bouncing a bit, in her bed. "Viktory dance," she whispered, while watching the nurse check her vitals.

The nurse had trouble hearing her breath and heart in the stethoscope, because she wouldn't settle down. Calling for help, other nurses came, and Faith just smiled at them wiggling her eyebrows and toes. She was ecstatic to be back.

"Shhhh," one of them hissed.

"*I will not shhhh*," Faith hollered back. Her eyebrows nearly touched she was so cross, then burst out laughing again.

One nurse called for the doctor and the other called for security. Faith laid down then and put her hands up in surrender. "Okay. Okay. I'm sorry," she said, then giggled quietly, watching them tend to her.

The older nurse making small talk said, "You got quite a bump on the noggin. We thought we would lose you a few times. You're a lucky one." then smiled, even though Faith had just scared the life out of her.

"You've no idea how lucky I am!" Faith yelled.

Security already there, they waited to the side as the nurses did as needed but her yelling put them on high alert.

"Sorry! I'm just excited to be back and alive," Faith assured them.

They didn't budge from their positions, though.

When the nurse turned her back, Faith bounced a little, squishing her arms to her chest. "Smol viktory dance," she mouthed, as if in defiance, then straightened up when the nurse turned back around.

Having called the doctor, he rushed in to see a bizarre scene. Security, three nurses, and Faith there with a huge grin, bouncing.

The female doctor must be off, Faith thought. Him, her replacement for today. Weird but okay. The female doctor had been around for weeks and weeks she assumed . . . and where was Mary?

The doctor went to the bedside, checking her, and the machines. Clear eyes, no pains, motor skills fine. "You seem to be in good spirits. Your father will be thrilled."

What? She had no father. He committed suicide when Faith was very young, and Roger had died ten years ago. He must be mistaken. Anyway. No matter. Faith felt fantastic!

"Don't say I've woken up? I want it to be a surprise."

"That's not usually something we do. We have protocol."

Taking his fingers from her wrist, he checked things on the chart and wrote.

"Please . . . don't," she begged with her hand on his wrist now.

"I suppose this one time won't hurt. They'll be in anytime now anyway."

"Yay! What's to eat?" she asked with big eyes. It felt like forever since she'd tasted food.

The nurses looked at each other.

"That's some recovery," one told her.

The doctor asked what she remembered last, and Faith told him about Archer and the kids. Being attacked by Lacey, how she'd been kidnapped and beaten, about her life as a world-famous writer. Remembering her whole life, there were no *gaps*. She could have told them every single detail about her life and had no worries with what this test would reveal.

Writing in the chart that her memory may be affected, the doctor suggested Faith see the psychiatrist when they could get her in. Faith agreed. She needed to vent about what had happened in the shed with Lacey. Couldn't hurt.

"When can I get out of this damn bed? What happened to Lacey" Faith asked.

The doctor told her it would be at least a few days. Her muscles would need some therapy. They'd worked on her while she was asleep, but it would just keep them from getting stiff, also mentioning they didn't know who Lacey was.

"How long was I out?" Faith asked, more seriously and thought she'd find out eventually what happened to Lacey.

"It's been nearly a year," the doctor informed her.

Faith's mouth made a sound when she cupped her hand over it. "My god. Archer and the kids must be sick about it."

"Yes. We didn't think you were going to come out. A lot of money was spent keeping you going. You sure are loved. I shouldn't tell you, but they nearly went into the poorhouse to keep you."

What? Archer couldn't have had to spend all of his money to keep her going. There was no way her expenses were that high. He'd barely have seen a dent in his wallet.

When the doctor left, Faith asked the nurse for food, and was told she should be careful. Her stomach hadn't digested food in quite some time.

"I'm *dying* for some chowder," she exclaimed motioning with her hands open at her mouth like she was drooling. "And orange juice!"

The nurse said that wasn't so bad, but only a little, and that she'd check with the kitchen. If it wasn't available, she'd get it brought some other way, then, as the nurse was leaving, Faith asked for the paper and her name.

"Oh, dear. I'm sorry. My name is Ada, and if you meant the news paper, I'll bring you that. You stay in that bed. I'm not kidding," she warned.

"I know an Ada. From the diner."

"Strange, it's a very uncommon name," she remarked and went for the chowder, stressing again for Faith to stay in bed.

Maybe she'd get to meet Mary soon. She was so sweet to Archer. There was barely a conversation where Faith hadn't heard her comforting everyone. Archer was in for such a big surprise, she thought, taking the remote for the TV to entertain herself. She'd been in that silence and the hum for so long now. Clicking the button, the news came on. That would do for now.

The weatherman talked of the storm coming in, Quincy, Illinois?! Bizarre that no other stations came in on the little TV.

Buzzing, the nurse answered, "Yes, Ms. McKay? Is there a problem?"

Faith laughed. *These people are blooming idiots. Can't get anything right about me.* She wondered how they'd managed to keep her going, then.

"No. I just wondered if I could get more stations on this TV?"

"You have to order it. There's a book in the drawer on how to do that," the voice replied.

No difference, the paper is coming, Faith thought and thanked her in a sweet voice.

Looking out the window, the snow was pretty coming down and thought of Archer and the tree in the yard, Grace, and Jesse. Faith couldn't wait to tell Grace she'd done such a good job helping Archer find her.

Ada walked in then. "I have chowwwwwder," she sang and waving the paper in her hand. "This too."

Faith's mouth watered thinking about the taste, as Ada set the bag down on the wheely cart, with the paper underneath, and rolled it to her. "This is gonna be sooo good."

Not recognizing the emblem on the front of the bag, Faith thought, *Whatever*, as she scooped the food out from it. It was hot, and the steam rose through the air when she took the lid off.

"Oooohhh, thank you *so* much Ada. It smells heavenly!"

Ada thought she looked like an amazed kid at Christmas, but couldn't imagine how Faith was feeling, though. Her brain was starved for textures, sounds, smells, and flavours.

"Thank you again Ada," Faith said with a big smile and praying hands.

"You're welcome, dear," Ada replied back and rubbed Faith's arm. "Your regular visitors will be here in no time. I wish I could see their faces! Take that very slow. Okay?"

Her hand felt like Ada's at the diner, and it was nice. Familiar.

"Okay," she promised, and Ada left while Faith stirred in the pepper she'd covered on the whole top. Barely seeing chowder underneath it.

Listening as the plastic spoon scraped the sides of the paper take-out bowl, Faith enjoyed everything. Blowing on the chowder, she watched the steam disappear. It was so pretty, and she'd taken so many things for granted.

Smelling the chowder slowly and deeply, Faith took it all in along with her surroundings and when the spoonful she' d scooped had cooled some, she ate. The flavour. Oh! The flavour.

Taking a few slow bites and watching the steam, Faith was in her own little world of senses. Reborn. When her belly growled, she thought she thought it best to do as Ada had said, and so put it away.

Taking the paper, it read Illinois? *What the hell?*, Faith thought and went through the pages quickly. Sports, politics, local events. All Illinois . . .

Ada popped her head in just then and smiled. "Found these ones lost in the halls," she joked.

Putting it all down, Faith pushed the cart out of the way for the kids to rush in and give her hugs. She dreamed of Archer's arms around her for so long, in the place she'd no name for.

When Ada opened the door all the way, a woman came in with an older man.

"*Faith*!" the woman said and rushed to hug her.

The smiled wiped right off her face when Faith put her hands up to stop her and looking cross, which stopped her in her tracks alright.

"Faith?" she said looking puzzled.

"Yes . . . You are?" Faith inquired snobbily, looking her up and down.

"Oh. You were always a good kidder," she remarked with a slight chuckle.

Faith had no idea who she was, or how she knew Faith was a joker.

"Gimme a hug," she smiled with arms open again

Faith pulled her arms back in and crossed them over her chest, guarding her body. "You are?" she repeated.

"It's me . . . Barb . . ." she answered, pulling the old man under her arm. "And Dad."

He couldn't have been even ten years older than her, maybe closer to six.

"Maybe we should go slower," Ada suggested.

"No! What the actual *fuck* is going on here?" Faith yelled, shaking the newspaper. They all just looked at each other when Faith threw the tv remote. "Like, why does everything say Illinois?"

Ada got in front of the strangers protectively,

"*Faith*! That is no way to talk to your family."

Peering around Ada's side, eyeballing these obvious actors, Faith was furious.

"This isn't funny . . . Who are they?" she asked waving her hand with a limp wrist. "And where's my husband?!"

"Maybe we should go, Dad," Barb proposed.

"Yeah, you fucking should! Barrrrbb," Faith said rudely then, in no mood for this shit.

"Faith!" Ada snarled, then looking to the strangers she took Barb's arm to help them leave. "I'm sorry. Maybe tomorrow would be a better day. I'm so, so sorry."

As she shut the door, Faith began to cry. "What is going on? This is all wrong. It's *all* wrong!"

"Don't you yell at *me*, missy!" Ada growled.

Faith felt bad for putting Ada in that position then.

"I'm sorry, Ada. Something isn't right. In fact, it all seems to be wrong."

"Faith . . ." Ada said in a kinder voice as she came closer.

She noticed Ada's wobble . . . Like from the diner. And that shuffling sound . . .

"There's nothing wrong, dear. You're just confused maybe. What do you see that's wrong, besides the people?"

"All of it. The food bag, the TV, the paper. These people . . ." Faith sobbed. "Is this a joke? Like . . . is this a stage?"

Ada sat beside her. "I'd never do that to anyone. That would be cruel. This hospital is very real. So am I."

"No, no, no . . . this isn't happening," Faith cried, shaking her head. Was she still in the coma? "I just want my husband and kids. I want to talk to Archer."

"Whose Archer, dear?"

"My husband . . ." Faith answered looking very seriously at Ada, as tears streamed down her face. "Please, Ada . . ."

"Faith, you're not married. Nor have you got kids. I'd know."

"I am *so* married," Faith growled and pulled her hand up to show Ada her wedding band, but her finger was bare. "Where is it?"

"What?"

"My ring? Did I lose it?"

"You had no jewellery when you came in," Ada informed her. "Maybe we should get the on-call psychiatrist."

"Yes. Let's straighten this out," Faith agreed. "There has to be a mistake. Archer and the children will be worried sick. I don't know how I even got here. This is way too far from home. I need to get back," she said in a desperate tone.

"I'll be right back," Ada said and shuffled to the door.

"Yes. Please. Ada, I'm scared."

"We'll sort this out. Don't worry your head," she comforted, before leaving,

He was only gone a few minutes and when she returned, Faith was standing at the window with her IV out.

"Faith. You can't be doing that," she warned.

Very concerned, Ada went over to help her back to the bed and Faith grumbled never turning from the window.

"It was itchy."

"You should be sitting."

Then plunking herself on the window ledge, Faith softly said, "There."

Ada moved closer to her, as Faith looked out the window watching the flakes drift lazily to the ground. She thought of the view Archer had made in the yard with the pole and the trees. How the branches drooped from the weight of the snow. How it flung some into the air when it finally fell off, having bent too far. Gravity in full effect.

Noticing Ada's walk Faith imagined the diner in her head and thought. "*Wha . . . It couldn't be.*"

Snapping her eyes shut to listen, the image of the shake she'd gotten from Ada at the diner came into view. Even the fingerprints left behind in the frost of the cup. Then Ada touched her arm.

Those hands . . . She'd felt them before. "No no no no no!" Faith whispered.

Immediately thinking of Dorothy in The Wizard of Oz, she knew now how Dorothy must have felt repeating the phrase, "there's no place like home. there's no place like home."

Bursting into tears, Ada hugged her a little. Though it wasn't right for them to do that but did it anyway. "The doctor will be here shortly."

It was no comfort at all. The only thing that could fill the hole in Faith's heart was Archer and the kids and her home. This whole place was alien to her.

Ada asked Faith to get back into the bed, she'd have physio on the morning, and they'd work on her strength. Faith did as Ada asked, and the psychiatrist came soon after and checked the chart.

"Tell me everything you remember."

Faith spoke about her real father. How he'd committed suicide, that her mother died when she was seventeen, in an accident. Then about Jonsie, selling the house, going to PEI and meeting Archer. How she played all kinds of instruments, is a singer, and a famous author. Also mentioning she'd never seen those people who, came earlier, in her entire life.

She told them about the cottage. His proposal. The gallery. Their home and friends. Then about the children, and the fateful night when Lacey kidnapped her, beating her with a bat. That Grace had found her psychically and saved her life.

They looked down the whole time. Faith lost more and more ground with everything she told them. Trying to find credibility, Faith told them of what it was like in her coma and that she woke up . . . here. None of it made sense to her now. Just the emotions existed and memories. She had to get it back.

The doctor confirmed all of Faith's darkest nightmares. This was actually her life. She'd somehow made up a whole world based off of the sounds around her as she was in her coma.

Faith had mentioned many names of staff that had been in her room. Ada would know. Disconnected, the memory of the life she'd lived had faded into some void and was told they'd work to get it back, informing her that it was her father, who'd kept them going on her. They'd lost hope she'd recover, discussed pulling the plug to let Faith go naturally but her father wouldn't hear if it, saying that "grace" would bring her back to him.

Knowing Faith thought she was over forty, now, Ada took the mirror from the drawer and passed it to her. It was her alright. But not forty-three . . . she looked barely in her twenties. Her mind tripped over itself. But . . . Archer . . .

It's a nightmare, Faith told herself, pinching her arm so hard she shook. Ada fought with her to stop.

She might be old, but she wasn't one to be trifled with. That's for sure. The doctor knew and waited for Faith to give up. She would. He'd seen Ada in action before, wrestling full-grown men to the ground with barely any effort.

Faith gave up. Taking a pillow and hugging it close, she threw herself to the bed and said, "Just leave me alone."

All of her expression gone, she stared out the window.

The doctor got up saying he'd be back and that they can work it out to get her recovered fully, then wrote in her charts that she was delusional and now lethargic. Very concerning.

As far as Faith was concerned her memory had no flaws. She didn't want to recover. She wanted them to put her back. Maybe this was an alternate reality.

Ada talked softly at the door, saying they could help her by searching the internet for her name and book titles. The doctor agreed.

Faith didn't care what they'd said. Her world was shattered, and she didn't know what to do about it. Nothing *could* be done and she felt like dying then.

Going through the full course of physio, Faith got stronger. Enough that she left the hospital in a few weeks and moved in with her so called father, as her apartment and job were gone now, insisting he could handle it. After all, he did raise her and knew her well.

Continuing with an out-patient program, the psychiatrist set her up with a counsellor to see once a week, but she was beyond help now.

Maybe she was in another body. Like a double. Maybe swapped with whoever owned this body in this dimension. She in Archer's arms, thinking it as her and living her life. It made Faith furious to consider. She had to get back and stay back.

Just a shell of herself, compared to when she'd felt alive with Archer, Faith cried herself to sleep every night, not knowing how to start living again. Living for her.

She'd taken up jogging and for whatever reason, her father said, became obsessed with guitar. He had no idea how, but she was really, really good. Especially since she'd never put her hands on one before. Her singing was horrible, but if it helped, he'd put up with it and not complain.

Faith drove for hours to get to the shore, and had jars of sea glass all over the house and started drinking . . . a lot!

They'd argue when he tried to talk to her about it, making attempts to reason with her, but it was pointless. She'd just smashing things and when Faith broke her mother's urn, his heart shattered with it.

"That will be enough. I don't know who you are anymore," he cried, picking up the pieces. "That was the last straw. I'll help you get an apartment for yourself and move. You won't be welcome in my house again. I never thought I'd have to give you tough love, but it seems that's the only way to get through to you. My angel. You were always my angel," he spoke gently, then stood and yelled, "But I *won't* let you continue to destroy the home your mother and I built for you girls!"

Sitting on the stairs crying into his hands he muttered, "You were the light of her life. Even over me," he sobbed.

His emotions were tumultuous as he spoke more.

"I swore I would do everything for you . . . and I'm sorry, love," he whispered holding his hands to the sky and looking at the ceiling, the to Faith, "You're going to have to learn to help yourself. I can't do it anymore. You're breaking my home . . . and my heart."

Softly she said, "Fine," then stomped up the stairs and before slamming the door, screamed, "*Nobody understands!*"

Going to the stairs her father yelled, "*You won't let us!*" and fell to his knees.

All night he prayed for her, while listening to her cry and break things, until finally she went to bed.

Faith got her apartment and shut everyone out and stopped seeing the counsellor. It was no use talking about it over and over, it just kept it fresher in her mind. Even on her doctor's suggestion, Faith didn't care about anything or anyone's opinions. She jogged every morning and drank every night, crying herself to sleep, though most nights, the alcohol made her pass out.

Memories haunting her, nightmares when she slept, the only music Faith ever listened to was Snow Patrol. That was the only thing that was real for her anymore.

One morning, as she jogged, Faith had a thought that stopped her in her tracks. Breathless, she took out her phone and typed in the name of Archer's gallery. Why hadn't she thought of it before?

Nothing came up. Damn.

Running her usual circuit, Faith's mind reeled and after getting home, she entered PEI into her browser. It was too late to sit and look, so she changed, went to work and would check it later.

The day sucked, as usual, and was more difficult with PEI on her mind. Those screeching neon lights drove her nuts. One of them hummed constantly . . . like in the coma when she tried to wake up.

After getting home, Faith cracked a drink and sat at her laptop. Finding everything she could, then checking her budget, if she stopped drinking and took her tax refund, she could go for a visit.

Cutting all corners Faith saved, pinched pennies wherever she could, and joined AA.

It wasn't as hard as she'd thought it would be and didn't agree with everything but felt a sense of community and belonging. Like they understood her pain somehow, and instead of crying herself to sleep, Faith dreamt of him. It wasn't perfect, but it was better than slowly killing herself with alcohol, and instead of trying to forget him, she let herself drown in his memory.

Spring came, and Faith filed her taxes. When it came back, she checked her savings and budget again. She'd saved more than enough. Nearly twice what she'd planned.

Going to the internet and finding some cottages near the gallery, though not as nice as what she'd stayed in, or not stayed in, before, she booked a few weeks then hopped up from the desk and did the "smol viktory dance".

That Saturday she dressed nice, did her hair, and put on some makeup. The way Archer liked it. It made her feel more alive.

Driving to her father's house Faith knocked on the door, not expecting it to open, but then the curtains moved on the tiny window of the door, and he peeked out.

Feeling like she'd waited an eternity; he finally opened it. Faith stood there shaking her head, still not knowing how to start and just cried, not even being able, to utter the words "I'm sorry," though she tried. Her voice wouldn't come out.

He didn't need her to and just took her to him, hugging her, rocking, and saying, "My girl . . . my girl . . ."

Faith confessed everything to her father and apologized for the hell she'd put him through. He wept as she emptied her mind and soul to him and couldn't believe his ears.

"This was so real for you, sweetheart, it's no wonder, you acted like you did."

His face contorted, to one who had just suffered the worst pain a human could. There was a wheezing sound from his throat as he spoke.

"All this time and you were suffering alone," he sobbed into his hands. "I can't even imagine your pain. When your mother died, I'd have died too, if it weren't for you girls. I had to live . . . for you."

Faith knew now he'd suffered alone, though she couldn't recall and now felt horrible for the way she'd treated him. She had hope. He didn't.

"Aww. Dad."

It broke him to hear her call him that, for the first time since the accident and had a complete meltdown. Faith slid over to hold him, even though it still felt awkward, but had promised herself she'd try, though.

"I've waited so long to hear you call me that . . ." he sobbed into her neck.

Faith felt him wipe tears behind her back and she held onto hers. For his sake.

"I'm so sorry. You deserved better than that, from me."

"Water under the bridge, angel," he comforted, collecting himself. "So! You're going to PEI?"

"Yep!" Faith answered happily.

"What exactly do you hope to find there?"

"Some solace. Though I don't know what that means, or what it will look like, I have to do something. I just feel like . . . There's nothing for me now. I don't even know who I am without . . . Him."

"Archer," he confirmed and nodded. "It's okay, honey. Just tell me everything. I'm not judging you."

"Yes. Archer."

"I understand, but Faith?" he questioned with his head sideways. "You need to be prepared. If you go there, and for some *strange* reason, this man exists? He may have a wife and family. Or it could be that he's a bad cat. You have to be guarded."

Faith sighed, "You're right. I have nothing left right now, though, and . . . if he exists . . . To see him smile would be enough. I could find some peace. To close the book."

"Are you sure? If you see him, you may not feel this way."

Sighing, Faith knew he was right. She couldn't just sit there and drink herself into oblivion, though.

"Do you know or remember why we called you Faith?"

Faith shook her head "no" and he went on to tell her.

"We tried for so long to have a child. One after another, her body rejected them. Your mother had so many miscarriages. The doctor told her, if she didn't stop, it may take her life. It was a dangerous game. She had so much to give, and she wanted so badly to have a child and *never* lost her "Faith," and so, you came to be. We couldn't think of a better name for you. Every day, you showed us what that word really meant," a softness coming over his face as he went on, "When I saw you there, nearly dead, I couldn't bear it. All I could hear was your mother calling you, and the vision of you, bolting across the yard to come in. So strong. So free. That wild, red hair flipping in the air. It echoes in my head constantly. I had to find 'My Faith' again . . ."

"Dad . . ."

"No, no. Listen here. I'd do it all again if I was given the choice. I regret nothing. It almost cost me my home, my retirement savings are gone and anything extra I was keeping for you girls, for when I'd no longer be here, and joined your mother again. You were lashing out. Now understood. It tore me apart. I wanted you to be happy again and I couldn't help. I see, now, that you had to help yourself. Somehow, in my heart, I knew that. The father in me, wanted to fix it for you, though," he paused, then looked her all around, "I see now, you're stronger than you ever were. All I could see was my li'l muffin, though."

Faith covered her mouth as she realized how much she'd made up in her mind. From little bits of memories to things going on around her, while she was out "on vacay." That's what she'd started calling it.

"You do what you need to, cupcake, but I want a call every single day. You hear?"

"Yes." She smiled.

"Go then. See PEI, take pictures and send vids, or whatever you kids call them now, to your sister. I don't know how to work that stuff," he laughed.

Then hugging him, Faith went home, and called Barb to apologize. She'd forgiven Faith, before she'd even said the words.

Going online, and booking her train, just like she remembered, though not being able to afford taking her car, rented a small, okay one. That was expensive enough for the month, with the mileage she planned to put on it, while there.

Counting down the days, Faith's agenda was fairly full. Canada Day celebrations, music, arts. The best was the gallery, hoping it would be like she imagined or remembered.

Growing more and more excited crossing the days off the calendar, Faith wondered why she hadn't done more with what she knew. *Remembered*, she corrected herself. She'd need to keep doing that, if anything was going to be laid down to rest. Face reality.

Canada Day seemed like it would be fun and scheduled to leave a few days before, to unpack and try to settle in a bit. Maybe not get lost when she went to town that day.

The night before, she didn't get a wink of sleep and thought to catch up on the train, though. It'd take a few days anyway, and then the bus from Halifax, if she hadn't. Everythong packed, Faith tried to get as close as she could to the memory, or dream. Whatever. To make it more real.

CHAPTER TWENTY-EIGHT
In Search of Closure

Faith took the day before her trip off from work, to have a small break before the travelling. Spending the day out, she went downtown for breakfast at her favourite restaurant, surfing through the web pages on the laptop making notes, of all the things she wanted to do while there, besides what had already been planned. The gallery was definitely a place she was going to hit first. "The Dunes" they called it. The farmer's markets looked splendid too.

Tourist pages gabbed on about Victoria Row. The shops, food, and music. They'd cut off the street, from spring to fall and people ate outdoors on the cobblestone street. The Theatre of the Arts was right there too, and The Guild.

The beaches and fields looked amazing. There was one rock that was special. Teacup Rock. It didn't tickle her fancy, but thought she'd see it anyway. Though it wasn't the pillar.

Nothing stood out as real for her, yet still had hope that some things would be like she remembered. All of it truly real, though. It was like another dimension, where things were slightly off.

Knowing how her book sold, wherever she'd been, Faith thought to write it out. Maybe even try and write another about being in an alternate dimension. Slipping in and out. Even if not for others, for herself.

She'd go to the gallery, get some soap and sea glass jewellery. Maybe find those coasters she "had." Imbue the person she was with Archer. Possibly make it an annual retreat, if it went well.

Thinking about it all, Faith sighed, missing him still. *But*, she had an idea, which made her feel a sense of power.

Leaving the restaurant, Faith finished her coffee walking through the mall. Passing a window, she saw a blue sunhat. It looked like the one she'd lost that day. The one archer rescued from the ocean.

Going right in, she bought it, already knowing what it would look like, after all. A little expensive, but what the hell. She felt pretty in it, and was trying, so hard, to get closer.

Told she'd never heard of PEI from her family or classes, it existed. Then, the blue hat, well, that was just peculiar. With everything in her, Faith hoped it was a premonition. A vision of the future. Time travelling.

The hat put a little skip in her step on her way home to check everything off the list and managed to kill nearly the whole day. Now, shopping for a few new outfits, Faith looked forward to sleep, or no sleep. Whatever.

Once the train had left the station, she relaxed a bit. Taking out the laptop, Faith began writing and thought, maybe she could write a story about her coma life and everything that happened afterwards. It was quite traumatic but had to figure out what to do with herself first.

Everyone wanted her to forget and just drop it. To her, though, it was like just forgetting a whole lifetime. Impossible . . . but, maybe it would help someone who was struggling with trauma and addictions, or a great romance novel.

She'd definitely take care of her dad, if she'd struck it rich. Pay him back for everything he'd done for her. Even when Faith was a little witch to him.

Watching the scenery pass, she was inspired by the beauty of it, and took notes as she thought of things.

Not wanting to be hung up on missing him again, she made plans to start the book at the cottage. Like *his* Faith did. She *was* Faith. *Forever his Faith*. No matter what the current reality was.

Thinking about what that meant, finally wondering who she was before the accident, it had never mattered to her. So distraught then, but now, it seemed a curious thing.

Was she very in touch with herself? Was that who she always was? Was she the same in this life, as in her coma?

All Faith knew was, she'd finally started to get in touch with her soul. But wasn't she already? Everything she'd learned with Archer, was still very much alive in her, though, couldn't pull it out to get over him, or her children, feeling as though it was betrayal. Very much alive, Faith felt their pain of missing her, it seemed, and wanted to comfort them, but there was no way. To her knowledge, they didn't even exist. Such a torn place to live, in her mind.

Wanting to know what kind of person she was, her dad had told her, he wasn't looking at his Faith. Drinking. Angry. So, who was she really? Mind kept occupied, she'd find time to do some soul-searching, even after coming so far in the last year of her sobriety.

After getting settled in the cottage, Faith was going to call her dad, get him to tell her about some things from the past, wanting to know for the first time since she'd woken up, what her life had held before. Anything he remembered.

All she wanted before, was to get back to Archer, or to forget about him. One impossible, the other unrealistic, in her opinion. Nothing else was on her mind. It was tearing her apart and was slowly killing her.

Always in a fog of depression, anger her first reaction, it was under control now that she'd been meditating. Like Archer said he did. Like she remembered doing. Feeling more grounded, like Archer had told her he was, and she had felt before, Faith pondered now about what this meant to her. There were so many heavy questions that needed answers.

Had it existed inside her or had it come when her mind was finally quiet?, having read how that can happen. Being in AA was beneficial, though lacked a great deal to her. So much left untouched.

What Faith had learned in her time with Archer was phenomenal. In this reality? She had to dig to find out if it was true and studied things on meditation, watched shows on quantum mechanics and entanglement, finally finding what she considered to be the cream of the crop. It made everything else make sense. The things this person said blew her mind. Manifest your life. She'd do her best.

Hearing about some miracle stories of healing. Mental, physical, and financial. Nothing was off the table, and Faith wanted that . . . To heal.

Why had she not done exactly as she'd done in the coma. Why hadn't she started a house-cleaning business, she knew the money was good. Why didn't she write the book? It could have flopped or been as successful as in the coma. Was she dumb?

So much didn't make sense, but she was after finding out, though. Feeling a bit better, more questions flooded her mind. She'd been so selfish. Never asking about her mother, or sister. Why did her father continue to support her?

She didn't even flip through any photo albums, or yearbooks. Was she the outcast she remembered? Teased? Or was she something different? Maybe she'd been popular.

Having no answers, Faith put the questions on paper, and took the train ride. She'd use the time to make notes for what was needed for the book. Maybe it would help someone.

Closing the notebook full of questions, Faith sat on the train, trying to quietly enjoy the ride some and take in some scenery.

The ride seemed short, and time passed quickly while typing. She'd gotten a lot done too. In her years, as a writer, or not a writer, Faith found she could type very fast. More questions. Was that from her time in the coma, or was it something she always had?

The train reached its destination, she took her bags and called a cab to get to the bus in Halifax, that headed to Prince Edward Island.

Once in Charlottetown, Faith got her car and started for the cottage in Brackley Beach, wanting to unpack, then have a look around before getting groceries.

Super excited, Faith thought about the reality of the situation, as it loomed, like a dark cloud threatening to rain. If it did. She'd handle it . . . she hoped.

Having taken her "piece of crap" guitar to play outside, like in her, whatever, Faith wasn't even going to try to explain it to herself if it could be helped. It just was what it was.

Once out of town, she noticed it smelled like . . . did she dare say it? Yes . . . like it always had.

So much so, that it swept her away with it. It felt as though she floated through the place, taking in her bags and guitar, it was bigger than it looked in the walk-through she'd seen on the website. It didn't relate the openness, now seeing it with her own eyes. Pictures sometimes not worth a thousand words.

The towels were folded, all the same, the ends of the beds tucked in, and the blankets turned down folded over themselves, neatly, at the foot of the bed, and overstuffed with fluffy, down-filled pillows that felt like air. Soft rugs ran the lengths of the beds. Rustic rope mats in the kitchen and dining area. The toilet paper was twisted into flowers and slabs of homemade soap laid on the counters, any place you'd wash your hands.

It smelled amazing too. Each one stamped with the cottage owner's business name and the maker of the soap.

Satisfied, Faith got back in the car and went for food. It was sweltering outside now that she'd been in the air conditioning a little while.

Windows open, music blasting, her cool rock star shades, and hair whipping around in the car, she felt amazing. The gallery would be the first stop, though. She'd passed it on the way to the cottage.

Pulling in, and feeling excitement, Faith hoped it would be something like she expected. They did have a gallery and cafe. The gardens were lovely and all, but not what Archer had done. The fountain was a little pool. The furniture, though! Huge chunks of carved wood. Benches, lounges, tables, and chairs.

Wishing she could afford it; she'd have taken some of them home. The food smelled great, and so Faith went inside.

Right inside the door, she was in the gallery so walked through . . . like before . . .

There were copious amounts of people inside and Jamaican music played. It was quite nice.

Buying things, as she'd done before, soap, a small piece of pottery and a little tray. Even though she'd saved double what was needed for the trip, an emergency might happen and she didn't have money like before, but felt she just needed to go through the motions and make a new ending for herself, and for her sanity.

Shown to a table and given a menu, Faith looked around while waiting for her food. It was a short trip. The meal made up for it though, and the servers were pleasant. Not Archer's staff, but nice, nonetheless.

The cafe was tiny compared to the rest of the areas. It did have a spot on top, where the owners stayed, when at home. A loft that overlooked the gardens. So strange the similarities. There was also a room for pottery, with classes.

Every silver lining, has a cloud, she thought, but how could it be so similar? It was truly bizarre and boggled her mind, so took another stroll through, before leaving for the farmer's market, which was buzzing with people.

There was a lineup for everything. It took her hours to get through and was much more than expected, having gone through the website for that also. Just a few more things from the pharmacy and grocery store, Faith could sit.

The town was nice. The roads, not so much. Supposing the sandstone was soft and probably needed a lot of maintenance, she was happy there were no toll booths.

Loading the car up and finally headed back for the cottage, since it was beginning to get dark, Faith figured she'd just make a bunch of food. "Stuff her face," she giggled. Archer laughed so many times, when she'd used the term . . . ugh, she growled at herself for continuing to say it, but didn't know anything else to say.

Slumped in her seat now, Faith thought, maybe just put on some music and try the ketchup chips. She'd seen videos of people trying foods from other countries. It was quite interesting and had filled at least one bag with what she could find, between the grocery store and pharmacy.

Once back, she struggled with the paper bags, since plastic was banned and Faith found herself digging under the car for a few things, because she'd been too rough . . . and trusting of them.

Putting everything away, she then ran a bath. The tub was gorgeous. It sat on its own and had an egg-like oval shape to it, that dropped where you hold onto the sides. A pretty whitewashed wooden beaded chandelier, hung above the tub.

Having bought candles at the store she lit them, then poured a glass of wine. Yes. She'd stopped drinking. This was a holiday, though. She'd really only "been a drunk" because she wasn't coping with the loss of . . . *Sigh*! Having gotten strong, she now found in certain areas, weakened.

The candles smelled great once they burned some. They smelled the way . . . he did . . . swishing the water a minute, Faith got in the tub.

Taking her wine and laying back, the hot water felt good. The train had sucked, actually, and she was happy to be relaxing. Taking a sip of the wine, Faith sighed again and feeling the warmth fill her up, she set the glass down and slid under the water. All that could be seen was hair floating around. Coming up, she breathed another deep sigh, then rested her head, drifting off into memories, and began to feel weepy so stopped herself.

Taking a big drink now, she sat in a ball, with her knees tucked in, assuring herself this was going to be fun. The water dripped from the tap, and she felt herself be pulled in by it. Like the clocks. Tick, tick, tick . . .

Sitting there until the water chilled and the wine, now warm, Faith then washed her hair and got out. Wrapping as much as possible into the towel, she grabbed the glass and walked out, naked. The drapes were closed, and no one would see. Archer loved when she did it. He'd fight himself off, as long as he could, and she'd be sorry for it. "Good and sorry," she joked out loud.

Drying her hair, Faith grabbed the snacks, then laying out a soft blanket that she'd bought especially for this, sat on the sofa.

Thinking she should send her dad some videos, that she didn't think would be horrible, Faith flipped through all she taken.

Having a few more glasses that night she fell asleep on the sofa. Like when Archer taken her home that first night, she slept like a baby.

That morning, she'd almost forgotten where she was. Then, it sank in, and Faith sighed, happily this time, and did her smol viktory dance.

Her hair was awful, so grabbed a tie and made a messy bun, then got dressed to have breakfast at the lovely island that separated the kitchen from the living room.

The marble was cold. She was cold. Opening a window, the trees rustled, and a beautiful warm breeze came in. Along with the humidity. It was fine, though.

After finishing breakfast, Faith got the remote to find music. It was complicated and took awhile, but finally finding what she wanted, she sat cross-legged to meditate. Her clothes were loose and soft, and the trees sounded nice. Not like the city, cars, horns, and swearing, Faith found herself going into a deep trance. Deeper than ever.

Feeling as though she'd left her body, Faith was filled with a happiness she had never known. Tears soaked her top and she didn't wipe a single one away, just being "aware" of them. More aware of her body, her emotions were like shadows in the background, wrapped in a love that was like no other. Familiar, though, somehow.

Then she heard a voice. "Child, why do you always come to me with your head down?"

"Because I'm being humble," she replied.

The voice said, "Child, I did not create you to be small. You are just as I had intended.

As you intended. Remember . . ."

"Remember what?" she asked.

"Remember our agreement. I live through you. All of you. Children do not come with their heads down in humility. They come joyfully and without shame. Exuberant. They are excited and full of wonder. Your life was intended to be that."

Faith cried hard now, still not moving. "I don't know how to do that."

"Yes, you do. Your father just told you, how you would come bolting through the yard when your mother called to you. Remember that girl. She's inside of you."

Faith began to understand as the words unfolded in her mind.

"Your mother is waiting. To hold your hand. You are braver than you have ever known. You are not forsaken, nor do you require forgiveness, child. That is unconditional love. Find it in your heart to forgive yourself. You didn't know better."

In a moment it had left her, but Faith felt full of light and love, so sat in it for hours. Until she felt it slip away from her gently, then sat in the memory of it, just a little bit more. With the mother she remembered and the one she didn't.

Listening to the music, Faith felt the room again. Then, the blankets under her feet, her clothes, and the weight of her hair. She'd lost all sensations.

Now flooding back to the awareness of everything around her, Faith realized how much she'd never noticed about herself. What of the things she couldn't remember? Was it even worth asking now? Knowing who she was, it might be best to leave it alone and move forward. Yes . . . move forward . . .

Stretching her arms up, twisting her back, then putting her hands to the floor Faith slid them out as far as she could, arching her back. Pulling in a fluid movement, she stood up feeling very alive.

Today, she'd planned to go to the beach after lunch, then get an ice cream. First on the list was RELAX in bold letters. Feel good first and then everything else there was time for and then, did just that.

Playing guitar and singing horribly for a few hours, Faith knew she was bad, but *damn* could she play guitar!

While eating lunch she put on the radio. CBC Radio, they said, as she clicked it on. A show called "The Debaters." Came on. She hadn't laughed that hard in . . . well . . . quite some time now.

CBC had classical music, which was nice, it was the local musicians Faith was interested in, as she had plans to go out and hear some.

The Buzz magazine was on the table in the entrance of the cottage. Flipping through, she bought tickets to see Scott Parsons.

Having overheard some people discussing a guy name Roland while at the market, Faith went to her social media page and typed in his name. It came right up Roland Beaulieu.

Can't pronounce that, she thought. He was playing in Kinkora. *No idea how to pronounce that either*, she laughed and then just took the date, and time he was playing.

The beach was just a few steps away, really, so decided to leave the car and walk. The forest lane was thick with the smell of the fir trees, which reminded her of Christmas, when she'd told Archer she was pregnant and the look on his face realizing they'd have a baby. Faith smiled the whole way down the lane to the beach.

Kids could be heard yelling from there as it rolled over the dunes. She hummed and listened to her flip-flops. Flip, flip, flip, and the sound of the rocks under them. She felt amazing after that meditation, and bounced the idea around in her head, if maybe she'd had an encounter with god. It wasn't the one everyone talked about. This was lovely.

Going down the wooden walkway to the beach, Faith listened to every footstep. Like she was walking in her own footsteps, again.

The sand was hot when she'd finally made it. There was a jar in her bag, in case she hit a jackpot with sea glass or something. Doubtful, though.

The beach was littered with people and walked a long way before finding a private place, then piling her things near the water, she took to it.

It wasn't cold . . . but it wasn't warm either, but she'd not be in for long, though. There weren't any rocks like she was familiar with. It was just sandbars, and she could visibly see the changes in the water where there was one. In between was a little warmer there too.

Floating around, mostly, Faith found herself bored and got out. Coming from the water she noticed a huge dune and climbed the side to find it was hard to get up by herself. Archer had always helped her.

At the top, she found a crater. Like at the hidey haven Archer had shown her. Just tiny, though. Thinking, she stood and looked down into it. No one was near . . . she'd hear them coming.

Running down, Faith watched the sand slide out from under her feet, and it whistled. Like the hidey haven. Remembering the vision of tumbling down and how they laid at the bottom of the dune laughing, it warmed her even more than when it had actually happened.

Taking her things, Faith went down a several metres further and looked back. No one had seen her, so she ran up the tiny hill and came from the side of the dune, back to where she had been.

Dropping her things as she got into the tiny crater, Faith pulled out her blanket and spread it, then stripped off to nothing. Ooooohhh, it felt so good.

Laying there sweating in the hot sun, she was dripping and didn't care. Flipping onto her belly, the towel felt like sandpaper. *Better get the back too*, she thought.

Satisfied, Faith laid in the hole until she felt the same sting on her back side. The towel soaked with sweat now, stuck to her as she got up.

"Well, now . . . That was nice."

Packing everything up and not wanting to get dressed, Faith guessed it was better than getting a fine for indecency, which made her laugh all the way back down the dune, Then all down the dirt road and into the cottage, as a matter of fact. Leaving the bags at the door, she got a tall cold drink.

Looking on maps for beaches, Faith logged them into her phone for the next few days. She'd be looking for that rock.

Tomorrow, Canada Day, Faith planned to stick in town for the fireworks. Stripping off, for a cooler shower, would be good for her now burnt skin. It was gonna look *so* good once it browned against her red hair and green eyes.

Putting on a loose, soft dress she'd bought before leaving her "hometown," Faith cooked dinner, and got done up for the show that night. Scott was playing in Mount Stewart, a thirty-minute drive, and she was pushing it.

Slapping on some eye shadow and mascara, Faith tied her hair into a braid. When it laid on her skin, it hurt her burnt shoulders. One strand would be more than enough torture for now.

Starting the car and turning on the air conditioning, she then let it sit awhile, running back into the house to grab her things as it cooled. It was like an oven in there.

Only taking what she needed in her purse, a few dollars for some mussels and a soda, plus an extra thirty for a CD, if they had them.

Hopping into the now cool car, merely uncomfortable in her skin with the burn and the heat, the air conditioning was nice. Pulling into Mount Stewart, Faith was greeted with a tiny town. Maybe six streets. The buildings were old. A fishing village, no doubt, for most of its life. It was right on the river.

The place was packed. Showing her ticket from the email they'd sent her after purchase, they sat her at a table with music scores under the glass top. The stage had barn boards on the walls and was tucked in the corner.

The outside of the building was barn shaped, at the tables, all the chairs were old. Not one the same and every one a different colour. Ordering a soda for now, Faith took in the atmosphere. On stage were bongo drums, electric guitar, bass, and one acoustic guitar.

"Niicceee!" she mumbled under her breath, while her neck wobbled. Like a bird does as they walk.

When her drink came, they said something and she barely heard them over the people talking and asked them to repeat it.

"Will that be all?"

"Yes. I'll keep the menu, though," Faith told them as she waved it in the air.

Men walked through the place, touching people and talking briefly on the way to the stage. Faith got excited and sat up straight to see better. *C'mon, you guys!* she whined in her head. She was anxious to hear.

She'd only seen a few videos of Scott on the app and was curious now. In the video she found, it was just him alone, but sounded like he had several players. She was in for a show, she suspected.

Everyone took their places and Scott strapped his guitar on, while thanking everyone for coming out. His voice had a bit of a crackle to it. As the band took to the stage, Faith recalled seeing them outside smoking.

The bongo player had long, white hair and a super long beard. She'd never have taken them for the musicians. Thinking again, though, she felt dumb for *not* thinking they were! They seemed eccentric, and obvious, the more she thought.

Scott told stories, all night, about the songs. He'd lived quite a life, from what she could gather. One of the songs called "Darkies Hollow" was something that made her feel happy and bizarre at the same time.

They played well together, and she particularly liked the song "Fish Bar." It was a sailors tune for sure and sounded almost haunting.

All night long, they continued to play the most excellent tunes. One after the other, Faith found herself not having a favourite anymore. The lyrics were fantastic, and she was puzzled by the way he played.

It looked like he was doing nearly nothing, but amazing sounds came from the guitar, and his voice ... oh, his voice ... it was so unique, with a bit of a lisp. She was buying the CD for sure!

Instead of getting mussels, she got their bruschetta. Homemade bread, toasted just right, served with fresh veggies and dressing to dip.

As they finished up, Faith was impressed with the whole experience. Everyone gathered outside as she followed them out to thank Scott for such good music.

"Why thank you. Thank you so much," he replied with a big smile, bobbing his head like in agreement.

So cute, she thought. Charming man. Dreamily, she went to her car and put the windows down. The sky was clear, the stars were plentiful with the darkness in the country. Fresh cut grass, lots of people talking and laughing. No brawls. The way she remembered life on The Island.

Fighting in her head, again, about her other life, she started the car and went back to the cottage, ready to check that bed out tonight. Maybe make her dad a video of the snacks she'd gotten. Anything to get those thoughts from her head.

During the show, Faith had taken a few short videos. Ones of the band while they played to share with Dad, promising she'd send him videos and Barb would be there to help him, having talked with her earlier about it. There were also the ones she'd done of the beach and yesterday at the gallery.

The time difference wasn't too bad. Being somewhat of a night owl since she'd left the hospital, Faith had no recall of it before.

It didn't seem late for her to be up when he was about to go to bed. The drive home was nice, but the car was covered in bugs.

Calling, Faith told him about the day and since Barb was over, she had a short talk with her too saying she was sending pics and vids, while they were on the phone. In a few minutes, she could hear it playing in the back, and her dad clapping, making Faith cry.

She'd been so mean to him. Then, remembering the vision from the morning. "Forgive yourself," rang in her head like a gong.

It wouldn't be easy, but knew she had to. Barb passed him the phone and he went on about how good it was, and how much he liked the way the place looked, happy she was having a good time. She was happy that he was happy.

Knowing it was late, he told her to go get some rest. The holiday was tomorrow, and Faith had a big day planned. Plus, the fireworks and the drive back to the cottage.

"Make sure you turn the lights out," he reminded her, before saying he was proud and that he loved her.

"Love you too, Dad."

He knew she meant it and said goodbye with a crack in his voice. Faith was glad she'd said it. More weight off her chest.

Crawling into bed, she clicked on a movie, then pulled up the feather duvet, it crinkled and puffed, then drifted slowly back down onto her. She was asleep before it had totally settled.

CHAPTER TWENTY-NINE
A Way Around?

Faith woke a few times through the night. Nightmares came, now and then, of Lacey and the barn. Fearing for the children and Archer was her biggest concern. Every time she woke, she'd have to get herself back to this life. No way around it and eating away at her. Even when she was laughing, her soul was crying in agony.

She'd just get back to sleep and fall right back in. By five in the morning, Faith had had enough. Remembering the vision, she tried to get back to that place. It had washed her clean of everything.

Wanting to make connections to Archer, the place with no name, the way she knew about little things on PEI, that she shouldn't have, Faith's mind wouldn't let her. She'd beaten and wrestled it to the ground and was stuck with the outcome. Unresolved forever, she dreaded.

Putting coffee, from the market, in the grinder, it smelled good when she opened the lid. Tempted to stick her finger in and taste it like cake batter in . . . her mom's bowl! She'd remembered something! "Yes!" she shouted.

The coffee was as sweet as the memory. Not knowing what that would mean for her, to get memories back, she wanted to let go but everything in her told her not to. *Bittersweet*, she thought.

Popping homemade bread in the toaster, Faith leaned on the counter smelling it as it wafted up and under the cupboard. When it popped, it startled her a bit, so she cleared her throat, as though to pretend it didn't happen.

Yep. Not edgy at all. She was so tired. Slowly, buttering the toast, then clicking some music on, she dragged her slippers on the floor. Maybe a short nap before the festivities. That coffee had kick, though.

Faith would call it "no smack jack" like Devon would have made. All hyped up now, she was ready for the fireworks, but the fireworks weren't ready for her. Not having done anything with herself yet Faith didn't want to rush with her hair and whatnot.

It took a lot to keep her patience. Her feet nearly wanting to run out from underneath her like, *let's go then*! Certain she'd give a squirrel a run for their money.

Standing in the mirror, Faith told herself to calm down. Maybe more toast would do her some good.

Popping in a few more slices of bread, she thought to keep an eye out for roadside stands with jams or jellies on any of her travels. Buttering the slices, she gobbled them down and tried to get back to doing her hair. *Messy bun again*, she thought, after three tries.

Up with it now, and slipping on some shorts, tight on the waist, but like a skirt at the bottom, with a wraparound top that showed some of her cleavage. Smoothing it out, Faith felt like she was cheating on Archer, so, put on some cotton pants and a tank top. He still owned her.

A small fair at the harbour in Charlottetown, she got some cotton candy. More sugar. Good idea.

There were some dart games and ring toss. Winning a small key chain, she put the cottage key on it, so to not lose it. Walking the streets, she saw some kids had their faces painted. There must have been a one at the fair she hadn't noticed. It remined her of the party Archer had thrown for the staff when they'd first met.

Following the blue line on the sidewalk, it took her to another part of the harbour, with many food trucks. One had samosas, which she'd never heard of, so got a couple. They burned her mouth, nearly off.

Hot from the oil, the spices in the sauce were worse. Stopping at the next booth, she got poffertjes. Little puffy pancakes, with a dab of butter, sprinkled with powdered sugar. They were delicious and soothed her tongue some! Then Faith tried some Lil' Orbit donuts.

Watching them go into the grease through an automated machine, they rolled down through the narrow fryer trough, one by one, and it flipped them as they cooked, amusing her.

The stand owner, and her daughter, scrambled to keep up to the buyers, offering a wide assortment of toppings. Buying six of them to go, she only ate one, as she was getting full now.

The blue line went the entire way of the boardwalk. From Hillsborough Bridge to Victoria Park, where the main event was. Watching some boys play Frisbee, kids ran around with balloons. There was a small amphitheatre, and the music was great. So energetic.

Getting closer, Faith watched as two guys sang Taylor Swift's "Blank Space." Then introduced themselves.

Brandon Gillis. A stalky guy, with a voice that kind of quivered. He hit some great high notes and paired nicely with the thinner guy, Dave Woodside. A smoky voice that swooped around the notes Brandon sang. Bopping along with their fast ones;

the slower ones made her want to just sway.

Shortly after, Brandon's wife, Jenn, came to sing with them, doing some old '80s tunes. Faith loved her voice and was kind of jealous. Jenn's group name was The Sirens.

That was Archer's pet name for her, and now, she sounded like shit. Wondering if she could fix that, Faith went to the internet to find vocal coaches in her area, as she kept listening. Some free videos came up and she bookmarked the page but felt little hope.

When darkness came, she sat at the harbour watching the fireworks. Kids cried and people ooohhh'ed. It took her forever to get out and was nearly one in the morning before she got back to the cottage. No sleep and up way too early, Faith just went to bed and hoped tomorrow would be better. It would take a bomb to get her up tonight.

Opening her eyes that morning, she laid in the bed awhile, just enjoying the comforters. A feeling of being well rested was refreshing. She'd started to settle in some now.

The trip there and back took nearly half a week of her vacation. Plus, the day before she'd taken off. Now half this day was wasted. It was rounding up on noon.

Throwing herself from the bed Faith made coffee. While it brewed, she got dressed and put on a little makeup. After the coffee was poured, she ate some toast and took the new sandals she'd bought from their box. They were super comfortable, then got in the car and took a few hundred dollars with her to go to the farmer's market downtown, wanting to bring home gifts for her dad and sister.

The drive in was nice and she'd gotten rid of the feeling of panic about the time. Being active in her quest to find some preferred ending, Faith battled with herself about whether Archer was real or not. If she'd find him or not. Should she hurry up? She might miss him. Should she slow down? She might miss him. Follow her plan? Or follow her intuition? Too many questions. Just do "stuff" Faith told herself.

The parking was awful on her first trip round, so she decided to just take a spot farther away and walk, rather than waste god knows how much time trying to get closer.

Every decision could be fatal to her answers. She'd come to find resolution. The only thing that would bring it was him or passing over the keys to her rental car.

Walking the lovely streets with old brick buildings, Faith found the sweetest smell. Cow's dairy bar. The line was way too long. Maybe on the way back she'd grab an ice cream.

The streets blocked off; she watched an older guy with a Kermit puppet say some things. Though she didn't catch what he'd said but sounded just like him. She watched a second, with the market ahead of her, four streets long. She'd be there awhile.

Vendors tents crackled in the wind. The air from the harbour at the end of the street, brought the cool of the ocean with it. Her sunhat helped and was glad she'd bought it.

Her burn was just starting to brown, and Faith thought it best to keep it from the sun, to let it heal.

Buying a turned little cup that almost looked like a flower, the bark still on the top edge and bottom rim, Faith moved to the next vendor. Beef jerky titled with the names of Greek gods. He'd given her some samples and they were so good she bought a few kinds. It came in a paper cup that he folded in front of her, simply closed with a fold. A little expensive, but delicious.

A leather craftsman had belts closed by interlacing the ends together. Like the one she'd bought for Archer, to help him get through metal detectors and not have to nearly strip down. How could she have known that? Had she seen it before in a commercial or something?

Faith took his card. He was nice to look at and pleasant. A great energy came from him. High but controlled and calm . . . like him.

She'd decided to stop saying his name. Not knowing if he was real and looking for peace, Faith wasn't getting it. She'd have to make it happen. A little scared, she distracted herself by asking about how he'd started making his things, and what else he did.

Thinking maybe she'd save some money right now and order something to be shipped back to her, Faith couldn't help to buy *something*. A wallet maybe. Then she saw a bracelet. Passing the money, he gave it to her, and she put it right on, then continued to stroll the streets.

Hand-made cards, paintings, soap, fresh veggies, and snack wagons. Still a bit hungry, she bought a sausage from the meat vendor. It was incredible and she wanted to buy more, but still had the drive to the country.

A young girl played guitar and sang. Stopping to listen, Faith watched as people threw change and bills in her jar. She was quite good.

Faith sat on the grass eating her sausage, listening awhile before leaving, she asked the girl's favourite song to sing.

"Oh, that would have to be 'Ophelia,'" she told Faith.

"Could you play it?"

"Well, I did when I got here, but, yeah, I can do it again," she told Faith with a smile.

Listening to her play, the strings buzzed a bit and her fingers looked awkward getting to make the chords. Lovely all the same, though.

A memory formed for her, of, the other life. Something almost identical, though she put a large sum in the girl's jar.

When she'd finished, Faith put a twenty in her container and thanked her, then went on her way, looking at pottery and dream catchers.

Going through faster than she thought she would, Faith had made it back up to the man with the Kermit puppet in no time. He was talking again.

Listening a bit, he started singing "The Rainbow Connection."

Faith remembered it. A feeling of not having a care in the world came over her. Like when she was a kid. No bills, no school, or worries about being unpopular and picked on. Or of the abusive she'd had over the years. Crying, she didn't care if anyone saw, she was lost in the moment.

When the song was over, Faith put a fifty in his hat. Kermit looked at her then.

"Hey, lady, don't cry . . ." he said, and the people laughed.

Not at her, though. At him. Then, an old man came beside her and rubbed her arm. Then stayed with his arm around her.

What the hell?

Fighting the urge to sob out loud, Faith nodded to him with a smile, and he looked at her with eyebrows raised, as if to say, "Are you sure you're okay?" Which made her feel better.

Giving Faith a tissue, she dried her eyes, blew her nose and was happy she came, Then after leaving, she thought about it all. Her dad would be so happy to get the video of Kermit and the girl on guitar.

With a big sigh, Faith realized, she'd had a memory. Of being a kid. Of being bullied and teased. Not for her hair, though, for not being wealthy, like the cool kids. Her parents had enough for them. They weren't poor. They just couldn't afford brand name clothes.

The men she'd been with were abusive. Calling her names to put her down. She'd shown jealousy, then found out later they were cheating on her. Faith stayed with them until she couldn't take anymore.

Remembering one she'd dated and lived with for five years, how he always came home late, reeking of alcohol. She'd challenged him a few times, not scared of anyone, but he grabbed her by the throat and threw her across the room, scraping her leg on the coffee table. Remembering the cut, Faith pulled up her skirt, there was the scar.

Kermit had made her feel good, and she wanted to keep that going, so stood in line and waited to get an ice cream. The cone was fantastic. Hand-made. The ice cream was, well, ice cream.

Having eaten it all by the time she'd gotten to the car Faith decided to head out to Kinkora, to catch Roland, whatever his last name was. Only stopping for gas, she went straight out.

The town was cute. All of them she'd seen so far were. Going inside the tavern, where he was playing, it was quiet. Just a few people. He was setting up and chatting with others, like he knew them.

Faith just watched and ordered a glass of wine, deciding to stay for the whole show. It would give her two hours. One glass wouldn't hurt.

Roland played everything under the sun. A few times he'd clicked a pedal with his foot, instantly having backup singers. Happy and animated, he asked for requests, then delivered every one of them. Like a jukebox.

Before leaving, Faith told him how much she enjoyed it, and he thanked her for coming.

Roland went around the room saying hi to people, before getting himself a drink, then sat at a table with a group, maybe family, or friends.

Faith hopped back into the car and thought she'd go to the next town. It was closer than the cottage and enjoyed the way she was feeling.

Coming to it, she was greeted with the same quaint buildings. One had a liquor store and pub. There were also local artisan shops. Entering, Faith found some sweet stained glass and bought one that looked like a thong flip-flop, then chose to call it a day.

Typing in the address for the cottage, she decided to take the scenic route instead of the highway, which brought her all along a coastal drive. When coming up over a hill, Faith looked across to see . . . what? The pillar rock?!

Pulling over, she looked to see how to get to it or if there were power lines running down to cottages. *Anything.*

With nothing to show the way, she pulled up the map. Now, all she saw were fields. If she had to trek them, she friggin' would.

In satellite view Faith could see some of the houses on the maps, but some weren't. Could be that it hadn't been updated in awhile. There might very well be a road, so she drove until it was getting dark, still not finding it.

She'd be back, bright and early, though. How could this be? Something strange had happened. Not knowing how to get to the bottom of it, Faith decided to let it go, for now.

The next day, she realized the rest of her vacation would probably go out the window. She'd seen enough and now with the pillar rock, nothing else was on her mind. It was where she met "him" and that was all that mattered anymore.

With a towel, flashlight, and her robe, in case she found it that day, Faith was off to chase that rock. It was quite a ways away from where she was staying. Best get a bite to eat in the closest town.

Driving for hours back and forth, one lane after another took her just to the sides of it and the cliffs were way too high to be climbing. Vertical drops too. It made her feel nauseous to look over the edges. Walking the lengths from the shore wasn't safe. The tide could come in farther than she'd have liked.

Starving now, Faith went to Kensington and had all-you-can-eat Chinese food. It was fantastic. She also stopped for bug spray, and something for the mosquito bites she'd already gotten, almost being eaten alive.

No matter, though. Her heart soared and she felt like she was in a zone. Going back, Faith spent another day, until dark, trying to find it. It was slow driving on the lanes and took a lot of the day just to be too far from it.

Getting back to the cottage, she spent the evening zooming in. Trying to get a fix on the roads she'd taken and where they led and drawn out a make-do map, marking the roads she'd gone down already, so to not do it again.

Some of them had almost just gone in a circle, or she had to walk through tall weeds to get to the cliff. Only to be disappointed again. She wasn't about to quit, though, so called her dad and updated him. They sat on the phone together as he watched her videos. Barb had bought a laptop for him to do video chats, if he felt brave enough.

After getting off with him, Faith laid in bed, staring at the ceiling. She had five days left. Three to travel.

It filled her with anxiety then but then remembered how Archer had said that she attracted things by being in the right mind. So put on some bamboo flute music and sat cross-legged on the bed to do some meditation. Find her center and the sense of unconditional love again. Making it serve her.

Surprisingly, she got in fast. Which also heightened the sense of familiarity for her. Easy to get into, meant available. It was a choice. The peace had made her take a leap of progress. The cars had always distracted. They never would again.

Experience teaches, Faith remembered. Deeper she went. Feeling a calm sweep over her now, she laid down, but kept her vision going. Until just dozing off.

When she woke that morning, being grateful to be alive again, Faith didn't remember ever feeling that way except . . . whatever.

Doing her best to let it go, Faith continued to dismiss him and the thoughts. Best to not notice that he wasn't there yet. Filling in the gaps meant building a bridge, and so she sang happily. It was such a contradiction, forgetting him to bring him to her.

Humming the whole time, she cooked a huge breakfast. Something that would last. Bacon, eggs, toast, coffee, a huge pile of fruit, and a tall glass of milk.

She wanted to rush, but her intuition said, take your time and enjoy your food. *Hm*, Faith thought. Maybe the patience would do her some good. To keep her in that calm place and draw her right to it. Right to him! Like the sea glass stopper.

True or not, made no difference, Faith felt it was possible and it gave her hope. Truth is what you believe, she'd come to realize.

With everything still in the car from the day before; Faith took some water. The drive felt shorter every time.

Maybe she needed a better plan. Stopping on one side of the road, to look, the first road that took her furthest wasn't it. Checking them over, she marked off ones that were wrong by name, to be certain.

With no luck, she drove to the highest hill and looked over. She could see a tractor trail through the tall grass, which went down over a hill and disappeared.

There were only a few fields, and now, that was her only hope. All the roads led to nowhere. She'd have to risk the field. It hadn't rained in awhile, so the dirt tracks wouldn't be slick. No sliding or sinking, she hoped, but would go by foot if needed.

This one had tall grass in the centre. It clicked under the car, and she prayed there were no rocks, not wanting to pay damages on the rental car.

One field, two fields. The going was slow.

Sitting up close to the window nearing the top of the hill, she'd stopped breathing and hadn't notice, until she saw the tracks and the curve of the cliff, then tried to get a deep breath. Her lungs were already full, though. Hopeful now, Faith went over and down the hill. Slowly.

Keep your calm. Take your time. Use your patience. Don't waver from the place, she kept telling herself.

At the bottom, the grass wasn't so long now, like someone had been keeping it. Then getting out from the car, Faith walked to the edge.

The white top came into view, right in front of her this time. She danced, hands in the air, slowly turning as if to say thank you. Then, going to the edge and looking down the vertical drop, Faith walked along the entire edge to see how to get down.

Going to the right, there was nothing, because it was a bit of a point, she could see down to the sand and the shore was pretty short. Walking back then, to the left, she found . . . *stairs*! Just her luck!

No way! she thought and rushed to make sure it was real, then going back to the car, Faith got her things and went to the stairs. They were wobbly and almost as straight as the cliff. It wasn't going to stop her, though.

Once at the bottom, she put everything on the sand and took her phone out. The reception was horrible, but it was the camera she wanted anyways, and after taking some pictures, Faith laid out her towel, then stood there all . . . alone. She'd hadn't felt *more* alone. Not the day she married Archer or when she'd woken up. Even the whole next year, not being able to relate to anyone, or them to her, she stopped trying to explain. The liquor was the only thing that kept her half sane. This "alone" was the worst by far.

Tonight, was a full moon. Mostly full the next night. Then, it would be time to go. Her bus was leaving at one that afternoon. Then . . . it was over. It'd be time to face the facts.

So much had been relative to the "dream" she'd had in her coma and, no doubt would get hellbent, on how to put those pieces where they belong. For now, she had the pillar rock and things, kind of close, to what she knew. Now all there was to do was wait.

Midnight skinny dip in the plans, Faith had a few dunks under the water. It was super hot down there and now that her burn was healed, she laid out. A lot. When bored, she wrote in her book, till the battery died on the laptop.

The sun going down now, excitement filled her. Taking more pictures, she'd never seen a more beautiful sunset. There was a large flat rock exposed when the tide had gone out all the way. Taking pictures, Faith then checked them to edit.

It looked like they were taken way out in the water. Maybe on a boat. There wasn't a cliff to be seen from where she sat. She really should have gotten wood to make a fire. It was all long the roadside every few kilometres.

Remembering the way Faith groped Archer teasingly that first night they had the bonfire, she could hear his fake scream, making her smile. The night when he fell in love with her. It really felt like yesterday, and she hadn't smiled like that in so very long.

Planning for the next day, Faith made a note to get wood. There were lots of rocks she could pull together, to make a pit and could just throw the wood from the cliff top, leave whatever was left over, and take the plastic bag they were in, back with her.

Dark now, she sat and watched the moon get brighter. When it came over the horizon fully, it looked four times bigger than it ended up being, and tried to get some pictures, but it refused to be captured.

Satisfied, though, Faith stripped off her clothes, waded in, and left the flashlight on to see the shore. Familiar with the tide, she didn't worry. They'd done this a hundred times.

Sighing, she pushed it from her head needing to enjoy this. Hope was dwindling. Maybe, grace would bring him back, the way her dad had said, it would bring her back to him.

Staying till two in the morning, having gone into the water a few times, she'd gotten cold and sat with the robe wrapped around her. It always felt sticky to her. The salt water did that.

Figuring she'd need to get some sleep; it was time to leave. One more dip, though. Wading into the water again, Faith heard a rustling in the grass above her, and just froze, listening a moment. Again, the rustle.

Dipping low into the water to hide her naked body, then, after a minute, realized she was being silly. No one was coming down there, making her feel alone again, but at the same time, a bit of closure came. Relief. As small as it was, it was noticed and appreciated.

Now, most of the way back to the shore, the rustling again.

Could be an animal. A bird maybe. The wind. Faith took her robe, wrapped it around her, and listened.

When it was gone, she took her things and went for the arduous task of getting back up. The wobbling made her nervous, but she made it, very slowly, then put her things in the car. The rustling again. It definitely *wasn't* the wind.

Starting the car, she took to the long drive home. With the lane ahead, it would be even longer. It was three thirty in the morning before Faith got to the cottage, packed her things and had them by the door. Now or later didn't matter. Good to go to the shore early, get food in Kensington and go back, have the car packed and ready for the bus.

No coming back, the plan was to stay all night long, have a fire, some hot dogs and chips. Her last night and her last hope, she'd make the absolute most of it.

Sleeping till 8 a.m., four hours would have to do. Maybe she could take a nap at the shore. If anyone, and by anyone she meant Archer, showed up, she'd hear them on the stairs for sure.

The car loaded now, coffee brewed, Faith did all the dishes. It'd just be the pot and the cup left to clean. Doing a short meditation, then enjoying the coffee, she said goodbye to the cottage, left a note how lovely it was, and put a twenty on the table beside it. With not much money left Faith wanted to do something nice.

The laundry was also done, and the towels were folded, the way she'd found them. Like some of the cottage guests had *not* done for her, because it was a "dream".

The bed clothes were washed and in the dryer for the cleaner. Just a little something to help. She hadn't left a mess either and before locking the door, Faith took one last look around. Her heart was heavy, but there were still a few hours left. How life could change in the blink of an eye.

Dropping the trash in the bin, Faith got in the car and headed for the pillar, praying the whole way there. Not for something she was missing. Not that life would change, or that she may find closure.

What she prayed for was the peace, love, joy, and the wonder she'd felt so intensely, within all of her memories, leaving out the part that made it seem to be a dream. A delusion. She left out all that had been before.

Never saying any of their names. Archer, Grace, or Jesse.

Having watched some videos about how attraction is based on thoughts and emotions, to leave out all that you don't want, to be healed, you don't ask for healing. You just feel the feeling of wellbeing. It wasn't easy and Faith struggled all the while.

Now and then, she'd get lost in the smell of the watermelon grass, the feel of the wind, and how it sounded blasting in her ear at 100 kilometres an hour. What was a ticket at this point?

There was a cute stand on the side of the road across from the gallery. Pulling in, she could smell the onion rings, making her belly growl, but didn't have much of an appetite. Her nerves were on the edge of snapping but, all day and night, is a long time. Better to fuel up and grab some snacks.

The fries were heaping on the burger platter she ordered. The meat slid out the end of the bun when she bit in. It was loaded with everything. Going out with a bang sounded good.

It kind of felt good too. Anything to keep the momentum going in her mind. It *was* delicious. The bun was browned on the grill with butter, it was shiny and had just a touch of crunch to it.

Getting where she wanted to be, Faith felt as though one more thing was checked from the list. The onion rings were hand-made. Measuring them, she thought she'd never seen a thicker one. They were *colossal*. It was all washed down with lemonade, and before leaving, she asked for a few more cans to-go.

Getting back in the car, it was now ten in the morning. The gas station, up the road, had a small grocery store, and stopping in, Faith filled the tank.

She remembered Greg and how she'd whacked him and regretted not enjoying that life more than she had. Knowing that the road behind is clearer after having travelled it.

Picking up some peanuts, a few pieces of fruit, along with some chips and Cheezies, Faith remembered having an argument with one of her exes, about whether they were called Cheezies or cheese sticks. Then, when he'd thoroughly pissed her off, she started calling them cheezitz to bug him, knowing she was wrong, he did too. Dispute over. They both win.

It came back to her in bits and pieces as she roamed the aisles for snacks. Picking up hot dogs and buns, and grabbed a handful of ketchup from the stand for them, for later. Plus a few more in case anyone came around.

Full of food and anxiety now about getting there, she took what was in her hand cart and left. She'd be at the beach soon.

Grabbing some wood on the way, she threw it in the trunk with the food. It was going to be a few trips up and down the wretched stairs to get this done. No big thing, though. She was after a feeling and the work would be done, happily.

Faith enjoyed the drive up the fields listening to the grass scrape and ting under the car.

Covering herself in bug spray, throwing the wood over the side, along with the bag that had the pillow and blanket she'd bought, intending to sleep there. Maybe the tide would take her out and drown her.

"*Stop!*" Faith cried out loud, not wanting to play the "good feeling gone" game. It would be, what it would be. She'd have to settle with the outcome.

Where did the cynicism come from? Why did it always seem to taint everything in this life. She'd beaten it down while with Archer. How did it have its grips in her after all she'd worked for?

Maybe the installed program? Maybe the body she was in and the life it had lived. Bits and pieces lingering like ghosts.

Knowing her spirit was one of joy, maybe the body *is* just a computer. If those people were right about creating reality, though, now would be a great time to prove it.

"All I ever wanted was to feel content and happy. No need for living it all at once. I'll take all the roads you lead me down," she said out loud.

The "god encounter" had made her believe that all she had to do was trust and love. Unconditionally. Everything would come to her, based on that foundation. Then, learn the rest as she went.

Filled with hope, Faith began singing a song about being a believer that she'd heard on the radio. It rang true to her soul right then.

Setting the food bag down, she went back up for the guitar. It wasn't as bad a job as she'd imagined it would be. Up? Well. It would be okay, she figured. Empty garbage, plus the bag with pillow and blanket, wasn't so heavy. The guitar was just awkward.

Once down at the beach, there was no reception, so she put on some downloaded music. Keeping the wood on some slabs of rock, in case the sand made them wet, Faith then built her firepit.

There was tons of driftwood and sticks to use to get the fire going. She remembered how, from her "other life" she'd decided to call it, how Archer always got the fire started.

The day was glorious, and she laid in the sun, had some chips and cheezitz, and washed them down with lemonade. It was warm now and made her teeth feel dry. Still tasty, though.

Once the sun had started going down, she double-checked everything to make sure there were no more trips to the car. Daylight was better for that.

Satisfied she had what was needed, Faith broke sticks and got the fire going. Stacking them like a teepee to entertain herself, they lit up quick, but burned quick also.

Making a stack to burn while there, she put them on either side of the fire, then laid three on top of the flames, with space between for air. They went up quickly, and soon she had a nice bed of coals. It kept the bugs away too.

Now and then, the smoke would get in her eyes when the breeze changed. It burned, but Faith welcomed every second. It let her know she was still alive. The memory would be part of her soul forever, no matter how it went.

Watching the sun go down over the horizon, the stars were reborn after losing the battle in the morning before. The moon was brighter than it had ever been, to her.

Taking out her guitar, Faith went over all the songs that made her happy. Save one, for the end of the night. Or a special reason. Quickly Faith swooped her mind from going there. Things akin are drawn together, she kept repeating.

With faith in her heart, she understood, now, what her name meant. Her mother could have died, and she wouldn't have cared. She was having a baby, no matter what. Faith was determined to have her way, as well. Even if it killed her and it very well may.

Taking her mind from the passing thoughts, she stripped down and sat on the rocks with her beautiful bonfire, which lit up the pillar rock. Hot dogs on a stick and wrapped in a warm soft robe. Definitely a night to remember. Who gets to do this?

Having set an alarm for midnight, it went off. Faith unrobed herself as she headed for the water, the moon sparkled on the tiny waves that came in.

Watching them a few minutes before pushing through them, she never did catch them, but sitting below the surface, Faith remembered Archer the night he prayed to have his wife and child. How he begged for mercy.

Once she'd risen, she floated, like before. Finding the feeling place instead of the actions but using them to create the emotions. Like a two-way street.

After an hour, she felt a little down and decided to sit on the rock that became exposed from the tide going out, thinking of him and how they ended that night, touching him in her mind. Faith and hope dwindling.

Once satisfied, she took a few more minutes to swim as the fire died some, then dried off, threw in more wood.

When it grew enough, she stood on front of it, and it felt good on her naked body, with no intention of getting dressed, unless she had to.

Watching how long the fire took to die, she noted it and set an alarm to feed it more, supposing there wasn't enough for the night. The robe and her blanket would keep her warm, though. If not, she had the car. Worse come to worse, she still had the cottage till ten that morning.

Faith laid down feeling tired. The waves and the cracking fire soothing the aches in her heart. The night was chilly, but not bad.

Laying on the blanket, she wore the robe, but could still feel the ground beneath her so manipulated it with her body to take the shape.

Thinking of how she'd manipulated everything this whole time, trying to find relief, here she was, at the last second, finally feeling her way through.

When Faith woke, the fire had been out awhile. She had some lemonade and cheezits for breakfast thinking she should have gotten some muffins or something.

Packing everything up, she watched the sun rise. Fire in the sky, stars disappearing, one by one. Like the dreams she'd had of getting back what was lost. Birds chirping and crickets joining the song, she took everything but the guitar up to the stairs. Save one. Chasing cars and then back to real life.

Staying there as long as she could, Faith played her song and cried. When starting the car, she promised that it was over. No looking back and no regret. Not a single thing!

Halfway back to town, she pulled over. Mind reeling, tears not stopping, she screamed. Weary and disheveled, Faith pulled on her eyelashes. The lids slopped around, like the thoughts in her head. "FUCK IT! FUCK IT! FUCK IT!" she yelled.

Turning the car around, she tore out, rocks and dust flying behind the tires on the road. Faith drove up the fields without caring at all. Snaps and cracks came from under the car, as she bounced through the dips in the ground.

Parking in the field now, she got out and left the door wide open. It dinged in the air behind her as she walked to the cliff and stared at the pillar.

"It's all done."

Sticking out both her hands, as if to reach out and touch it. Closer to the edge than anyone would be comfortable with, she felt as though she *could* touch it.

Visions rolled through her head, wreaking havoc. Smashing down all she'd built, coming here. Archer's face was just there. It seemed so real. Stroking in the air, she realized it was just her mind, but leaned forward just a little more.

Right over the side.

She meant to.

"I love you," Faith said, on her way to the rocky bottom.

Someone had screamed at her, and she didn't care. Laying there, in excruciating pain, Faith waited for it to stop forever. Like when the doctors operated on her after the ambulance brought her into the hospital.

Feeling the life slipping away, it wasn't soon enough for her taste. There was more screaming, and all she could do was lay there. Her neck was broken. Among other things.

Hearing him struggling with the 9-1-1 operator, as he described where they were, his sandals seemed heavy on the rock with her ear on it.

"She's not moving."

He was panic stricken, as she faded in and out of consciousness.

Rolling her over to check her eyes, they googled under her lids and there was blood coming from them. Her breathing garbled, like when Jonsie was in the kitchen, after Archer had had his way with him.

"Please don't help me," she begged, but all he heard was choking.

"Please hurry!"

She'd heard that before. That voice.

Struggling to open her eyes, she managed to see out of one.

"They're on the way," he soothed. "Just keep holding on. I won't leave you."

He asked her a lot of questions. Nothing but garbled words came out, drowned by the blood seeping into her lungs.

Faith just stared at him. Not able to take back what she'd done, and said, "I love you so much" in her garbled voice.

It was him.

"I've missed you, every single day," she spoke then in her head, hoping he would hear her, like Grace did.

He had no clue as to how much he could love or be loved by her, breaking her heart. She'd failed him in the end.

Floating up and out of her body, Faith watched, as he sat on the rocks with his head in his hands. There was nothing she could do for him and nothing he could do for her now.

About the Cover Artist

Susan Christensen is a painter, primarily in acrylics. She's also created works of art in oils, water colours and printmaking. Her main subject of inspiration has been the landscapes of her native home, Prince Edward Island, Canada. In recent years, her landscape paintings have been moved away from impressionistic realism to her own unique style of minimalist representation. Her new work has been inspired by the works of Lawren Harris from the Group of Seven. Through solid bands in colors of gradients, this work has captured the essence of The Islands landscape, as well as the hearts of people who are residents as well as visitors and share in her passion of the arts and for the landscapes of Prince Edward Island. Susan uses only primary colours in her work, and many have said that her colours are what draw them to her art. A new area of endeavour, the Ekphrastic practice of creating poetry inspired by painting, Susan has been creating paintings inspired by the poetry of Lucy Maud Montgomery. She will then engage six island poets to create new poetry inspired by her paintings. Susan has found that stretching herself in this new direction has challenged both her imagination and technical skills. This is the third time Susan will have created a body of work using poetry as her inspiration.

To see more of her work, you can visit her website.
www.susanchristensenart.com

More about the cover

In the making of this book, I had wanted to use more images. Situationally, my device made it difficult to collect the images I wanted to use. Fortunately, on prompting from my editing specialist I went looking for images.

Susan had been written into this book. I had never even thought to look and see who the artist was in the gallery in which I had first seen them. On every visit to the gallery, I would always been drawn to them and would gaze at them for very long periods. Lost in the emotion they inspired in me.

One day in the middle of production to create this book for all to read, I saw one of her paintings come through my social media page and began to follow her. Regularly I would see the paintings develop in stages as she shared them with the public. It excited me so much to see them as they happened. When asked about my images for the book I decided to ask her if I could use one for the cover. A specific one of the dunes we have on Prince Edward Island title The Dunes PEI.

Taking the chance to ask her for use I sent a message not expecting her to even get back to me. She has quite a large following and thought I'd get buried by others inquiring about purchasing her paintings. To my delight she messaged me back immediately asking me to tell her about the book. Agreeing to let me use the dunes painting we got into a conversation. She recognized me as a kindred spirit. We messaged back and forth all day. In the end we both had things to get done and were about to end the discussion when I asked if I could give her a sea glass necklace which I make. I had only started a week or so before and felt I wanted to gift her.

I asked her favorite colour, and she said blue. Which is also my favourite colour. Picking the best one I started making it that evening.

When I asked how I could get it to her she mentioned that she came to Charlottetown from Summerside often and that she would be around in the next week. A day or so later Susan messaged me that she'd be in Charlottetown and would I like to go for lunch. I said yes in a heartbeat. I had admired her for so long. We worked out a time that suited us both and met for dinner. We talked for four hours, barley eating. She had hardly even sipped on her tea.

During the conversation she showed me a painting she was working on of an elderly woman from a poem by Lucy Maud Montgomery about the lines on your face, how they tell the story of your life. I was then even more fascinated by her talent.

She then scrolled through her phone and showed me her painting of The Rock at Sea View. I was covered in goosebumps as I scrolled through my phone to show her the image I had of the same rock. The one that this book begins and ends with.

I was tickled by this for several days and decided I wanted to use it for the cover of this book. Our meeting had been so serendipitous to me that to have it on the cover was the only option I had. Nothing else would have done. It was perfect.

In this book Faith lives just across from the rock where she's renting the cottage. Susan mentioned the house belongs to a family member and I was shocked.

Life is magical and when you dedicate yourself to your passions you begin to see the relativity of your thought and emotions develop into something you can see, smell, taste, touch and hear. Which is what I intended to describe in this book. Some of the experiences are mine. The visions, ideas about life and the process I've taken to get to this book. It's been a wild ride.

Susan and I have an ongoing relationship. A beautiful friendship of support and kindness. No doubt ringing through all of space and time. I can't thank her enough for softly coming into my life, which has shown me some of the power I wield in creating my life experience. Which we all have.

I hope that this book can inspire you to start asking the question: "What would truly make me happy?" and that it inspires you to become the powerful creator of your life that you were intended to be and that you find joy at every corner, in every opportunity, and that you seize it.

About the Author

Debut author Sharon Follows is inspired by art in all its forms, from drawing, making soap and poetry, to creating music and writing this novel. She identifies with her lead character of Faith and used aspects of her own life as inspiration. Sharon currently lives in Charlottetown, PEI.

9 781039 172586